The Best
AMERICAN
SHORT
STORIES
1979

To Bob Bason—
Joyce
Carol
Oates

The Best
AMERICAN
SHORT
STORIES
1979

Selected from
U.S. and Canadian Magazines
by Joyce Carol Oates
with Shannon Ravenel

With an Introduction by Joyce Carol Oates
Including the Yearbook of the
American Short Story

1979

Houghton Mifflin Company Boston

"The New Music" from *Great Days* by Donald Barthelme. First published in *The New Yorker*. Copyright © 1978, 1979 by Donald Barthelme. Reprinted with the permission of Farrar, Straus & Giroux, Inc.

"A Silver Dish" by Saul Bellow. First published in *The New Yorker*. Copyright © 1978 by Saul Bellow.

"The Eye" by Paul Bowles. First published in *The Missouri Review*. Copyright © 1978 by Paul Bowles.

"The Wedding Week" by Rosellen Brown. First published in *Boston University Journal*. Copyright © 1978 by Rosellen Brown.

"Falling Off the Scaffold" by Lyn Coffin. First published in the *Michigan Quarterly Review*, Vol. 17, No. 1 Winter 1978. Copyright © 1979 by Lyn Coffin.

"The Middle Place" by Mary Hedin. First published in *Southwest Review*. Copyright © 1978 by Mary Hedin.

"A Short Walk into Afternoon" by Kaatje Hurlbut. First published in *Southwest Review*. Reprinted by permission of McIntosh and Otis, Inc. Copyright © 1978 by Kaatje Hurlbut.

"The Missing Person" by Maxine Kumin. First published in *TriQuarterly*. Copyright © 1978 by Maxine Kumin.

"Some Manhattan in New England" by Peter LaSalle. First published in *The Georgia Review*. Copyright © 1979 by Peter LaSalle.

"Home Is the Hero" by Bernard Malamud. First published in *The Atlantic*. Copyright © 1977 by Bernard Malamud.

"Seasons" by Ruth McLaughlin. First published in *California Quarterly*. Copyright © 1978 by Ruth McLaughlin.

"Spelling" by Alice Munro. First published in *Weekend Magazine*. Copyright © 1978 by Alice Munro. All rights reserved.

"An Exile in the East" by Flannery O'Connor. Copyright © 1978 by Regina O'Connor; other versions of this story copyright © 1965, 1971 by the Estate of Mary Flannery O'Connor. Reprinted with the permission of Farrar, Straus & Giroux, Inc.

Contents

Introduction

THIS VOLUME lays claim to being a collection of the "best" North American short stories published in the past year, and of course it is a claim most gracefully made with some qualifications. Though Shannon Ravenel read 1494 stories published in some 153 periodicals, and out of these 1494 stories selected 125 to send along to me, it is obviously the case — given the unstable, even protean nature of small-press publishing in America — that we were unable to read each story published in 1978. In *TriQuarterly*'s recent 750-page special issue, Michael Anania estimates that there are approximately 1500 little magazines being published at the present time. Not all of these publish fiction, of course, and not all of these will survive more than a few issues, but the fact of their existence constitutes a staggering challenge to anyone who purports to be bringing together an anthology of short stories that are both excellent and representative. And there is the matter, too, of subjectivity in selection — Shannon Ravenel's and my own — for which we cannot apologize but about which, a little further on, I will explain.

Months of reading and rereading and brooding and indecision, letters back and forth between Shannon and me (though our tastes coincided in remarkable ways, they were, of course, hardly identical) . . . and here it is, the collection of twenty-five stories, each memorable in its own way, all of them distinct in voice and vision. Some are quite clearly and forthrightly modest, excellent "minor" fiction — two or three (there could not be more, probably, in a given year) strike me as small masterpieces. Confined within the covers of this book, which has become, over the thirty-six years of Martha Foley's distinguished editorship, a publishing tradition, they will — and should — quarrel with one another. Even if my tastes in fiction were not so catholic as they are I would have sought out, for this occasion, stories whose "voices" differ greatly from one another.

An anthology of the best fiction published in North America in any given year must be a kaleidoscopic affair: one might compare it to a museum gallery in which works of art of greatly varying sizes, techniques, and styles — modest line drawings, immense polychromatic oil paintings, water colors, lithographs, pencil sketches — have been hung side by side and are competing for the viewer's attention. A museum gallery so arranged would be an aesthetic error, an affront to the senses as well as to the intellect, but an anthology that sets out to reprint representative work must be as various, as democratic, even as motley as possible — within the limits set, of course, by the standard of excellence claimed by the title. And so it is the case that while certain periodicals are represented year after year, and with justification — *The New Yorker, Esquire, The Atlantic Monthly* — I have made an attempt to bring in more of the little magazines, some of them, such as *Quarterly West* and *Gallimaufry,* quite unknown to me, and many of them, I suspect, unknown to the general reader. Among the twenty-two periodicals represented are three published in Canada — *The Malahat Review, The Ontario Review,* and *Weekend Magazine* — and more Canadian periodicals appear in the "100 Other Distinguished Short Stories of the Year" list selected by Shannon Ravenel. The reader with a particular interest in the wide variety of creative work being written and published in North America is advised to consult the *TriQuarterly* volume and William Henderson's yearly anthology, *The Pushcart Prize: Best of the Small Presses.*

*

So much has been said in recent years about the function of art, particularly of fiction — that it should serve society as a moral force, or that it should stand apart from society as an end in itself, with no moral function whatsoever — that I would like in this preface to make a statement, necessarily abbreviated, about the writer's freedom; and I would like to present the stories I have selected as illustrations of the essential health and sound judgment that characterize the writer's freedom.

Though much is routinely said about the troubled state of contemporary fiction — as it is said, routinely, about the troubled state of contemporary politics, religion, morality, education, and television — it seems to me self-evident that we are living in an era of particularly well crafted creative work, whether fiction or poetry. More good work is being done by more gifted writers than ever before. More magazines are being published; more public readings (of prose as well as poetry) are being given, often to packed auditoriums. I know that it is fashionable to lament the passing of a literate order — I know that one is supposed to worry aloud about the malefic effect of the media and "eroding standards" in public schools, and the fact that notorious nonbooks or ghostwritten concoctions are best sellers while the sales of an award-winning collection of poems are distressingly low. Yet it has always seemed to me that such observations fail to take into consideration that the audience for serious literature at any given time has been fairly limited, and the audience for difficult literature has always been extremely limited. Decades ago, people say, there was a far larger market for short fiction — *The Saturday Evening Post, Collier's,* among others, paid high prices for stories — while today the market has been severely curtailed. Once upon a time a writer such as Scott Fitzgerald could make a handsome living by his short stories, but today he would certainly have to produce novels if he wanted to survive. The laments are familiar: we have heard them many times. But what they fail to acknowledge is that mass magazines of the twenties and thirties were primarily interested in slick, formula fiction, the sort of thing that now goes directly into television and would never qualify as "serious." *The Saturday Evening Post* and *Collier's were* the television of their time, and if writers such as Fitzgerald, Faulkner, Hemingway, Saroyan, Irwin Shaw, O'Hara, and others could make a living from them, it was perhaps to the detriment of their art. (See Faulkner's *Selected Letters,* for instance, which makes dismaying reading: he exhausted himself churning out stories he considered trash for the high-paying *Post,* in order to finance the writing of his novels — which were, of course, commercial failures.)

In the past, "experimental" writing was not welcome in any of the mass-market magazines, whereas today self-consciously experimental work (for whatever it is worth: one can see that much of it has degenerated into a new sort of formulaic fiction) can appear anywhere — in magazines once considered conservative, such as

The Atlantic Monthly and *The New Yorker*, as well as in such periodicals as *Partisan Review, The Paris Review,* the new *Georgia Review,* the new *Mississippi Review,* and innumerable others with small circulations. The audience for serious fiction has definitely increased: it has certainly become more sophisticated. Whereas at one time only meticulously crafted fiction in the Jamesian or Chekhovian mode was considered acceptable — because obviously "literary" — we now have a cultural climate hospitable to fictions that may take the form of surrealist monologues or Dadaist fantasies, or, in the case of Borges, fanciful commentaries on nonexistent books. A gap of sorts has widened between what might be called traditional fiction, with its emphasis on psychologically "realistic" characters in recognizable settings who are moved, usually with some direction, through time and space, and what might be called meta-fiction: prose that aspires to the bodiless condition of poetry, or pure sound, the "new music" of Barthelme's story, which is no longer entirely new, though its dissonances and relentless non sequiturs make claims of newness. ("There are certain criticisms," Barthelme's eloquent voice says, "the Curator of Archetypes thinks I don't quite cut it, thinks I'm shuckin' and jivin' when what I should be doing is attacking, attacking, attacking . . .")

     Short fiction, in my opinion, can aspire to any condition whatsoever: as an editor of this volume, and as a chronic reader, I have no prejudices except that a story, as a construct of words, make some claim for uniqueness. I was deeply moved by Saul Bellow's "A Silver Dish," one of the most beautiful, and beautifully crafted, stories I have come across in years; it seemed to me so incontestably masterful a work that I wanted to organize the entire anthology around it. Yet I see no difficulty in choosing as a companion piece for it the laconic, chill, passionless "The Eye," by Paul Bowles, which reads as if it had no narrator at all, and aspires to a condition of sheer narrative bereft of character — a tale told by no one in particular about no one in particular (its "hero," never directly glimpsed, is dead before the story opens), which nevertheless possesses an uncanny suspenseful power. Bellow's story, like Bowles's, is anecdotal, even conversational; one might see Bellow's as a brilliant variation on the stereotypical *New Yorker* reminiscence, a lesson in sheer genius, performed in Bellow's inimitable voice. (For Bellow's fiction is all voice: one can hear its rhythms, its nuances, and would recognize the Bellow sound anywhere.)

Had there been meta-fictions of comparable uniqueness among this year's published fiction I would have been grateful to reprint them, but it seems to me that meta-fiction's ironies have begun to run out, or to repeat themselves with dismaying frequency. (Nearly every "experimental" story one encounters today reads like an undergraduate imitation of Ionesco, or Beckett, or Borges, or one of their American counterparts. Postsixties "fictions" have dwindled into patterns as rigid as O. Henry's, in which an arbitrary proposition — a dwarf elephant, for instance, has been elected President of the United States — is threaded through with exotic motifs or mock symbols — a Yamaha grand piano, a tap-dancing team from the forties, Salvador Dali's waxed mustache, let us say — in a story of not less than five pages or more than eight. Presumably someone reads these "fictions," but not more than once, for they dissolve sadly on a second reading, and often midway through the first, when their single parodic theme becomes transparent. But so uncertain are editorial standards today that I came across a version of Robert Coover's high-spirited "The Babysitter" set in a zoo, and, in a highly respectable magazine, a diluted recycling of Shirley Jackson's classic "The Lottery," both of which were presented by their editors, if not by their authors, as original works.)

In his introduction to last year's *The Best American Short Stories* Ted Solotaroff, by way of explaining both his own background (as editor, over a ten-year period, of *New American Review*) and his professional standards for the "best" stories, said some important things about the state of contemporary fiction. Like many of us, he had seen the short story undergo a violent metamorphosis in a single decade — so violent a metamorphosis that it became more or less unhelpful to draw a line between fiction and nonfiction. Writers boldly experimented with fictions that presented themselves as essays, often on absurd or nonexistent subjects; there were fictions in the form of questions-and-answers, or interviews, or rambling monologues in the style of Beckett's nameless narrators; there were false memoirs, meditations, recipes; even the liner notes (fictitious, of course) to a record album. In short, all that wasn't conspicuously poetry might be considered prose — whatever "poetry" and "prose" now meant. (A special issue of *TriQuarterly* billed itself "Post-*Wake*": and, indeed, the fictions published were by a variety of writers all of whom sounded as if *Finnegans Wake* had been in a way their own, and they were doomed to self-conscious pseudo-Joycean posturings of the kind literary critics now call Post-Modernist.)

It was revealing, however, that in selecting twenty-odd stories for this volume, Solotaroff thought it most pragmatic to limit his definition of "story" to a fairly conservative model. With such a dizzying profusion of fictional forms to choose from he decided he wanted "genuine" stories and nothing else — "stories with a strong narrative movement that clearly gets somewhere, preferably to a point that is both unpredictable and right." This definition I thought a particularly astute one, though it might eliminate stories that repudiate motion in favor of stasis, and certain gemlike works (in this volume, Rosellen Brown's "The Wedding Week") that aspire to the condition of poetry. But it is good to know an editor's preferences, even if, as in the case of Solotaroff, he *sounds* more conservative than he really is. (For the 1978 *Best American Short Stories* contained highly idiosyncratic work — genuine stories, certainly, but told in arresting ways, in a wonderful variety of voices.)

When asked to speak in public about the short story, or about fiction in general, I often hear myself saying — if I have been unable to avoid the vaporous topic — that fiction, the story, all of art itself, cannot be determined. Definitions are quite meaningless. One can *say* that a novel is this or that, based upon the novels one has happened to have read; one can *say* that the short story must be this but not that, it "must" have an ending, or characters, or a coherent linear development; one can say anything at all. But commentary on art can help only to elucidate already existing art: it cannot prescribe, and it certainly cannot predict. Art is an expression of imaginative freedom. Not all artists, of course, enjoy freedom — not all artists are worthy of their art, in fact. But art itself comes before any of its commentators, be they helpful or censorious. Plato's small-minded malice in wishing to rid the well-regulated State of its poets is often quoted, and sometimes in an approving way, but I see no reason to refrain from noting that Plato's vision of the well-regulated State (and, indeed, of the well-regulated cosmos) is about as appealing to most of us, poets or nonpoets, as the prospect of spending the rest of our lives in straitjackets or solitary confinement. Plato meant to eradicate from the State all change, all innovation, all imaginative thinking — he aligned himself with political tyranny, which was, of course, his option. We need not ban Plato and his disciples from the poet's state: only, let their ideas be freely contested.

The short story, as it is one of the many manifestations of the human spirit, simply cannot be defined. Art *is*: it springs forth from the soul, usually in mysterious ways; and it addresses itself to an audience, sometimes in humility, very often in arrogance. Anyone who attempts to define art reveals himself first of all as lamentably conservative, and secondly as a critic or commentator rather than as an artist. (When great artists — among them Joyce, Lawrence, Mann, Kafka — speak of art they are usually struggling to define their own practice, and to set it against the practice of their contemporaries and predecessors.) If I say that this volume's spare, terse, almost too elliptical "Home and Native Land," by Seán Virgo, seems to me an unusually effective story, I am not saying at the same time that Virgo's practice of his art should be raised into a principle for others. If I say that William Styron's wonderful "Shadrach" — so rich it has the feel of a novel — is an unforgettable story, I am not saying that Styron's art is superior to that of, say, Jean Thompson in "Paper Covers Rock," which seems to me an unsettling work of fiction in many ways, not least because it captures, in its muted, passionless tones, a lifelessness at the core of our world's "liberated" life that is appalling. I said earlier that the stories' many voices quarrel, and this is true enough — but they also constitute a larger harmony.

Unlike Ted Solotaroff, I am not especially disposed to stories with a strong narrative movement, nor do I particularly want or need fiction to have characters, or a clearly evoked setting, or, in fact, much of a "point" at all. I suppose I want simply the sense, which the writer conveys only through the skill of his language, that *something* unique is being offered. Some illumination, some droll observation, the authenticity of *what it feels like* from a position alien to my own: the fiction can be straight autobiography or absolute fantasy, it can attempt to delineate, in detailed prose, the experience of suffering the literal deterioration of one's heart (as in the late Herbert Wilner's "The Quarterback Speaks to His God"), or the experience of terror in a modern city (as in Maxine Kumin's parablelike "The Missing Person," in which apprehension — one might call it neurotic — is refined into art), or the experience, presented only obliquely, and breezily, of living alone, in Robley Wilson Jr.'s "Living Alone." Narrative movement is buried in Louis D. Rubin Jr.'s "Finisterre," and characterization too is minimal: but the evocation of place, the feel, the *texture* of Rubin's world! Bear with the fourteen-year-old protagonist's experience, and it will become your own, so meticulous, so thoughtful is the writer's art.

Rubin's art, like that of Mary Hedin in "The Middle Place," is slow to reveal itself. Sensing beforehand that there will be no surprises — the fiction will not explode into meta-fiction, it will not coyly question its own reason for being — the reader simply succumbs to the spell of its language, and thus lives the life of the story along with the fictional characters. Lynne Sharon Schwartz's beautifully modulated "Plaisir d'Amour," like Peter LaSalle's brilliant "Some Manhattan in New England," is fantasy securely grounded in naturalism; or is it naturalism subtly grounded in fantasy . . . ? (Last year's *Best American Short Stories* contained a story by Schwartz, "Rough Strife," that seems to me even more powerful than "Plaisir d'Amour." And I must confess a predilection for Schwartz's fiction, since I am an editor of *The Ontario Review*, in which both these stories first appeared.)

The art of Bernard Malamud's "Home Is the Hero" is an art that hides itself. Malamud is a highly sophisticated stylist, whose fantasy and surrealism are seamlessly employed in narratives that otherwise have the appearance, and the authenticity, of straightforward naturalism. He moves from one plane to another so adroitly, with so little self-conscious fuss, that one can be deceived into thinking that his achievements come easily. So too with Isaac Bashevis Singer's "A Party in Miami Beach" (and another fine story, "The Bus," included in the list of 100 other distinguished short stories of 1978), in which autobiography and fiction appear to be blended. Malamud presents his hero's experiences in language that is part his hero's and part Malamud's (see, for instance, the story's fascinating conclusion, in which Dubin wanders, lost, in a snowstorm), while Singer appears to have refined himself out of existence, allowing his characters their long, rich, manic, monologues.

Another art that disguises itself in artlessness is that of Alice Munro in "Spelling" (and in a companion story, "Characters," on the distinguished-stories list). In earlier works, Munro brought to near perfection the kind of story that summed up a life in carefully chosen scenes; here her tone is one of scrupulous meanness (to use Joyce's phrase), life is reduced to a gesture or two, and emotion is withheld. These are strange, unsettling stories that might appear to the inattentive reader to have no "point." They are naturalistic works so intensely evoked, with so little apparent sentiment, that they have the passionless force of prose poems, in which images, not characters, are drawn. Narrative movement, though it can certainly be traced, is hardly the issue here.

Similarly with Silvia Tennenbaum's poignant "A Lingering Death," in which the shadow of death, thrown back upon an immensely rich and complex life, has the paradoxical effect of illuminating that life: and with what rigorous, faultless language! "A song of praise escaped from her mouth" — so the utterly believable Amalie slips into the oblivion of death; yet her story is not at all self-pitying or depressing. (And it doesn't harangue us like Tolstoy's *The Death of Ivan Ilyitch,* which it peripherally resembles.) Lyn Coffin's "Falling off the Scaffold" has, in a sense, no characters at all, only the projected personae of two people unknown to each other; yet it respects the contours of reality and gives us, in a most unusual form, a story about illusion and self-deception, timely in its relatedness to current thinking about male-female roles. "Trip in a Summer Dress," "The Quail," and "A Short Walk into Afternoon" are exquisitely rendered stories about deliberately modest subjects, subjects that cannot be described in language other than their own: their "stories" are simply beside the point. One must read them with care and sympathy to appreciate their achievement.

"Seasons," the title of Ruth McLaughlin's delicate, haunting, and finally rather disturbing story, might well serve as a subtitle for this volume. For most of the stories I have discussed, as well as Flannery O'Connor's "An Exile in the East" and Jayne Anne Phillips's "Something That Happened," focus upon arrested moments in the seasons of a protagonist's life that illuminate the entirety of that life, or of the life of someone close to him or her. It seems to have occurred in our modern tradition that the most popular of *literary* stories (in contrast to mass-market fiction) employ the synecdochic method, in which the near-at-hand serves magically to summon forth the whole, the universal. Sometimes the Chekhovian or Joycean "epiphany" is made fairly explicit, as in "The Middle Place"; sometimes, as in Alice Munro's and Seán Virgo's stories, it must be inferred. One might argue for a traditional, even classical structure behind the enigmatic dialogue of talking heads in Barthelme's "The New Music," and it isn't unreasonable to suspect that Barthelme shares with a number of others in this volume certain obsessive cares about the nature of language in a culture of relentless novelty.

"An Exile in the East" — which admirers of Flannery O'Connor's fiction will recognize as an early version of the magisterial "Judgement Day" — was written in 1954 and published, for the first time, in *The South Carolina Review* of November 1978 (it was found among O'Connor's papers at Georgia College). Written between "The Displaced Person" and "The Artificial Nigger," "An Exile in the East" shares concerns with both, and with the visionary pathos of "Judgement Day." Yet it is a far more human story — virtually the most "realistic" of all O'Connor's fiction. That it was ultimately transformed into "Judgement Day" should not obscure the fact that it is a complete story in itself, and that in 1954 Flannery O'Connor considered it important enough to be included in her first collection of short stories, *A Good Man Is Hard to Find.* (It was later pulled from the collection to make room for a newer story, "Good Country People," which O'Connor evidently preferred.) In this poignant story the themes of racial conflict, spiritual exile, and loneliness are treated unsentimentally through the person of old Tanner, one of O'Connor's most sympathetic characters, one with whom she evidently felt a deep kinship.

Perhaps it is the case that most successful stories, in this volume or elsewhere, employ a synecdochic method that allows the particular to evoke the universal. O'Connor's exiled Tanner cannot state the degree of his loneliness, but his human suffering is made dramatically clear by the story's artful understatement. Another exile, the breezy, chatty Max Flederbush of Singer's "A Party in Miami Beach," speaks in entertaining monologues on the subject of Jewish concentration-camp survivors who now sit, by the hundreds, awaiting death in Miami Beach — "in a certain sense, it's worse here than in the camps. There, at least, we all hoped" — and his suffering is no less poignant for being floridly overstated.

Old Morris of Bellow's "A Silver Dish," idiosyncratic as he is, is at the same time emblematic of all fathers. No matter that he is a singular and singularly maddening, old man — he is simultaneously *all* old men; and his son, Woody's, grief becomes, through the subtlety of Bellow's art, our universal grief for all that we must lose, despite the desperate strength of our love. That we *cannot* preserve those whom we cherish, but must, in the end, surrender them to death: this is the hidden meaning of Bellow's story, the foundation that supports, but never intrudes upon, the irresistibly entertaining material.

It is not my prejudice that a story, to be complete, must so deftly employ the synecdochic method that one is reading both about an individual and a universal condition, but certainly such fiction has the power to move us greatly — it is really fiction as a kind of communion.

*

Though I have set forth with apparent confidence and, I hope, with reasonable clarity, my standards in choosing these stories, I want to say too that I found the task challenging; it was not at all an easy one. Certain stories, of course, immediately struck me as marvelous — I wanted at once to show them to other people, to share them, to talk about them. Others impressed me as well worth preserving in an anthology of this nature, but it was difficult — *very* difficult — to draw a line between those that would be reprinted and those that, because of space limitations, would have to be rejected. (If the anthology could have accommodated thirty-five stories the situation would have been far more congenial.) Many of the stories I reluctantly excluded from the volume are, it might be argued, as good as any included, and perhaps in another year, or in another few weeks, I will reread one of them and regret my decision. So be it. My position as this year's editor of *The Best American Short Stories* amplifies the frustrations I ordinarily feel as an editor of *The Ontario Review,* which receives more good material than it can possibly publish; and I suspect that my experience is shared by most editors. Ours is, doom sayers to the contrary, not only a highly literate age: it is also a highly *literary* age. More people are writing, and writing well, than ever before in our history, and there are simply not enough channels of publication open to them. When critics say smugly that the state of contemporary prose or poetry is poor, one really should challenge them to list the books and periodicals they have actually recently read. To how many magazines do they subscribe? Do they know that the *Kenyon Review* has returned? Have they discovered the gorgeous new *Bennington Review,* the new *Agni Review,* and others such as *Canto, Fiction, Antæus, Exile, Story Quarterly, The New England Review, Ploughshares, Pequod, New Letters* . . . ?

It is to be hoped that the reader, approaching this anthology, will honor the important differences between the writers by *not* reading the stories one after another as if the book were a novel.

Run hurriedly together, the voices of Bellow and O'Connor and Virgo and Hurlbut and the rest will lose their distinctiveness, and consequently their art; and the reader will be cheated of the revelation each story offers. Properly executed, the act of reading is not only a creative act; it aspires to the condition of what might be called a mystic communion. "A book is an ax," says Kafka, "for the frozen sea within." And so indeed it is.

JOYCE CAROL OATES

The Best
AMERICAN
SHORT
STORIES
1979

SAUL BELLOW

A Silver Dish

(FROM THE NEW YORKER)

WHAT DO YOU DO about death — in this case, the death of an old father? If you're a modern person, sixty years of age, and a man who's been around, like Woody Selbst, what do you do? Take this matter of mourning, and take it against a contemporary background. How, against a contemporary background, do you mourn an octogenarian father, nearly blind, his heart enlarged, his lungs filling with fluid, who creeps, stumbles, gives off the odors, the moldiness or gassiness of old men. I *mean!* As Woody put it, be realistic. Think what times these are. The papers daily give it to you — the Lufthansa pilot in Aden is described by the hostages on his knees, begging the Palestinian terrorists not to execute him, but they shoot him through the head. Later they themselves are killed. And still others shoot others, or shoot themselves. That's what you read in the press, see on the tube, mention at dinner. We know now what goes daily through the whole of the human community, like a global death-peristalsis.

Woody, a businessman in South Chicago, was not an ignorant person. He knew more such phrases than you would expect a tile contractor (offices, lobbies, lavatories) to know. The kind of knowledge he had was not the kind for which you get academic degrees. Although Woody had studied for two years in a seminary, preparing to be a minister. Two years of college during the Depression was more than most high-school graduates could afford. After that, in his own vital, picturesque, original way (Morris, his old man, was also, in his days of nature, vital and picturesque) Woody had read up on many subjects, subscribed to *Science* and other magazines that gave real information, and had taken night courses at De Paul and Northwestern in ecology, criminology, existential-ism. Also he had travelled extensively in Japan, Mexico, and Africa, and there was an African experience that was especially relevant to mourning. It was this: On a launch near the Murchison Falls in Uganda, he had seen a buffalo calf seized by a crocodile from the bank of the White Nile. There were giraffes along the tropical river, and hippopotamuses, and baboons, and flamingos and other brilliant birds crossing the bright air in the heat of the morning, when the calf, stepping into the river to drink, was grabbed by the hoof and dragged down. The parent buffaloes couldn't figure it out. Under the water the calf still threshed, fought, churned the mud. Woody, the robust traveller, took this in as he sailed by, and to him it looked as if the parent cattle were asking each other dumbly what had happened. He chose to assume that there was pain in this, he read brute grief into it. On the White Nile, Woody had the impression that he had gone back to the pre-Adamite past, and he brought reflections on this impression home to South Chicago. He brought also a bundle of hashish from Kampala. In this he took a chance with the customs inspectors, banking perhaps on his broad build, frank face, high color. He didn't look like a wrongdoer, a bad guy; he looked like a good guy. But he liked taking chances. Risk was a wonderful stimulus. He threw down his trenchcoat on the customs counter. If the inspectors searched the pockets, he was prepared to say that the coat wasn't his. But he got away with it, and the Thanksgiving turkey was stuffed with hash-ish. This was much enjoyed. That was practically the last feast at which Pop, who also relished risk or defiance, was present. The hashish Woody had tried to raise in his back yard from the Africa seeds didn't take. But behind his warehouse, where the Lincoln Continental was parked, he kept a patch of marijuana. There was no harm at all in Woody but he didn't like being entirely within the law. It was simply a question of self-respect.

After that Thanksgiving, Pop gradually sank as if he had a slow leak. This went on for some years. In and out of the hospital, he dwindled, his mind wandered, he couldn't even concentrate enough to complain, except in exceptional moments on the Sun-days Woody regularly devoted to him. Morris, an amateur who once was taken seriously by Willie Hoppe, the great pro him-self, couldn't execute the simplest billiard shots anymore. He could only conceive shots; he began to theorize about impossible three-cushion combinations. Halina, the Polish woman with whom Morris had lived for over forty years as man and wife, was too old herself now to run to the hospital. So Woody had to do it. There was Woody's mother, too — a Christian convert — needing care; she was over eighty and frequently hospitalized. Everybody had diabetes and pleurisy and arthritis and cataracts and cardiac pacemakers. And everybody had lived by the body, but the body was giving out.

There were Woody's two sisters as well, unmarried, in their fifties, very Christian, very straight, still living with Mama in an entirely Christian bungalow. Woody, who took full responsibility for them all, occasionally had to put one of the girls (they had become sick girls) in a mental institution. Nothing severe. The sisters were wonderful women, both of them gorgeous once, but neither of the poor things was playing with a full deck. And all the factions had to be kept separate — Mama, the Christian convert; the fundamentalist sisters; Pop, who read the Yiddish paper as long as he could still see print; Halina, a good Catholic. Woody, the seminary forty years behind him, described himself as an agnostic. Pop had no more religion than you could find in the Yiddish paper, but he made Woody promise to bury him among Jews, and that was where he lay now, in the Hawaiian shirt Woody had bought for him at the tilers' convention in Honolulu. Woody would allow no undertaker's assistant to dress him but came to the parlor and buttoned the stiff into the shirt himself, and the old man went down looking like Ben-Gurion in a simple wooden coffin, sure to rot fast. That was how Woody wanted it all. At the graveside, he had taken off and folded his jacket, rolled up his sleeves on thick freckled biceps, waved back the little tractor standing by, and shovelled the dirt himself. His big face, broad at the bottom, narrowed upward like a Dutch house. And, his small good lower teeth taking hold of the upper lip in his exertion, he performed the final duty of a son. He was very fit, so it must have been emotion, not the shovelling, that made him redden so. After the funeral, he went home with Halina and her son, a decent Polack like his mother, and talented, too — Mitosh played the organ at hockey and basketball games in the Stadium, which took a smart man because it was a rabble-rousing kind of occupation — and they had some drinks and comforted the old girl. Halina was true blue, always one hundred per cent for Morris.

Then for the rest of the week Woody was busy, had jobs to run, office responsibilities, family responsibilities. He lived alone; as did his wife; as did his mistress: everybody in a separate establishment. Since his wife, after fifteen years of separation, had not learned to take care of herself, Woody did her shopping on Fridays, filled her freezer. He had to take her this week to buy shoes. Also, Friday night he always spent with Helen — Helen was his wife de facto. Saturday he did his big weekly shopping. Saturday night he devoted to Mom and his sisters. So he was too busy to attend to his own feelings except, intermittently, to note to himself, "First Thursday in the grave." "First Friday, and fine weather." "First Saturday; he's got to be getting used to it." Under his breath he occasionally said, "Oh, Pop."

But it was Sunday that hit him, when the bells rang all over South Chicago — the Ukrainian, Roman Catholic, Greek, Russian, African-Methodist churches, sounding off one after another. Woody had his offices in his warehouse, and there had built an apartment for himself, very spacious and convenient, in the top story. Because he left every Sunday morning at seven to spend the day with Pop, he had forgotten by how many churches Selbst Tile Company was surrounded. He was still in bed when he heard the bells, and all at once he knew how heartbroken he was. This sudden big heartache in a man of sixty, a practical, physical, healthy-minded, and experienced man, was deeply unpleasant. When he had an unpleasant condition, he believed in taking something for it. So he thought, What shall I take? There were plenty of remedies available. His cellar was stocked with cases of Scotch whiskey, Polish vodka, Armagnac, Moselle, Burgundy. There were also freezers with steaks and with game and with Alaskan king crab. He bought with a broad hand — by the crate and by the dozen. But in the end, when he got out of bed, he took nothing but a cup of coffee. While the kettle was heating, he put on his Japanese judo-style suit and sat down to reflect.

Woody was moved when things were *honest*. Bearing beams were honest, undisguised concrete pillars inside high-rise apartments were honest. It was bad to cover up anything. He hated faking. Stone was honest. Metal was honest. These Sunday bells were very straight. They broke loose, they wagged and rocked, and the vibrations and the banging did something for him — cleansed his insides, purified his blood. A bell was a one-way throat, had only one thing to tell you and simply told it. He listened.

He had had some connections with bells and churches. He was
after all something of a Christian. Born a Jew, he was a Jew facially,
with a hint of Iroquois or Cherokee, but his mother had been
converted more than fifty years ago by her brother-in-law, the
Reverend Dr. Kovner. Kovner, a rabbinical student who had left
the Hebrew Union College in Cincinnati to become a minister and
establish a mission, had given Woody a partly Christian upbring-
ing. Now Pop was on the outs with these fundamentalists. He said
that the Jews came to the mission to get coffee, bacon, canned
pineapple, day-old bread, and dairy products. And if they had to
listen to sermons, that was O.K. — this was the Depression and you
couldn't be too particular — but he knew they sold the bacon.

The Gospels said it plainly: "Salvation is from the Jews."

Backing the Reverend Doctor were wealthy fundamentalists,
mainly Swedes, eager to speed up the Second Coming by converting all Jews. The foremost of Kovner's backers was Mrs. Skoglund,
who had inherited a large dairy business from her late husband.
Woody was under her special protection.

Woody was fourteen years of age when Pop took off with Halina,
who worked in his shop, leaving his difficult Christian wife and his
converted son and his small daughters. He came to Woody in the
back yard one spring day and said, "From now on you're the man
of the house." Woody was practicing with a golf club, knocking off
the heads of dandelions. Pop came into the yard in his good suit,
which was too hot for the weather, and when he took off his fedora
the skin of his head was marked with a deep ring and the sweat
was sprinkled over his scalp — more drops than hairs. He said,
"I'm going to move out." Pop was anxious, but he was set to go —
determined. "It's no use. I can't live a life like this." Envisioning
the life Pop simply *had* to live, his free life, Woody was able to
picture him in the billiard parlor, under the "L" tracks in a crap
game, or playing poker at Brown and Koppel's upstairs. "You're
going to be the man of the house," said Pop. "It's O.K. I put you
all on welfare. I just got back from Wabansia Avenue, from the
Relief Station." Hence the suit and the hat. "They're sending out a
caseworker." Then he said, "You got to lend me money to buy
gasoline — the caddie money you saved."

Understanding that Pop couldn't get away without his help,
Woody turned over to him all he had earned at the Sunset Ridge
Country Club in Winnetka. Pop felt that the valuable life lesson he
was transmitting was worth far more than these dollars, and when-

ever he was conning his boy a sort of high-priest expression came down over his bent nose, his ruddy face. The children, who got their finest ideas at the movies, called him Richard Dix. Later, when the comic strip came out, they said he was Dick Tracy.

As Woody now saw it, under the tumbling bells, he had bankrolled his own desertion. Ha ha! He found this delightful; and especially Pop's attitude of "That'll teach you to trust your father." For this was a demonstration on behalf of real life and free instincts, against religion and hypocrisy. But mainly it was aimed against being a fool, the disgrace of foolishness. Pop had it in for the Reverend Dr. Kovner, not because he was an apostate (Pop couldn't have cared less), not because the mission was a racket (he admitted that the Reverend Doctor was personally honest), but because Dr. Kovner behaved foolishly, spoke like a fool, and acted like a fiddler. He tossed his hair like a Paganini (this was Woody's addition; Pop had never even heard of Paganini). Proof that he was not a spiritual leader was that he converted Jewish women by stealing their hearts. "He works up all those broads," said Pop. "He doesn't even know it himself, I swear he doesn't know how he gets them."

From the other side, Kovner often warned Woody, "Your father is a dangerous person. Of course, you love him; you should love and forgive him, Voodrow, but you are old enough to understand he is leading a life of wice."

It was all petty stuff: Pop's sinning was on a boy level and therefore made a big impression on a boy. And on Mother. Are wives children, or what? Mother often said, "I hope you put that brute in your prayers. Look what he has done to us. But only pray for him, don't see him." But he saw him all the time. Woodrow was leading a double life, sacred and profane. He accepted Jesus Christ as his personal redeemer. Aunt Rebecca took advantage of this. She made him work. He had to work under Aunt Rebecca. He filled in for the janitor at the mission and settlement house. In winter, he had to feed the coal furnace, and on some nights he slept near the furnace room, on the pool table. He also picked the lock of the storeroom. He took canned pineapple and cut bacon from the flitch with his pocketknife. He crammed himself with uncooked bacon. He had a big frame to fill out.

Only now, sipping Melitta coffee, he asked himself — had he been so hungry? No, he loved being reckless. He was fighting Aunt

Rebecca Kovner when he took out his knife and got on a box to reach the bacon. She didn't know, she couldn't prove that Woody, such a frank, strong, positive boy who looked you in the eye, so direct, was a thief also. But he was also a thief. Whenever she looked at him, he knew that she was seeing his father. In the curve of his nose, the movements of his eyes, the thickness of his body, in his healthy face she saw that wicked savage, Morris.

Morris, you see, had been a street boy in Liverpool — Woody's mother and her sister were British by birth. Morris's Polish family, on their way to America, abandoned him in Liverpool because he had an eye infection and they would all have been sent back from Ellis Island. They stopped awhile in England, but his eyes kept running and they ditched him. They slipped away, and he had to make out alone in Liverpool at the age of twelve. Mother came of better people. Pop, who slept in the cellar of her house, fell in love with her. At sixteen, scabbing during a seamen's strike, he shovelled his way across the Atlantic and jumped ship in Brooklyn. He became an American, and America never knew it. He voted without papers, he drove without a license, he paid no taxes, he cut every corner. Horses, cards, billiards, and women were his lifelong interests, in ascending order. Did he love anyone (he was so busy)? Yes, he loved Halina. He loved his son. To this day, Mother believed that he had loved her most and always wanted to come back. This gave her a chance to act the queen, with her plump wrists and faded Queen Victoria face. "The girls are instructed never to admit him," she said. The Empress of India, speaking.

Bell-battered Woodrow's soul was whirling this Sunday morning, indoors and out, to the past, back to his upper corner of the warehouse, laid out with such originality — the bells coming and going, metal on naked metal, until the bell circle expanded over the whole of steelmaking, oil-refining, power-producing mid-autumn South Chicago, and all its Croatians, Ukrainians, Greeks, Poles, and respectable blacks heading for their churches to hear Mass or to sing hymns.

Woody himself had been a good hymn singer. He still knew the hymns. He had testified, too. He was often sent by Aunt Rebecca to get up and tell a church full of Scandihoovians that he, a Jewish lad, accepted Jesus Christ. For this she paid him fifty cents. She made the disbursement. She was the bookkeeper, fiscal chief, general manager of the mission. The Reverend Doctor didn't know a thing about the operation. What the Doctor supplied was the fervor. He was genuine, a wonderful preacher. And what about Woody himself? He also had fervor. He was drawn to the Reverend Doctor. The Reverend Doctor taught him to lift up his eyes, gave him his higher life. Apart from this higher life, the rest was Chicago — the ways of Chicago, which came so natural that nobody thought to question them. So, for instance, in 1933 (what ancient, ancient times!) at the Century of Progress World's Fair, when Woody was a coolie and pulled a rickshaw, wearing a peaked straw hat and trotting with powerful, thick legs, while the brawny red farmers — his boozing passengers — were laughing their heads off and pestered him for whores, he, although a freshman at the seminary, saw nothing wrong, when girls asked him to steer a little business their way, in making dates and accepting tips from both sides. He necked in Grant Park with a powerful girl who had to go home quickly to nurse her baby. Smelling of milk, she rode beside him on the streetcar to the West Side, squeezing his rickshaw puller's thigh and wetting her blouse. This was the Roosevelt Road car. Then, in the apartment where she lived with her mother, he couldn't remember that there were any husbands around. What he did remember was the strong milk odor. Without inconsistency, next morning he did New Testament Greek: The light shineth in darkness — *to fos en te skotia fainei* — and the darkness comprehended it not.

And all the while he trotted between the shafts on the fairgrounds he had one idea — nothing to do with these horny giants having a big time in the city: that the goal, the project, the purpose was (and he couldn't explain why he thought so; all evidence was against it), God's idea was that this world should be a love-world, that it should eventually recover and be entirely a world of love. He wouldn't have said this to a soul, for he could see himself how stupid it was — personal and stupid. Nevertheless, there it was at the center of his feelings. And at the same time Aunt Rebecca was right when she said to him, strictly private, close to his ear even, "You're a little crook, like your father."

There was some evidence for this, or what stood for evidence to an impatient person like Rebecca. Woody matured quickly — he had to — but how could you expect a boy of seventeen, he wondered, to interpret the viewpoint, the feelings of a middle-aged woman, and one whose breast had been removed? Morris told him that this happened only to neglected women, and was a sign. Morris said that if titties were not fondled and kissed they got cancer in protest. It was a cry of the flesh. And this had seemed true to Woody. When his imagination tried the theory on the Reverend Doctor, it worked out — he couldn't see the Reverend Doctor behaving in that way to Aunt Rebecca's breasts! Morris's theory kept Woody looking from bosoms to husbands and from husbands to bosoms. He still did that. It's an exceptionally smart man who isn't marked forever by the sexual theories he hears from his father, and Woody wasn't all that smart. He knew this himself. Personally, he had gone far out of his way to do right by women in this regard. What nature demanded. He and Pop were common, thick men, but there's nobody too gross to have ideas of delicacy.

The Reverend Doctor preached, Rebecca preached, rich Mrs. Skoglund preached from Evanston, Mother preached. Pop also was on a soapbox. Everyone was doing it. Up and down Division Street, under every lamp, almost, speakers were giving out: anarchists, Socialists, Stalinists, single-taxers, Zionists, Tolstoyans, vegetarians, and fundamentalist Christian preachers — you name it. A beef, a hope, a way of life or salvation, a protest. How was it that the accumulated gripes of all the ages took off so when transplanted to America?

And that fine Swedish immigrant Aase (Osie, they pronounced it), who had been the Skoglunds' cook and married the eldest son to become his rich, religious widow — she supported the Reverend Doctor. In her time she must have been built like a chorus girl. And women seem to have lost the secret of putting up their hair in the high basketry fence of braid she wore. Aase took Woody under her special protection and paid his tuition at the seminary. And Pop said . . . But on this Sunday, at peace as soon as the bells stopped banging, this velvet autumn day when the grass was finest and thickest, silky green: before the first frost, and the blood in your lungs is redder than summer air can make it and smarts with oxygen, as if the iron in your system was hungry for it, and the chill was sticking it to you in every breath — Pop, six feet under, would never feel this blissful sting again. The last of the bells still had the bright air streaming with vibrations.

On weekends, the institutional vacancy of decades came back to the warehouse and crept under the door of Woody's apartment. It felt as empty on Sundays as churches were during the week. Before each business day, before the trucks and the crews got started, Woody jogged five miles in his Adidas suit. Not on this day still reserved for Pop, however. Although it was tempting to go out and run off the grief. Being alone hit Woody hard this morning. He thought, Me and the world; the world and me. Meaning that there always was some activity to interpose, an errand or a visit, a picture to paint (he was a creative amateur), a massage, a meal — a shield between himself and that troublesome solitude which used the world as its reservoir. But Pop! Last Tuesday, Woody had gotten into the hospital bed with Pop because he kept pulling out the intravenous needles. Nurses stuck them back, and then Woody astonished them all by climbing into bed to hold the struggling old guy in his arms. "Easy, Morris, Morris, go easy." But Pop still groped feebly for the pipes.

When the tolling stopped, Woody didn't notice that a great lake of quiet had come over his kingdom, the Selbst Tile Warehouse. What he heard and saw was an old red Chicago streetcar, one of those trams the color of a stockyard steer. Cars of this type went out before Pearl Harbor — clumsy, big-bellied, with tough rattan seats and brass grips for the standing passengers. Those cars used to make four stops to the mile, and ran with a wallowing motion. They stank of carbolic or ozone and throbbed when the air compressors were being charged. The conductor had his knotted signal cord to pull, and the motorman beat the foot gong with his mad heel.

Woody recognized himself on the Western Avenue line and riding through a blizzard with his father, both in sheepskins and with hands and faces raw, the snow blowing in from the rear platform when the doors opened and getting into the longitudinal cleats of the floor. There wasn't warmth enough inside to melt it. And Western Avenue was the longest car line in the world, the boosters said, as if it was a thing to brag about. Twenty-three miles long, made by a draftsman with a T-square, lined with factories, storage buildings, machine shops, used-car lots, trolley barns, gas stations, funeral parlors, six-flats, utility buildings, and junk yards, on and on from the prairies on the south to Evanston on the north. Woodrow and his father were going north to Evanston, to Howard Street, and then some, to see Mrs. Skoglund. At the end of the line they would still have about five blocks to hike. The purpose of the trip? To raise money for Pop. Pop had talked him into this. When they found out, Mother and Aunt Rebecca would be furious, and Woody was afraid, but he couldn't help it.

Morris had come and said, "Son, I'm in trouble. It's bad."

"What's bad, Pop?"

"Halina took money from her husband for me and has to put it back before old Bujak misses it. He could kill her."

"What did she do it for?"

"Son, you know how the bookies collect? They send a goon. They'll break my head open."

"Pop! You know I can't take you to Mrs. Skoglund."

"Why not? You're my kid, aren't you? The old broad wants to adopt you, doesn't she? Shouldn't I get something out of it for my trouble? What am I — outside? And what about Halina? She puts her life on the line, but my own kid says no."

"Oh, Bujak wouldn't hurt her."

"Woody, he'd beat her to death."

Bujak? Uniform in color with his dark-gray work clothes, short in the legs, his whole strength in his tool-and-die-maker's forearms and black fingers; and beat-looking — there was Bujak for you. But, according to Pop, there was big, big violence in Bujak, a regular boiling Bessemer inside his narrow chest. Woody could never see the violence in him. Bujak wanted no trouble. If anything, maybe he was afraid that Morris and Halina would gang up on him and kill him, screaming. But Pop was no desperado murderer. And Halina was a calm, serious woman. Bujak kept his savings in the cellar (banks were going out of business). The worst they did was to take some of his money, intending to put it back. As Woody saw him, Bujak was trying to be sensible. He accepted his sorrow. He set minimum requirements for Halina: cook the meals, clean the house, show respect. But at stealing Bujak might have drawn the line, for money was different, money was vital substance. If they stole his savings he might have had to take action, out of respect for the substance, for himself — self-respect. But you couldn't be sure that Pop hadn't invented the bookie, the goon, the theft — the whole thing. He was capable of it, and you'd be a fool not to suspect him. Morris knew that Mother and Aunt Rebecca had told Mrs. Skoglund how wicked he was. They had painted him for her in poster colors — purple for vice, black for his soul, red for Hell flames: a gambler, smoker, drinker, deserter,

screwer of women, and atheist. So Pop was determined to reach
her. It was risky for everybody. The Reverend Doctor's operating
costs were met by Skoglund Dairies. The widow paid Woody's
seminary tuition; she bought dresses for the little sisters.

Woody, now sixty, fleshy and big, like a figure for the victory of
American materialism, sunk in his lounge chair, the leather of its
armrests softer to his fingertips than a woman's skin, was puzzled
and, in his depths, disturbed by certain blots within him, blots of
light in his brain, a blot combining pain and amusement in his
breast (how did *that* get there?). Intense thought puckered the skin
between his eyes with a strain bordering on headache. Why had he
let Pop have his way? Why did he agree to meet him that day, in
the dim rear of the poolroom?

"But what will you tell Mrs. Skoglund?"

"The old broad? Don't worry, there's plenty to tell her, and it's
all true. Ain't I trying to save my little laundry-and-cleaning shop?
Isn't the bailiff coming for the fixtures next week?" And Pop
rehearsed his pitch on the Western Avenue car. He counted on
Woody's health and his freshness. Such a straightforward-looking
boy was perfect for a con.

Did they still have such winter storms in Chicago as they used to
have? Now they somehow seemed less fierce. Blizzards used to
come straight down from Ontario, from the Arctic, and drop five
feet of snow in an afternoon. Then the rusty green platform cars,
with revolving brushes at both ends, came out of the barns to
sweep the tracks. Ten or twelve streetcars followed in slow proces-
sions, or waited, block after block.

There was a long delay at the gates of Riverview Park, all the
amusements covered for the winter, boarded up — the dragon's-
back high-rides, the Bobs, the Chute, the Tilt-a-Whirl, all the fun
machinery put together by mechanics and electricians, men like
Bujak the tool-and-die-maker, good with engines. The blizzard was
having it all its own way behind the gates, and you couldn't see far
inside; only a few bulbs burned behind the palings. When Woody
wiped the vapor from the glass, the wire mesh of the window
guards was stuffed solid at eye level with snow. Looking higher,
you saw mostly the streaked wind horizontally driving from the
north. In the seat ahead, two black coal heavers both in leather
Lindbergh flying helmets sat with shovels between their legs, returning from a job. They smelled of sweat, burlap sacking, and
coal. Mostly dull with black dust, they also sparkled here and there.

There weren't many riders. People weren't leaving the house. This was a day to sit legs stuck out beside the stove, mummified by both the outdoor and the indoor forces. Only a fellow with an angle, like Pop, would go and buck such weather. A storm like this was out of the compass, and you kept the human scale by having a scheme to raise fifty bucks. Fifty soldiers! Real money in 1933.

"That woman is crazy for you," said Pop.

"She's just a good woman, sweet to all of us."

"Who knows what she's got in mind. You're a husky kid. Not such a kid either."

"She's a religious woman. She really has religion."

"Well, your mother isn't your only parent. She and Rebecca and Kovner aren't going to fill you up with their ideas. I know your mother wants to wipe me out of your life. Unless I take a hand, you won't even understand what life is. Because they don't know — those silly Christers."

"Yes, Pop."

"The girls I can't help. They're too young. I'm sorry about them, but I can't do anything. With you it's different."

He wanted me like himself, an American.

They were stalled in the storm, while the cattle-colored car waited to have the trolley reset in the crazy wind, which boomed, tingled, blasted. At Howard Street they would have to walk straight into it, due north.

"You'll do the talking at first," said Pop.

Woody had the makings of a salesman, a pitchman. He was aware of this when he got to his feet in church to testify before fifty or sixty people. Even though Aunt Rebecca made it worth his while, he moved his own heart when he spoke up about his faith. But occasionally, without notice, his heart went away as he spoke religion and he couldn't find it anywhere. In its absence, sincere behavior got him through. He had to rely for delivery on his face, his voice — on behavior. Then his eyes came closer and closer together. And in this approach of eye to eye he felt the strain of hypocrisy. The twisting of his face threatened to betray him. It took everything he had to keep looking honest. So, since he couldn't bear the cynicism of it, he fell back on mischievousness. Mischief was where Pop came in. Pop passed straight through all those divided fields, gap after gap, and arrived at his side, bent-nosed and broad-faced. In regard to Pop, you thought of neither sincerity nor insincerity. Pop was like the man in the song: he wanted what he wanted when he wanted it. Pop was physical; Pop was digestive, circulatory, sexual. If Pop got serious, he talked to you about washing under the arms or in the crotch or of drying between your toes or of cooking supper, of onions, of draw poker or of a certain horse in the fifth race at Arlington. Pop was elemental. That was why he gave such relief from religion and paradoxes, and things like that. Now Mother *thought* she was spiritual, but Woody knew that she was kidding herself. Oh, yes, in the British accent she never gave up she was always talking to God or about Him — please-God, God-willing, praise-God. But she was a big substantial bread-and-butter, down-to-earth woman, with down-to-earth duties like feeding the girls, protecting, refining, keeping pure the girls. And those two protected doves grew up so overweight, heavy in the hips and thighs, that their poor heads looked long and slim. And mad. Sweet but cuckoo — Paula cheerfully cuckoo, Joanna depressed and having episodes.

"I'll do my best by you, but you have to promise, Pop, not to get me in Dutch with Mrs. Skoglund."

"You worried because I speak bad English? Embarrassed? I have a mockie accent?"

"It's not that. Kovner has a heavy accent, and she doesn't mind."

"Who the hell are those freaks to look down on me? You're practically a man and your dad has a right to expect help from you. He's in a fix. And you bring him to her house because she's big-hearted, and you haven't got anybody else to go to."

"I got you, Pop."

The two coal trimmers stood up at Devon Avenue. One of them wore a woman's coat. Men wore women's clothing in those years, and women men's, when there was no choice. The fur collar was spiky with the wet, and sprinkled with soot. Heavy, they dragged their shovels and got off at the front. The slow car ground on, very slow. It was after four when they reached the end of the line, and somewhere between gray and black, with snow spouting and whirling under the street lamps. In Howard Street, autos were stalled at all angles and abandoned. The sidewalks were blocked. Woody led the way into Evanston, and Pop followed him up the middle of the street in the furrows made earlier by trucks. For four blocks they bucked the wind and then Woody broke through the drifts to the snowbound mansion, where they both had to push the wrought-iron gate because of the drift behind it. Twenty rooms or more in this dignified house and nobody in them but Mrs. Skoglund and her servant Hjordis, also religious.

As Woody and Pop waited, brushing the slush from their sheepskin collars and Pop wiping his big eyebrows with the ends of his scarf, sweating and freezing, the chains began to rattle and Hjordis uncovered the air holes of the glass storm door by turning a wooden bar. Woody called her "monk-faced." You no longer see women like that, who put no female touch on the face. She came plain, as God made her. She said, "Who is it and what do you want?"

"It's Woodrow Selbst. Hjordis? It's Woody."

"You're not expected."

"No, but we're here."

"What do you want?"

"We came to see Mrs. Skoglund."

"What for do you want to see her?"

"Just to tell her we're here."

"I have to tell her what you came for, without calling up first."

"Why don't you say it's Woody with his father, and we wouldn't come in a snowstorm like this if it wasn't important."

The understandable caution of women who live alone. Respectable old-time women, too. There was no such respectability now in those Evanston houses, with their big verandas and deep yards and with a servant like Hjordis, who carried at her belt keys to the pantry and to every closet and every dresser drawer and every padlocked bin in the cellar. And in High Episcopal Christian Science Women's Temperance Evanston no tradespeople rang at the front door. Only invited guests. And here, after a ten-mile grind through the blizzard, came two tramps from the West Side. To this mansion where a Swedish immigrant lady, herself once a cook and now a philanthropic widow, dreamed, snowbound, while frozen lilac twigs clapped at her storm windows, of a new Jerusalem and a Second Coming and a Resurrection and a Last Judgment. To hasten the Second Coming, and all the rest, you had to reach the hearts of these scheming bums arriving in a snowstorm.

Sure, they let us in.

Then in the heat that swam suddenly up to their muffled chins Pop and Woody felt the blizzard for what it was; their cheeks were frozen slabs. They stood beat, itching, trickling in the front hall that *was* a hall, with a carved rural post staircase and a big stained-glass window at the top. Picturing Jesus with the Samaritan woman. There was a kind of Gentile closeness to the air. Perhaps when he was with Pop, Woody made more Jewish observations than he would otherwise. Although Pop's most Jewish characteristic was that Yiddish was the only language he could read a paper in. Pop was with Polish Halina, and Mother was with Jesus Christ, and Woody ate uncooked bacon from the flitch. Still now and then he had a Jewish impression.

Mrs. Skoglund was the cleanest of women — her fingernails, her white neck, her ears — and Pop's sexual hints to Woody all went wrong because she was so intensely clean, and made Woody think of a waterfall, large as she was, and grandly built. Her bust was big. Woody's imagination had investigated this. He thought she kept things tied down tight, very tight. But she lifted both arms once to raise a window and there it was, her bust, beside him, the whole unbindable thing. Her hair was like the raffia you had to soak before you could weave with it in a basket class — pale, pale. Pop, as he took his sheepskin off, was in sweaters, no jacket. His darting looks made him seem crooked. Hardest of all for these Selbsts with their bent noses and big, apparently straightforward faces was to look honest. All the signs of dishonesty played over them. Woody had often puzzled about it. Did it go back to the muscles, was it fundamentally a jaw problem — the projecting angles of the jaws? Or was it the angling that went on in the heart? The girls called Pop Dick Tracy, but Dick Tracy was a good guy. Whom could Pop convince? Here, Woody caught a possibility as it flitted by. Precisely because of the way Pop looked, a sensitive person might feel remorse for condemning unfairly or judging unkindly. Just because of a face? Some must have bent over backward. Then he had them. Not Hjordis. She would have put Pop into the street then and there, storm or no storm. Hjordis was religous, but she was wised up, too. She hadn't come over in steerage and worked forty years in Chicago for nothing.

Mrs. Skoglund, Aase (Osie), led the visitors into the front room. This, the biggest room in the house, needed supplementary heating. Because of fifteen-foot ceilings and high windows, Hjordis had kept the parlor stove burning. It was one of those elegant parlor stoves that wore a nickel crown, or mitre, and this mitre, when you moved it aside, automatically raised the hinge of an iron stove lid. That stove lid underneath the crown was all soot and rust, the same

as any other stove lid. Into this hole you tipped the scuttle and the
anthracite chestnut rattled down. It made a cake or dome of fire
visible through the small isinglass frames. It was a pretty room,
three-quarters panelled in wood. The stove was plugged into the
flue of the marble fireplace, and there were parquet floors and
Axminster carpets and cranberry-colored tufted Victorian upholstery, and a kind of Chinese étagère, inside a cabinet, lined with
mirrors and containing silver pitchers, trophies won by Skoglund
cows, fancy sugar tongs and cut-glass pitchers and goblets. There
were Bibles and pictures of Jesus and the Holy Land and that faint
Gentile odor, as if things had been rinsed in a weak vinegar solution.

"Mrs. Skoglund, I brought my dad to you. I don't think you ever
met him," said Woody.

"Yes, Missus, that's me, Selbst."

Pop stood short but masterful in the sweaters, and his belly sticking out, not soft but hard. He was a man of the hard-bellied type.
Nobody intimidated Pop. He never presented himself as a beggar.
There wasn't a cringe in him anywhere. He let her see at once by
the way he said "Missus" that he was independent and that he knew
his way around. He communicated that he was able to handle
himself with women. Handsome Mrs. Skoglund, carrying a basket
woven out of her own hair, was in her fifties — eight, maybe ten
years his senior.

"I asked my son to bring me because I know you do the kid a lot
of good. It's natural you should know both of his parents."

"Mrs. Skoglund, my dad is in a tight corner and I don't know
anybody else to ask for help."

This was all the preliminary Pop wanted. He took over and told
the widow his story about the laundry-and-cleaning business and
payments overdue, and explained about the fixtures and the at-
tachment notice, and the bailiff's office and what they were going
to do to him; and he said, "I'm a small man trying to make a living."

"You don't support your children," said Mrs. Skoglund.

"That's right," said Hjordis.

"I haven't got it. If I had it, wouldn't I give it? There's bread
lines and soup lines all over town. Is it just me? What I have I divvy
with. I give the kids. A bad father? You think my son would bring
me if I was a bad father into your house? He loves his dad, he
trusts his dad, he knows his dad is a good dad. Every time I start a

little business going I get wiped out. This one is a good little business, if I could hold on to that little business. Three people work for me, I meet a payroll, and three people will be on the street, too, if I close down. Missus, I can sign a note and pay you in two months. I'm a common man, but I'm a hard worker and a fellow you can trust."

Woody was startled when Pop used the word "trust." It was as if from all four corners a Sousa band blew a blast to warn the entire world. "Crook! This is a crook!" But Mrs. Skoglund, on account of her religious preoccupations, was remote. She heard nothing. Although everybody in this part of the world, unless he was crazy, led a practical life, and you'd have nothing to say to anyone, your neighbors would have nothing to say to you if communications were not of a practical sort, Mrs. Skoglund, with all her money, was unworldly — two-thirds out of this world.

"Give me a chance to show what's in me," said Pop, "and you'll see what I do for my kids."

So Mrs. Skoglund hesitated, and then she said she'd have to go upstairs, she'd have to go to her room and pray on it and ask for guidance — would they sit down and wait. There were two rocking chairs by the stove. Hjordis gave Pop a grim look (a dangerous person) and Woody a blaming one (he brought a dangerous stranger and disrupter to injure two kind Christian ladies). Then she went out with Mrs. Skoglund.

As soon as they left, Pop jumped up from the rocker and said in anger, "What's this with the praying? She has to ask God to lend me fifty bucks?"

Woody said, "It's not you, Pop, it's the way these religious people do."

"No," said Pop. "She'll come back and say that God wouldn't let her."

Woody didn't like that; he thought Pop was being gross and he said, "No, she's sincere. Pop, try to understand; she's emotional, nervous, and sincere, and tries to do right by everybody."

And Pop said, "That servant will talk her out of it. She's a toughie. It's all over her face that we're a couple of chisellers."

"What's the use of us arguing," said Woody. He drew the rocker closer to the stove. His shoes were wet through and would never dry. The blue flames fluttered like a school of fishes in the coal fire. But Pop went over to the Chinese-style cabinet or étagère and

tried the handle, and then opened the blade of his penknife and in
a second had forced the lock of the curved glass door. He took out
a silver dish.

"Pop, what is this?" said Woody.

Pop, cool and level, knew exactly what this was. He relocked the
étagère, crossed the carpet, listened. He stuffed the dish under his
belt and pushed it down into his trousers. He put the side of his
short thick finger to his mouth.

So Woody kept his voice down, but he was all shook up. He went
to Pop and took him by the edge of his hand. As he looked into
Pop's face, he felt his eyes growing smaller and smaller, as if something were contracting all the skin on his head. They call it hyper-
ventilation when everything feels tight and light and close and
dizzy. Hardly breathing, he said, "Put it back, Pop."

Pop said, "It's solid silver; it's worth dough."

"Pop, you said you wouldn't get me in Dutch."

"It's only insurance in case she comes back from praying and
tells me no. If she says yes, I'll put it back."

"How?"

"It'll get back. If I don't put it back, you will."

"You picked the lock. I couldn't. I don't know how."

"There's nothing to it."

"We're going to put it back now. Give it here."

"Woody, it's under my fly, inside my underpants, don't make
such a noise about nothing."

"Pop, I can't believe this."

"For Cry-99, shut your mouth. If I didn't trust you I wouldn't
have let you watch me do it. You don't understand a thing. What's
with you?"

"Before they come down, Pop, will you dig that dish out of your
long johns."

Pop turned stiff on him. He became absolutely military. He said,
"Look, I order you!"

Before he knew it, Woody had jumped his father and begun to
wrestle with him. It was outrageous to clutch your own father, to
put a heel behind him, to force him to the wall. Pop was taken by
surprise and said loudly, "You want Halina killed? Kill her! Go on,
you be responsible." He began to resist, angry, and they turned
about several times when Woody, with a trick he had learned in a
Western movie and used once on the playground, tripped him and

they fell to the ground. Woody, who already outweighed the old man by twenty pounds, was on the top. They landed on the floor beside the stove, which stood on a tray of decorated tin to protect the carpet. In this position, pressing Pop's hard belly, Woody recognized that to have wrestled him to the floor counted for nothing. It was impossible to thrust his hand under Pop's belt to recover the dish. And now Pop had turned furious, as a father has every right to be when his son is violent with him, and he freed his hand and hit Woody in the face. He hit him three or four times in mid-face. Then Woody dug his head into Pop's shoulder and held tight only to keep from being struck and began to say in his ear, "Jesus, Pop, for Christ sake remember where you are. Those women will be back!" But Pop brought up his short knee and fought and butted him with his chin and rattled Woody's teeth. Woody thought the old man was about to bite him. And, because he was a seminarian, he thought, "Like an unclean spirit." And held tight. Gradually Pop stopped threshing and struggling. His eyes stuck out and his mouth was open, sullen. Like a stout fish. Woody released him and gave him a hand up. He was then overcome with many many bad feelings of a sort he knew the old man never suffered. Never, never. Pop never had these grovelling emotions. There was his whole superiority. Pop had no such feelings. He was like a horseman from Central Asia, a bandit from China. It was Mother, from Liverpool, who had the refinement, the English manners. It was the preaching Reverend Doctor in his black suit. You have refinements, and all they do is oppress you? The hell with that.

The long door opened and Mrs. Skoglund stepped in, saying, "Did I imagine, or did something shake the house?"

"I was lifting the scuttle to put coal on the fire and it fell out of my hand. I'm sorry I was so clumsy," said Woody.

Pop was too huffy to speak. With his eyes big and sore and the thin hair down over his forehead, you could see by the tightness of his belly how angrily he was fetching his breath, though his mouth was shut.

"I prayed," said Mrs. Skoglund.

"I hope it came out well," said Woody.

"Well, I don't do anything without guidance, but the answer was yes, and I feel right about it now. So if you'll wait I'll go to my office and write a check. I asked Hjordis to bring you a cup of coffee. Coming in such a storm."

And Pop, consistently a terrible little man, as soon as she shut the door said, "A check? Hell with a check. Get me the greenbacks."

"They don't keep money in the house. You can cash it in her bank tomorrow. But if they miss that dish, Pop they'll stop the check, and then where are you?"

As Pop was reaching below the belt Hjordis brought in the tray. She was very sharp with him. She said, "Is this a place to adjust clothing, Mister? A men's washroom?"

"Well, which way is the toilet, then?" said Pop.

She had served the coffee in the seamiest mugs in the pantry, and she bumped down the tray and led Pop down the corridor, standing guard at the bathroom door so that he shouldn't wander about the house.

Mrs. Skoglund called Woody to her office and after she had given him the folded check said that they should pray together for Morris. So once more he was on his knees, under rows and rows of musty marbled cardboard files, by the glass lamp by the edge of the desk, the shade with flounced edges, like the candy dish. Mrs. Skoglund, in her Scandinavian accent — an emotional contralto — raising her voice to Jesus-uh Christ-uh, as the wind lashed the trees, kicked the side of the house, and drove the snow seething on the windowpanes, to send light-uh, give guidance-uh, put a new heart-uh in Pop's bosom. Woody asked God only to make Pop put the dish back. He kept Mrs. Skoglund on her knees as long as possible. Then he thanked her, shining with candor (as much as he knew how) for her Christian generosity and he said, "I know that Hjordis has a cousin who works at the Evanston Y.M.C.A. Could she please phone him and try to get us a room tonight so that we don't have to fight the blizzard all the way back? We're almost as close to the Y as to the car line. Maybe the cars have even stopped running."

Suspicious Hjordis, coming when Mrs. Skoglund called to her, was burning now. First they barged in, made themselves at home, asked for money, had to have coffee, probably left gonorrhea on the toilet seat. Hjordis, Woody remembered, was a woman who wiped the doorknobs with rubbing alcohol after guests had left. Nevertheless, she telephoned the Y and got them a room with two cots for six bits.

Pop had plenty of time, therefore, to reopen the étagère, lined with reflecting glass or German silver (something exquisitely delicate and tricky), and as soon as the two Selbsts had said thank you and goodbye and were in mid-street again up to the knees in snow, Woody said, "Well, I covered for you. Is that thing back?"

"Of course it is," said Pop.

They fought their way to the small Y building, shut up in wire grille and resembling a police station — about the same dimensions. It was locked, but they made a racket on the grille, and a small black man let them in and shuffled them upstairs to a cement corridor with low doors. It was like the small-mammal house in Lincoln Park. He said there was nothing to eat, so they took off their wet pants, wrapped themselves tightly in the khaki army blankets, and passed out on their cots.

First thing in the morning, they went to the Evanston National Bank and got the fifty dollars. Not without difficulties. The teller went to call Mrs. Skoglund and was absent a long time from the wicket. "Where the hell has he gone," said Pop.

But when the fellow came back he said, "How do you want it?"

Pop said, "Singles." He told Woody, "Bujak stashes it in one-dollar bills."

But by now Woody no longer believed Halina had stolen the old man's money.

Then they went into the street, where the snow-removal crews were at work. The sun shone broad, broad, out of the morning blue, and all Chicago would be releasing itself from the temporary beauty of those vast drifts.

"You shouldn't have jumped me last night, Sonny."

"I know, Pop, but you promised you wouldn't get me in Dutch."

"Well, it's O.K., we can forget it, seeing you stood by me."

Only, Pop had taken the silver dish. Of course he had, and in a few days Mrs. Skoglund and Hjordis knew it, and later in the week they were all waiting for Woody in Kovner's office at the settlement house. The group included the Reverend Dr. Crabbie, head of the seminary, and Woody, who had been flying along, level and smooth, was shot down in flames. He told them he was innocent. Even as he was falling, he warned that they were wronging him. He denied that he or Pop had touched Mrs. Skoglund's property. The missing object — he didn't even know what it was — had probably been misplaced, and they would be very sorry on the day it turned up. After the others were done with him, Dr. Crabbie said until he was able to tell the truth he would be suspended from the seminary, where his work had been unsatisfactory anyway. Aunt Rebecca took him aside and said to him, "You are a little crook, like your father. The door is closed to you here."

To this Pop's comment was "So what, kid?"

"Pop, you shouldn't have done it."

"No? Well, I don't give a care, if you want to know. You can have the dish if you want to go back and square yourself with all those hypocrites."

"I didn't like doing Mrs. Skoglund in the eye, she was so kind to us."

"Kind?"

"Kind."

"Kind has a price tag."

Well, there was no winning such arguments with Pop. But they debated it in various moods and from various elevations and perspectives for forty years and more, as their intimacy changed, developed, matured.

"Why did you do it, Pop? For the money? What did you do with the fifty bucks?" Woody, decades later, asked him that.

"I settled with the bookie, and the rest I put in the business."

"You tried a few more horses."

"I maybe did. But it was a double, Woody. I didn't hurt myself, and at the same time did you a favor."

"It was for me?"

"It was too strange of a life. That life wasn't *you*, Woody. All those women — Kovner was no man, he was an in-between. Suppose they made you a minister? Some Christian minister! First of all, you wouldn't have been able to stand it, and, second, they would throw you out sooner or later."

"Maybe so."

"And you wouldn't have converted the Jews, which was the main thing they wanted."

"And what a time to bother the Jews," Woody said. "At least *I* didn't bug them."

Pop had carried him back to his side of the line, blood of his blood, the same thick body walls, the same coarse grain. Not cut out for a spiritual life. Simply not up to it.

Pop was no worse than Woody, and Woody was no better than Pop. Pop wanted no relation to theory, and yet he was always pointing Woody toward a position — a jolly, hearty, natural, likable, unprincipled position. If Woody had a weakness, it was to be unselfish. This worked to Pop's advantage, but he criticized Woody for it, nevertheless. "You take too much on yourself," Pop was always saying. And it's true that Woody gave Pop his heart because Pop was so selfish. It's usually the selfish people who are loved the most. They do what you deny yourself, and you love them for it. You give them your heart.

Remembering the pawn ticket for the silver dish, Woody startled himself with a laugh so sudden that it made him cough. Pop said to him after his expulsion from the seminary and banishment from the settlement house, "You want in again? Here's the ticket. I hocked that thing. It wasn't so valuable as I thought."

"What did they give?"

"Twelve-fifty was all I could get. But if you want it you'll have to raise the dough yourself, because I haven't got it anymore."

"You must have been sweating in the bank when the teller went to call Mrs. Skoglund about the check."

"I was a little nervous," said Pop. "But I didn't think they could miss the thing so soon."

That theft was part of Pop's war with Mother. With Mother, and Aunt Rebecca, and the Reverend Doctor. Pop took his stand on realism. Mother represented the forces of religion and hypochondria. In four decades, the fighting never stopped. In the course of time, Mother and the girls turned into welfare personalities and lost their individual outlines. Ah, the poor things, they became dependents and cranks. In the meantime, Woody, the sinful man, was their dutiful and loving son and brother. He maintained the bungalow — this took in roofing, pointing, wiring, insulation, air-conditioning — and he paid for heat and light and food, and dressed them all out of Sears, Roebuck and Wieboldt's, and bought them a TV, which they watched as devoutly as they prayed. Paula took courses to learn skills like macramé-making and needlepoint, and sometimes got a little job as recreational worker in a nursing home. But she wasn't steady enough to keep it. Wicked Pop spent most of his life removing stains from people's clothing. He and Halina in the last years ran a Cleanomat in West Rogers Park — a so-so business resembling a laundromat — which gave him leisure for billiards, the horses, rummy and pinochle. Every morning he went behind the partition to check out the filters of the cleaning equipment. He found amusing things that had been thrown into the vats with the clothing — sometimes, when he got lucky, a locket chain or a brooch. And when he had fortified the cleaning fluid, pouring all that blue and pink stuff in from plastic jugs, he read the *Forward* over a second cup of coffee, and went out, leaving Halina in charge. When they needed help with the rent, Woody gave it.

After the new Disney World was opened in Florida, Woody treated all his dependents to a holiday. He sent them down in separate batches, of course. Halina enjoyed this more than anybody else. She couldn't stop talking about the address given by an Abraham Lincoln automaton. "Wonderful, how he stood up and moved his hands, and his mouth. So real! And how beautiful he talked." Of them all, Halina was the soundest, the most human, the most honest. Now that Pop was gone, Woody and Halina's son, Mitosh, the organist at the Stadium, took care of her needs over and above Social Security, splitting expenses. In Pop's opinion, insurance was a racket. He left Halina nothing but some out-of-date equipment.

Woody treated himself, too. Once a year, and sometimes oftener, he left his business to run itself, arranged with the trust department at the bank to take care of his Gang, and went off. He did that in style, imaginatively, expensively. In Japan, he wasted little time on Tokyo. He spent three weeks in Kyoto and stayed at the Tawaraya Inn, dating from the seventeenth century or so. There he slept on the floor, the Japanese way, and bathed in scalding water. He saw the dirtiest strip show on earth, as well as the holy places and the temple gardens. He visited also Istanbul, Jerusalem, Delphi, and went to Burma and Uganda and Kenya on safari, on democratic terms with drivers, Bedouins, bazaar merchants. Open, lavish, familiar, fleshier and fleshier but (he jogged, he lifted weights) still muscular — in his naked person beginning to resemble a Renaissance courtier in full costume — becoming ruddier every year, an outdoor type with freckles on his back and spots across the flaming forehead and the honest nose. In Addis Ababa he took an Ethiopian beauty to his room from the street and washed her, getting into the shower with her to soap her with his broad, kindly hands. In Kenya he taught certain American obscenities to a black woman so that she could shout them out during the act. On the Nile, below Murchison Falls, those fever trees rose huge from the mud, and hippos on the sandbars belched at the passing launch, hostile. One of them danced on his spit of sand, springing from the ground and coming down heavy, on all fours. There, Woody saw the buffalo calf disappear, snatched by the crocodile.

Mother, soon to follow Pop, was being light-headed these days. In company, she spoke of Woody as her boy — "What do you think of my Sonny?" — as though he was ten years old. She was silly with him, her behavior was frivolous, almost flirtatious. She just didn't seem to know the facts. And behind her all the others, like kids at the playground, were waiting their turn to go down the slide; one on each step, and moving toward the top.

Over Woody's residence and place of business there had gathered a pool of silence of the same perimeter as the church bells while they were ringing, and he mourned under it, this melancholy morning of sun and autumn. Doing a life survey, taking a deliberate look at the gross side of his case — of the other side as well, what there was of it. But if this heartache continued, he'd go out and run it off. A three-mile jog — five, if necessary. And you'd think that this jogging was an entirely physical activity, wouldn't you? But there was something else in it. Because, when he was a seminarian, between the shafts of his World's Fair rickshaw, he used to receive, pulling along (capable and stable), his religious experiences while he trotted. Maybe it was all a single experience repeated. He felt truth coming to him from the sun. He received a communication that was also light and warmth. It made him very remote from his horny Wisconsin passengers, those farmers whose whoops and whore-cries he could hardly hear when he was in one of his states. And again out of the flaming of the sun would come to him a secret certainty that the goal set for this earth was that it should be filled with good, saturated with it. After everything preposterous, after dog had eaten dog, after the crocodile death had pulled everyone into his mud. It wouldn't conclude as Mrs. Skoglund, bribing him to round up the Jews and hasten the Second Coming, imagined it but in another way. This was his clumsy intuition. It went no further. Subsequently, he proceeded through life as life seemed to want him to do it.

There remained one thing more this morning, which was explicitly physical, occurring first as a sensation in his arms and against his breast and, from the pressure, passing into him and going into his breast.

It was like this: When he came into the hospital room and saw
Pop with the sides of his bed raised, like a crib, and Pop, so very
feeble, and writhing, and toothless, like a baby, and the dirt already
cast into his face, into the wrinkles — Pop wanted to pluck out the
intravenous needles and he was piping his weak death noise. The
gauze patches taped over the needles were soiled with dark blood.
Then Woody took off his shoes, lowered the side of the bed, and
climbed in and held him in his arms to soothe and still him. As if
he were Pop's father, he said to him, "Now Pop. Pop." Then it was
like the wrestle in Mrs. Skoglund's parlor, when Pop turned angry
like an unclean spirit and Woody tried to appease him, and warn
him, saying, "Those women will be back!" Beside the coal stove,
when Pop hit Woody in the teeth with his head and then became
sullen, like a stout fish. But this struggle in the hospital was weak
— so weak! In his great pity, Woody held Pop, who was fluttering
and shivering. From those people, Pop had told him, you'll never
find out what life is, because they don't know what it is. Yes, Pop
— well, what is it, Pop? Hard to comprehend that Pop, who was
dug in for eighty-three years and had done all he could to stay,
should now want nothing but to free himself. How could Woody
allow the old man to pull the intravenous needles out? Willful Pop,
he wanted what he wanted when he wanted it. But what he wanted
at the very last Woody failed to follow, it was such a switch.

After a time, Pop's resistance ended. He subsided and subsided.
He rested against his son, his small body curled there. Nurses came
and looked. They disapproved, but Woody, who couldn't spare a
hand to wave them out, motioned with his head toward the door.
Pop, whom Woody thought he had stilled, only had found a better
way to get around him. Loss of heat was the way he did it. His heat
was leaving him. As can happen with small animals while you hold
them in your hand, Woody presently felt him cooling. Then, as
Woody did his best to restrain him, and thought he was succeeding,
Pop divided himself. And when he was separated from his warmth
he slipped into death. And there was his elderly, large, muscular
son, still holding and pressing him when there was nothing anymore to press. You could never pin down that self-willed man.
When he was ready to make his move, he made it — always on his
own terms. And always, always, something up his sleeve. That was
how he was.

FLANNERY O'CONNOR

An Exile in the East

(FROM THE SOUTH CAROLINA REVIEW)

OLD TANNER lowered himself into the chair he was gradually molding to his own shape and looked out the window ten feet away at another window framed by blackened red brick. The brim of his black felt hat was pulled down sharply to shade his eyes from the grey streak of sunlight that dropped in the alley. He was a heavy old man and he had almost ruined their chair already. He had heard the son-in-law, in his nasal yankee whisper, call him "the cotton bale in there." He would have liked to be thin to be less in their way. He didn't eat any more of their food than he had to but no flesh had fallen off him since he had come. He was still walled up in it. Since he had been here, he had only got pale, or rather yellow with brown spots, whereas at home, his spots had been red and purple.

His daughter wouldn't let him wear his hat inside except when he sat like this in front of the window. He told her it was necessary to keep the light out of his eyes; which it was not: the light here was as weak as everything else. He had bought the hat new to come here in and whenever he thought how he had actually been that foolish, he would catch both arms of the chair and lean forward, gasping as if he could not get enough air. His face was large and bloated and his pale grey eyes, far under the hat brim, were as weak as the sunlight. His vision reached as far as the other window ledge across the alley and stopped. He never tried to look into the other window. He waited every morning, sitting here, for them to put their geranium on the ledge. Nothing else they had could interest him and they had no business with a geranium as they didn't know how to take care of it. They put it out every morning

about ten and took it in at five-thirty or so. It reminded him of the
Grisby child at home who had polio and was set out in the sun like
that every morning to blink. These people across the alley thought
they had something in this sick geranium that they didn't know
how to take care of. They let the sun slow-cook it all day and they
set it so near the edge that any sudden wind could have done for
it. At home where the sunlight was strong, the geraniums were red
and tough. Every morning after breakfast he sat down in the chair
in front of the window and waited, as if he were waiting for a
performance to begin, for the pair of hands to put the geranium
in the window. He pulled a large watch from his pocket and looked
at the time. It was four minutes after ten.

His daughter came in and stood in the door, rubbing a yellow
dishrag over the bottom of a pan while she watched him with her
air of righteous exhaustion. She was lean and swaybacked.

"Why don't you go out for a stroll?" she asked.

He didn't answer. He set his jaw and looked straight ahead. A
stroll. He could barely manage to stay upright on his feet and she
used the word *stroll.*

"Well huh?" she said. She always waited to be answered and
looked at as if something could come of answering her or looking
at her.

"No," he said in a voice that was wavery, almost reed-like. If his
eyes began to water, she would see and have the pleasure of
looking sorry for him. She enjoyed looking sorry for herself too;
but she could have saved herself, old Tanner thought, and shifted
his weight so abruptly in the chair that the spring on one side gave
a raucous creak. If she'd just have let him alone and not been so
taken up with her damn duty, let him stay where he was and not
been so taken up with her damn duty, she could have spared
herself this.

She gave the pan one more lingering rub and then left the door
with a sigh that seemed to remain suspended in the room for some
seconds to remind him that it was actually his own fault he was
here; he hadn't had to come; he had wanted to. This thought
tightened his throat so quickly that he leaned forward and opened
his mouth as if he had to let air into himself or choke. He unbuttoned his collar and twisted his huge neck and then his hand fell,
shaking at the wrist, on the mound of stomach that lay in his lap.

He could have got out of coming. He could have been stubborn and said to her that helpless or not helpless he'd spend his life where he'd always spent it, send him or don't send him a check every month, he'd continue on as he'd continued on before. He had raised up five boys and this girl with sawmilling and farming and one thing and another and the result of it was the five boys were gone, two to the devil and one to the asylum and two to the government and there was nobody left but the daughter, married and living in New York City like a big woman, and ready, when she came home and found him the way he was, to take him back with her. She was more than ready, he had told Coleman, she was hog-wild. She was thirsting to have some duty to do. When she had found him in a shack made entirely of tin and crates, but large enough for a cook stove and a cot and a pallet for the nigger — and the nigger, she said, that filthy Coleman, half the time in there drunk on the pallet — when she had seen this, his deplorable conditions, she had shivered all over with duty.

"How do you stand that nigger?" she had wailed. "How do you stand that drunk stinking nigger, right there beside you? I can't stay in that place two minutes without getting sick!"

"I'd been dead long since if he hadn't been waiting on me hand and foot," he said. "Who you think cooks? Who you think empties my slops?"

"You don't have to live like this," she said. "If you ain't got any pride, I have and I know my duty and I've been raised to do it."

"Who raised you?" he asked.

"Righteous people though poor," she said. "Where'd you get that awful nigger anyway? Why's he stay with you? You can't pay him. He's the one feeding you. Do you think I want to see my own father living off a nigger? The both of them eating stolen chickens?"

"I give him a roof," he said. "This is my shack. I made it myself."

"It looks like you made it," she said.

It was true that he had been on a nigger's hands more or less but he had not thought of it that way until she appeared. Before that Coleman had been on his hands for forty years. They were both old now, him sewed up in a wall of flesh and the other twisted double with no flesh at all. Between them they made out. It was his shack and if he ate what the nigger could find for them to eat, he was still providing the roof and giving the orders.

Since he had been up here he had got one post card from

Coleman that said, "This is Coleman. X. How do boss. Coleman," and the other side was a picture of a local monument put up by the Daughters of the American Revolution. Coleman had marked the X and got somebody to write the rest of it for him. Old Tanner had sent him a post card in return with, "This place is alrite if you like it. Franklyn R.T. Tanner," written on it. The other side was a picture of General Grant's tomb. He kept Coleman's card stuck behind the inside band of his hat.

At home he had lived in a shack but here she didn't even live in a house. She lived in a building with more other people than could be counted living in the same building with her and that building in the middle of a row of buildings all alike, all blackened red and grey with rasp-mouthed people hanging out their windows looking at other windows with other rasp-mouthed people hanging out looking back at them. And this was the way the whole city was. It kept on going on this way for miles around itself.

Sometimes he would sit and imagine showing New York to Coleman. He didn't imagine further than their walking down the street and his turning every now and then to say, "Keep to the inside or these people'll knock you down. Keep right behind me or you'll get left. Keep your hat on," and the negro coming on with his bent running shamble, panting and muttering, "Just lemme get away from here, just lemme get back where I was, just lemme offen this walk, just lemme be back where I come from, why you brung me here?" and him saying, "It was your idea. Keep your eyes on my back. Don't take your eyes off my back or you'll get lost."

She might say he was living off a nigger but he had been putting up with that nigger for forty years. They had first come across each other forty years ago when Coleman was twice his present size and known for a trouble-maker, a big black loose-jointed nigger who had been hanging around the edge of his sawmill for a week, not working, just stirring up the other hands and boasting. He had known it was no nigger to hang around his sawmill and not work, no matter how big or black or mean. He was a thin man then and he had some disease that caused his hand to shake. He had taken to whittling to steady the hand and he managed his sawmill niggers entirely with a very sharp pen knife. This Coleman finally got them all discontented enough to sit down on the job — six niggers off in the middle of the woods, against one white man with a shaky hand — but the other five were willing for the trouble to be between him and Coleman. They were as sorry a crew as he had ever worked. They were willing to lie back against the sawdust pile and watch and the big black one, Coleman, he was willing to lean against a tree in full sight and wait until he was accosted, because he had never been accosted before, only ignored. He thought here was one white man afraid of him and with good reason as this didn't appear to be much of a white man, gaunt and yellow-grey and shaking in the wrist. The others had been content just to sit and wait and so they sat and waited and he was in no hurry himself he remembered and the nigger against the tree was in no hurry and if they all wanted a show, they could take their ease and wait until he was ready to begin it.

He had eyed that nigger once and then he had started hunting on the ground with his foot for a piece of bark to whittle on. He had found two or three and thrown them away until he found a piece about four inches long and a few inches wide and not very thick and then he had begun to cut, making his way closer to that black leaning nigger all the time but not paying him any attention. His hand with the knife in it probably worked as fast as an old woman's with a tatting needle and it must have looked wild to the nigger. He finally got up to him and stopped and stood there in front of him, gouging two round holes out of the piece of bark and then holding it off a little way and looking through the holes past a pile of shavings into the woods and on down to where he could see the edge of the pen they had built to keep their mules in. He began to carve again with the nigger watching his hand.

He rounded the holes from inside and out and the nigger never quit watching his hand. "Nigger," he could have said, "this knife is in my hand now but it's going to be in your gut in a few minutes," but that was not what he had said. He had said, "Nigger, how is your eyesight?" and he hadn't waited for any answer; he had begun to scrape around with his foot on the ground, looking for a piece of wire. He turned over a small piece of haywire and then another shorter piece of a heavier kind and he picked these up and began to prick out openings on either end of the bark to attach them to. When he finished he had a large pair of pine bark spectacles.

"I been watching you hanging around here for about a week," he said, "and I don't think you can see so good and I hate to see anybody can't see good. Put these on," and for the first time he had actually looked up at that nigger and what he saw in his eyes was more than pure admiration, it was a kind of awe for the hand and the spectacles. That nigger had reached out for the spectacles and had put them on his nose and attached the wire bows behind his ears in a slow careful way and then he had stood there, looking as if he saw the white man in front of him for the first time.

"What you see in front of you?"

"See a man," the nigger had said.

"Is he white or black?"

"He white."

"Well you treat him like he was white. Now you see better than you been seeing?"

"Yesshh."

"Then get to work," he had said, "and get these others to work because I've took all I'm going to take from them," and the nigger had said, "Is these my glasses now?" and he had said, "Yes, what's your name?" and the nigger had said, "Coleman."

He had been able to make the spectacles in a few minutes but he could not carve now at all because his hands were too swollen. By the time he had left home, he could not do anything at all but sit and he had been fool enough to think it would be better to sit in a new place. He couldn't even fire a gun anymore. Coleman's hands were twisted but he could still hunt. Coleman still had plenty he could do. All he himself could do was sit. The geranium was late today. He pulled out the watch again and looked at the time. It was ten-thirty and they usually had it out by ten. The shade of the window where they put it out was always halfway down so that he never saw anything but a pair of arms thrust it out on the ledge, sometimes a man's, sometimes a woman's. The man always put it too near the ledge. It was the only thing he had seen growing since he had come to the city. At home any woman could have set it out in the ground and made something of it. We got real ones of them at home, he wanted to holler whenever the hands stuck it out on the ledge. We'd stick theter thang in the ground, Lady, and have us a real one.

He put the watch back in his pocket. Outside a woman shrieked something unintelligible and a garbage can fell on one of the fire escapes and banged to the concrete. Then inside, the door to the next apartment slammed and he heard a sharp distinct footstep clip down the hall. "That's the nigger," he muttered, "yonder he goes somewheres," and he sat forward as if he might get up suddenly.

The nigger lived in the next apartment. He had been here a month when the nigger moved in. That Thursday he had been standing in the door, looking out into the empty hall when a big light brown baldheaded but young nigger walked into the next apartment, which was vacant. He had on a grey business suit and a tan tie. His collar was white and made a clear cut line across his neck and his shoes were shiny tan and matched his skin — he was the kind rich people would dress up for a butler but there were no rich people in this building. Then he had seen the manager of the building come up the steps and go in the apartment behind the nigger and then he had heard, with his own ears, the nigger *rent* the apartment. For some time after he had heard it, he still didn't believe it. Then when it finally came down on him that the nigger was actually going to rent the apartment, he had gone and got the daughter by the arm and brought her to the door to listen. The voices were still going on in there, the manager's and the nigger's, and he had held her by the arm in the door while they listened. Then he had shut it, and stood looking at her.

Her big square face had cracked in a silly grin and she had said, "Now don't you go getting friendly with him. I don't want any trouble with niggers. If you have to live next to them, just mind your own business and they'll mind theirs. Everybody can get along if they just mind their business. Live and let live," she said. "That's my motto. Up here everybody just minds their own business and everybody gets along. That's all you have to do."

He had stood there, hardly able to endure looking at her. Then he had raised his hand and tried to tighten it into a fist. He had felt the breath come wheezing into his windpipe and he had said in a throaty squeak that should have been thundery, "You ain't been raised thataway!" He had had to sit down before he could say any more. He had backed onto a straight chair by the door. "You ain't been raised to live next to niggers that rent the same as you. And you think I would go taking up with one of that kind! You ought to move. You ought to get out of this building and go where there ain't any. You ain't been raised to live with renting niggers just like you. You ain't been raised thataway!" Finally he had realized that he was moving his mouth but that the sound had stopped coming out.

She had stood there repeating, "I live and let live, I live and let live," as if she were trying to remember a better argument she had and couldn't. Then it hit her. Her face looked as if she had discovered gold. "Well, you should squawk!" she shouted. "You should squawk! You living in the same room with that nasty stinking filthy Coleman!"

He couldn't endure to look at her. Every day he thought he couldn't endure it through the day if he had to look at her one more time.

He did not get out of the chair. The nigger's footsteps died away, and he sat back. The daughter was making a clatter in the kitchen. She was always banging something. All he could do anymore was sit and listen to her noise and wait on the flower to be put in the window. He pulled out the watch again, impatient with the people across the alley. He wondered if something could have happened in there. He didn't care anything about flowers but he had got in the habit of expecting this one to be put out and they ought to put it. The first day he had seen it, he had been sitting there thinking that if he could ever get out of the city far enough, a truck going South might pick him up. He would probably be dead by the time he got halfway there but it would be better to be dead halfway home than to be living here. And then while he was thinking this, a hand had appeared with no warning and put the pale pink flower in the window across the alley and he had reached forward as if he thought it were being handed to him. After that they put it out every day. He put the watch back in his pocket.

The daughter came in and leaned on the door facing him again. She was never satisfied until she had got him out of the chair. A doctor had told her if he didn't use his feet he would forget how. "Listen," she said, "do me a favor. Go down to the second floor and ask Mrs. Schmitt to gimme back the pattern I lent her. Take it easy and the stroll'll do you good."

She would stand there and wait until he pulled himself out of the chair and shuffled off. It was better to get up and go than to have to turn and look at her. He didn't want to leave until they put out the geranium but he leaned forward and caught the arms of the chair and hoisted himself up. Once standing, he pulled the black hat lower on his face and then moved off, watching his feet under him as if they were two small children he was encouraging to get out of his way.

He was always afraid that when he went creeping out into the hall, a door would open and one of the snipe-nosed men that hung off the window ledges in his undershirt would ask him what he was snooping around for. The door to the nigger's apartment was cracked and he could see a dark woman with rimless glasses sitting in a chair by the window. She didn't look like a nigger to him, more like a Greek or a Jew or maybe she was a red Indian, he didn't give a damn what she was anyway. He turned down the first flight of stairs, gripping the greasy banister and lowering his feet carefully one beside the other onto the linoleum-covered steps. As he set each foot down he felt needles floating up his legs. The nigger's wife could be a Chinese for all what he cared; she could be part giraffe.

A white woman, drinking something grape out of a bottle, passed him on the flight of steps and gave him a stare without taking her mouth from around the bottle. He had learned that you don't speak to them unless they speak to you and that they don't speak to you unless you're in their way.

After he had gone down two flights of stairs, he found the door he was supposed to go to and knocked on it. A foreign boy, ten or twelve years old, opened it and said nobody was at home and gave him an appraising look out of one eye before he shut it again.

Going up the steps was harder for him than going down. He was one flight from the street. He could go down one more flight and be in the street and then he could keep walking straight in front of him until in maybe a month he would be outside the city. He did not have any money and he would not ask the daughter for any. In other plans he had made to run away, he had decided to sell his hat and watch. He stood for a few minutes on the second floor, looking down the last flight of stairs and out into a crack of street, before he turned and started back up again. The trip back to the room would probably take him half an hour. Every time he got himself up a step, he might have just lifted a hundred-pound sack, he thought, and if he could do that he was good for something but he was not good for anything because he was not a hundred-pound sack. In one plan he had made to run away, he had imagined that he would pretend he was dead and have his body shipped back and when he arrived he would knock on the inside of the box and they would let him out. Coleman would stand there with his red eyeballs staring out and think he had rose from the dead.

Thinking about this appealed to him so much that he began to imagine it as he pulled himself up one step after another in the blank hall. He saw the train getting in early in the morning and Coleman waiting on the platform where he had written him to wait for the body. He saw Hooten, the station master, running with the rattling baggage wagon down to the freight end of the train. They would shove the coffin off and inside he would feel the fresh early morning air coming in through the cracks of the pine box but he wouldn't make a noise yet. The big train would jar and grate and slide on off until the noise was lost in the distance and he would feel the baggage wagon rumbling under him, carrying him on back up to the station. Then they would slide the coffin onto the platform where Coleman was waiting and Coleman would creep over and stand looking down on it and he would make a small noise inside and Coleman would say, "Open hit." And Hooten would say, "Why open it? He's as dead as he's ever going to get," and Coleman would say, "Open hit," and Hooten would go for a hammer and all the time, he would be feeling the light cool early morning air of home coming through the cracks of the wooden box, and Hooten would come mouthing back with the hammer and begin to pry open the lid and even before he had the upper end pried Coleman would be jumping up and down, not saying anything yet, only jumping up and down, panting like a horse, and then the lid would fly back and Coleman would shout out, "Hiiiiiiieeeee!"

Old Tanner shouted it into the hollow hall. His high voice made a piercing sound that echoed shrilly on the other floors and then in the quiet that followed, he was aware of the clipping footsteps that had been coming all the time behind him. He slipped and grabbed the banister and then turned his head just enough to see the big light brown baldheaded nigger back of him, grinning.

"What kind of game are you playing, Pardner?" the big nigger asked in a well-oiled yankee voice. He had a small trimmed mustache and a tan tie with brown flecks in it and his collar was white.

Old Tanner turned his head again and remained bent over, looking at the floor and clenching the banister with both hands. His hat entirely hid his face.

"Ah wouldn't be playing Indians on these steps if ah were you, old pal," the nigger drawled in a mock Southern accent. "Now ah sho' nuf wouldn't be a-doing that," and he patted old Tanner on the shoulder and then went up the steps. His socks had brown flecks in them. Once around the bend, he began to whistle "Dixie," but the sound stopped as he shut his own door behind him.

Old Tanner turned his face to the opposite wall without unbending. There were two trickles of water running over his tight cheeks and he leaned farther forward and let them fall on the steps as if his head were a pitcher he was emptying. Then he began to move on up the steps, like a cotton bale with short legs and a black hat. Finally he got to his own door and went in.

The daughter was nowhere in sight. He moved to the chair by the window and lowered himself into it. His face was expressionless but water was still coming out of his eyes. After a few seconds, he realized a man was sitting in the window across the alley. The shade was up all the way and the man was sitting in the window in his undershirt, watching him, head-on. He was leaning out, his upper lip twisted, as if he were trying to decide if the old man were actually crying.

"Where is thet flower?" old Tanner piped.

"Fell off," the man said.

The man couldn't see too much of old Tanner's face because the black hat almost covered his eyes but he saw his mouth begin to work as if he were talking. Then in a second, a high voice came out of him. "You shouldn't have put it so near the ledge!" he said.

"Listen, I put it where I please," the man said. "Who're you to be telling me where I'll put it? Maybe I knocked it off? Maybe I'm sick of the damn thing?"

Old Tanner hoisted himself out of the chair and leaned over the window ledge. The cracked pot was scattered on the concrete at the bottom of the alley. The pink part of the flower was lying by itself and the roots were lying by the paper bow.

"I seen you before," the man in the window said. "I seen you sitting in that chair every day, staring out in the window into my apartment. What I do in my apartment is my business, see? I don't like people looking at what I do." He paused a minute and then he said, "I don't like people watching me."

It was at the bottom of the alley with its roots in the air.

"I only tell people once," the man said and stood up and pulled down the shade all the way.

SEÁN VIRGO

Home and Native Land

(FROM THE MALAHAT REVIEW)

THE TWO MEN were far down the beach — wavering, indistinct black figures, stooping to dig clams by the low tide mark. Their boat swung on its chain out in the inlet and their dinghy was stranded on the sand, ten yards above them. After a while they looked up and one of them waved. They spoke together and started up the beach, dumping their sacks and shovels in the dinghy.

Ron had been home for two days. He sat moodily round the house all the time, every so often swearing angrily to himself, springing up and pacing to the door and back. He kept watching out the window, going out the door and then coming back to slump on the old wooden seat by the stove. His shirt-back was always dark and limp with sweat.

Dickie heard him walking about in the night, too. The outbursts of sudden, muttered curses punctuating the close darkness. When he looked out into the room before dawn the first night, Ron had fallen asleep by the stove, all the wood used up, a cigarette drooping from his stained hand with a curved inch of ash upon it. Dickie had stepped over one of the dogs and gently removed the still-smoking butt before it burnt his brother's hand. Then he'd gone back to bed.

An hour later he'd woken again, hearing "Oh fucking, *fucking* hell" hollowly from the front room, and a scrambling away of the dogs onto the porch. His mother called out "Who there?" and there was no answer. He heard someone scuffing through the salmonberry bushes by the gate and then he slept again. Ron was the same all day. If you talked to him, even Mumma, he'd just grunt, or sometimes stare into your head as if you were a mile off, on the horizon, and he didn't know whether to notice you.

This morning he had fidgeted round the house for an hour, didn't eat anything, then motioned to Dickie from the porch. They set off walking down to the point, toward the old village. One of the dogs followed them warily. Ron led the way, and said nothing — he was thinner than he'd been before he went away: when the curtain of irritation wasn't trembling before his face there was something almost transparent about him. And he smelt of Vancouver, even now out above the exposed beds of weed and mussels: his clothes were worn-out cheap versions of city style — his feet canted clumsily over on ruined cuban heels.

"You're the only fucker round here I can stand anymore" was all he said as they scrambled together on the puddingstone rocks where the path ended. He said it not as a confidence, but with his eyes straying vaguely out to sea down the shrunken inlet, one hand stiff against his hip as though to control something.

He was sick, but he was beautiful. Dickie had never seen an Indian grow his hair long before: the black, shining frame down the cheek bones looked proud.

Ron touched his arm and waited for the two men to come up to them. He stood tautly, his nostrils flared like a hound's, questing at the suspicion of a familiar scent. Not a smell, though, something more shimmering than that. Dickie could sense it too, though he did not recognize it. When the men came closer and that feeling grew stronger, Ron seemed to slip far away from him — Dickie felt that he was the outsider and that his brother and the two white men formed a circle that pushed him out. But the pride was gone from Ron as the circle closed: at that moment Dickie saw a vision of him at a sidewalk looking across to him over a broad street, where cars shuttled past every second, like waves hiding and staining his stranger eyes.

One of the men was big and fair — under his fringe his eyes slewed round to meet yours and then cannoned off again like a pool-ball. When he spoke his eyelids fluttered all the time — his words came clear and easy but the stutter had moved up into his eyes. His face was hairless as an Indian's, his fringe was swept to cover baldness, and one day soon he'd be fat. He wanted something.

His companion was smaller, less assertive but more at ease. He related more to his surroundings: the deserted sands here, life on a boat, the beer he had been drinking: but he was second fiddle, no doubt of it, and had a sheepish kind of awe for the big one. His want was slighter, more detached. He was inclined to turn to Dickie, to let the circle break up into pairs, but the boy turned away, shut them out of his head and went to stare at the water.

Sandpipers were hurtling along the foreshore — east to west and back, black to white and back, rising and falling, sometimes disappearing against the dark sea, never settling. The tide was just ready to die, to lie for an hour at ebb and then come rushing back at the rocks across the waste of sand. Down a ways, two gulls were swooping at a big bird dragging a horse clam off the tide line. Probably the eagle. And crows were shouting in the young trees that grew over the old village.

Behind him Ron was nervous and animated. What they wanted, what they had, must be out in the open now. The smaller white man offered Dickie a draw on the cigarette — holding it out to him mutely, his lips compressed, nodding, trying to hold back a cough from his own inhaling. Ron's attention focussed on him for a moment with a kind of anxiousness and then shrugged away. Dickie refused.

Ron was pointing down past the old village. "The second island out," he said, grinning with mask-like camaraderie into the big man's face. "There'll be no water round it for two hours maybe. You could take your boat round anyway."

"Nobody about for sure, eh?"

"Nah, no one ever comes this way. Too scared." They both laughed in an idiot way at this invented superstition.

The big man handed over the plastic bag, swinging it for a moment or two over Ron's palm. "Right," he said. "Thanks." "Sure thing, mister," Ron said. Then the man swung away and back down the drying, steaming sand toward the dinghy. His companion shadowed his brisk footsteps, but did have eyes for Dickie. Who looked away.

When they were down by the dinghy, "What they doing out there?" he asked. Ron was sitting on the sand, easing his bare feet out of his cowboy boots, contemplating his stretching toes and digging them in.

"What did they want?"

Ron looked up. His eyes came back from a million miles, a vague smile hovered and he looked back again at the sand. His hair hung in a dense tent of blackness over his downturned face. "They were looking for burial grounds," he said and shrugged his shoulders and laughed.

"Why'd you tell them? Why?"

"Hell, they likely want them old blue-bead necklaces. They can sell them to the museums. But they're all in the cave by the old village. I didn't say that." Then he looked hard at Dickie, like he used to before he went away, when he was mad at him or wanted to show him something important. His brown eyes were hard, they held you still. "Anyways, Dick, there ain't no necklaces left neither. Johnny Grey and me took them long ago."

"But why did you say about the island?"

"Look, kiddo, when they get there and find a lot of new boxes they'll just take off. They're not expecting that."

The picket fence and the pile of boxes. No earth to dig them into. "There's stuff in the boxes too," he blurted.

Ron didn't move. But Dickie felt that strange shimmer round his brother. He was thinking — not Ron thoughts; ways of thinking from the prison or something. Dickie couldn't see in there and he didn't want to. The circle was still closed.

Ron stood up and held his brother's arm. Tightly. He was hurting his shoulder. Dickie said so and Ron didn't answer. "I'll see you at home, kid," he said suddenly and set off running down the beach. The men were dragging the skiff slowly toward the water. The eagle flapped heavily down the beach above their heads, the white gulls still dipping and screaming round him. Ron's hair leaped on his shoulders, his lean legs stretched above the sand. "Hey guys," he yelled, "Hey wait I'll bring you there." One moment he was a movie hero striking lithely over the sands, next the sea-mirage rose past his legs and he was a puppet, stiffly, erratically working. "Hey wait," he called. The men looked up and waited for him to help with the dinghy.

Dickie turned back past the point. The dog appeared again from a patch of salal and ran beside him. He didn't look back but he heard the boat's engine rumbling over the water, heard that circle clench as tight as a bear-trap. As the houses came into sight again he heard out behind them the shriek of some sea bird and the rising gabble of loons. The cry echoed in his head — he heard in it the screech of a box lid opening.

"You're getting like your brother," Mumma said. He'd been lying on the couch most of the afternoon, watching the grain in the roof-planks.

"I feel sick, Mumma," he said.

"Would you cut me some wood," she said snappily. She was helpless but she saw things. He got up and went out to the shed. Ron was back in the village, back in his cuban heels. He waved from the porch at Sharon Grey's but he didn't come back till supper. He sat on the couch, smoking, while the others ate. He was moody again, but the shimmer was round him. Dickie put down his fork. "Goin' out tomorrow," Ron said, "on the bus."

"Where you goin'?" said Mumma. So weary, she might as well not have asked.

"Goin' out," said Ron.

Dickie looked out at dawn again and Ron was asleep by the dead stove. The boy took a rug off the couch and went to cover his brother up. He was sprawled out on the chair, one leg straight, one knee bent. On his lap was a tarnished silver bracelet, almost black. Dickie picked it up and traced out the lines through the tarnish. An eagle's head, etched firmly, the beak slightly open, a claw stretched out before it as though to strike. He looked at it closely in the half-light, seeing the eye patterns fitted perfectly upon the folded wings, before the smell of it came shimmering sickly up into his face.

Ron died in the city a week later. If he hadn't been in the city, or if there'd been any money, or if they'd heard in time, he would have been laid to rest on the island. But they didn't hear about it for two weeks. Dickie rowed out to the island the next day. He nailed back two of the lids before he had to run. His cousin Mary, nine years old and two years dead. They had left her jawbone beside the little box because it still had skin upon it.

KAATJE HURLBUT

A Short Walk into Afternoon

(FROM SOUTHWEST REVIEW)

THE MONTH'S VISIT with Aunt Jeanette in her New York apartment was in its last week. She had twice asked Margaret if she would not like to stay longer. Embarrassed for want of a tactful answer, Margaret, who was eight, assumed a very polite expression as she shook her head. The thought of being impolite to Aunt Jeanette was alarming because she never showed annoyance or anger; she only smiled. The smile was very bright.

This was the first time Margaret had ever been away from her mother and father, her brothers, and the long airy house in New Hampshire surrounded by giant trees which, according to her father, whispered about the doings of the mountains. It was the first time she had ever been in a place that was never quiet.

She observed the routine she encountered here as solemnly as if she were in church, except for the afternoon "rest," which she privately considered preposterous and which she accomplished by sitting in a blue wing chair beside an open window in the living room and unhappily submitting to the afternoon's dreary mingling of noise and heat. It was August.

After Mrs. Peel had cleared away lunch and made preparations for dinner, she would say in her paper voice: "We'll just rest now until auntie comes home." (Aunt Jeanette would be in her gallery downtown.) She would then glide down the hall to the maid's room and close the door, and Margaret would go to stand in the living room doorway where, for a moment, she would stubbornly resist the short walk that would carry her into the afternoon.

She had invented a way of prolonging the walk. There were four carpets of stealthy color and neat design which Aunt Jeanette had explained (as she explained everything in the apartment: furniture, paintings, engravings, objects of all kinds), and one of them was a prayer rug. Margaret could not remember which one, so she respectfully trod the borders of all the rugs, saying prayers as she went. When this became exasperatingly tiresome, she would spin in circles and say: "Matthew, Mark, Luke and John, hold the horse while I get on," and "Amen, brother Ben, shot at a goose and killed a hen," after which she would stick out her tongue as far as it would go.

Finally seated in the blue chair, there was little to see except the blind windows of the apartments opposite (at which faces appeared now and then to stare vacantly before melting back into the gloom) or the courtyard three stories below where a narrow iron gate revealed a segment of the sidewalk.

The second-story windows were enclosed by narrow balconies. The balcony just below Margaret's window belonged to a violin student who, Aunt Jeanette had explained, had been in Europe most of the summer. They had passed him on the street in the evening three days ago; Aunt Jeanette had nodded coolly, and he had returned an impudent grin. Margaret thought him bad and wild-looking. He never came out on his balcony, and none of the other people ever seemed to use theirs. She marveled at this and longed for one of her own to play on, or just to stand on, and be outside and high up and look down on things.

At the beginning of each afternoon, she did two things with stern deliberation. First, she maintained to herself that the afternoons were not part of the real visit. The real visit was in the morning when Mrs. Peel took her to the park or to the smelly, bustling market where a huge fat man in a filthy apron called her sweetheart and gave her peaches, and always smiled at her in a way that made her profoundly happy. The real visit was in the evening, uncomfortable but interesting, when Aunt Jeanette's friends often came — strange people, sharp and sad under their good manners and quiet laughter. The best of the real visit was on weekends when Aunt Jeanette was free and took her to concerts and galleries and curious shops on narrow steets, and on rambling walks to see monuments of men and horses frozen in terrible greatness, and fountains, and buildings shouting up into the sky, and the endless faces of people, never to be seen again, never to be forgotten. Impossibly, she absorbed it all and went to sleep at night with her enormous mind revolving above her, tumbling its wondrous burden. In the morning she would pretend her brothers sat on the foot of her bed while she whispered amazing things to them.

The second thing she did each afternoon was to say to herself with great firmness: "I'm still me. I'm just like I always was," and lift the hot shawl of her hair from her back and violently shake her head. At home she wore pigtails so long she could tuck them into the belt of her jeans or stand beside one of her brothers and spin so the pigtails slapped him across the face if he didn't duck.

The first thing Aunt Jeanette had done on Margaret's arrival was to shampoo her hair and brush it until it shone like pale satin and curled at the tips below her waist. Then she bought her dresses (to match her hair, she said) of creamy white, pale apricot, and lemon. Aunt Jeanette tried the dresses on her and looked at her, not saying anything. The look made Margaret's skin feel tight. Aunt Jeanette's hands had shaken as she buttoned and tied, and unbuttoned and untied.

The pretty dresses made her squirm, but she decided that wearing them for Aunt Jeanette's company in the evening was the same as pretending the afternoons were fun. ("What did you do all afternoon, dear?" "I had fun. I played.") It was all part of being kind, as her mother had said she knew she would be. ("Aunt Jeanette has no family. She is lonely. You'll be very kind, won't you?") So Margaret suffered the hot shawl of her hair, the pale dresses, the dreary afternoons, and felt kind.

But she did not feel kind about Aunt Jeanette brushing her hair so much. She did not like the way she brushed it wildly, laughing her dark laugh. She brushed with long, hard strokes until Margaret's neck ached from holding her head against the pull of the brush. Faster and faster she brushed until the hair crackled and flew. She wrapped the shining bands around her wrists, and took handfuls and buried her face in them. Margaret had to clench her fists and her teeth to keep from yelling and hitting. Later, lying in the dark with her neck aching no matter how she turned her head, she hated her hair and jerked it until she made herself cry, quietly and fiercely. Instead of feeling kind, she wanted to tear Aunt Jeanette's arms off as she had once torn the wings off a bumblebee that had stung her on the sole of her foot.

Today was Thursday. When Mrs. Peel had shut herself in her room, Margaret accomplished the elaborate journey to the blue wing chair by the window. She didn't want to be drawn into the weary turmoil of the street noises; she hated the sounds of afternoon. So she said *Thursday* to herself and thought about the calendar her father had given her. He had marked it, showing the days and weeks of the visit. Three square-marked days from today was Sunday, over which he had written in large letters: GOING HOME DAY. As she thought of this, she grinned suddenly and widely, but immediately a tight pain in her throat warned her not to think about the calendar any more. For something to do she inspected the ceiling, but found it just a plain white ceiling. She looked to each side of the chair's curving back, and decided if those curves were the wings of this wing chair, they would never be able to fly it. Many of Aunt Jeanette's chairs had names: a round-shouldered one was called Empire; polite-looking ones in the dining room were called Fiddlebacks; and a very important chair across the room was called The Chippendale, and nobody except company was supposed to sit on it — as long as the company wasn't too fat. If the company was fat, Aunt Jeanette stood in front of The Chippendale and smiled brightly and blinked and the company would go and sit somewhere else.

She could force people to do anything by looking right at them and smiling. She made Margaret eat terrible things, like a fish with its head still on at the table, just by smiling; she could make her talk about very private family matters, like that baby that was coming and her mother crying about it; in the evening when company was there and someone argued with Aunt Jeanette about a painter or a book, she would smile suddenly and blink until the person was embarrassed and stopped arguing — all except Miss Ledbetter, who had a deep voice and wore men's shoes. Miss Ledbetter would say, "Oh, come on, Jenny," and Aunt Jeanette would turn away with a blank face.

Like a tired voice calling, an automobile horn dragged her attention back to the afternoon sounds. They were unlike the brisk clatter of morning, unlike the night sounds which were as merry and secret as the lights winking throughout the city. In the glare and heat the horns sounded lonely; the squeal of brakes was the fearful sound of being hurt; voices rising from the street were innocent of the dangers that stalked; the profound whisper of a passing jet plane trailed on unknowable sorrow.

For two days there had been a new sound, brief and disturbing:

that of the violin student in the apartment below, practicing. It didn't alarm her; it wasn't sad; but it was more demanding than the other sounds. It made her restless. When the violin lashed out, she thought of his bad face, and the fiddle he would hold down with his chin, and the bow he would use like a whip. The brief bursts of music snatched and stung. But in a fierce way, it was much better than the other noises.

As the heat and the dreary din pushed through the window, Margaret lifted the hot shawl of hair and opened her mouth to yawn. As the yawn arched in her throat, the violin cut through the afternoon like a rusty knife. It startled her, releasing a rush of anger.

The anger felt good in the sad afternoon, and she thought suddenly of her brothers, and the tumbling, digging, slapping, shouting battles she had with them, and of her mother's voice, sharp and furious: *"Stop that this minute!"*

She scrambled out of the chair and leaned out the window to glare down at the small balcony below. Breathing hard, she waited for a pause in the violin's raucous frenzy, and when it came, she said furiously and distinctly:

"Stop that this minute!"

In the silence, she waited, still breathing hard, watching the balcony. Presently the student's head appeared; he looked down, from side to side, and then up. His tilted eyes gave him a sharp look, even in astonishment. When he began to laugh, deeply and uncontrollably, she clamped her mouth tight and frowned to keep from giggling. She liked his bad face and wanted to give it a good slap. His eyes matched his teeth, which were bright and sharp; the corner ones were pointed, like a dog's.

When he stopped laughing, he watched her expectantly, as if he might laugh again. With unsmiling deliberation, she stuck her tongue out as far as it would go and withdrew it.

The dog teeth showed again. "Was I disturbing you, beautiful?"

His speaking sent a flutter from her stomach into her throat, and she scrambled back into the blue chair. She sat very still waiting for something to happen.

As she waited, the whine of an engine stretched thinly through the heat; a hollow footstep of someone who might be dead and not know it echoed in the court; a weary voice called and was answered by a distant siren.

With a leap, the violin pounced upon the noises of afternoon and sent them running for their lives. They scattered as they fled, but merged again into a scuttling band of fright as it chased them into a narrow road and followed fast upon their heels, gaining on them, pursuing them along the edge of a precipice, skidding around corners in its wild chase, grabbing for them as they madly rushed to a mountain top, and fled into the air to escape. Gone! They were gone!

On the mountain top the violin performed a joyous, taunting dance — and paused. Then it began to descend, idle and happy, kicking stones down the slope, bounding over a stream, tumbling through a feathery patch of grass. Margaret sitting with her head back, smiling, followed him down the mountain — strolling, dancing, running past trees and snatching handfuls of leaves, and spinning, pigtails flying as she spun. At the foot of the mountain she sat down against a giant tree, and round and round her he went and bound her to the tree with gentle threads of music.

In the evening Aunt Jeanette said that because she had taken a nice nap (she had found her asleep in the blue chair), she might sit up and help entertain.

As usual, Miss Ledbetter and the fat person came, and, among others, a beautiful, sulky girl called Ann, who looked through walls and never smiled; everyone treated her like a spoiled child. Margaret found herself tired of the company as soon as it had arrived and folded her hands in her lap in order to appear polite.

The only interesting thing about the evening was waiting to see if Aunt Jeanette would have to keep the fat person from sitting on The Chippendale, but this did not happen. The fat person, who wore a wildly flowered dress, laughed almost continuously and never looked at anybody, threw herself in the corner of a sofa, and behind the laughing her restless eyes swept back and forth all evening.

As time went on Margaret was scarcely aware of the people in the room; their voices were waves of noise with phrases bobbing on the crests. The fat person kept calling Miss Ledbetter "sweetie"; Ann's voice emerged without disturbing her lips as she murmured, "Oh, but *really,*" from time to time; a dark, hairy woman with a low forehead and a foreign accent offered a bass "haw-haw" when amused and called Ann "liddle one."

Squirming delicately in the blue chair, her hair like a woolen shawl, Margaret wanted only to go to bed, where in the cool dark she could think about the violin student. Even with the windows open, cigarette smoke and the sharp, oily smell of whiskey drifted in layers through the room. She was about to drop her head, pretending to be overcome with sleepiness so she would be sent to bed, when Miss Ledbetter pushed an ottoman near her chair and sat down.

"I'm going to sit at the feet of this little princess," she said in her deep musical voice. Margaret liked her handsome sun-browned face and the short dark hair licked with silver at the temples; she liked her voice: it was a gentle, circling voice, as a warm hand is gentle circling the wrist.

"Do you use this little, little bone? Does it actually work?" Miss Ledbetter asked with a musing frown.

Margaret found it hard not to stare at Miss Ledbetter. (Her mother said staring was almost as rude as slapping.) But she felt compelled to discover whether Miss Ledbetter was mostly a woman or mostly a man. Sometimes, instead of trousers, she wore severe-looking skirts to match her coat, and she was *Miss* Ledbetter. Otherwise, she was a man — shoes, necktie, and all. Margaret put this by as another amazing thing to tell her brothers.

As they idly discussed school, her family, and the problems encountered in climbing cedar trees, Miss Ledbetter slipped a finger through the curling tip of Margaret's hair. All at once she stopped talking and stood up to face Aunt Jeanette, who had suddenly appeared beside the chair. She was looking straight at Miss Ledbetter, smiling brightly and blinking.

Miss Ledbetter held her gaze a moment and said quietly: "Oh for God's sake, Jenny," and moved away.

Margaret felt suffocated all at once and announced firmly to no one in particular that she was going to bed. She didn't care if it was impolite.

The next afternoon she walked straight to the blue chair without lingering on the rugs and waited. It was a short wait and a tingling one. Quickly and gaily the violin seized the afternoon. Margaret dashed to her room and returned with a box of wooden mosaics and a frame of small squares and made designs while she listened, half smiling, spellbound. For the first time during the visit, she "played" all afternoon, just as she always told Aunt Jeanette she did.

They spoke once. During a lull in the music, she leaned out the window and softly called: "Hey." He appeared almost at once. "Hey," he said, grinning. "Was I disturbing you again?" "No," she said breathlessly, shaking her head. Her hair tumbled over the sill. He laughed gently and gazed at her for a moment, then kissed his hand to her. Shyly, in haste, she kissed her hand to him and returned to the blue chair. Presently he resumed playing.

At dinner that evening, after listening to Margaret's account of the day (she did not mention the student), Aunt Jeanette laid her hand on Margaret's arm, holding it there until Margaret put down her fork and looked at her.

"I have a lovely surprise for you, dear."

"Shall I guess?"

"You'd never guess." She watched her closely as she said: "It's this: if you would like, and of course I know you would, you don't have to go home."

She continued to watch her, directly and widely, seeing her, seeing around her, like a fence of eyes. Margaret's skin grew tight; she knew she must speak but she did not know what to say. She opened her mouth, trusting some remark to emerge, but her jaws were stiff and no words came.

Aunt Jeanette took her hand and spoke hurriedly: "You see, dear, when you left home, your mother wasn't well, and she is not any better — just yet. And so one less child to care for —"

"Is Mom sick?" she bluntly interrupted.

"Not exactly. You see —" she glanced away — "she was going to have another dear little baby —" Margaret nodded impatiently. "Yes. You knew that. Well. Something happened and the little baby isn't coming after all. So for the next little while, it might be easier for your mother if —"

"Did Mom say for me not to come home?" She deliberately interrupted again, looking her in the eye as a good hot lump of anger gathered in her stomach. Aunt Jeanette let go her hand and sat up very straight. She said coldly and evenly:

"No, Margaret. I suggested it."

They looked steadily at each other. Margaret's mouth tightened and her teeth clenched. Suddenly Aunt Jeanette smiled.

The lump of anger in Margaret's stomach sickened her for a moment, but before the smile it flattened and flattened, until it was no more than a thin, red ache. She doubled up her toes and turned to stare blindly at the wall.

She dreamed that night that her mother had fallen out of a nest with some baby birds and died. She woke from the dream crying and kicking at the covers to find Aunt Jeanette standing over her. When she bent down to try to stroke her head, Margaret told her crossly to go away. It was the only time she had been openly defiant; she was grateful for the dark: she wouldn't be able to see the smile.

The next day was Saturday — next to GOING HOME DAY. All day Saturday and all day Sunday there was not a pause in the going and seeing and doing. It began with breakfast on the terrace of the zoo, where Aunt Jeanette, lighthearted and joking and planning, set the hours spinning like a wheel with colored spokes. They saw a slam-bang puppet show. They took a brave ride on the prow of a ferry. They went to the Museum of Natural History, where in a glass cage of watery light a Siberian tiger snarled coldly at the whole world; Indians were there: at the top of a flight of stairs, startling, silent, crouched in a teepee around a smokeless fire as red as blood, their eyes alive with listening — eyes fiercer than anything they feared. They shopped for a lavender dress, and a book — any book she wanted. Margaret chose a book of the old fairy tales, but with pictures so vivid and strange that she knew the stories would be better in this book.

The sleeping beauty lay like marble, but a spider startled by the prince was live and hairy. As Rumpelstiltskin stamped himself into the ground, his eyes bulged with rage, but the young mother-queen smiled a sly, silver smile. The eyes of the hiding witch burned with hatred as she watched the prince, splendid in his swirling cloak, call to Rapunzel in the tower:

"Rapunzel, Rapunzel, let down your hair!"

Throughout the weekend, the possibility of not going home lay in the bottom of her mind like a stone. Her thought, swept along by what she saw and did and heard, went round it and over it, always touching it. She could not speak of it — and Aunt Jeanette would not. As she tired, the weight became unbearable and forced slow tears. But Aunt Jeanette looked away and talked brightly.

Sunday night nothing was said. Aunt Jeanette brushed her hair until her head rolled with the pull of the brush, and read to her from the new book after she was in bed. When sleep dragged her down, she dreamed of Rapunzel in the tower, and of her mother holding her brothers by the hand, weeping bitterly because she could not guess Rumpelstiltskin's name.

When Monday morning came, she saw nothing to release her from the weekday routine and stepped helplessly into the measured squares of time. She looked for a broken hour somewhere, or a blank square in which something would happen that would make going home the *next* thing. She tried to ready the event in her mind in case it needed a way to happen: Aunt Jeanette could telephone from the gallery: "I've changed my mind. You can go home." Or a letter could come from her mother: "You must come home. I need you right away." Or a telegram from her father: "Come home at once. No matter what."

But the hours did not swerve or crack or open at all. They plodded on to lunchtime, and afterward, when Mrs. Peel went down the hall and sealed herself away, Margaret crossed the living room to the blue chair and sat down.

The dreary afternoon noises crowding through the window mingled with the heaviness inside her and became part of her own pain and her mother's; horns and solitary shouts were the voices of her brothers calling in distress; the warning squeals of brakes were swift dangers overtaking her father.

As she gasped against a strangling sob, it tore into the afternoon, cruel and raging — the fury of the violin under the savage little whip. He leapt into her mind — the student — his bad face scowling down on the instrument, ready to snap with his sharp teeth. He lashed it and it growled threateningly; he lashed again and the growl rose to a howl of anguish and, with a broken sound, subsided into a piteous moan. But in a changing moment it was the whip that spoke, using the strings for voice. Softly it murmured with pity in its breath, a cruel pity, prolonged, manipulating, dangerous, but presently it relented and lightened, until at last it wept tears of forgiveness. Tenderness flowered between whip and ardent strings, and they sang together in happiness until, with a gasp, a laugh broke forth to be followed by a shout, and then a wild joy exploded into a spinning, whirling dance. Faster and faster the dancing went until the dancers cleared the ground, leaving the astonished earth below.

In the abrupt silence, Margaret was surprised by the sound of her own laughing. She was leaning out the window, breathless, helpless with laughter. The student came out at once and laughed too. She laughed until she was weak and her head dropped on the sill and her hair hung down over the ledge.

"So you like Bruch, do you?" he said, with his head cocked and his tilted eyes merry.

She didn't know or care what Bruch was, but nodded and took a deep breath, seeking something to say. She was afraid he would go in.

"I have two brothers," she said tentatively. He looked keenly at her and stopped smiling. He nodded encouragingly. "And I'm going home tomorrow," she said. "I think. I'm almost sure."

He said quickly: "No. No. Don't cry." He shook his head and pleaded, "Don't!"

"I'm not," she said crossly, and ground her teeth. He was looking at her the way her brothers did when they unintentionally hurt her. So she stuck out her tongue at him and he laughed again, and she flopped over the sill and giggled. Surprisingly the tears erupted again and she blinked them back, sniffing mightily.

"What do you do all day, Goldilocks?" He leaned against the iron railing and folded his arms. He wasn't going in.

"My father says Goldilocks was a nitwit."

He chuckled. "Well, what's your name, then?"

"Anyway," she was sure of his attention, "anyway, Goldilocks had tons of curls, and I only have some at the ends." She shook her head, rippling the shining mass.

His face lost its sharp look and smiling he stretched up his hand; he was looking not at her face, but at her hair.

"It won't reach," she said. "Not even halfway. If it reached, would you grab hold and climb up here with me?"

"If it reached, I'd cut off enough to restring my bow."

She gazed solemnly at him. "You would?" He nodded, still smiling. After a moment she said shortly: "Do you know the witch?"

His eyes narrowed; he watched her intently. Her gaze, fixed on him, widened until she no longer saw him. Involuntarily she drew an uneven breath and focused her eyes again, but vaguely. She whispered: "I have to go now."

She tiptoed swiftly down the hall to Aunt Jeanette's room and took a pair of scissors from a leather case on the bureau. She returned to the blue chair in the living room and sat on the edge, breathing heavily.

The afternoon noises were louder now, bustling and urgent —
later sounds, more horns blowing, futile but insistent. The desolate
cry of a paper boy dragged at the hurrying footsteps, but the
footsteps hurried faster, hurrying home. It was late.

She took a handful of hair close to her head and cut. As it came
whispering away in her hand, she looked at it in sudden fright and
thrust it from her, out the window. Then she cut the other side
and the back, her hand shaking violently. When she had dropped
the last pale shock among the others, she looked down at the
sprawling mass; it moved as a slight breeze stirred. She sat down
again quickly and was shaken by her heart banging against the thin
wall of her chest.

Presently the student would see her hair on the balcony; she
knew he wouldn't string his bow with it; it didn't matter. Presently
Aunt Jeanette would walk into the room and see, and she would be
very, very angry, and smile the terrible smile; it didn't matter.
What mattered was that now Aunt Jeanette would let her go home.

WILLIAM STYRON

Shadrach

(FROM ESQUIRE)

MY TENTH SUMMER ON EARTH, in the year 1935, will never leave my mind because of Shadrach and the way he brightened and darkened my life then and thereafter. He turned up as if from nowhere, arriving at high noon in the village where I grew up in Tidewater Virginia. He was a black apparition of unbelievable antiquity, palsied and feeble, blue-gummed and grinning, a caricature of a caricature at a time when every creaky, superannuated Negro grandsire was (in the eyes of society, not alone the eyes of a small Southern white boy) a combination of Stepin Fetchit and Uncle Remus. On that day when he seemed to materialize before us, almost out of the ether, we were playing marbles. Little boys rarely play marbles nowadays but marbles were an obsession in 1935, somewhat predating the yo-yo as a kids' craze. One could admire these elegant many-colored spheres as potentates admire rubies and emeralds; they had a sound yet slippery substantiality, evoking the tactile delight — the same aesthetic yet opulent pleasure — of small precious globes of jade. Thus, among other things, my memory of Shadrach is bound up with the lapidary mineral feel of marbles in my fingers and the odor of cool bare earth on a smoldering hot day beneath a sycamore tree, and still another odor (ineffaceably a part of the moment): a basic fetor, namely the axillary and inguinal smell which that squeamish decade christened B.O., and which radiated from a child named Little Mole Dabney, my opponent at marbles. He was ten years old, too, and had never been known to use Lifebuoy soap, or any other cleansing agent.

Which brings me soon enough to the Dabneys. For I realize I must deal with the Dabneys in order to try to explain the encompassing mystery of Shadrach — who after a fashion was a Dabney himself. The Dabneys were not close neighbors; they lived nearby down the road in a rambling weatherworn house which lacked a lawn. On the grassless, graceless terrain of the front yard was a random litter of eviscerated Frigidaires, electric generators, stoves, and the remains of two or three ancient automobiles whose scavenged carcasses lay abandoned beneath the sycamores like huge rusted insects. Poking up through these husks were masses of weeds and hollyhocks, dandelions gone to seed, sunflowers. Junk and auto parts were a sideline of Mr. Dabney, he also did odd jobs; but his primary pursuit was bootlegging.

Like such noble Virginia family names as Randolph and Peyton and Tucker and Harrison and Lee and Fitzhugh and a score of others, the patronym Dabney is an illustrious one, but with the present Dabney, born Vernon, the name had lost almost all of its luster. He should have gone to the University of Virginia; instead, he dropped out of school in the fifth grade. It was not his fault; nor was it his fault that the family had so declined in status. It was said that his father (a true scion of the distinguished old tree but a man with a "character defect" and a weakness for the bottle) had long ago slid down the social ladder, forfeiting his F.F.V. status by marrying a half-breed Mattaponi or Pamunkey Indian girl from the York River, accounting perhaps for the black hair and sallowish muddy complexion of the son.

Mr. Dabney — at this time, I imagine he was in his forties — was a runty, hyperactive entrepreneur with a sourly intense, purse-lipped, preoccupied air and a sometimes rampaging temper. He also had a ridiculously foul mouth, from which I learned my first dirty words. It was with delectation, with the same sickishly delighted apprehension of evil which beset me about eight years later when I was accosted by my first prostitute, that I heard Mr. Dabney in his frequent transports of rage use those words forbidden to me in my own home. His blasphemies and obscenities, far from scaring me, caused me to shiver with their splendor. I practiced his words in secret, deriving from their amalgamated filth what, in a dim pediatric way, I could perceive was erotic inflammation. "Son of a bitch whorehouse bat shit Jesus Christ pisspot asshole!" I would screech into an empty closet, and feel my little ten-year-old pecker rise. Yet as ugly and threatening as Mr. Dabney might sometimes appear, I was never really daunted by him for he had a humane

and gentle side. Although he might curse like a stevedore at his
wife and children, at the assorted mutts and cats that thronged the
place, at the pet billy goat which he once caught in the act of
devouring his new three-dollar Thom McAn shoes, I soon saw that
even his most murderous fits were largely bluster.

Oh how I loved the Dabneys! I visited the Dabney homestead as
often as I could, basking in its casual squalor. I must avoid giving
the impression of Tobacco Road, the Dabneys were of better quality. Yet there were similarities. The mother, named Trixie, was a
huge sweaty generous sugarloaf of a women, often drunk. It was
she, I am sure, who propagated the domestic sloppiness. But I
loved her passionately just as I loved and envied the whole Dabney
tribe and that total absence in them of the bourgeois aspirations
and gentility which were my own inheritance. I envied the sheer
teeming multitude of the Dabneys — there were seven children —
which made my status as an only child seem so effete, spoiled and
lonesome. Only illicit whiskey kept the family from complete destitution, and I envied their near poverty. Also their religion. They
were Baptists: as a Presbyterian I envied that. To be totally im-
mersed — how wet and natural! They lived in a house devoid of
books or any reading matter except funny papers — more envy. I
envied their abandoned slovenliness, their sour unmade beds, their
roaches, the cracked linoleum on the floor, the homely cur dogs
leprous with mange that foraged at will through house and yard.
My perverse longings were — to turn around a phrase unknown
at the time — downwardly mobile. Afflicted at the age of ten by
nostalgie de la boue, I felt deprived of a certain depravity. I was too
young to know, of course, that one of the countless things of which
the Dabneys were victim was the Great Depression.

Yet beneath this scruffy facade, the Dabneys were a family of
some property. Although their ramshackle house was rented, as
were most of the dwellings in our village, they owned a place
elsewhere, and there was occasionally chatter in the household
about "the Farm," far upriver in King and Queen County. Mr.
Dabney had inherited the place from his dissolute father and it
had been in the family for generations. It could not have been
much of a holding, or else it would have been sold years before,
and when, long afterwards, I came to absorb the history of the
Virginia Tidewater — that primordial American demesne where
the land was sucked dry by tobacco, laid waste and destroyed a

whole century before golden California became an idea, much less
a hope or a westward dream — I realized that the Dabney farm
must have been as nondescript and as pathetic a relic as any of the
scores of shrunken, abandoned "plantations" scattered for a
hundred miles across the tidelands between the Potomac and the
James. The chrysalis, unpainted, of a dinky, thrice-rebuilt farmhouse with a few mean acres in corn and second-growth timber —
that was all. Nonetheless it was to this ancestral dwelling that the
nine Dabneys, packed like squirming eels into a fifteen-year-old
Model T Ford pockmarked with the ulcers of terminal decay,
would go forth for a month's sojourn each August, as seemingly
bland and blasé about their customary estivation as Rockefellers
decamping to Pocantico Hills. But they were not entirely vacation-
ing. I did not know then but discovered later that the woodland
glens and lost glades of the depopulated land of King and Queen
were every moonshiner's dream for hideaways in which to decoct
white lightning, and the exodus to "the Farm" served a purpose
beyond the purely recreative: each Dabney of whatever age and
sex had at least a hand in the operation of the still, even if it was
simply shucking corn.

All of the three Dabney boys bore the nickname of Mole, being
differentiated from each other by a logical nomenclature — Little,
Middle, and Big Mole; I don't think I ever knew their real names.
It was the youngest of the three Moles I was playing marbles with
when Shadrach made his appearance. Little Mole was a child of
stunning ugliness, sharing with his brothers an inherited mixture
of bulging thyroid eyes, mashed-in, spoon-like nose and jutting jaw
which (I say in retrospect) might have nicely corresponded to
Cesare Lombroso's description of the criminal physiognomy.
Something more remarkable — accounting surely for their collec-
tive nickname — was the fact that save for their graduated sizes
they were nearly exact replicas of each other, appearing less related
by fraternal consanguinity than as monotonous clones, as if Big
Mole had reproduced Middle who in turn had created Little, my
evil-smelling playmate. None of the Moles ever wished or was ever
required to bathe and this accounted for another phenomenon. At
the vast and dismal consolidated rural school we attended, one
could mark the presence of any of the three Dabney brothers in a
classroom by the circumambience of empty desks which caused
each Mole to be isolated from his classmates who, edging away

without apology from the effluvium, would leave the poor Mole abandoned in his aloneness, like some species of bacteria on a microscope slide whose noxious discharge has destroyed all life in a circle around it.

By contrast — the absurdity of genetics! — the four Dabney girls were fair, fragrant in their Woolworth perfumes, buxom, lusciously ripe of hindquarter, at least two of them knocked up and wed before attaining full growth. Oh, those lost beauties . . .

That day Little Mole took aim with a glittering taw of surreal chalcedony; he had warts on his fingers, his odor in my nostrils was quintessential Mole. He sent my agate spinning into the weeds.

Shadrach appeared then. We somehow sensed his presence, looked up and found him there. We had not heard him approach, he had come as silently and portentously as if he had been lowered on some celestial apparatus operated by unseen hands. He was astoundingly black. I had never seen a Negro of that impenetrable hue: it was blackness of such intensity that it reflected no light at all, achieving a virtual obliteration of facial features and taking on a mysterious undertone which had the blue-gray of ashes. Perched on a fender, he was grinning at us from the rusted frame of a demolished Pierce-Arrow. It was a blissful grin which revealed deathly purple gums, the yellowish stumps of two teeth and a wet mobile tongue. For a long while he said nothing but, continuing to grin, contentedly rooted at his crotch with a hand warped and wrinkled with age: the bones moved beneath the black skin in clear skeletal outline. With his other hand he firmly grasped a walking stick.

It was then that I felt myself draw a breath in wonder at his age, which was surely unfathomable. He looked older than all the patriarchs of *Genesis* whose names flooded my mind in a Sunday school litany: Lamech, Noah, Enoch, and that perdurable old Jewish fossil, Methuselah. Little Mole and I drew closer, and I saw then that the old man had to be at least partially blind; cataracts clouded his eyes like milky cauls, the corneas swam with rheum. Yet he was not entirely without sight, I sensed the way he observed our approach; above the implacable sweet grin there were flickers of wise recognition. His presence remained worrisomely Biblical; I felt myself drawn to him with an almost devout compulsion, as if he were the prophet Elijah sent to bring truth, light, the Word.

The shiny black mohair mail-order suit he wore was baggy and frayed, streaked with dust; the cuffs hung loose, and from one of the ripped ankle-high clodhoppers protruded a naked black toe. Even so, the presence was thrillingly ecclesiastical and fed my piety.

It was midsummer, the very trees seemed to hover on the edge of combustion; a mockingbird began to chant nearby in notes rippling and clear. I walked closer to the granddaddy through a swarm of fat green flies supping hungrily on the assorted offal carpeting the Dabney yard. Streams of sweat were pouring off the ancient black face. Finally I heard him speak in a senescent voice so faint and garbled that it took moments for it to penetrate my understanding. But I understood: "Praise de Lawd. Praise His sweet name! Ise arrived in Ole Virginny!"

He beckoned to me with one of his elongated, bony, bituminous fingers; at first it alarmed me but then the finger seemed to move appealingly, like a small harmless snake. "Climb up on ole Shad's knee," he said. I was beginning to get the hang of his gluey diction, realized that it was a matter of listening to certain internal rhythms; even so, with the throaty gulping sound of Africa in it, it was nigger talk I had never heard before. "Jes climb up," he commanded. I obeyed. I obeyed with love and eagerness, it was like creeping up against the bosom of Abraham. In the collapsed old lap I sat happily, fingering a brass chain which wound across the grease-shiny vest; at the end of the chain, dangling, was a nickel-plated watch upon the face of which the black mitts of Mickey Mouse marked the noontime hour. Giggling now, snuggled against the ministerial breast, I inhaled the odor of great age — indefinable, not exactly unpleasant but stale like a long-unopened cupboard — mingled with the smell of unlaundered fabric and dust. Only inches away the tongue quivered like a pink clapper in the dark gorge of a cavernous bell. "You jes a sweetie," he crooned. "Is you a Dabney?" I replied with regret, "No," and pointed to Little Mole. "That's a Dabney," I said.

"You a sweetie, too," he said, summoning Little Mole with the outstretched forefinger, black, palsied, wiggling. "Oh, you jes de sweetest thing!" The voice rose joyfully. Little Mole looked perplexed. I felt Shadrach's entire body quiver; to my mystification he was overcome with emotion at beholding a flesh-and-blood Dabney and as he reached toward the boy I heard him breathe again: "Praise de Lawd! Ise arrived in Ole Virginny!"

Then at that instant Shadrach suffered a cataclysmic crisis — one that plainly had to do with the fearful heat. He could not, of course, grow pallid but something enormous and vital did dissolve within the black eternity of his face; the wrinkled old skin of his cheeks sagged, his milky eyes rolled blindly upward, and uttering a soft moan he fell back across the car's ruptured seat with its naked springs and its holes disgorging horsehair.

"Watah!" I heard him cry feebly, "*Watah!*" I slid out of his lap, watched the scrawny black legs no bigger around than pine saplings begin to shake and twitch. "Watah, please!" I heard the voice implore, but Little Mole and I needed no further urging; we were gone — racing headlong to the kitchen and the cluttered, reeking sink. "That old nigger's dying!" Little Mole wailed. We got a cracked jelly glass, ran water from the faucet in a panic, speculating as we did: Little Mole ventured the notion of a heat stroke, I theorized a heart attack. We screamed and babbled, we debated whether the water should be at body temperature or iced. Little Mole added half a cupful of salt, then decided that the water should be hot. Our long delay was fortunate, for several moments later, as we hurried with the terrible potion to Shadrach's side, we found that the elder Dabney had appeared from a far corner of the yard and, taking command of the emergency, had pried Shadrach away from the seat of the Pierce-Arrow, dragged or carried him across the plot of bare earth and propped him up against a tree trunk where he now stood sluicing water from a garden hose into Shadrach's gaping mouth. The old man gulped his fill. Then Mr. Dabney, small and fiercely intent in his baggy overalls, hunched down over the stricken patriarch, whipped out a pint bottle from his pocket and poured a stream of crystalline whiskey down into Shadrach's gorge. While he did this he muttered to himself in tones of incredulity and inwardly tickled amazement: "Well, kiss my ass! Who are you, old uncle? Just who in the God damned hell *are* you?"

We heard Shadrach give a strangled cough, then he began to try out something resembling speech. But the word he was almost able to produce was swallowed and lost in the hollow of his throat.

"What did he say? What did he say?" Mr. Dabney demanded impatiently.

"He said his name is Shadrach!" I shouted, proud that I alone seemed able to fathom this obscure Negro dialect further muddied by the crippled cadences of senility.

"What's he want?" Mr. Dabney said.

I bent my face toward Shadrach's, which looked contented again. His voice in my ear was at once whispery and sweet, a gargle of beatitude: "Die on Dabney ground."

"I think he said," I told Mr. Dabney at last, "that he wants to die on Dabney ground."

"Well I'll be God damned," said Mr. Dabney.

"Praise de Lawd!" Shadrach cried suddenly, in a voice that even Mr. Dabney could understand. "Ise arrived in Ole Virginny!"

Mr. Dabney roared at me: "Ask him where he came from!"

Again I inclined my face to that black shrunken visage upturned to the blazing sun; I whispered the question and the reply came back after a long silence, in fitful stammerings. At last I said to Mr. Dabney: "He says he's from Clay County down in Alabama."

"*Alabama!* Well, kiss my ass!"

I felt Shadrach pluck at my sleeve and once more I bent down to listen. Many seconds passed before I could discover the outlines of the words struggling for meaning on the flailing ungovernable tongue. But finally I captured their shapes, arranged them in order.

"What did he say now?" Mr. Dabney said.

"He said he wants you to bury him."

"*Bury him!*" Mr. Dabney shouted. "How can I bury him? He ain't even dead yet!"

From Shadrach's breast there now came a gentle keening sound which, commencing on a note of the purest grief, startled me by the way it resolved itself suddenly into a mild faraway chuckle; the moonshine was taking hold. The pink clapper of a tongue lolled in the cave of the jagged old mouth. Shadrach grinned.

"Ask him how old he is," came the command. I asked him.

"Nimenime," was the glutinous reply.

"He says he's ninety-nine years old," I reported, glancing up from the ageless abyss.

"*Ninety-nine!* Well, kiss my ass! Just kiss my ass!"

Now other Dabneys began to arrive, including the mother, Trixie, and the two larger Moles, along with one of the older teen-age daughters, whale-like but meltingly beautiful as she floated on the crest of her pregnancy, and accompanied by her hulking, acne-cratered teen-age spouse. There also came a murmuring clutch of neighbors — sun-reddened shipyard workers in cheap sport shirts, scampering towhead children, a quartet of scrawny housewives in sack-like dresses, bluish crescents of sweat beneath their arms. In my memory they make an aching tableau of those exhausted years. They jabbered and clucked in wonder at Shadrach, who, immobilized by alcohol, heat, infirmity and his ninety-nine Augusts, beamed and raised his rheumy eyes to the sun. "Praise de Lawd!" he quavered.

We hoisted him to his feet and supported the frail, almost weightless old frame as he limped on dancing tiptoe to the house, where we settled him down upon a rumpsprung glider which squatted on the back porch in an ambient fragrance of dog urine, tobacco smoke and mildew. "You hungry, Shad?" Mr. Dabney bellowed. "Mama, get Shadrach something to eat!" Slumped in the glider, the ancient visitor gorged himself like one plucked from the edge of critical starvation: he devoured three cantaloupes, slurped down bowl after bowl of Rice Krispies, and gummed his way through a panful of hot cornbread smeared with lard. We watched silently, in wonderment. Before our solemnly attentive eyes he gently and carefully eased himself back on the malodorous pillows and with a soft sigh went to sleep.

Sometime after this — during the waning hours of the afternoon, when Shadrach woke up, and then on into the evening — the mystery of the old man's appearance became gradually unlocked. One of the Dabney daughters was a fawn-faced creature of twelve named Edmonia; her fragile beauty (especially when contrasted with ill-favored brothers) and her precocious breasts and bottom had caused me — young as I was — a troubling, unresolved itch. I was awed by the ease and nonchalance with which she wiped the drool from Shadrach's lips. Like me, she possessed some inborn gift of interpretation, and through our joint efforts there was pieced together over several hours an explanation for this old man — for his identity and his bizarre and inescapable coming.

He stayed on the glider, we put another pillow under his head. Nourishing his dragon's appetite with Hershey bars and, later on, with nips from Mr. Dabney's bottle, we were able to coax from those aged lips a fragmented, abbreviated but reasonably coherent biography. After a while it became an anxious business for, as one of the adults noticed, old Shad seemed to be running a fever; his half-blind eyes swam about from time to time, and the clotted phlegm which rose in his throat made it all the more difficult to understand anything. But somehow we began to divine the truth. One phrase, repeated over and over, I particularly remember: "Ise a Dabney." And indeed those words provided the chief clue to his story.

Born a slave on the Dabney plantation in King and Queen County, he had been sold down to Alabama in the decades before the Civil War. Shadrach's memory was imperfect regarding the date of his sale. Once he said "fifty," meaning 1850, and another time he said "fifty-five," but it was an item of little importance; he was probably somewhere between fifteen and twenty-five years old when his master — Vernon Dabney's great-grandfather — disposed of him, selling him to one of the many traders prowling the worn-out Virginia soil of that stricken bygone era; and since in his confessional to us, garbled as it was, he used the word "coffle" (a word beyond my ten-year-old knowledge but one whose meaning I later understood), he must have journeyed those six hundred miles to Alabama on foot and in the company of God knows how many other black slaves, linked together by chains.

So now, as we began slowly to discover, this was Shadrach's return trip home to Ole Virginny — three-quarters of a century or thereabouts after his departure from the land out of which he had sprung, which had nurtured him, and where he had lived his happy years. Happy? Who knows? But we had to assume they were his happy years — else why this incredible pilgrimage at the end of his life? As he had announced with such abrupt fervor earlier, he wanted only to die and be buried on "Dabney ground."

We learned that after the war he had become a sharecropper, that he had married three times and had had many children (once he said twelve, another time fifteen; no matter, they were legion); he had outlived them all, wives and offspring. Even the grandchildren had died off, or had somehow vanished. "Ah was dibested of all mah plenty" was another statement I can still record verbatim. Thus divested and (as he cheerfully made plain to all who gathered around him to listen) sensing mortality in his own shriveled flesh

and bones, he had departed Alabama on foot — just as he had
come there — to find the Virginia of his youth.

Six hundred miles! The trip, we were able to gather, took over
four months, since he said he set out from Clay County in the early
spring. He walked nearly the entire way, although now and then
he would accept a ride — almost always, one can be sure, from the
few Negroes who owned cars in the rural South of those years. He
had saved up a few dollars, which allowed him to provide for his
stomach. He slept on the side of the road or in barns, sometimes a
friendly Negro family would give him shelter. The trek took him
across Georgia and the Carolinas and through Southside Virginia.
His itinerary is still anyone's conjecture. Because he could not read
either road sign or road map, he obviously followed his own north-
ward-questing nose, a profoundly imperfect method of finding
one's way (he allowed to Edmonia with a faint cackle) since he once
got so far astray that he ended up not only miles away from the
proper highway but in a city and state completely off his route —
Chattanooga, Tennessee. But he circled back and moved on. And
how, once arrived in Virginia with its teeming Dabneys, did he
discover the only Dabney who would matter, the single Dabney
who was not merely the proprietor of his birthplace but the one
whom he also unquestioningly expected to oversee his swiftly approaching departure, laying him to rest in the earth of their mutual
ancestors? How did he find *Vernon Dabney?* Mr. Dabney was by no
means an ill-spirited or ungenerous man (despite his runaway
temper), but was a soul nonetheless beset by many woes in the
dingy threadbare year 1935, being hard pressed not merely for
dollars but for dimes and quarters, crushed beneath an elephan-
tine and inebriate wife along with three generally shiftless sons and
two knocked-up daughters plus two more in the offing, and living
with the abiding threat of revenue agents swooping down to ter-
minate his livelihood and, perhaps, get him sent to the Atlanta
penitentiary for five or six years. He needed no more cares or
burdens, and now in the hot katydid-shrill hours of the summer
night I saw him gaze down at the leathery old dying black face with
an expression that mingled compassion and bewilderment and
stoppered-up rage and desperation, and then whisper to himself:
"He wants to die on Dabney ground! Well, kiss my ass, just kiss my
ass!" Plainly he wondered how, among all his horde of Virginia
kinfolk, Shadrach found *him,* for he squatted low and murmured:

"Shad! Shad, how come you knew who to look for?" But in his fever Shadrach had drifted off to sleep, and so far as I ever knew there was never any answer to that.

The next day it was plain that Shadrach was badly off. During the night he had somehow fallen from the glider, and in the early morning hours he was discovered on the floor, leaking blood. We bandaged him up. The wound just above his ear was superficial, as it turned out, but it had done him no good; and when he was replaced on the swing he appeared to be confused and at the edge of delirium, plucking at his shirt, whispering and rolling his gentle opaque eyes at the ceiling. Whenever he spoke now his words were beyond the power of Edmonia or me to comprehend, faint high-pitched mumbo-jumbo in a drowned dialect. He seemed to recognize no one. Trixie, leaning over the old man as she sucked at her first Pabst Blue Ribbon of the morning, decided firmly that there was no time to waste. "Shoog," she said to Mr. Dabney, using her habitual pet name (diminutive form of Sugar), "you better get out the car if we're goin' to the Farm. I think he ain't gone last much longer." And so, given unusual parental leave to go along on the trip, I squeezed myself into the back seat of the Model T, privileged to hold in my lap a huge greasy paper bag full of fried chicken which Trixie had prepared for noontime dinner at the Farm.

Not all of the Dabneys made the journey — the two older daughters and the largest Mole were left behind — but we still comprised a multitude. We children were packed sweatily skin to skin and atop each other's laps in the rear seat, which reproduced in miniature the messiness of the house with this new litter of empty RC Cola and Nehi bottles, funny papers, watermelon rinds, banana peels, greasy jack handles, oil-smeared gears of assorted sizes and wads of old Kleenex. On the floor beneath my feet I even discerned (to my intense discomfort, for I had just learned to recognize such an object) a crumpled, yellowish used condom, left there haphazardly, I was certain, by one of the older daughters' boyfriends who had been able to borrow the heap for carnal sport. It was a bright summer day, scorchingly hot like the day preceding it, but the car had no workable windows and we were pleasantly ventilated. Shadrach sat in the middle of the front seat. Mr. Dabney was hunched over the wheel, chewing at a wad of tobacco and driving with black absorption; he had stripped to his undershirt, and I thought I could almost see the rage and frustration in the tight bunched muscles of his neck. He muttered curses at the balky gearshift but otherwise said little, rapt in his guardian misery. So voluminous that the flesh of her shoulders fell in a freckled cascade over the back of her seat, Trixie loomed on the other side of Shadrach; the corpulence of her body seemed in some way to both enfold and support the old man, who nodded and dozed. The encircling hair around the shiny black head was, I thought, like a delicate halo of the purest frost or foam. Curiously, for the first time since Shadrach's coming, I felt a stab of grief and achingly wanted him not to die.

"Shoog," said Trixie, standing by the rail of the dumpy little ferry that crossed the York River, "what kind of big birds do you reckon those are behind that boat there?" The Model T had been the first car aboard, and all of us had flocked out to look at the river, leaving Shadrach to sit there and sleep during the fifteen minute ride. The water was blue, sparkling with whitecaps, lovely. A huge gray naval tug with white markings chugged along to the mine depot at Yorktown, trailing eddies of garbage and a swooping flock of frantic gulls. Their squeals echoed across the peaceful channel.

"Seagulls," said Mr. Dabney. "Ain't you never recognized seagulls before? I can't believe such a question. Seagulls. Dumb greedy bastards."

"Beautiful things," she replied softly, "all big and white. Can you eat one?"

"So tough you'd like to choke to death."

We were halfway across the river when Edmonia went to the car to get a ginger ale. When she came back she said hesitantly: "Mama, Shadrach has made a fantastic mess in his pants."

"Oh Lord," said Trixie.

Mr. Dabney clutched the rail and raised his small, pinched, tormented face to heaven. "Ninety-nine years old! Christ almighty! He ain't nothin' but a ninety-nine years old *baby*!"

"It smells just awful," said Edmonia.

"Why in the God damned hell didn't he go to the bathroom before we left?" Mr. Dabney said. "Ain't it bad enough we got to drive three hours to the Farm without — "

"*Shoosh*!" Trixie interrupted, moving ponderously to the car. "Poor ol' thing, he can't help it. Vernon, you see how you manage your bowels fifty years from now."

*

Once off the ferry we children giggled and squirmed in the back seat, pointedly squeezed our noses, and scuffled amid the oily rubbish of the floorboards. It was an awful smell. But a few miles up the road in the hamlet of Gloucester Court House, drowsing in eighteenth-century brick and ivy, Trixie brought relief to the situation by bidding Mr. Dabney to stop at an Amoco station. Shadrach had partly awakened from his slumbrous trance. He stirred restlessly in his pool of discomfort, and began to make little fretful sounds, so softly restrained as to barely give voice to what must have been his real and terrible distress. "There now, Shad," Trixie said gently, "Trixie'll look after you." And this she did, half-coaxing, half-hoisting the old man from the car and into a standing position, then with the help of Mr. Dabney propelling his skinny scarecrow frame in a suspended tiptoe dance to the rest room marked COLORED, where to the muffled sound of rushing water she performed some careful rite of cleansing and diapering. Then they brought him back to the car. For the first time that morning Shadrach seemed really aroused from that stupor into which he had plunged so swiftly hours before. "Praise de Lawd!" we heard him say, feebly but with spirit, as the elder Dabneys maneuvered him back onto the seat, purified. He gazed about him with glints of recognition, responding with soft chuckles to our little pats of attention. Even Mr. Dabney seemed in sudden good humor. "You comin' along all right now, Shad?" he howled over the rackety cluttering sound of the motor. Shadrach nodded and grinned but remained silent. There was a mood in the car of joy and revival. "Slow down, Shoog," Trixie murmured indolently, gulping at a beer, "there might be a speed cop." I was filled with elation, and hope tugged at my heart as the flowering landscape rushed by, green and lush with summer and smelling of hay and honeysuckle.

The Dabney country retreat, as I have said, was dilapidated and rudimentary, a true downfall from bygone majesty. Where there once stood a plantation house of the Palladian stateliness required of its kind during the Tidewater dominion in its heyday, there now roosted a dwelling considerably grander than a shack yet modest by any reckoning. Box-like, paintless, supported by naked concrete blocks and crowned by a roof of glistening sheet metal, it would have been an eyesore almost anywhere except in King and Queen County, a bailiwick so distant and underpopulated that the house was scarcely ever viewed by human eyes. A tilted privy out back lent another homely note, junk littered the yard here too. But the soft green acres that surrounded the place were Elysian; the ancient fields and the wild woods rampant with sweet gum and oak and redbud had reverted to the primeval glory of the time of Pocahontas and Powhatan; grapevines crowded the emerald-green thickets which bordered the house on every side, a delicious winey smell of cedar filled the air, and the forest at night echoed with the sound of whippoorwills. The house itself was relatively clean, thanks not to any effort on the part of the Dabneys but to the fact that it remained unlived in by Dabneys for most of the year.

That day after our fried chicken meal we placed Shadrach between clean sheets on a bed in one of the sparsely furnished rooms, then turned to our various recreations. Little Mole and I played marbles all afternoon just outside the house, seeking the shade of a majestic old beech tree; after an hour of crawling in the dirt our faces were streaked and filthy. Later we took a plunge in the millpond, which, among other things, purged Little Mole of his B.O. The other children went fishing for perch and bream in the brackish creek which ran through the woods. Mr. Dabney drove off to get provisions at the crossroads store, then vanished into the underbrush to tinker around his well-hidden still. Meanwhile Trixie tramped about with heavy footfalls in the kitchen and downed half a dozen Blue Ribbons, pausing occasionally to look in on Shadrach. Little Mole and I peered in, too, from time to time. Shadrach lay in a deep sleep and seemed to be at peace, even though now and then his breath came in a ragged gasp and his long black fingers plucked convulsively at the hem of the sheet which covered him to his breast like a white shroud. Then the afternoon was over. After a dinner of fried perch and bream we all went to bed with the setting of the sun. Little Mole and I lay sprawled naked in the heat on the same mattress, separated by a paper-thin wall from Shadrach's breathing, which rose and fell in my ears against the other night sounds of this faraway and time-haunted place: katydids and crickets and hoot owls and the reassuring cheer — now near, now almost lost — of a whippoorwill.

Late the next morning the county sheriff paid a visit on Mr. Dabney. We were not at the house when he arrived, and so he had to wait for us; we were at the graveyard. Shadrach still slept, with the children standing watch one by one. After our watch Little

Mole and I had spent an hour exploring the woods and swinging on the grapevines, and when we emerged from a grove of pine trees, a quarter of a mile or so behind the house, we came upon Mr. Dabney and Trixie. They were poking about in a bramble-filled plot of land which was the old Dabney family burial ground. It was a sunny, peaceful place, where grasshoppers skittered in the tall grass. Choked with briars and nettles and weeds and littered with tumbledown stone markers, unfenced and untended for countless decades, it had been abandoned to the encroachments of summer after summer like this one, when even granite and marble had to give way against the stranglehold of spreading roots and voracious green growing things.

All of Mr. Dabney's remote ancestors lay buried here, together with their slaves, who slept in a plot several feet off to the side — inseparable from their masters and mistresses, but steadfastly apart in death as in life. Mr. Dabney stood amid the tombstones of the slaves, glaring gloomily down at the tangle of vegetation and at the crumbling lopsided little markers. He held a shovel in his hand but had not begun to dig. The morning had become hot, and the sweat streamed from his brow. I peered at the headstones, read the given names, which were as matter-of-fact in their lack of patronymic as spaniels or cats: *Fauntleroy, Wakefield, Sweet Betty, Mary, Jupiter, Lulu. Requiescat in Pace. Anno Domini 1790 . . . 1814 . . . 1831.* All of these Dabneys, I thought, like Shadrach.

"I'll be God damned if I believe there's a square inch of space left," Mr. Dabney observed to Trixie, and spat a russet gob of tobacco juice into the weeds. "They just crowded all the old dead uncles and mammies they could into this piece of land here. They must be shoulder to shoulder down there." He paused and made his characteristic sound of anguish — a choked dirge-like groan. "Christ almighty! I hate to think of diggin' about half a ton of dirt!"

"Shoog, why don't you leave off diggin' until this evenin'?" Trixie said. She was trying to fan herself with a soggy handkerchief, and her face — which I had witnessed before in this state of drastic summer discomfort — wore the washed-out bluish shade of skim milk. It usually preceded a fainting spell. "This sun would kill a mule."

Mr. Dabney agreed, saying that he looked forward to a cool glass of iced tea, and we made our way back to the house along a little

path of bare earth that wound through a field glistening with gold-
enrod. Then, just as we arrived at the back of the house, we saw
the sheriff waiting. He was standing with a foot on the running
board of his Plymouth sedan; perched on its front fender was a
hulkingly round, intimidating silver siren (in those days pronounced si-*reen*). He was a potbellied middle-aged man with a
sun-scorched face fissured with delicate seams and he wore steel-
rimmed spectacles. A gold-plated star was pinned to his civilian
shirt, which was soaked with sweat. He appeared hearty, made an
informal salute and said: "Mornin', Trixie. Mornin', Vern."

"Mornin', Tazewell," Mr. Dabney replied solemnly, though with
an edge of suspicion. Without pause he continued to trudge toward
the house. "You want some ice tea?"

"No thank you," he said. "Vern, hold on a minute. I'd like a
word with you."

I was knowledgeable enough to fear in a vague way some involvement with the distillery in the woods, and I held my breath,
but then Mr. Dabney halted, turned, and said evenly: "What's
wrong?"

"Vern," the sheriff said, "I hear you're fixin' to bury an elderly
colored man on your property here. Joe Thornton down at the
store said you told him that yesterday. Is that right?"

Mr. Dabney put his hands on his hips and glowered at the sheriff. Then he said: "Joe Thornton is a God damned incurable blab-
bermouth. But that's right. What's wrong with that?"

"You can't," said the sheriff.

There was a pause. "Why not?" said Mr. Dabney.

"Because it's against the law."

I had seen rage, especially in matters involving the law, build up
within Mr. Dabney in the past. A pulsing vein always appeared
near his temple, along with a rising flush in cheeks and brow; both
came now, the little vein began to wiggle and squirm like a worm.
"What do you mean, it's against the law?"

"Just that. It's against the law to bury anybody on private property."

"*Why* is it against the law?" Mr. Dabney demanded.

"I don't *know* why, Vern," said the sheriff, with a touch of exas-
peration. "It just *is*, that's all."

Mr. Dabney flung his arm out — up and then down in a stiff,
adamant, unrelenting gesture, like a railroad semaphore.

"Down in that field, Tazewell, there have been people buried for nearabout two hundred years. I got an old senile man on my hands. He was a slave and he was born on this place. Now he's dyin' and I've got to bury him here. And I am."

"Vern, let me tell you something," the sheriff said with an attempt at patience. "You will not be permitted to do any such a thing, so please don't try to give me this argument. He will have to be buried in a place where it's legally permitted, like any of the colored churchyards around here, and he will have to be attended to by a licensed colored undertaker. That's the *law*, Commonwealth of Virginia, and there ain't any which whys or wherefores about it."

Trixie began to anticipate Mr. Dabney's fury and resentment even before he erupted. "Shoog, keep yourself calm — "

"*Bat shit!* It is an *outrage!*" he roared. "Since when did a taxpaying citizen have to answer to the gov'ment in order to bury a harmless sick old colored man on his own property! It goes against every bill of rights I ever heard of — "

"Shoog!" Trixie put in. "*Please* — " She began to wail.

The sheriff put out placating hands and loudly commanded: "*Quiet!*" Then when Mr. Dabney and Trixie fell silent he went on: "Vern, me an' you have been acquainted for a long time, so please don't give me no trouble. I'm tellin' you for the last time, this. Namely, you have *got* to arrange to get that old man buried at one of the colored churches around here, and you will also have to have him taken care of by a licensed undertaker. You can have your choice. There's a well-known colored undertaker in Tappahannock and also I heard of one over in Middlesex, somewhere near Urbanna or Saluda. If you want, I'll give them a telephone call from the courthouse."

I watched as the red rage in Mr. Dabney's face was overtaken by a paler, softer hue of resignation. After a brooding long silence, he said: "All right then. *All right!* How much you reckon it'll cost?"

"I don't know exactly, Vern, but there was an old washer woman worked for me and Ruby died not long ago, and I heard they buried her for thirty-five dollars."

"*Thirty-five dollars!*" I heard Mr. Dabney breathe. "Christ have mercy!"

Perhaps it was only his rage which caused him to flee, but all afternoon Mr. Dabney was gone and we did not see him again until that evening. Meanwhile, Shadrach rallied for a time from his deep slumber, so taking us by surprise that we thought that he might revive completely. Trixie was shelling peas and sipping beer while she watched Little Mole and me at our marble game. Suddenly Edmonia, who had been assigned to tend to Shadrach for an hour, came running from the house. "Come here you all, real quick!" she said in a voice out of breath. "Shadrach's wide awake and talking!" And he was: when we rushed to his side we saw that he had hiked himself up in bed and his face for the first time in many hours wore an alert and knowing expression, as if he were at least partially aware of his surroundings. He had even regained his appetite. Edmonia had put a daisy in the buttonhole of his shirt, and at some point during his amazing resurrection, she said, he had eaten part of it.

"You should have heard him just now," Edmonia said, leaning over the bed. "He kept talking about going to the millpond. What do you think he meant?"

"Well, could be he just wants to go see the millpond," Trixie replied. She had brought Shadrach a bottle of RC Cola from the kitchen and now she sat beside him, helping him to drink it through a paper straw. "Shad," she asked in a soft voice, "is that what you want? You want to go see the millpond?"

A look of anticipation and pleasure spread over the black face and possessed those old rheumy eyes. And his voice was high-pitched but strong when he turned his head to Trixie and said: "Yes ma'am, I does. I wants to see de millpond."

"How come you want to see the millpond?" Trixie said gently.

Shadrach offered no explanation, merely said again: "I wants to see de millpond."

And so, in obedience to a wish whose reason we were unable to plumb but could not help honor, we took Shadrach to see the millpond. It lay in the woods several hundred yards to the east of the house — an ageless murky dammed-up pool bordered on one side by a glade of moss and fern, spectacularly green, and surrounded on all its other sides by towering oaks and elms. Fed by springs and by the same swiftly rushing stream in which the other children had gone fishing, its water mirrored the overhanging trees and the changing sky and was a pleasurable ordeal to swim in, possessing the icy cold that shocks a body to its bones. For a while we could not figure out how to transport Shadrach down to the place; it plainly would not do to try to let him hobble that long distance, propelled, with our clumsy help, on his nearly strengthless legs in their dangling gait. Finally someone thought of the wheelbarrow, which Mr. Dabney used to haul corn to the still. It was fetched from its shed, and we quickly made of it a not unhandsome and passably comfortable sort of a wheeled litter, filling it with hay and placing a blanket on top.

On this mound Shadrach rested easily, with a look of composure, as we moved him gently rocking down the path. I watched him on the way: in my memory he still appears to be a half-blind but self-possessed and serene African potentate being borne in the fullness of his many years to some longed-for, inevitable reward.

We set the wheelbarrow down on the mossy bank, and there for a long time Shadrach gazed at the millpond, alive with its skating waterbugs and trembling beneath a copper-colored haze of sunlight where small dragonflies swooped in nervous filmy iridescence. Standing next to the wheelbarrow, out of which the shanks of Shadrach's skinny legs protruded like fragile black reeds, I turned and stared into the ancient face, trying to determine what it was he beheld now that created such a look of wistfulness and repose. His eyes began to follow the Dabney children, who had stripped to their underdrawers and had plunged into the water. That seemed to be an answer, and in a bright gleam I was certain that Shadrach had once swum here too, during some unimaginable August nearly a hundred years before.

I had no way of knowing that if his long and solitary journey from the Deep South had been a quest to find this millpond and for a recaptured glimpse of childhood, it may just as readily have been a final turning of his back on a life of suffering. Even now I cannot say for certain, but I have always had to assume that the still-young Shadrach who was emancipated in Alabama those many years ago was set loose, like most of his brothers and sisters, into another slavery perhaps more excruciating than the sanctioned bondage. The chronicle has already been a thousand times told about those people liberated into their new and incomprehensible nightmare: of their poverty and hunger and humiliation, of the crosses burning in the night, random butchery and, above all, the unending dread. None of that madness and mayhem belongs in this story, but without at least a reminder of these things I would not be faithful to Shadrach. Despite the immense cheerfulness with which he had spoken to us of being "dibested of mah plenty," he must have endured unutterable adversity. Yet his return to Virginia, I can now see, was out of no longing for the former bondage, but to find an earlier innocence. And as a small boy at the edge of the millpond I saw Shadrach not as one who had fled darkness, but had searched for light refracted within a flashing moment of remembered childhood. As Shadrach's old clouded eyes gazed at the millpond with its plunging and calling children, his face was suffused with an immeasurable calm and sweetness, and I sensed that he had recaptured perhaps the one pure, untroubled moment in his life. "Shad, did you go swimming here too?" I said. But there was no answer. And it was not long before he was drowsing again; his head fell to the side and we rolled him back to the house in the wheelbarrow.

On Saturday nights in the country the Dabneys usually went to bed as late as ten o'clock. That evening Mr. Dabney returned at suppertime, still sullen and fretful but saying little, still plainly distraught and sick over the sheriff's mandate. He did not himself even pick up a fork. But the supper was one of those ample and blessed meals of Trixie's I recall so well. Only the bounty of a place like the Tidewater backcountry could provide such a feast for poor people in those hard-pressed years: ham with red-eye gravy, grits, collard greens, okra, sweet corn, huge red tomatoes oozing juice in a salad with onions and herbs and vinegar. For dessert there was a delectable bread pudding drowned in fresh cream. Afterward, a farmer and bootlegging colleague from down the road named Mr. Seddon R. Washington arrived in a broken-down pickup truck to join with Mr. Dabney at the only pastime I ever saw him engage in — a game of dominoes. Twilight fell and the oil lanterns were lit. Little Mole and I went back like dull slugs to our obsessive sport, scratching a large circle in the dust beside the porch and crouching down with our crystals and agates in a moth-crazed oblong of lantern light, tiger-yellow and flickering. A full moon rose slowly out of the edge of the woods like an immense, bright, faintly smudged balloon. The clicking of our marbles alternated with the click-click of the dominoes on the porch bench.

"If you wish to know the plain and simple truth about whose fault it is," I heard Mr. Dabney explain to Mr. Washington, "you can say it is the fault of your Franklin D for Disaster Roosevelt.

The Dutchman millionaire. And his so-called New Deal ain't worth a jugful of warm piss. You know how much I made last year — legal, that is?"

"How much?" said Mr. Washington.

"I can't even tell you. It would shame me. They are colored people sellin' deviled crabs for five cents apiece on the streets in Newport News made more than me. There is an injustice somewhere with this system." He paused. "Eleanor's near about as bad as he is." Another pause. "They say she fools around with colored men and Jews. Preachers mainly."

"Things bound to get better," Mr. Washington said.

"They can't get no worse," said Mr. Dabney.

Footsteps made a soft slow padding sound across the porch and I looked up and saw Edmonia draw near her father. She parted her lips, hesitated for a moment, then said: "Daddy, I think Shadrach has passed away."

Mr. Dabney said nothing, attending to the dominoes with his expression of pinched, absorbed desperation and muffled wrath. Edmonia put her hand lightly on his shoulder. "Daddy, did you hear what I said?"

"I heard."

"I was sitting next to him, holding his hand, and then all of a sudden his head — it just sort of rolled over and he was still and not breathing. And his hand — it just got limp and — well, what I mean, cold." She paused again. "He never made a sound."

Mr. Washington rose with a cough and walked to the far edge of the porch, where he lit a pipe and gazed up at the blazing moon. When again Mr. Dabney made no response, Edmonia lightly stroked the edge of his shoulder and said gently: "Daddy, I'm afraid."

"What're you afraid about?" he replied.

"I don't know," she said with a tremor. "Dying. It scares me. I don't know what it means — death. I never saw anyone — like that before."

"Death ain't nothin' to be afraid about," he blurted in a quick, choked voice. "It's life that's fearsome! *Life!*" Suddenly he arose from the bench, scattering dominoes to the floor, and when he roared "*Life!*" again I saw Trixie emerge from the black hollow of the front door and approach with footfalls that sent a shudder through the porch timbers. "Now, *Shoog* — " she began.

"*Life* is where you've got to be terrified!" he cried as the unplugged rage spilled forth. "Sometimes I understand why men commit suicide! Where in the God damned hell am I goin' to get the money to put him in the ground? Niggers have always been the biggest problem! God damn it, I was brought up to have a certain respect and say *colored* instead of *niggers* but they are always a problem, these niggers! They will just drag you down, God damned black bastards! Nigger assholes! I ain't got thirty-five dollars! I ain't got *twenty-five* dollars! I ain't got *five* dollars!"

"*Vernon!*" Trixie's voice rose, and she entreatingly spread out her great creamy arms. "Someday you're goin' to get a *stroke!*"

"And one other thing! Franklin D. Roosevelt is the worst nigger lover of them all!"

Then suddenly his fury — or the harsher, wilder part of it — seemed to evaporate, sucked up into the moonlit night with its soft summery cricketing sounds and its scent of warm loam and honeysuckle. For an instant he looked shrunken, runtier than ever, so light and frail that he might blow away like a leaf, and he ran a nervous, trembling hand through his shock of tangled black hair. "I know, I know," he said in a faint unsteady voice edged with grief. "Poor old man, he couldn't help it. He was a decent, pitiful old thing, probably never done anybody the slightest harm. I ain't got a thing in the world against Shadrach. Poor old man."

Crouched below the porch I felt an abrupt, smothering misery. The tenderest gust of wind blew from the woods and I shivered at its touch on my cheek, mourning for Shadrach and Mr. Dabney, and slavery and destitution, and all the human discord swirling around me in a time and place I could not understand. As if to banish my fierce unease, I began to try — in a seizure of concentration — to count the fireflies sparkling in the night air. Eighteen, nineteen, twenty . . .

"And anyway," Trixie said, touching her husband's hand, "he died on Dabney ground like he wanted to. Even if he's got to be put away in a strange graveyard."

"Well, he won't know the difference," said Mr. Dabney. "When you're dead nobody knows the difference. Death ain't much."

ROSELLEN BROWN

The Wedding Week

(FROM BOSTON UNIVERSITY JOURNAL)

NEXT SATURDAY NIGHT at this time I will be married. I am not afraid of that — it may be unfashionable but I haven't a doubt we are doing the right thing, we shall be at our best as husband and wife, if not in the old style then in the new.

To be blunt, what worries me is my father. How can I explain this?

How must he appear to the woman who is to be my wife? When she met the two of them it was, of course, my mother she remembered. My mother is small; she looks as though her very bones are dense; thrown into a pool of water she would surely sink like a stone, were she not so enterprising that she would raise the dead to come to her assistance. She wastes neither inches of flesh nor steps nor movements. They are, like all things, scarce, so they are only spent on work she fancies must be done, much of it scrub-work (into the dawn — God, from my bed I used to hear her harrowing the refrigerator's poor skin long past midnight) or cook-work to keep the holy fires stoked in our stomachs. She is the blower upon the one flame of life, digestion. This feisty little immigrant *balabuste* who started in Poland and continued in Hester Street en route to East New York — nonetheless she has a noisy dignity about her. I recognize that; she moves about, shapeless, in ugly shoes, haggling and bearing grudges at every street-corner, but with a nun's certainty that she is doing God's work. (And more efficiently, too — with no thoughts wasted on God.) The old story. From the sight of my mother's print housedresses and shopping bags one could derive a view of my childhood that would have to be correct, as it is clichéd, in some if not all of its details.

What else, I asked my wife-to-be. What could she say about my father after a single meeting?

Kind. Frightened, she said. Of me?

Of the moon, I told her. The months. The mice. Start anywhere. The heat of his own mouth. All of it makes him hide. A gentle man, terrified of the command to breathe and keep on breathing. A rabbit on his way to the stew pot.

You have his arms, she says.

I do?

His legs probably. And more. Precisely. Down to the way the dark hairs lie. For all I can tell you trade one pair of arms between you when I look away.

I am downcast and intrigued, hot and cold. What else do we share? I have a voice and I use it, though with little ease. I have shoulders he never dreamed of having, and in my muscles a history of basketball, of five-sewer stickball. Also, a will in which my mother's red blood runs hard. But I am so visibly his son. If he is a rabbit I am a lamb — his fears are my second-thoughts and third, his cringing has become my following. My wife and I will move into a house which would have been a palace to him on his wedding night. It will have a niche at the turning of the stairs in which we could place a statue — *The Winged Victory* — but will probably mock with a collage of beer cans or a giant mousetrap. If our doorway has a *mezuzah* tacked on with little nails, it will only be so that my father can visit us here. But I am going nowhere on my own, though I may punish myself for knowing it, with my second-generation self-consciousness. Updated vices. Each of us is just a shadow too helpless for whatever dreams we need.

I must assume he was a boy once. I ask him, he kicks himself for answer. Why do you want to know, he asks. Such memories no one needs. Think ahead. Think happy. I insist. His head goes into his shoulders. He could never wiggle his ears like some fathers but he could wrinkle his neck like an ancient turtle. He seems to think he deserved his past.

Always, apparently, the ground was frozen. (It will do you good to know? You need it for something, maybe a paper?) Summers he doesn't remember, nor any of the colors of summer. Maybe there were flowers, maybe not. Nor does he remember the pogroms, though Szeliezin suffered its necessary share. Mostly it was local hooligans, out with torches and jugs of foul local wine, nothing to

be dignified with a word like pogrom. Good luck, who wants to
remember?

But those days and nights, so weighted with flung stones, sank to
the bottom of his memory and lie there now. He brims and brims
with his ready tears that make me cringe. He had fur at the top of
his boots — my father in boots! and a sort of Russian pea-coat with
a fur collar, double-breasted — but holes at the bottom. The floor
of his house was made of dirt, certainly. It had never occurred to
me. Only the synagogue was whole and the houses of most of the
goyim — out there, across a moat full of, what? drunks? rapists?
assassins? A few of the Jews in the village had wooden floors — the
rebbe, after all . . .

He swears he ran in the stiff stripped fields, he climbed, fought,
made mischief. The youngest son always makes trouble, you know.
Also he beat his breast in shul beside his father. He must have
listened too well to the Yom Kippur chant of self-excoriation: *For
the sin which we have committed before thee by the stretched-forth neck of
pride; for the sin which we have committed before thee by levity; and for the
sins for which we are liable to the penalty of forty stripes . . . to the penalty
of excision and childlessness . . . to the penalty of death by the hand of
heaven. . . .* He never met most of his brothers, nor did he replace
them. Could it really be — while I, his child, climbed his steep
sides, he was back inside his balding head, getting his firm foothold
on a tree that still stands, leaning a long way down over the frozen
river Szeliezin?

And then he woke up here? Was it like that? Yes, one long lurch
of a crossing, boring, full of squabbling with strangers, and the
smell of puke in your pores, a dream in which you suffered like
cattle. Who has a new word for it — what should you say, you
suffered like silkworms? No one ever said it was poetry. Cattle.
Shoyin.

So the sidewalks here were frozen — worse than home in Szeliezin, at least he'd had those boots. But he didn't bring such things
to the new world, *shmates*. So he was always cold. He lived on the
ice. No matter how he sweated. All those shabbos candles, what did
they ever melt? Not a heart, not a winter. Only his own heart
dripped down in waxy tears, his mother covered her eyes and wept
and prayed and wept. Never trust what's underfoot (his one long
lesson to his only son — does it have anything to do with me,
learned as he slid and tumbled down Delancey Street?). You slip,

you slide, *greeneh*! You guess it all wrong, none of it's yours. *Go home, sheeny*! It's not for you to choose, this feast, this America — none of it's kosher — nobody said! — none of it's cheap. For fifty years you walk hunched forward ready to fall and break your skull, and never relax in the language. What more do I know of him? I search him out like a father so long dead I never met him. All that's left to tell is this part that terrifies me. I go to her, my almost-wife, she holds my hand as though nothing is going to happen. She doesn't see.

I know, I think, when my father stopped his climbing games, when he closed the trapdoor over his head, when he learned the rabbit jerk and began to wait for the axe's shadow on the ice. It was this week in his life, the one I'm beginning today. Do you see? This week exactly. Listen.

He lived at home. He was the only child still with his parents, his sisters married, his brothers scattered, one even gone off somewhere without a trace, without a how-are-you. He brought his paycheck home from the shop and gave it to his mother whole. Finally he would bite off a corner of it, he had a girl, a possibility. He felt guilty about leaving them, he delayed the proposal that hung in the air until the girl made moves to break the whole thing off; she was wasting her time, she had obligations to her parents too, the first of which was marriage . . . That was my mother, of course, with long hair and a round face, my mother from the pictures at Bear Mountain wearing knickers, smiling in a tumult of fallen leaves. Everyone I know has pictures of their parents young at Bear Mountain, I have been to Bear Mountain myself with a camera around my neck . . . My father looks a foot taller in those pictures, his lips were full and his nose assertive, his eyes gave off complicated lights, refracted by evident laughter. He was a funny man, my mother has told me, more incredulous, even, than I. In Yiddish he would make word plays, jokes on people's names, nobody got away without being renamed. Really.

Then his father died. His father died on a Monday morning, coughing black blood.

It wasn't enough. His mother choked on the bone of that death and died — echo, obedient echo! — all in the week of his wedding. *He didn't intend to start his marriage sitting shiva.* The dancers in the mirrors stopped in their tracks, the looking glasses went dark, locked up what they had seen like memories behind blind eyes. It is forbidden to see yourself in mourning. *He didn't intend to lie down in the earth when he had a marriage-bed*, like a servant, a widow, a dog. But the youngest son is sewed to his parents' bones with the strongest thread of their life.

Like a man whose hair goes gray in a single night, my father's life — can you see it? — drained down, to water their graves. They must have beanstalks on those graves, for all they took of his passion, for the little they left behind. There was a year that dragged like a terminal illness; then slowly, beginning again, my father remembered he had almost had a wife. So they were married.

Now, you see, whether I believe it or not — this is the week of my wedding. Deep winter coughs and chatters and washes down the air with killing cold. My father's bad eyes are clenched against an angel with better things to do (I say) than hang around for a chat where he's got no customer. The *malachamuviss* doesn't haggle. But my father, small as a boy, ducks under his 50 mg. of bottled sleep. He goes looking, shaking the bedclothes, beating the louvered closet doors, sniffing for the doom that slouches, still, just out of eyeshot.

I take his shoulders, in his old striped sweater that's buttoned wrong. Papa, the world is full of unlucky men! I swear he regrets he is not one, once and for all. His forehead is gray, the veins are lavender. I don't think he has pain in him, only aches. Not anger, just apology. The way my mother, all her life, has had not tragedies but "aggravations" . . .

I pull myself up, above him like a father: Will it make you happy, papa, you want a disaster? What would you like? You want me to say it, I will — here. The floor of your house, no matter what, will always, now and forever, be made of dirt.

Sonny, what do you want? What do you want from me. He shrugs, weakly, one shoulder, to get me off him.

He doesn't know. I am fighting for his life, for mine. I want him to marry my mother again, all of us together under the *chupa*, the arbor of good wishes. Begin again, start fresh, drink the wine of his children, be blessed with our hope against hope. I want him to have a honeymoon of lust and sun and wine prodigally spilled. *I want him to promise me, promise me like a man, not like a shivering rabbit, that he is not going to die.*

ISAAC BASHEVIS SINGER

A Party in Miami Beach

(FROM PLAYBOY)

Translated from the Yiddish by Joseph Singer

MY FRIEND the humorist Reuben Kazarsky called me on the telephone in my apartment in Miami Beach and asked, "Menashe, for the first time in your life, do you want to perform a *mitzvah?*"

"Me a *mitzvah?*" I countered. "What kind of word is that — Hebrew? Aramaic? Chinese? You know I don't do *mitzvahs,* particularly here in Florida."

"Menashe, it's not a plain *mitzvah.* The man is a multimillionaire. A few months ago, he lost his whole family in a car accident — a wife, a daughter, a son-in-law and a baby grandchild of two. He is completely broken. He has built here in Miami Beach, in Hollywood and in Fort Lauderdale maybe a dozen condominiums and rental houses. He is a devoted reader of yours. He wants to make a party for you, and if you don't want a party, he simple wants to meet you. He comes from somewhere around your area — Lublin or how do you call it? To this day, he speaks a broken English. He came here from the camps without a stitch to his back, but within fifteen years, he became a millionaire. How they manage this I'll never know. It's an instinct like for a hen to lay eggs or for you to scribble novels."

"Thanks a lot for the compliment. What can come out from this *mitzvah?*"

"In the other world, a huge portion of the leviathan and a Platonic affair with Sarah, daughter of Tovim. On this lousy planet, he's liable to sell you a condominium at half price. He is loaded and he's been left without heirs. He wants to write his memoirs and for you to edit them. He has a bad heart; they've implanted a pacemaker. He goes to mediums or they come to him."

"When does he want to meet me?"

"It could even be tomorrow. He'll pick you up in his Cadillac."

At five the next afternoon, my house phone began to buzz and the Irish doorman announced that a gentleman was waiting downstairs. I rode down in the elevator and saw a tiny man in a yellow shirt, green trousers and violet shoes with gilt buckles. The sparse hair remaining around his bald pate was the color of silver, but the round face reminded me of a red apple. A long cigar thrust out of the tiny mouth. He held out a small, damp palm, pressed my hand once, twice, three times, then said, in a piping voice:

"This is a pleasure and an honor! My name is Max Flederbush."

At the same time, he studied me with smiling brown eyes that were too big for his size — womanly eyes. The chauffeur opened the door to a huge Cadillac and we got in. The seat was upholstered in red plush and was as soft as a down pillow. As I sank down into it, Max Flederbush pressed a button and the window rolled down. He spat out his cigar, pressed the button again and the window closed.

He said, "I'm allowed to smoke about as much as I'm allowed to eat pork on Yom Kippur, but habit is a powerful force. It says somewhere that a habit is second nature. Does this come from the Gemara? The Midrash? Or is it simply a proverb?"

"I really don't know."

"How can that be? You're supposed to know everything. I have a Talmudic concordance, but it's in New York, not here. I'll phone my friend Rabbi Stempel and ask him to look it up. I have three apartments — one here in Miami, one in New York and one in Tel Aviv — and my library is scattered all over. I look for a volume here and it turns out to be in Israel. Luckily, there is such a thing as a telephone, so one can call. I have a friend in Tel Aviv, a professor at Bar-Ilan University, who stays at my place — for free, naturally — and it's easier to call Tel Aviv than New York or even someone right here in Miami. It goes through a little moon, a Sputnik or whatever. Yes, a satellite. I forget words. I put things down and I don't remember where. Our mutual friend, Reuben Kazarsky, no doubt told you what happened to me. One minute I had a family, the next — I was left as bereft as Job. Job was apparently still young and God rewarded him with new daughters, new camels and new asses, but I'm too old for such blessings. I'm sick, too. Each day that I live is a miracle from heaven. I have to guard myself with every bite. The doctor does allow me a nip of whiskey, but only a drop. My wife and daughter wanted to take me along on that ride, but I wasn't in the mood. It actually happened right here in Miami. They were going to Disney World. Suddenly, a truck came up driven by some drunk and it shattered my world. The drunk lost both of his legs. Do you believe in Special Providence?"

"I don't know how to answer you."

"According to your writings, it seems you do believe."

"Somewhere deep inside, I do."

"Had you lived through what I have, you'd grow firm in your beliefs. Well, but that's how man is — he believes and he doubts."

The Cadillac had pulled up and a parking attendant had taken it over. We walked inside a lobby that reminded me of a Hollywood supercolossal production — rugs, mirrors, lamps, paintings. The apartment was in the same vein. The rugs felt as soft as the upholstery in the car. The paintings were all abstract. I stopped before one that reminded me of a Warsaw rubbish bin on the eve of a holiday when the garbage lay heaped in huge piles. I asked Mr. Flederbush what and by whom this was, and he replied:

"Trash like the other trash. Pissako or some other bluffer."

"Who is this Pissako?"

Out of somewhere materialized Reuben Kazarsky, who said, "That's what he calls Picasso."

"What's the difference? They're all fakers," Max Flederbush said. "My wife, may she rest in peace, was the expert, not me."

Kazarsky winked at me and smiled. He had been my friend even back in Poland. He had written a half-dozen Yiddish comedies, but they had all failed. He had published a collection of vignettes, but the critics had torn it to shreds and he had stopped writing. He had come to America in 1939 and later had married a widow 20 years older than he. The widow died and Kazarsky inherited her money. He hung around rich people. He dyed his hair and dressed in corduroy jackets and hand-painted ties. He declared his love to every woman from 15 to 75. Kazarsky was in his 60s, but he looked no more than 50. He let his hair grow long and wore side whiskers. His black eyes reflected the mockery and abnegation of one who has broken with everything and everybody. In the cafeteria on the Lower East Side, he excelled at mimicking writers, rabbis and party leaders. He boasted of his talents as a sponger. Reuben Kazarsky suffered from hypochondria and because he was by nature a sexual philanthropist, he had convinced himself that he was impotent. We were friends, but he had never introduced me to his benefactors. It seemed that Max Flederbush had insisted that Reuben bring us together. He now complained to me:

"Where do you hide yourself? I've asked Reuben again and again to get us together, but according to him, you were always in Europe, in Israel or who knows where. All of a sudden, it comes out that you're in Miami Beach. I'm in such a state that I can't be alone for a minute. The moment I'm alone, I'm overcome by a gloom that's worse than madness. This fine apartment you see here turns suddenly into a funeral parlor. Sometimes I think that the real heroes aren't those who get medals in wartime but the bachelors who live out their years alone."

"Do you have a bathroom in this palace?" I asked.

"More than one, more than two, more than three," Max answered. He took my arm and led me to a bathroom that bedazzled me by its size and elegance. The lid of the toilet seat was transparent, set with semiprecious stones and a two-dollar bill implanted within it. Facing the mirror hung a picture of a little boy urinating in an arc while a little girl looked on admiringly. When I lifted the toilet-seat lid, music began to play. After a while, I stepped out onto the balcony that looked directly out to sea. The rays of the setting sun scampered over the waves. Gulls still hunted for fish. Far off in the distance, on the edge of the horizon, a ship swayed. On the beach, I spotted some animal that from my vantage point, 16 floors high, appeared like a calf or a huge dog. But it couldn't be a dog and what would a calf be doing in Miami Beach? Suddenly, the shape straightened up and turned out to be a woman in a long bathrobe digging for clams in the sand.

After a while, Kazarsky joined me on the balcony. He said, "That's Miami. It wasn't he but his wife who chased after all these trinkets. She was the businesslady and the boss at home. On the other hand, he isn't quite the idle dreamer he pretends to be. He has an uncanny knack for making money. They dealt in everything — buildings, lots, stocks, diamonds, and eventually she got involved in art, too. When he said buy, she bought; and when he said sell, she sold. When she showed him a painting, he'd glance at it, spit and say, 'It's junk, they'll snatch it out of your hands. Buy!' Whatever they touched turned to money. They flew to Israel, established Yeshivas and donated prizes toward all kinds of endeavors — cultural, religious. Naturally, they wrote it all off in taxes. Their daughter, that pampered brat, was half-crazy. Any complex you can find in Freud, Jung and Adler, she had it. She was born in a DP camp in Germany. Her parents wanted her to marry a chief rabbi or an Israeli prime minister. But she fell in love with a gentile, an archaeology professor with a wife and five children. His wife wouldn't divorce him and she had to be bought off with a quarter-million-dollar settlement and a fantastic alimony besides. Four weeks after the wedding, the professor left to dig for a new Peking man. He drank like a fish. It was he who was drunk, not the truck driver. Come, you'll soon see something!"

Kazarsky opened the door to the living room and it was filled with people. In one day, Max Flederbush had managed to arrange a party. Not all the guests could fit into the large living room. Kazarsky and Max Flederbush led me from room to room and the party was going on all over. Within minutes, maybe 200 people had gathered, mostly women. It was a fashion show of jewelry, dresses, pants, caftans, hairdos, shoes, bags, make-up, as well as men's jackets, shirts and ties. Spotlights illuminated every painting. Waiters served drinks. Black and white maids offered trays of hors d'oeuvres.

In all this commotion, I could scarcely hear what was being said to me. The compliments started, the handshakes and the kisses. A stout lady seized me around and pressed me to her enormous bosom. She shouted into my ear, "I read you! I come from the towns you describe. My grandfather came here from Ishishok. He was a wagon driver there and here in America, he went into the freight business. If my parents wanted to say something I wouldn't understand, they spoke Yiddish, and that's how I learned a little of the language."

I caught a glimpse of myself in the mirror. My face was smeared with lipstick. Even as I stood there, trying to wipe it off, I received all kinds of proposals. A cantor offered to set one of my stories to music. A musician demanded I adapt an opera libretto from one of my novels. A president of an adult-education program invited me to speak a year hence at his synagogue. I would be given a plaque. A young man with hair down to his shoulders asked that I recommend a publisher, or at least an agent, to him. He declared, "I *must* create. This is a physical need with me."

One minute all the rooms were full, the next — all the guests were gone, leaving only Reuben Kazarsky and myself. Just as quickly and efficiently, the help cleaned up the leftover food and half-drunk cocktails, dumped all the ashtrays and replaced all the chairs in their rightful places. I had never before witnessed such perfection. Out of somewhere, Max Flederbush dug out a white tie with gold polka dots and put it on.

He said, "Time for dinner."

"I ate so much I haven't the least appetite," I said.

"You must have dinner with us. I reserved a table at the best restaurant in Miami."

After a while, the three of us, Max Flederbush, Reuben Kazarsky and I, got into the Cadillac and the same chauffeur drove us. Night had fallen and I no longer saw nor tried to determine where I was being taken. We drove for only a few minutes and pulled up in front of a hotel resplendent with lights and uniformed attendants. One opened the car door ceremoniously, a second fawningly opened the glass front door. The lobby of this hotel wasn't merely supercolossal but supersupercolossal — complete to light effects, tropical plants in huge planters, vases, sculptures, a parrot in a cage. We were escorted into a nearly dark hall and greeted by a headwaiter who was expecting us and led us to our reserved table. He bowed and scraped, seemingly overcome with joy that we had arrived safely. Soon, another individual came up. Both men wore tuxedos, patent-leather shoes, bow ties and ruffled shirts. They looked to me like twins. They spoke with foreign accents that I suspected weren't genuine. A lengthy discussion evolved concerning our choice of foods and drinks. When the two heard I was a vegetarian, they looked at each other in chagrin, but only for a second. Soon they assured me they would serve me the best dish a vegetarian had ever tasted. One took our orders and the other wrote them down. Max Flederbush announced in his broken English that he really wasn't hungry, but if something tempting could be dredged up for him, he was prepared to give it a try. He interjected Yiddish expressions, but the two waiters apparently understood him. He gave precise instructions on how to roast his fish and prepare his vegetables. He specified spices and seasonings.

Reuben Kazarsky ordered a steak and what I was to get, which in plain English was a fruit salad with cottage cheese.

When the two men finally left, Max Flederbush said, "There were times if you would have told me I'd be sitting in such a place eating such food, I would have considered it a joke. I had one fantasy — one time before I died to get enough dry bread to fill me. Suddenly, I'm a rich man, alas, and people dance attendance on me. Well, but flesh and blood isn't fated to enjoy any rest. The angels in heaven are jealous, Satan is the accuser and the Almighty is easily convinced. He nurses a longtime resentment against us Jews. He still can't forgive the fact that our great-great-grandfathers worshiped the golden calf. Let's have our picture taken."

A man with a camera materialized. "Smile!" he ordered us.

Max Flederbush tried to smile. One eye laughed, the other cried. Reuben Kazarsky began to twinkle. I didn't even make the effort. The photographer said he was going to develop the film and that he'd be back in three quarters of an hour.

Max Flederbush asked, "What was I talking about, eh? Yes, I live in apparent luxury, but a woe upon this luxury. As rich and as elegant the house is, it's also a Gehenna. I'll tell you something; in a certain sense, it's worse here than in the camps. There, at least, we all hoped. A hundred times a day we comforted ourselves with the fact that the Hitler madness couldn't go on for long. When we heard the sound of an airplane, we thought the invasion had started. We were all young then and our whole lives were before us. Rarely did anyone commit suicide. Here, hundreds of people sit, waiting for death. A week doesn't go by that someone doesn't give up the ghost. They're all rich. The men have accumulated fortunes, turned worlds upside down, maybe swindled to get there. Now they don't know what to do with their money. They're all on diets. There is no one to dress for. Outside of the financial page in the newspaper, they read nothing. As soon as they finish their breakfasts, they start playing cards. Can you play cards forever? They have to, or die from boredom. When they get tired of playing, they start slandering one another. Bitter feuds are waged. Today they elect a president, the next day they try to impeach him. If he decides to move a chair in the lobby, a revolution breaks out. There is one touch of consolation for them — the mail. An hour before the postman is due, the lobby is crowded. They stand with their keys in hand, waiting like for the Messiah. If the postman is late, a hubbub erupts. If one opens his mailbox and it's empty, he starts to grope and burrow inside, trying to create something out of thin air. They are all past seventy-two and they receive checks from Social Security. If the check doesn't come on time, they worry about it more than those who need it for bread. They're always suspicious of the mailman. Before they mail a letter, they shake the cover three times. The women mumble incantations.

"It says somewhere in the Book of Morals that if man will remember his dying day, he won't sin. Here you can as much forget about death as you can forget to breathe. Today I meet someone by the swimming pool and we chat. Tomorrow I hear he's in the other world. The moment a man or a woman dies, the widow or widower starts right in looking for a new mate. They can barely sit out the shivah. Often, they marry from the same building. Yesterday they maligned the other with every curse in the book, today they're husband and wife. They make a party and try to dance on their shaky legs. The wills and insurance policies are speedily rewritten and the game begins anew. A month or two don't go by and the bridegroom is in the hospital. The heart, the kidneys, the prostate.

"I'm not ashamed before you — I'm every bit as silly as they are, but I'm not such a fool as to look for another wife. I neither can nor do I want to. I have a doctor here. He's a firm believer in the benefits of walking and I take a walk each day after breakfast. On the way back, I stop at the Bache brokerage house. I open the door and there they sit, the oldsters, staring at the ticker, watching their stocks jump around like imps. They know full well that they won't make use of these stocks. It's all to leave in the inheritance, and their children and grandchildren are often as rich as they are. But if a stock goes up, they grow optimistic and buy more of it.

"Our friend Reuben wants me to write my memoirs, I have a story to tell, yes I do. I went through not only one Gehenna but ten. This very person who sits here beside you sipping champagne spent three quarters of a year behind a cellar wall, waiting for death. I wasn't the only one — there were six of us men there and one woman. I know what you're going to ask. A man is only a man, even on the brink of the grave. She couldn't live with all six of us, but she did live with two — her husband and her lover — and she satisfied the others as best as she could. If there had been a machine to record what went on there, the things that were said and the dreams that were played out, your greatest writers would be made to look like dunces by comparison. In such circumstances, the souls strip themselves bare and no one has yet adequately described a naked soul. The *szmalcowniks*, the informers, knew about us and they had to be constantly bribed. We each had a little money or some valuable objects and as long as they lasted, we kept buying pieces of life. It came to it that these informers brought us bread, cheese, whatever was available — everything for ten times the actual price.

"Yes, I could describe all this in pure facts, but to give it flavor requires the pen of a genius. Besides, one forgets. If you would ask me now what these men were called, I'll be damned if I could tell you. But the woman's name was Hilda. One of the men was called Edek, Edek Saperstein, and the other — Sigmunt, but Sigmunt what? When I lie in bed and can't sleep, it all comes back as vivid as if it would have happened yesterday. Not everything, mind you.

"Yes, memoirs. But who needs them? There are hundreds of such books written by simple people, not writers. They send them to me and I send them a check. But I can't read them. Each one of these books is poison, and how much poison can a person swallow? Why is it taking so long for my fish? It's probably still swimming in the ocean. And your fruit salad first has to be planted. I'll give you a rule to follow — when you go into a restaurant and it's dark, know that this is only to deceive. The headwaiter is one of the Polish children of Israel, but he poses as a native Frenchman. He might even be a refugee himself. When you come here, you have to sit and wait for your meal, so that later on the bill won't seem too excessive. I'm neither a writer nor a philosopher, but I lie awake half the nights and when you can't sleep, the brain churns like a mill. The wildest notions come to me. Ah, here is the photographer! A fast worker. Well, let's have a look!"

The photographer handed each of us two photos in color and we sat there quietly studying them.

Max Flederbush asked me, "Why did you come out looking so frightened? That you write about ghosts, this I know. But you look here as if you'd seen a real ghost. If you did, I want to know about it."

"I hear you go to séances," I said.

"Eh? I go. Or, to put it more accurately — they come to me. This is all bluff, too, but I *want* to be fooled. The woman turns off the lights and starts talking, allegedly in my wife's voice. I'm not such a dummy, but I listen. Here they come with our food, the Miami *szmalcowniks.*"

The door opened and the headwaiter came in leading three men. All I could see in the darkness was that one was short and fat, with a square head of white hair that sat directly on his broad shoulders, and with an enormous belly. He wore a pink shirt and red trousers. The two others were taller and slimmer. When the headwaiter pointed to our table, the heavy-set man broke away from the others, came toward us and shouted in a deep voice:

"Mr. Flederbush!"

Max Flederbush jumped up from his seat.

"Mr. Albeginni!"

They began to heap praises upon each other. Albeginni spoke in broken English with an Italian accent.

Max Flederbush said, "Mr. Albeginni, you know my good friend, Kazarsky, here. And this man is a writer, a Yiddish writer. He writes everything in Yiddish. I was told that you understand Yiddish!"

Albeginni interrupted him. "*A gezunt oyf dein kepele . . . Hock nisht kein tcheinik . . . A gut boychik . . .* My parents lived on Rivington Street and all my friends spoke Yiddish. On Sabbath, they invited me for gefilte fish, *cholent,* kugel. Who do you write for — the papers?"

"He writes books."

"Books, eh? Good! We need books, too. My son-in-law has three rooms full of books. He knows French, German. He's a foot doctor, but he first had to study math, philosophy and all the rest. Welcome! Welcome! I've got to get back to my friends, but later on we'll —"

He held out a heavy, sweaty hand to me. He breathed asthmatically and smelled of alcohol and hair tonic. The words rumbled out deep and grating from his throat. After he left, Max said:

"You know who he is? One of the Family."

"Family?"

"You don't know who the Family is? Oh! You've remained a greenhorn! The Mafia. Half Miami Beach belongs to them. Don't laugh, but they keep order here. Uncle Sam has saddled himself with a million laws that, instead of protecting the people, protect the criminal. When I was a boy studying about Sodom in heder, I couldn't understand how a whole city or a whole country could become corrupt. Lately, I've begun to understand. Sodom had a constitution and our nephew, Lot, and the other lawyers reworked it so that right became wrong and wrong — right. Mr. Albeginni actually lives in my building. When the tragedy struck me, he sent me a bouquet of flowers so big it couldn't fit through the door."

"Tell me about the cellar where you sat with the other men and the only woman," I said.

"Eh? I thought that this would intrigue you. I talked to one of the writers about my memoirs and when I told him about this, he said. 'God forbid! You must leave this part out. Martyrdom and sex don't mix. You must write only good things about them.' That's the reason I lost the urge for the memoirs. The Jews in Poland were people, not angels. They were flesh and blood just like you and me. We suffered, but we were men with manly desires. One of the five was her husband. Sigmunt. This Sigmunt was in contact with the *szmalcowniks*. He had all kinds of dealings with them. He had two revolvers and we resolved that if it looked like we were about to fall into murderers' hands, we would kill as many of them as possible, then put an end to our own lives. It was one of our illusions. When it comes down to it, you can't manage things so exactly. Sigmunt had been a sergeant in the Polish army in 1920. He had volunteered for Pilsudski's legion. He got a medal for marksmanship. Later on, he owned a garage and imported automobile parts. A giant, six foot tall or more. One of the *szmalcowniks* had once worked for him. If I was to tell you how it came about that we all ended up together in that cellar, we'd have to sit here till morning. His wife, Hilda, was a decent woman. She swore that she had been faithful to him throughout their marriage. Now, I will tell you who her lover was. No one but yours truly. She was 17 years older than me and could have been my mother. She treated me like a mother, too. 'The child,' that's what she called me. The child this and the child that. Her husband was insanely jealous. He warned us he'd kill us both if we started anything. He threatened to castrate me. He could have easily done it, too. But gradually, she wore him down. How this came about you could neither describe nor write, even if you possessed the talent of a Tolstoy or a Zeromski. She persuaded him, hypnotized him like Delilah did Samson. I didn't want any part of it. The other four men were furious with me. I wasn't up to it, either. I had become impotent. What it means to spend 24 hours out of the day locked in a cold, damp cellar in the company of five men and one woman, words cannot describe. We had to cast off all shame. At night we barely had enough room to stretch our legs. From sitting in one place, we developed constipation. We had to do everything in front of witnesses and this is an anguish Satan himself couldn't endure. We had to become cynical. We had to speak in coarse terms to conceal our shame. It was then I discovered that profanity has its purpose. I have to take a little drink. So . . . *L'chayim*!

"Yes, it didn't come easy. First she had to break down his resistance, then she had to revive my lust. We did it when he was asleep, or he only pretended. Two of the group had turned to homosexuality. The whole shame of being human emerged there. If man is formed in God's image, I don't envy God . . .

"We endured all the degradation one can only imagine, but we never lost hope. Later, we left the cellar and went off, each his own way. The murderers captured Sigmunt and tortured him to death. His wife — my mistress, so to say — made her way to Russia, married some refugee there, then died of cancer in Israel. One of the other four is now a rich man in Brooklyn. He became a penitent, of all things, and he gives money to the Bobow rabbi or to some other rabbi. What happened to the other three, I don't know. If they lived, I would have heard from them. That writer I mentioned — he's a kind of critic — claims that our literature has to concentrate only on holiness and martyrdom. What nonsense! Foolish lies!"

"Write the whole truth," I said.

"First of all, I don't know how. Secondly, I would be stoned. I generally am unable to write. As soon as I pick up a pen, I get a pain in the wrist. I become drowsy, too. I'd rather read what you write. At times, It seems to me you're stealing my thoughts.

"I shouldn't say this, but I'll say it anyway. Miami Beach is full of widows and when they heard that I'm alone, the phone calls and the visits started. They haven't stopped yet. A man alone and something of a millionaire, besides! I've become such a success I'm literally ashamed before myself. I'd like to cling to another person. Between another's funeral and your own, you still want to snatch a bit of that swinish material called pleasure. But the women are not for me. Some *yenta* came to me and complained, 'I don't want to go around like my mother with a guilt complex. I want to take every-

thing from life I can, even more than I can.' I said to her, 'The
trouble is, one cannot . . .' With men and women, it's like with
Jacob and Esau: When one rises, the other falls. When the females
turn so wanton, the men become like frightened virgins. It's just
like the prophet said, 'Seven women shall take hold of one man.'
What will come of all this, eh? What, for instance, will the writers
write about in five hundred years?"

"Essentially, about the same things as today," I replied.

"Well, and what about in a thousand years? In ten thousand
years? It's scary to think the human species will last so long. How
will Miami Beach look then? How much will a condominium cost?"

"Miami Beach will be under water," Reuben Kazarsky said, "and
a condominium with one bedroom for the fish will cost five trillion
dollars."

"And what will be in New York? In Paris? In Moscow? Will there
still be Jews?"

"There'll be only Jews," Kazarsky said.

"What kind of Jews?"

"Crazy Jews, just like you."

ROLF YNGVE

The Quail

(FROM QUARTERLY WEST)

THE QUAIL came just before the lilacs bloomed in the green time
of their first spring married. The morning was the first warm
morning with no frost, only dew. Feeling sun on the bed she rose
earlier than usual; when she saw the quail in the backyard she
woke him. He saw eight birds scratching earth and pecking in the
landlord's garden.

He told her they were California Quail. The hens were like
dowager women, plump and impeccably arrayed in brown and
grey. They were escorted by three portly males with grey vested
chests and an ascot of black plumage at their throats. Each bird
had one black plume feather bobbing on the forehead. They wandered the garden like a tour group, stopping to peck in the earth,
gliding, aimless and individual but coveyed together.

The couple dressed, whispering about the birds and watching
them peck breakfast from the lawn. He made coffee, warmed rolls
and they ate at the kitchen table where they could watch the covey.
He opened the window; they could smell the morning dampness
and apple blossoms. Sun came through the window; the rolls were
sweet with raisins and they did not have to say anything to each
other.

That evening, on his way home from work, he stopped at a feed
store and bought cracked corn. He explained to her that the quail
would stay as long as they were fed and well treated. He scattered
the corn near the kitchen window and at sunset the birds returned.
They came very close to the window, pecked at the corn, and took
rolling dirt baths in the landlord's garden. She asked him if the
birds would eat the landlord's seeds and plantings. He told her

that the garden was in no danger as long as they fed the birds cracked corn.

After the birds came, they began to set the alarm clock early. At first it was to give them more time for coffee, rolls and watching the covey. When the lilacs bloomed and the tulips came out they set the alarm earlier still and made love before rising. She would bathe after and he would make breakfast, put out more corn for the birds.

It was best watching the covey just after sunrise, before the traffic noises, before the landlord let his poodle out. The landlord lived next door with a chicken wire fence dividing the two yards. When he let the poodle out, it would be crazy to get at the quail, charging the fence, yapping the insane little dog's bark. The covey would rise, flailing air, then settle in the apple tree's low branches waiting for the dog to calm himself and drop back to the corn.

Before long he could put corn on the windowsill and the quail would join them for breakfast. If they were quiet and ate without sudden movement, the birds would flutter to the windowsill a foot from the coffee pot and roll basket. The birds pecked at the corn, eating one piece at a time. Their beaks tapped the sill and their eyes gleamed. He removed the screen to see if they would come inside.

The four cocks were bold, sometimes walking onto the table, preening, ruffling feathers, shaking their plumes. For weeks she tried to feed them sweet roll crumbs from her fingers. The males looked at it but it was a hen who finally ran to the offered scrap, eyed it sideways with her plume like a hat feather cocked over one eye, and took the crumb. There was the touch of the hen's beak on her fingers. She laughed aloud; the covey exploded from the windowsill. When a week passed and the birds finally began coming to the windowsill again, the hen always took one crumb.

Evenings they would sit in lawn chairs and watch the covey feed. When the early roses bloomed and the landlord's garden sprouted, they saw a hen mated. It was in the garden and they did not see the courtship, only the act when the cock, all grey and brown feathered with black throat feathers, twisted the hen's neck down with his bill. The hen writhed in the soil as the cock mounted her and beat her sides with his wings.

And the landlord's wife railed from inside the landlord's house, "Tom! They're in the garden again, TOM!" The landlord ran from his house, waving his arms, hissing, his neck wrinkled and old, his hair white stubble.

The birds rose flailing air.

His wife held the screen door open, leaned out screeching, "Tom you *got* to do something about them birds! We got to eat that damn garden this winter, now you want to eat this winter you *do* something!"

The screen door made a whacking slam and she was out, stooped, her poodle at her feet, her legs splayed, her dress a grey farm woman's dress with a stained apron. She sounded like the poodle.

"Dammit, *Tom*! You going to do something about them birds?"

The tenant and his wife sat in the lawn chairs watching, thinking *they* should do something. Tell the old woman, maybe, that the birds wouldn't bother the seedlings. But they thought she would fight with them, scream at them because she was angry and old. They thought it best to say something later, when she calmed herself.

The next day the landlord said he liked the birds and said the garden had grown enough to be out of danger. He said he had always liked quail. Even when he was a boy he had thought them beautiful and fine eating, but there was his wife. The landlord said his wife would most likely be better in a day or two and the garden was always a sore spot with her because they canned for winter.

When the poppies bloomed and the sweet peas came in, three broods were hatched. The first chicks appeared at breakfast with the hen leading a weaving path to the corn and the cock running half-circles behind them keeping the chicks in line. They counted ten new birds in the three families and they rose even earlier so they could linger over breakfast and smell the drying mustard weed behind the garden.

One hen led her chicks for evening strolls down the front sidewalk. She would promenade her family punctually at five-thirty. The landlord and his wife sat on the front porch one night not believing the hen would show as the tenant had described. They all laughed when the hen strutted by on cue. The landlord and his wife drank beer and told them about the depression when there was drought and they had to save everything. The old woman said she still had those habits and also said she had been overly concerned about the garden. The tenant couple thought the landlord's wife would be just fine.

When it was autumn, they canned apples and apple sauce. The landlord took in his squash, carrots, tomatoes, beets. The landlord's wife traded canned cherries for their canned apples. The landlord cut back the garden and the tenant helped the old man put up storms, turn the garden and clean the garage. He bought a fifty-pound bag of cracked corn and built a feeding trough of redwood. With the trough on the windowsill there was enough room for all eighteen quail even with the window closed.

The covey was in good shape for the winter. He told her the birds would have an easy winter with the cracked corn and said they would stay near food. The chicks had grown, they were well fed, sleek with new adult plumage. The original eight were rotund, fattened by the summer's corn. He assured her the birds would be fine for the winter.

When the leaves turned and there was frost again they closed the kitchen window. She could not feed the hen crumbs but they could talk now without frightening the birds. They talked about the summer with the quail waking them early. He told her he had hoped all his life that it would someday be like it had been that summer.

When there was hard frost and cold mornings they lingered in bed, awake, warm next to each other, thinking of the quail, thinking of the warmth.

The morning after the first snowfall, the quail were gone. He brushed the snow out of the feeding trough and replaced the wet corn. The covey did not come back that night and the corn had not been touched the next morning. He told her the quail had probably gone to the hills outside town for winter. He told her there was better cover in the hills and that the hunting season was over, so they would be fine. He told her the birds would be back in the spring and it would be the same again.

The tenant and his wife slept late and hard through the winter. The winter was dry, bleak, and cold. There was talk of drought for summer; the landlord hoarded water for his garden by storing it in old oil drums.

The tenant changed the corn often, spreading some on the frozen ground. But the quail did not return and sparrows and jays ate the corn. His wife said she knew the quail would be back in the spring and it would be the same.

When the ground thawed and there was the mud and dirt smell outside, the tenant saw the landlord cleaning his garage and went to help. When he saw the plastic bag full of grey and brown feathers: down feathers, plume feathers, some with bits of dried skin; when he saw that sack and the large chicken wire trap that had not been in the garage before, he asked the landlord how he had managed to catch all the birds at once. The landlord said it had been his wife's idea. They had waited for the first winter storm and trapped the birds when they were huddled together. He said they had been fine eating.

The tenant did not tell his wife about the bag or trap but it was as if she knew. After a while he quit putting out the corn and when the fifty-pound bag began to rot, he threw it on the trash.

PETER LA SALLE

Some Manhattan in New England

(FROM THE GEORGIA REVIEW)

I

OLD JOE ROCK, born LaRoque, had had the same dream for three nights running. In his dream, he wasn't in the Massachusetts mill city at all. He was a sailor again as he had been, so happily, some fifty years before on the Irish Sea. In a black watchcap and black knit sweater, he strolled the decks in the greenish night. He was on watch, and then he noticed that nobody else was. Nobody else even was awake. The pilot's cabin was lit yellow, but the pilot wasn't at his wheel. The coal-burning engine chugged rhythmically and, frightened that they were adrift, young Joe bounded down the stairs to the lower decks. He had done the same in the dream each night before. Walking the narrow hall with its glossily painted, riveted walls, he could hear the crew members snoring in their short beds stacked atop one another next to the engine room.

Somebody else *should* be on watch. What were they doing?

He shook the bodies bundled in damp wool blankets and even slapped a red stubbly face or two. But it did no good. One grunted, another druggedly waved a hand to shoo him off like an annoying fly. They rolled over and away from him. What were they doing? What were . . .

Every night, Joe Rock woke panicking like that. He was asleep himself, only to find he wasn't asleep.

The dawn December light glowed a weak orange behind the pulled shades. Around him were the shadows of the tortoiseshell dresser with edges fringed with cigarette burns, the porcelain hand sink, the steel bed's ladder-like footboard, and the two fireproofed sitting chairs of the room in the Bradford Hotel. He had lived in the run-down place on Textile Avenue for the last ten years. The dream.

He remembered the dream as the same recurring one. He closed his eyes to the now blank purple screen of his lids. He was more sure than ever that he would die soon.

II

What if it *were* true that sound waves never totally dissolve? When scientists first experimented with radio equipment not all so long ago, the opinion was common that voices hover somewhere in infinity. And all that one needs is the proper reception equipment to tune in on them, on all history, again. That theory, now only the basis for an occasional low-budget science-fiction film, could be applied to telling the story of Joe Rock. Or the story of any of us, for that matter. Just voices:

"Is that good?"

"Jackie, oh, Jackie."

"That?"

"Jackie, there are people. Don't."

"Heh, I'll be easy."

"Ohhh."

"That's good, isn't it."

"Oh there. Oh yes. Jackie."

"I told you. It will be nice."

"Ohhh. Ohhhhhhh. I love you."

"Shhh."

"I love you, Jackie."

"I told you."

"Ohhhhhhhhhhh."

Except, how would we identify the voices even if we could isolate a conversation? Such a scene, that exchange, could have been any one of certainly millions. Sure, you could peg the accents maybe. The male's voice educated and a little broad, the female's with a South Boston Irish inflection. But you never would know that this transpired in 1948 in the back seat of Jackie Rock's Packard soft-top. You never would know that this was a common skit in the alley behind Joe Rock's massive 990 Club after Jackie dropped out of

Dartmouth. In fact, possibly the female was the chorus girl involved in the 1950 paternity suit.

Or another voice:

"Joe Rock was the master of the quip. Lively. He once said to me, 'Father Spike, what would the Catholic priest do without Chesterton, that veritable Farmer's Almanac and general familiar quotable for every Sunday sermon. A Catholic maybe. A second-rate writer at best.' "

That was the nasal voice of Father Louis "Spike" LeFebvre. And even if sound does travel at so many hundreds of miles an hour, those words wouldn't be too far gone in the cosmos, comparatively speaking. Father Spike spoke them just last year to the New York reporter who drove up to interview people in the mill city who had known Joseph Rock. In truth, Father Spike hadn't.

Father Spike wore an ill-fitting mahogany toupee because, as he told the pastor of the mill city's French mother church to which he was assigned, "It has nothing to do with vanity, Father. The world is all youth now. I must identify." How the reporter ended up talking with the priest in his cluttered room upstairs in the yellow-brick rectory — it adjoined the huge stone church that took thirty-five years to build — is not hard to deduce. Father Spike was known for championing causes. And so, somebody coming from out of town naturally would have assumed he was an authority on the man in question. Father Spike really wasn't interested in talking about the old fellow he never had spoken to. He had only seen Joe Rock leaning against the plate-glass window of the Woolworth's in the Square in winter, trying with the rest of the ragged men to savor some weak warming rays. If you listened to the rest, you would have heard:

"Which?" That was Father Spike.

"I'm not sure. I mean I have to look at them." The reporter.

"That's just it. I don't want you to study them. Just a quick glance."

"Well, maybe the first."

"With the foetus inside the question mark?"

"I guess."

Again, what would the voices mean without the scene? To make sense out of the conversation you would have to see Father Spike holding up rough sketches he made himself for two proposed book jackets. Both worked on patterns involving a foetus with its tiny hands tucked to its head, a two-tone capsule that was Father Spike's idea of "The Pill," and that looping question mark. The bold print above each: *Father Spike*, "A Novel." The reporter rubbed the bridge of his nose where the wire-rimmed glasses had left twin teardrop-shaped marks, and he looked disinterestedly at the jackets again.

His novel would be published, Father Spike explained, by a vanity press under a name other than Father Spike's, understandably. Father Spike had received diocesan censure for his involvement in pro-abortion demonstrations on grassy Boston Common, and he said he didn't need any more trouble with the bishop. The book told the story of a married woman who has an abortion after receiving counsel from a priest named Father Spike. Three months later she becomes pregnant by her husband again, and eventually she has twins.

"You see," Father Spike emphasized excitedly, "the punch is that if she didn't have the abortion, only one child would have been born. The other would have been denied life."

III

Joe Rock didn't make his usual rounds that day after the third night he had the same dream. The realization that he might be dead this time tomorrow didn't alarm him. It almost relaxed him to the point where he was sure he must go to those places he hadn't visited in many years. He must make the *final* rounds.

His usual rounds weren't even usual in their utterly painful routine. They were, for the most part, a succession of various staring points. Staring from the Bradford Hotel at cars and buses below on Textile Avenue, staring at tan crockery coffee cups in the Merrimack Lunch or the pile of fiberglass trays in the Valois Cafeteria, or staring at the white-gloved traffic cop going through his mime in front of the Woolworth's in the Square. Though people knew Joe Rock, they never spoke with him. He was considered probably senile, possibly bonkers altogether.

He would go to his wife, Margaret's, grave that day. He also would go there — to the Club.

The morning sun had given way to a milky gray that promised only more snow. It was the kind of damp cold that you can smell, the kind that absorbs exhaust and tastes sooty. Black bare trees fringed the rounded hills to the north toward New Hampshire. An amber schoolbus returning from morning deliveries swerved around the corner in the French end of the city. The splash of color only emphasized the bleakness of both the day and the wood-framed three-story tenements.

Bedson Cemetery, known to everybody except the local Protestants as the Protestant Cemetery, was a good mile from the Bradford and the city center. Joe Rock's arthritic knees ached, and he silently cursed the sagging bed mattress in the Bradford for not giving proper support and so letting arthritis invade the slack joints. The Harrington plot at Bedson was not really a plot. It was more an entire end of the cemetery. Margaret was one of "the" Harringtons — not a Cabot or a Lowell, but of the second rank of long-generationed mill-owning families. Because they were not so well known, they actually considered themselves a more exclusive, less flaunting lot.

Pink stone slabs and gray granite crosses sprouted from the crusted snow that crunched under each step he took. In the end, he didn't go right up to the stone marking her grave, for fear of walking on anybody's grave. His own mother had taken him often to the French cemetery as a boy. His father was buried there, and she always told him to be careful. In her French she would say, "Yes, be careful, Ti Joseph. Be careful you don't walk on the beds of the dead." *Les lits des morts.*

He hadn't come to his wife's grave for nearly two years. His wife, Margaret, never did understand, he knew, why he blamed himself, why he assumed the paralyzing remorse for all those years after their son, Jackie, was killed in the car accident in Florida.

> *Margaret Harrington Rock*   *1905–1960*
> *Joseph Henri Rock*   *1901–*

Now he was at the cemetery and strangely he didn't even think about her. Maybe the sight of his own name already chiseled in stone struck him just then. He found himself basking in the knowledge that soon he would be dead. And it was as if he already were dead. He longed to be so.

He knew they didn't bury in December. They would leave him in the vault with its rusting steel doors that was set into the little knoll beside the black-lattice cemetery gates. It would have been easier in the spring when the cemetery grass turns emerald and others' relatives — he had none — trek out with wooden flower baskets and those tiny red-white-and-blue VFW flags. Yes, he wanted to be in that ground. He wanted this to be over. He was thinking that, but he was saying aloud something else. Lately, he often caught his lips mouthing words he didn't realize he was saying.

"You'd die again to know it, wouldn't you. You'd die to think Joe Rock was buried here. And they'll consecrate the ground because I'm baptized, you bastard. They'll consecrate my plot here in Bedson." He wasn't looking at his wife's grave anymore. It was the grave of her father, Adam Wells Harrington, who had forbidden his daughter to marry him. Joe Rock sensed a satisfying pang of the old one-upmanship, but it too was gone as soon as he recognized it. "And maybe you were right," he said.

He ate at the Merrimack Lunch. He was surprised to hear somebody "hello" him. As was said, the people who still knew him, knew he didn't want to converse. An acne-faced kid with a blood-spattered white paper hat scraped the black grill with what looked like a putty knife and peeled another frozen hamburger from between two waxy squares. Water from a faucet ran over a heap of unwashed plates. Snow melted muddily on the marbleized green linoleum floor, and fog steamed the front window.

"Hello! Why, Mr. Rock!" Joe Rock, sitting on a chrome-stemmed stool, looked up at the husky man who handed the tissuey green slip to the kid cook who now doubled as cashier. The man took his other hand, the fingers of which had been probing the jigger glass fanned with wooden toothpicks, and thrust the big thing out for a shake. Emil, Joe Rock thought. The name of the too-big ears came back to him instantly. But what had he done? An attendant in the lot? A barman or somebody on the staff of one of the Club's three restaurants?

"Ah, hello," he hesitated, "Emil."

"Jesus, Mr. Rock. It must be how long? How many years?"

"A long time, Emil." The man took his change without looking at it.

"And I never even get up here anymore. I usually drive between Boston and Providence." A trucker now, Joe Rock figured. "And the once I stop in this burg, I see you. I was going to swing by the place. Just to look." Joe Rock nodded. "That was the happiest time of my life, Mr. Rock. I can tell you that. Oh, those were the days, as the man says. You had a swank spot there all right. Mr. Rock. You look good."

"I'm old." The trucker didn't seem ready for the serious turn. He seemed to let it pass.

"Yeah, you look great. Jesus, who would have thought I'd see you, Mr. Rock." Joe Rock watched the man almost wince with the lie when he said, "you look great." He was glad when the bell atop the door stopped jingling and he was sure Emil was gone. Joe Rock left.

The sign on the high redbrick façade was visible from a distance. It had taken on a ghostly look. The outlines of brick underneath showed through the blue and yellow block letters saying JOE ROCK'S 990 CLUB. And under that in script, *Some Manhattan in New England*.

How long would it be there, Joe Rock asked silently as he started down the sidestreet, from the business district toward the mills. He knew the castle-like solidity of the building, of all the mills along the wide, frozen river. They were built late in the century before. And when Joe Rock was trying to convince the banks to finance his buying the abandoned Wellington Worsted, he escorted the Boston loan officers down to the bowels of the place himself. He pointed out the strength of the foot-square beams and the width of the stone-and-mortar foundation built on the river bed's strong granite. Joe Rock, like his father, had worked as a day carpenter for a textile company before going to sea at seventeen. He was Joseph-Henri LaRoque then. He returned to the mill city eight years later as Joe Rock and used his shipping contacts to build up a decent business wholesaling Canadian lumber.

That same lumber was used for the overlay on the streamlined "art deco" façade. Most of it had toppled to a mounding pile. But the galvanized awning frame for the gone awning in front still stood skeletally. The city had put up a chain-link fence years ago, and years ago kids had torn out chunks of the crisscrossing wire mesh. Since the bank had taken over the land again almost twenty years before, the gradually decaying ruins had served as subject for an annual, or at least biennial, tirade from a local councilman. Shaking his fist and making sure the reporters at the varnished press table were scribbling it down, the councilman would redden as he stood in the council chambers — the murky oils of past mayors lining the walls of the high-ceilinged room — and blasted the disgraceful state of that property. In the late fifties a half-witted child molester was apprehended with an eight-year-old boy there. More recently, a local attempt at a violent motorcycle gang cleared out what was once the men's smoking lounge and set up headquarters for a month till the police rousted them.

On June 15, 1953, almost two years after Jackie Rock was buried in Florida, Joe Rock, his father, saw him there in the ballroom. The Club had only recently been closed. Joe Rock and his son argued again. Joe Rock said that even if his son were alive, he would amount to nothing if he didn't change his ways. With slicked-back hair, dapper young Jackie only took a long drag on a cigarette and shook his head. He smiled.

"Don't you smile at me, you. I'm trying to tell you this for your own good!" Joe Rock had shouted.

"You're really a bore, do you know that? A real bore."

All the while, Joe Rock fully knew the boy was dead. But the unreality of his being gone taught Joe Rock that such things, any unreality, could happen.

Joe Rock planted each step carefully on the rubble blanketed with snow. He looked from outside. In the main ballroom the floorboards had rotted away, while the strong beams below remained intact. The plastered arcing shell over the bandstand had collapsed, avalanche-style, only the previous summer. That sparked another tirade from the councilman. To look at it now, you wouldn't imagine that the big-name bands all played there. "Swank," Emil had said to Joe Rock, and swank it had been. Above the dancefloor a balustrade studded with semi-circular upholstered booths had overlooked the scene. Blue lights played on the Italian cut-glass chandeliers. Every table was decorated with poinsettias flown in from Florida on fruit planes — back then when "flying in" anything was considered a marvel of modern technology. Out-of-town people never would believe that the sprawling club was once a textile mill. Joe Rock bought it in the Depression and soon there was dancing in dinner jackets and gowns in the thirties, khaki uniforms and knee-length dresses during the long War, and jackets and gowns again as the forties became the fifties and the post-War prosperity was on.

One wing off the ballroom had housed the three separate restaurants — "The Montmartre," "The Manhattan," and the "Hofbrau," which was a well-appointed snackbar. The other contained guest suites and a small gym, complete with steam room. Joe Rock headed that way.

That steam room was the only room still somewhat recognizable here. The walls showed some faded blue and yellow paint, the Club's color code, and rusting fixtures stuck out like stubble in the remaining stalls. Joe Rock heard the footsteps from the steam room. The late afternoon was pinkening, and a vagrant few flakes had begun to flurry.

Joe Rock simply knew it would be Jackie again. It was as if he had known all day that he would have to come to meet him. The steps, creaking over the not-too-safe floor, stopped.

"Jackie," he whispered. "Oh, Jackie. Boy, I'm here." He stepped into the roofless room, his breath puffing like smoke. "Jackie."

"Ahhhhh." It was a child crying. The woman and her child had flattened themselves behind a stall. The small girl buried her head in the woman's coat and bawled. The dark-haired woman had both arms wrapped around a brown paper grocery bag stuffed with wood. Her lips were red and full. A Puerto Rican living in one of the condemned, peak-roofed places, probably, behind the Greek church.

"We need thees wood, meester. Pleese, we need thees." Did she believe he was about to take it away? "My leetel girl, she has been so seeck." The child cried some more, though soon her moaning was drowned out by Joe Rock's own sobs.

He stood there, an old man with his hands in the pockets of the seedy overcoat. He stood in the monstrosity he had created, the place that was "Some Manhattan in New England," and he cried for his dead son, for himself, for the mother and child before him, for the mill city itself.

The woman dropped the bag in alarm.

"Meester, you are all right? Mia, come here now, don't run. Meester." She took his arm, maybe fearing he would fall. "Meester!"

IV

More voices, both female:

"No."

"Oh, isn't it the news, though. And true. Her father has cut her off completely. The man is a Frenchman, or a French-Canadian,

and a sailor. Or he once left the city to go to sea. Terribly hand-
some as those French can be, I hear. They all have Indian blood."
"Margaret Harrington. Meg. She would have been the last I
would have thought to do something like that."
"I also hear he has a tattoo. Look, is that Will Taylor over there?
Or maybe it's his younger brother. The one on the Harvard crew."
"And her father couldn't stop her?"
"Who?"
"Meg, of course."
"Oh darling, I see you are really quite in the dark about all of
this. She was three months gone then. I hear she's had a boy."
And that? Just two girls who knew Margaret Harrington at
Wellesley College for Women, where she was enrolled for two
years. The voices floated from Symphony Hall in Boston in 1928
during a concert intermission. If there were any identifying of
them in that forever of blackness, you maybe could tell by the
discordant tuning of violin strings and a squeaky oboe reed being
tested in the background.
    All those voices.

V

Recently, Mrs. Elizabeth Hennigan of Los Altos, New Mexico —
Joe Rock's sister's daughter — wrote a letter to Professor Edward
W. Lucoli of the University of Pennsylvania. Professor Lucoli edited the book of Joe Rock's poems, *Joe Rock, Né LaRoque: The Unknown Genius.* The volume appeared a year ago. Already, the
section called "The Aran Island Poems" is being reprinted sepa-
rately by the University of Pennsylvania Press — they brought out
the original — in paperback. In a recent article in *The New York
Times Book Review* entitled "If Eliot Had Read 'Upon Reading Dick-
ens in an Inishmore Cottage,'" Professor Lucoli argues that Joe
Rock had already voiced many of the observations on time and the
historical moment of Eliot's *Four Quartets* in his, Rock's, long, previously unpublished poem written in 1925. Of course all the Rock
poems were previously unpublished and written when he was a
young man and a sailor on the Irish Sea.
    Anyway, though Mrs. Hennigan had been friendly with Profes-
sor Lucoli when the latter rented a house in Los Altos during a
sabbatical leave, they definitely are no longer on speaking terms.

She had met the professor at a cocktail party and originally showed him the sheaf of poems handwritten on yellowing foolscap out of curiosity. She had found them among her uncle's personal belongings forwarded to her by the probate court that deemed her the closest surviving heir. The professor, a comparative literature scholar, was lucky indeed.

Now her lawyer is contesting Joe Rock's will that leaves all of the money nobody knew he had, nearly a quarter of a million dollars, to a trust to be presided over by the English department of the state college in the mill city. They will award grants as they see fit to "needy Massachusetts artists."

11 Flowering Yucca Drive
Los Altos, New Mexico
January 23, 1977

Professor Edward W. Lucoli
Department of Comparative Literature
University of Pennsylvania

Dear Professor Lucoli:

I am writing one letter in answer to your several letters sent to me recently. In fact, I believe that it is high time that I expressed myself on several matters.

My lawyer Frederick O. Blatt of Blatt and Blatt in Albuquerque did advise that I not correspond with you. But to protect myself now, I can tell you that he has read over this letter.

When I gave you *my* uncle's poems to look at three years ago, I did so because I thought then that I had no chance of contesting my uncle's will. When you said your university press would publish them, you assured me a book of poems never makes a profit. And believing you, and amazed that the poems interested you at all, I signed the release. Now I learn that the profits are going to the trust fund for supposedly "needy artists." The book sells well and I get nothing.

(Incidentally, that business of "needy artists" burns me up. My husband is a "needy" electrical engineer who works an eight-hour day at the energy laboratories here to try and honestly support his wife and three children.)

Now you have become an authority on *my* uncle. Well, I wish to tell you a few things. It was common knowledge in our family, and my mother was his sister afterall, that Joseph Rock never was mentally right after my cousin John was killed in the accident in Florida. My uncle went through the remainder of his life blaming himself that because he ran an entertainment club, his son — who hung out there and who, I can assure you, never was of any worth — turned out as he did. That Joseph Rock wasn't in full control of his faculties can be attested to by the way he let that successful business at the 990 Club slide into bankruptcy shortly afterwards. Also, consider his general behavior. Do you know that he honestly believed that he once met my dead cousin, his son, and the two chatted — several years after John was killed. Joseph Rock made my aunt miserable until she died and he moved into that hotel which only can be called a flea-bag. Does that sound like the rational action of a man with almost a quarter of a million dollars in the bank?

Last week I learned that you are taking up the cause of protecting this Rock Endowment for Massachusetts Artists against my claims for what is justly mine as the surviving heir. Granted my uncle wrote poems as a young man while a sailor working out of Liverpool. I personally fail to see much merit in the verse. But I also will grant that it probably has some merit, if critical response to the published book is to be trusted. But I certainly will not go along with your half-baked theories about *my* uncle and your saying that he was a poet all his life, even if he didn't write poems after the twenties. And so, you say, the legacy naturally should go to poets. Rubbish.

First of all, nobody even knew he had written poems. Secondly, nobody ever published a one of them. I am enraged when you get carried away with your conjecture, as in your so-called "Biographical Note." To quote you —

"The 990 Club itself, 'Some Manhattan in New England,' was Joe Rock's unpublished, but hauntingly concrete epic poem. Here the self-made man, so used to changing his sailor's experience into meaningful verse as a boy bard, changed the larger experience of his people's history, the mill experience, into a more meaningful entity. He built a veritable people's palace of enjoyment and happiness from a factory. It was a little heaven in itself, and what is poetry, but an attempt to show a glimpse of heaven to all of us in this larger sea of sadness? What happened was that the floodgates let loose and Joe Rock was drowned in the overwhelming tide of the sadness with the tragic auto death of his playboy son in 1951. He hadn't written a line of poetry for years; he never would live a moment of the poetry of his life again."

To repeat — rubbish! And I also wonder if you are all there. Joseph Rock was a poet *once*. He also was a businessman and a night club owner for most of his adult life. Why not set up the Joe Rock Endowment for Needy Night Spot and Cabaret Proprietors?

But, enough of this. All future correspondence should be addressed to my counsel, Mr. Blatt. My uncle was a sick man, Professor, when he made that ridiculous will. My only hope is that justice will be accomplished.

Mrs. Elizabeth Hennigan

VI

One more voice. But let's go a step further. If the voices of the living could last in infinity, what about those of the dead? Here is what Jackie Rock, who was interred in a municipal cemetery near Hialeah, Florida, before his father, Joe Rock, had even heard word of his death, says:

"I can never remember a moment when I didn't love my father. When I argued with him, hated him, I was hating me, not him. It was part of my having to admit he was somebody special, somebody I never would be. After I died, I returned to the mill city to visit him as a visible ghost on June 15, 1953. I loved him so much that I wanted to hug him right there. I wanted to tell him that although I was dead, real love somehow goes beyond that. But we argued again, and it never was said."

LYNNE SHARON SCHWARTZ

Plaisir d'Amour

(FROM THE ONTARIO REVIEW)

THEIR NAMES came to her in a dream, Brauer and Elemi. They were a couple, around thirty. In the dream they walked holding hands along the southern edge of Central Park, stopping to admire the restless buggy-horses pawing the pavement. Then they had breakfast in the Plaza Hotel: a waiter who bowed discreetly from the waist served them Eggs Benedict and ambrosial coffee. Afterwards they walked in the Park, where the smell of cut grass rose keen and fragrant. As if by telepathy, they stopped walking at the same moment and sat down on a bench to talk. Vera's first thought on awakening was that the dream had been so realistic; nothing happened in it that could not happen in real life.

She reached for an old plaid bathrobe — originally John's, but it had lost is aura of identity by now and felt anonymous. Vera, who was slim, had to fold over the excess fabric and belt it securely. In the kitchen she found her daughter, Jean, just sixteen, already finishing breakfast, peering through thick glasses at *Madame Bovary*. The pot of coffee was ready on the stove. Jean made it nearly every morning, using a filter, and it was excellent. When Vera praised it, as usual, Jean slowly closed the book, her eyes fixed on the vanishing page till the two halves snapped shut. All the years of inculcating good manners have worked, thought Vera.

"Thanks. Did you sleep all right? You didn't take any of those pills, did you?"

She was touched by her daughter's concern. Vera only occasionally took the sleeping pills prescribed when she left the hospital five months ago, but Jean was righteously wary of drugs. She also had strong feelings against cigarettes, abortion, and war. "No, I haven't taken them in over a week. I slept fine. I had a funny dream, though."

"Oh really? What?"

"This man and woman with very odd names who eat at the Plaza and walk in Central Park."

Jean leaned forward smiling, her face resting in her palms, some strands of loose blonde hair falling over her hands. "What were their names?" She was looking at her mother with almost the same eager attention she showed to her friends. Unprecedented and flattering though this was, Vera became aware that she did not wish to reveal the names of Brauer and Elemi.

"Oh, I forget. Except for the names it was a very ordinary dream, only I can't seem to shake it. Do you know that feeling?"

Her interest extinguished, Jean carried her plate and mug to the sink. Watching her, Vera received an abrupt flash of illumination: the name Brauer had something to do with the German word "Frau," and "Elemi" was a word she had often written in crossword puzzles. It meant a soft resin used in making varnish. Also, it was an auditory inversion of "Emily," the name of a beautiful girl she had known at college and since lost track of. She sensed at once that these connections were true and ingenious, but finally irrelevant.

Jean cast her mother a curious glance from the doorway. "You're going to work today, aren't you?"

"Oh, yes. It doesn't matter if I'm late. Howard is away this week and nobody else cares." She had worked in the advertising agency for seven years. When she needed to take six weeks off because of illness after her husband's death they had been very understanding. She noticed, though, that on her return Howard, the boss, had watched her closely for signs of instability, of which there were none. Vera was recovered; it would not happen again.

"I won't be back till around seven," Jean called from the hall. "I have the Dramatics Society." Then she dashed back to the kitchen. "Do you think we'll get a letter from Freddy today?"

"I hope so." Vera smiled at her. "Any day now." Jean's older brother, away for his first year in college, had mentioned possibly bringing a friend home over Easter, someone Jeanie might like, Freddy wrote, since he refused to do the vivisection experiment in zoology. Although boys were Jean's preoccupation, few met her ethical standards.

As the door finally clattered shut Vera realized that she had not even recalled Freddy's existence this morning before Jean spoke of him. That had something to do with the dream about Brauer and Elemi, which hovered about her still like a pleasant, warm fog. All other mornings now, when she woke she mentally ticked off the names of her two children, like a miser whose hoard has been plundered counting over with melancholy the few coins remaining. She had begun it in the hospital, spurred by a chance remark of one of the nurses: "But you're not all alone, Mrs. Leonard. Think of your children. You have a lot to live for." Vera had smiled wanly as the nurse, round, Oriental, efficient, smoothed unruly wrinkles in the sheets with a firm hand. Trite as her counsel was, it had helped, Vera had to admit.

Naming over her connections was not the only new habit to take hold since the painful weeks of her illness. With John gone, so many of her rooted personal customs had altered. (An "untimely" death, the minister had called it, and despite her suffering Vera almost grinned involuntarily: as a writer of copy she understood the lure of the ready-made phrase.) She no longer woke outrageously early on weekdays to start dinner simmering in the slow cooker; she could fix something simple for herself and Jean after work. She no longer tore the crossword puzzle out of the paper, or worried about underwear hanging in the bathroom for days or library books kept past their due date. She shopped in bits on the way home from work instead of massively on Saturdays. Magazines could be tossed out when she finished reading them, instead of accumulating in unsightly piles for John eventually to glance at. There was no need now to struggle with clothes packed tight in a narrow closet, or to feel hesitant about taking taxis home on rainy days, or talking at length to her older brother, long distance. All winter Vera had slept in flannel granny nightgowns, heedless of appearance, and let ashtrays overflow while she smoked in bed to her heart's content. In fact, as she often noticed guiltily, daily life was freer and easier without him. Yet she was lonely at night, and though she had tried she could not change the twenty-year habit of sleeping on one side of the bed, the right. If ever again she found herself in bed with a man, she thought in her more light-hearted moments, he had better approach her from the left or not at all.

On the bus going to work Vera let her eyes close and lapsed into a waking daze. She saw Brauer and Elemi again, this time following a Spanish building superintendent up the stairs to see a vacant apartment. It was spacious, with five good-sized rooms and large windows overlooking Central Park. The walls were dingy, but the super promised they would be freshly painted for the new tenants. Brauer and Elemi were holding hands as before, their faces glowing with joy. When they looked at each other they knew immediately, without words, that they would take it. Brauer spoke to the super and gave him ten dollars. Outside they stopped at the corner to buy frankfurters and orange drinks at a stand. Walking across the park, they passed the pond where miniature sailboats glided in the brilliant sunlight, then discovered a trio of students — violin, cello, and clarinet — playing ethereal chamber music under a grove of trees. Brauer tossed some coins into the hat and they walked on, holding hands, to the Frick Museum, where they sat down in the indoor sculpture garden. Vera was so enchanted that when she opened her eyes — some part of her mind attuned to the duration of the ride — she had to hurry through the crowd to get off at her stop. Again she was struck by the realism of the dream. She would have been less surprised had the dreams been re-creations of her own experience: there had been a phase, just after John's "untimely" death, when she brooded over episodes from their past. But she and John had not done any of the things that Brauer and Elemi did.

There were meetings with clients all morning, then a festive staff lunch honoring one of the young copywriters, whose wife had had a baby. Through it all Vera was suffused with a calm, happy glow which made her think of Eastern philosophies of acceptance, feeling beyond desire, the flow of being. These were things her son Freddy, home from college at Christmas, had talked about. Later, in the company library Will Pratt, one of the head accountants, approached her, slapping her warmly on the back so that she quivered. "Hey, Vera, you're certainly looking great today. I meant to tell you at lunch. What's up?"

"What do you mean? Nothing is up."

"Oh, come on. You don't get that glow just from martinis at lunch. You must be seeing somebody." He was gazing at her earnestly, with kindness beneath the brash grin, the nervous, swift dark eyes. She had known Will for years — he had been a help during the months of John's dying, letting her cry in his office, bringing her cups of coffee, even fixing her slipshod account sheets without complaint — so she shouldn't be alarmed by his bantering now. Nonetheless it made her eyelids twitch.

"No, really. No one."

"No one? Then you're a naturally beautiful woman. Lucky. Have a drink with me after work." Will had been divorced for some time and prided himself on his bachelorhood. She might have gone out with him now, as a friend — he asked her often — had he not also asked her often when John was alive and well.

"Thanks, Will, but I'm sorry. I've got to get home for Jean."

"Oh, Jean is no baby. What is it, Vera? Aren't we friends? Can't friends have a drink?" He came closer, frowning. She could feel his warm breath on her cheek, not unpleasant. When she kept silent his voice grew sharp and tight. "You've turned me down three times in a month. What the hell is suddenly wrong with me anyway, I'd like to know?"

Vera stepped back in fright, holding a large slick magazine before her as a shield. "Nothing is wrong with you, Will. Of course we're friends. It's just that evenings, you know, I'm tired. And I worry about Jean — she's lonely too. I'm sorry." Not yet, she was screaming inside her head. Not yet. Not ever.

Will was lighting a cigarette, his hands cupped around the match so a small glow was visible between his thick fingers, like a distant bonfire. He didn't answer.

Vera took another step back. A clasp had become unfastened; she felt the slow sliding of her hair down the back of her neck. In a moment it would be hanging loose. "Why don't we have lunch tomorrow, Will? Or Monday?" Lunch seemed less perilous than drinks after work.

"I'm generally tied up with business at lunch." Will moved to the door. "But I'll give you a buzz next week, maybe. Take care."

Vera breathed deeply, as though she had barely escaped anni-hilation by a massive natural phenomenon, an avalanche. Her hair tumbled to her shoulders and the clasp fell to the floor, but Will was gone by then.

On the bus that evening she closed her eyes as if in prayer and whispered, Brauer, Elemi. And they came. They were lying in bed under neatly arranged blankets, side by side, Brauer on the right and Elemi on his left. Vera waited, but they did not stir. They lay flat on their backs, holding hands, smiling and at peace. The peace that passeth understanding, Vera murmured, and wondered what she meant by that.

They came often in the days and weeks that followed. Brauer and Elemi did not make love, but they were certainly in love. There was no mistaking their constant hand-holding, their long searching glances, the soft sensual haze that floated about them. They furnished their new apartment with colorful wall hangings, lush ferns, and big floor pillows, and lay on the shag rug listening to chamber music and jazz. Other evenings they danced the latest dances in discotheques or went to Charlie Chaplin movies, where they shared bags of popcorn, laughed, and sometimes cried. They went ice-skating in Central Park, skimming along arm in arm through clusters of slower, more awkward skaters. Elemi, who was small and slight, wore a crimson velvet skating skirt with beige tights, a white turtleneck sweater, and a crimson beret. Tied to the laces of each skate were two red fur balls, which bounced as she moved. She was a delicate sight. Vera, who did not skate, wondered if it was too late to learn. One day Brauer and Elemi rode into the country on their new Mopeds — red for her, blue for him — and picnicked in a field under an elm tree. They tore chunks off a long French bread and drank red wine, then lay back to rest in the sun, with Brauer's head in Elemi's lap. She stroked his hair.

Vera was looking well, radiant, people told her, and she had stopped taking the sleeping pills altogether, which made Jean very happy. One of her women friends, less brash than Will, said Vera looked as though she were having a love affair. Vera shook her head and smiled, but inside she said, Yes, indeed I am.

Freddy brought Thomas, the boy who had refused to do the vivisection experiment, home for the Easter vacation. He was an amiable boy with a soft voice and long straight hair tied in a rubber band. Vera was glad to have him as a guest, and glad also to see Freddy thriving: his only complaints were about the dormitory food and the fact that he had no car. "I'd like at least to get a Moped, Mom."

"Mopeds are about four hundred dollars."

"I'll get a part-time job and pay you back, I promise."

"I'll think about it." She hated to refuse him — he was a good boy, hardworking, not greedy, and she still remembered with emotion how he had hated to leave her so soon after his father's death. It had been poignant, his young grief mingled with his eagerness to start college. Naturally Vera had urged him to go. It was only after he left that she became ill. But deserving as he was, she had to be careful with money: there were still some hospital bills, Jeanie wanted contact lenses, and in a year and a half she too would be going off to college. Vera shuddered at the thought of her daughter gone. But she would have to release her, and when the time came would do so bravely and cheerfully.

Freddy was kinder to his sister since he had been away, and Jean, to impress Thomas, was agreeable and unselfish. Vera was thankful for the peace. If only John could see the children now. Enraged at their nasty quarrels, which had persisted for several years of shared adolescence, he often used to shout, "Don't you two have any feeling for each other besides hate?" She had tried to placate him with assurances that it would pass. Had he lived, she could feel vindicated.

In the evenings the four of them would linger at the table over coffee and have long, animated discussions. Freddy was not so much "into" Eastern philosophy any more, he informed Vera. He was more into genetics, and he told of brilliant and daring experiments with DNA molecules. Thomas was into anarchy. After a while the young people would move to the living room and continue their talk sitting on the floor listening to records, while Vera finished cleaning up. They offered to help, but she said she didn't mind, it relaxed her. Besides, she didn't feel over-burdened. Thomas liked to cook, and several evenings she found an excellent dinner all prepared: eggplant casserole, soybean ragout, salads with bean sprouts and alfalfa. When she inquired, he told her shyly that he was also into health foods. Vera was interested in those talks that continued in the living room, but she was hesitant about intruding, and so she went to her room. Often, sitting up in bed holding a forgotten book, she would lapse into visions of Brauer and Elemi traveling on foot through the jungles of South America. There were many dangers: disease, snakes, losing their way in the rough, unfamiliar terrain, but they were unafraid.

Once she saw a man in a television commercial who looked remarkably like Brauer, with broad shoulders, sandy, lank hair, generous eyes, and a stubborn mouth that lost all stubbornness as soon as he smiled. Hot from tennis, the man was reaching for a glass of iced tea. Vera jumped out of bed to flick off the set before he could say a word. She clapped her hands over her ears, for sometimes a few dying words escaped after it was switched off.

Jean was delighted to have Thomas around. Vera could tell by the brightness in her eyes and by her clothing, only the newest jeans and sweaters. But after the first week the boys started to go out at night, leaving her at home. Jean sulked pathetically at the kitchen table, gnawing on a strand of hair.

Vera dried her soapy hands and sat down. "Listen, they're in college — they feel there's a great gap. In a year or two Thomas may think you're the most exciting person around."

"How can you be so idiotic as to think I care about that nerd," Jean replied coldly. "It's not him. It's me."

"What do you mean, it's you?"

"There is not one single boy in the entire junior or senior class who interests me at the moment, or who is interested in me. It makes life extremely tedious. But you wouldn't understand."

"I certainly do understand about being lonely," said Vera. "Things will change."

Jean leaped up and shrieked. "You always say that but they never do! No one will ever like me and I'll die a virgin! I'm ugly, who would ever want me!" She burst into tears and ran into her room, slamming the door. Vera followed. She sat near her on the bed and tried to take her hand, but Jean yanked it away.

"A virgin, how absurd. At sixteen! You have your whole life ahead of you. Lots of men — boys — will want you. Anyway, you're always telling me that women can have a full life without men, marriage is a trap, and so forth."

"I don't want to get married," Jean wailed, "I just want somebody to like me. I mean, look at this hair." She pulled at it wretchedly. "It's disgusting. Every girl in school has long blonde hair. If they don't have it they bleach it. I'm so ordinary."

"You could cut it," Vera suggested. "Then you'd look different."

"Oh you, you're impossible. You don't understand a thing. Would you please leave me alone in my room? I know you probably mean well but I'd prefer to be alone."

"All right," said Vera, shrugging her shoulders. "But I don't think you're ordinary." She understood perfectly the dynamics of these scenes: in the morning Jean would once more brew her fine coffee, having forgotten everything. Vera had pity for her daughter, as well as tolerance for the sputtering fireworks of a dying age. Still and all it was terribly wearing, terribly debilitating. When she finished in the kitchen she sat down at the table, cradled her head in her arms and closed her eyes. Brauer, Elemi, she murmured.

Suddenly, she didn't know how much time had passed, in the deep stillness of the apartment she thought she heard her name from far off. She didn't stir. The next moment someone was shaking her by the shoulder.

"Are you O.K., Mrs. Leonard? I'm sorry to wake you."

Baffled, she looked up at the thin, freckled face. Ah, of course, it was Thomas, the boy staying with them for Easter. He was into anarchy and natural foods. "That's all right, Thomas. I'm fine."

Brauer and Elemi had been sailing to Europe, where they planned to go backpacking through France and Italy. They had just returned from a tour of the ship's kitchen and were deciding whether they wanted to play shuffleboard or simply laze in the sun. Meanwhile they stretched out on deck chairs and drank bouillon. The shock of the intrusion made the blood pound behind Vera's eyes.

"I didn't mean to disturb you, but it's so late. You'll get a stiff neck sleeping like that."

She rose and rubbed her eyes with a tight fist. "Where's Freddy?"

"Freddy — uh — he gave me an extra set of keys." He walked quickly away from her to the sink, turned on the water and filled a glass. "He was taking this girl home. She lived very far out, I don't know how long . . ."

Vera could see his Adam's apple bobbing up and down as he gulped the drink. "That's quite all right, Thomas." She smiled. "I don't mean to pry. Turn out the lights, will you, when you're finished? Good night."

Climbing into bed, she thought to herself, You'd better watch it, Vera, with your Brauer and Elemi.

When the holidays were over and Freddy and Thomas returned to school, Jean acquired a boyfriend, a curly-haired, wildly energetic boy named Donald, who wore thick glasses too and was reputedly a mathematical genius. They spent long hours in her bedroom discussing intellectual and moral issues with the door open. Vera liked Donald, who often accosted her while waiting for Jean and elaborated complex mathematical theories.

"Mrs. Leonard, did you know that if the fastest rocket ship devised by man were to race the earth in one complete orbit around the sun it would arrive two years later?"

"Is that so?"

She was lost in his fevered explanation of objects hurtling through space at frenetic rates of speed — he paced rapidly as he spoke, occasionally bumping into furniture — but impressed by his mental stamina. When he left she felt as though a whirlwind had passed through the apartment, and she sank down in a chair, murmuring, Brauer, Elemi.

For they were her constant companions. More alone now that Jean had Donald, Vera took to strolling through Central Park. The days were growing longer and balmy. It stayed light till after seven. She would rush from the elevator after work, deliberately not looking around in case Will might be there, and walk the four blocks to the park, to find Brauer and Elemi waiting for her at their favorite entrance, East 64th Street, near the Zoo. Of course they didn't look at her directly or speak to her — they stayed slightly off to her left — but they knew she was there and didn't mind her walking near them. Sometimes they visited the animals. Brauer would call to the elephants, imitating their heavy stamping and the sullen arching of their trunks, while Elemi laughed and fed them peanuts. Vera watched from a few yards off. Later, if she stopped to buy an ice cream or a soft drink they paused and waited for her. They talked incessantly in soft whispers — what they said was not important, only the glow that enveloped them and that they were generous enough to share.

One evening when Vera came in at dusk, Jean, who was flipping hamburgers expertly, asked with an amused smile, "Come on, tell me, Mom, are you seeing somebody?"

"Of course not," Vera said sharply. "What makes you say that?"

"Well, you're out a lot, you come home all sort of rosy, and, like, your mind is elsewhere. I think it's great. You don't have to keep it a secret from me. We're both women."

"Don't be silly." Vera quickly laid the plates on the table. "There's nothing of the kind. I walked home through the park, that's all."

Late one afternoon at work Will buzzed her on the intercom. "Vera." It sounded like a command.

"Yes?" She should have sounded more confident, she thought immediately. After all, his was the question, hers the answer.

"How about a drink tonight? It's warm, we can sit outside at The Blue Door. I haven't seen you in ages."

"Thanks, Will, it's a nice idea. But I'm sorry. I've — " She took a deep breath for courage. "I've got a date."

"You've got a date."

"I'm afraid so."

"I see." He hung up.

In a moment he was in her doorway, glaring. "I'd like to say a few words to you." He shut the door firmly behind him. His shirt-sleeves were rolled up above his elbows and his loosened tie hung diagonally across his chest. "It's not like I'm some stranger trying to pick you up on the street, you know. It's not like I'm out to make you and then laugh it off." He was trying with strain to keep his voice down. His thick hair hung crazily over his forehead, and as he spoke, enraged, he wagged a finger at her. She noticed the dark hairs on his hands and felt an odd flicker of desire. He was much larger than she. Vera was afraid. "You know who I am, Vera. Aren't I good enough to pass an hour with, goddammit? I was good enough last year, when you needed a shoulder to cry on. Sure, that was fine. That was all for you, all taking and no giving. But when I ask for something, your company for an hour, that's all, oh no, that's asking too much. And you won't come straight out and say you don't want to, no, you give these phony excuses. You know what you are?" He wagged the hairy finger close to her face and she blinked in terror. "You are one helluva selfish, stuck-up bitch."

She didn't know what she could possibly say in reply. But she didn't need to say anything, for as soon as he finished speaking he stalked out of her office and slammed the door loudly behind him. The sound seemed to invade her body and made her shrink in her chair. She folded her arms on her desk and laid her head down. I can't, she thought. She was sorry about Will, but it was impossible, she was too afraid.

The very first time, she remembered, John had whispered, "Are you afraid?" And when she nodded he stroked her cheek and said, "It will be all right. I'll take care of you." She had grown used to him, so that the fear had shrunk very small, to the size of a shriv-eled pea, and then he died. He promised to take care of her but he broke his promise. She could not do it again with another, who might not take care. Even with John, twenty years, the small fear remained, each time he touched her. Sometimes it was so small, a speck at the bottom of a canyon, that she could pretend it wasn't there. But it always was, and she came to understand that she needed it; she was grateful for it. It was the small fear that held her body together and kept her from flying completely wild and perhaps shattering. She was more afraid of what she might do, how she might be, without her small fear, her amulet, the pea under the mattress.

Vera raised her head. There was still some work to finish before she could leave. Would they wait? They were accustomed to her arriving promptly at five-fifteen. She hurried through her papers, especially careful with the account sheets, though, with Will so angry. It would be disastrous if she messed them up, and Will told Howard, and Howard began watching. There were still the hospital bills, Jean's contact lenses, Freddy's Moped . . . At last she was finished and dashed out, not even bothering to wash her face or fix her hair, which had fallen again and hung loose down her back. Let it. It didn't matter, with Brauer and Elemi.

It was nearly five-forty-five when she reached the park entrance. They were still there, thank heaven, sitting on a bench in the shade. Elemi preferred the shade. Vera stopped in relief, panting. She had run all the way. When Brauer and Elemi saw her they rose instantly, joining hands, and began their evening stroll. Of course they had to wait, Vera realized as the slow walking calmed her senses. They are not real, they are mine. They can only do what I make them do. She laughed to herself, thinking of how foolish she had been to worry. They could not go off alone. They would always be there for her, and would do only what she wished and permitted, for they were her own invention.

Brauer was especially gentle toward Elemi this evening. He stroked her hand and picked out the softest, greenest patch of grass for her to sit on. When she twisted her ankle scrambling up a rock he rubbed it tenderly between his palms to ease the pain. Elemi tossed her head back, her long fair hair streaming out on the breeze, and looked up at Brauer with a gaze full of trust and gratitude. Tears came to Vera's eyes at the sight of them together.

Jean got her first real job, as a junior counselor at a summer camp in Maine. "What are you going to do on your vacation, Mom? Freddy will be working on the Cape, and you'll be all alone." They were drinking coffee together after dinner. Vera lit a cigarette and waved the smoke away from Jean, toward the open window.

"I don't know. Probably stay home and take it easy."

"You really ought to do something, Mom. You never go any-where. You could visit Uncle Matt on Fire Island. They always ask you. Or take a trip. San Francisco? You've never been out west."

"Maybe. I'll see."

The apartment was lonesome when Jean left, but once Vera was on vacation everything would be different. She had known for weeks what she wanted to do. The last evening after work, rather than leaving them on a park bench while she went dutifully home, she brought them right along with her: out the West Side entrance, down the street, into the lobby, up in the elevator. Brauer and Elemi, as usual, were serene, undisturbed by the change. They had been so many places that new adventures did not intimidate them. Vera's hand trembled as she fit the key in the lock. She was over-come with shyness. Should she speak? Welcome them with some joking remark? She decided definitely not. That would be going too far.

"Well, here we are," she muttered to herself. She kicked off her shoes, turned on the air conditioner, fixed a gin and tonic, and flopped down in an armchair in an ecstasy of relaxation, solitude, and freedom.

Brauer and Elemi passed a quiet evening browsing through the books on the shelves, playing Mozart on the stereo, childishly ex-ploring the bedrooms, Jean's, Freddy's, Vera's. As for Vera, it was the most beautiful evening she had spent in years, with nothing to be done, alone and yet not alone. She lay back in her chair listening to the music while they wandered about the apartment hand in hand, and she thought of all the things the three of them would do on her month off. They would go camping in Newfoundland, surfing on the beaches of Hawaii, ambling down the stone streets of Florence in the shadow of the great Cathedral, strolling in tran-quillity through the rock gardens of Kyoto. It was a summer of endless possibility.

At last Vera decided to go to bed: she was very tired. Brauer and Elemi could settle down anywhere they pleased — there was plenty of room. It was warm and the air conditioner was not work-ing well; she stripped off all her clothes and went to bed without a nightgown. She smoked a last cigarette as she did the daily cross-word puzzle, then turned off the bedside lamp. The dark seemed to make the room warmer and almost fragrant, as if there were flowers not far off. Her body felt light and smooth under the cool sheet. She remembered John and ran her hand over the sheet on his side of the double bed. It was odd how little she dwelt on John. She had thought about him so much when she was sick in the hospital that now there seemed nothing left to think about. She didn't even miss him particularly any more, though it had been better to sleep with someone than alone. She had missed him so much during the months of his dying that now there was no missing left in her. She missed only the feeling of missing him. Sometimes, from her great distance, she wondered if she had ever loved him. What was love? What did it feel like to love? Could real, flesh and blood people walk around forever holding hands, with stars in their eyes, like Brauer and Elemi? Of course not. They had to work, shop, prepare dinner, raise children. Her marriage, she judged, regarding it from her great distance, had been neither very unhappy nor very happy. It had been dull. Naturally there was a first flush of enchantment, but when that paled, it was dull, there was no use pretending otherwise. And even in that first flush of enchantment it had not been as beautiful as Brauer and Elemi. They never went places or did exciting things. Vera had dreams but John was practical, and she was afraid to burden him further with her dreams. She was even a little embarrassed by them, next to his practical ways. Probably she had loved him, she decided. She had always behaved like a loving wife. Perhaps real love was dull.

She was just falling asleep when she sensed that Brauer and Elemi were in the room. Strange, she had not noticed them enter. Brauer had his hands on Elemi's shoulders. He pulled her toward him, clasped her tightly and kissed her long on the mouth. Vera was surprised, and a trifle amused. Aha, she thought. So they are not such innocents. Elemi's arms closed around Brauer and she began caressing his back. Brauer bent and buried his face in her neck, roughly, and Elemi, her eyes closed, leaned her head back and gasped. Her fingers were taut and clutching at him. Vera's eyes began to pound. No, she thought in panic. Not yet. But they didn't stop. They sank down to the floor, where Brauer helped Elemi pull off her shirt, then put his lips to her breast. Elemi had her small white hand on the inside of his thigh. Vera shut her eyes tight but the vision remained. There was no way to get rid of them. Not yet, she tried to scream, but no sound would come. She felt herself grow inflamed, blood pounding and rushing to every surface. You want to see it, she whispered angrily. You know you want to see it. Yes, all along she had secretly wondered why, if they were so in love, they never made love. They must have done it behind her back, like naughty children. Why were they showing her now? Why now, she wanted to scream at them. But of course they would not hear. The pounding of her blood was unbearable. Her eyes were hot and every inch of her skin ached as she watched, for now they were intertwined in another long kiss, arms and legs groping, seizing. Vera placed a hand beneath her heart to calm herself, but the warm touch only made the throbbing worse. If it kept on she would soon burst from her skin.

Furious at herself, she snarled, If you want to see it so badly then take a good look. They were completely naked now. Vera cried out in fright — Brauer was so strong and hard, Elemi so white and frail. His fingers disappeared between her legs; Vera's spine jerked in a spasm of terror. Elemi seemed nearly faint in her abandon. In the park so pretty and childlike, now she had her legs spread apart, with her arms clinging around Brauer's neck and her open lips reaching for his. Then he was on top of her. Vera stiffened. Don't hurt Elemi, she whispered. Don't. Don't hurt. He began to push. She could see Elemi's face very clearly, the tight tendons of her arched neck, the trembling bluish-white of her eyelids, her mouth open as if in shock. Sweat glistened on Elemi's forehead. Brauer kept pushing, merciless, rhythmic. Elemi's face was so strained and twisted, Vera could not tell if it was misery or joy. Her own body began moving up and down in rhythm with Brauer's pushing and she could not stop it. No, not yet, she cried, but she was powerless to stop herself or them. They had escaped her. She had escaped herself.

On and on Brauer pushed — would he never stop? Vera ached to know what Elemi was feeling, poor Elemi, straining with him, pounding up and down on the floor so hard her frail body made a soft thudding sound. Was that wild face twisted in misery or joy? Somewhere within her she remembered that Elemi could feel only what she wished her to feel, yet Vera was powerless, trapped in their eternal rhythm, for she could not choose between misery or joy. Brauer kept pushing, and Elemi's face kept the terrible riddle, till Vera herself finally erupted from the inside out, shattering the bed, the room, the building, with her innards.

When it was finished she leaned back weakly and wiped her

streaming brow with the back of her hand, amazed to have survived. Her body was utterly limp and exhausted, but when she focused her eyes she saw that they, the dream, strained on. Still he pushed without respite and still she thudded beneath him. They would never stop.

LYN COFFIN

Falling off the Scaffold

(FROM THE MICHIGAN QUARTERLY REVIEW)

DEAR SIR:

I am enrolling in your correspondence course. Yours is the only ad that doesn't take a "writer's cheerleader" approach — "You too can write a sentence that sells," etc. I feel that someone who advertises his services in such a curt, laconic, or at least a "no nonsense" way may perhaps have something to offer me.

I would appreciate your not sending me the customary 'credentials' sheet, incidentally. I'm sure your credentials are excellent; if not, I have enough for both of us.

My check and my first submission (*At the Museum*) are enclosed.

Very truly yours,
e. trace

At the Museum

At the museum, looking at the mummy,
I think about mortality.
I think about
The hieroglyphs
Slow time has inscribed
On my moving face.
How did you feel,
Egyptian man?
You had long fingers,
Did you play the harp,
Cast the sticks,

Or were you a card shark?
The bones tell no story.
The linen, dissolving,
Tells no story.
I don't want it this way,
All up to the imagination!
Couldn't you have left a letter,
A suicide note
(All letters, poems, are ultimately suicide notes)
Saying
I was a painter of pyramids.
I got careless.
One day I fell off the scaffold
And got a fungus
And that fungus
Ate me up. I just shriveled away and
Died. But before I died, I picked out my favorite
Pots and knives and beads and here I am.
That's how I died, that's the way you see me.
Well, that would make me feel much better,
I could even get into that painter's trip,
Feel the scaffold slip —
The sudden drop, the scream —
Perhaps I'd die
And wouldn't you wonder
Seeing me curled up next to the mummy
In my turtleneck and bell-bottoms?

Dear Mr. or Ms. Trace:

Welcome to the course! My salutation is not meant to offend you in any way — merely to point out that presently I exist in a state of unawareness as to your gender, if I may put it that way.

Taking your most interesting and intriguing letter point by point (which is something I believe very strongly in doing), I feel that I must in all honesty admit that it was not considerations of *verbal* economy alone which led me to make my ad short and sweet. I'm sure you know what I mean!

As for the matter of credentials, I believe you spoke of having credentials enough for both of us. Well, all I have to say to *that* is, you must have quite a few! Seriously, I would like to know something about you — your gender, of course, as I mentioned above

— but that's just a beginning. The more I know about you, the more I can help you realize your own individual talent, and that's what we're both concerned with at this point, right? — Naturally, I don't expect you to tell me all the intimate details of your personal life — at least not yet! — as interesting as those details may be! But if you could tell me a little bit about the kind of education you've had, the kinds of things you're interested in writing about, etc. etc., I'd be in a much better position to advise you.

I'll bet you're wondering at this point just what I thought of *In The Museum.* Okay. Well, on the whole, I thought it was excellent. Really excellent. I just have a couple of points I'd like to make. First of all, I think you might be better off, if you're going to write poetry, to work within more or less traditional forms for a while. The poem as it is is too strung out, so to speak. I'm not sure that you have the poetic control (yet!) which one needs if one is going to write free verse. So that's one suggestion I'd like to make, that you try something in meter. Now, of course, *I* don't know (hint hint) what *you* know about matters of prosody. If you're interested, I can recommend several books on the subject, one of which I wrote myself!

Another thing. I think you run into a point-of-view problem at the end of the poem, when you address someone ("And wouldn't you be surprised") and the reader can't tell exactly who that some-one is. Up to that point, remember, the poet-you has been speaking directly to the mummy (I think that's one of the best things about the poem, that use of direct address!), so when you (the poet) say, "And wouldn't *you* be surprised," I don't think you can complete the line as you do, by saying, "Seeing me curled up here next to the *mummy.*"

As for the beginning, my honest feeling is that it should be cut! ("I think about mortality" is particularly bad. In poetry, especially, one has to "show — don't tell."*) I don't think you really hit your stride until the ninth or tenth line.

To sum it all up, I think you ought to try being less *casual,* less prosaic, as it were — assuming you still want to stick to poetry after all my discouraging comments!

I'm looking forward to your next submission and (one last re-minder) to learning more about you.

Happy writing!

K. C. Jedenacht

* Ditto, the line about all poems and letters being suicide notes.

You're perfectly right, of course, but being right is not at all the same as being poetic!

K. C. J.

Dear Prof. Jedenacht:

Thank you for your letter. I agree with everything you said about the poem. I disagree with everything else.

I am enclosing my poetic response to your poetic suggestions.

Very truly yours,
evelyn trace

The Catch

I swam the long sea
Down, a silver flash in deepest
Leagues of green, lifted by the swell
And surge, the strong, the sure, the slowly-rising
Tide. Exposed to seizures by a sudden ebb, your bare
Hands had me. I was cruelly beached. I dully thudded
Out my life against your bones and body strand-was
Cut, slit open by a most incisive blade. My Death
Was spasmodic-I labored like a girl
In frank breech birth.

Dear Ms. Trace:

Well, I must say that your second letter (?) intrigued me even more than the first! (And that's saying a lot!) As you will note by the salutation, I took your advice about trying to learn about you through your poems. Putting together some of the more obvious, shall we say, phrasings of your latest poem ("I was slit, cut open by your most incisive blade" and so on) with the name "Evelyn," I have come to the conclusion that you are a female-type person.

Also, judging from your address, you live in the suburbs. Going on the assumption that most women (your poems and letter are far too mature for a girl to have written them) who live in the suburbs are married and have a husband and children, I have concluded nothing less than that you are a married woman and a suburban mother! (How am I doing so far?)

As for the poem itself, I thought it was excellent, a real step up from the museum piece (if I may so phrase it)! *The Catch* shows a lot of thought and poetic craft. Still, it's not exactly the kind of thing I had in mind for you. The fish-shape, which (stupid me) I didn't see at first, represents an extremely ingenious bit of spatial engineering, of course, but I'm afraid emblem poems went out of style with Geo. Herbert and his bunch (c. the 1590's) and haven't come back in since! The line-raising ("ris^{ing}") and lowering ("Death") sort of thing never was in! Seriously, I'm afraid you suffer, as so many others of us do, from what I call "the curse of cleverness."

And, again, it seems to me, the poem takes too long to get off the ground. (Metaphorically speaking, of course!)

One last thing: I seem to remember your using a phrase like "my moving face" in your *Museum* poem. In *Catch*, you have words like "seizures" and "incisive" and "frank" and phrases like "had me," all of which are, it seems to me, more or less in the nature of puns. Perhaps you pun unconsciously, perhaps not. (My mother was a great one for unconscious puns. I remember she told me once she ironed her underwear because "I want my drawers to look neat.") Anyway, I think you ought to seriously consider how much, if at all, you want to use puns in a serious piece of writing.

To sum it all up, I would suggest your trying to write a more or less regular poem for your next submission, something I'm very much looking forward to reading.

Good luck,
"Sherlock" Jedenacht

Dear Sir:

Just a few items of possible interest: A) I agree with your criticisms of *The Catch*; B) "Evelyn" is a name which most authorities consider proper for either males *or* females; C) As so many other poets do, I "suffer from" a tendency to use *personae* in my work, a tendency which I should think you, as a detective if not as a fellow writer, would do well to keep in mind; D) George Herbert (1593–1633).

Enclosed is my latest submission. The puns are quite deliberate.

Very truly (and pseudonymously) yours,
e.d.t.

Presentation

> *Fluidly, they draw me out; I take it as it goes.*
> *They wrap my genitals with white so nothing manly shows.*
> *And in the padlock of my hands they place a waxy rose.*
> *In covered wagons, peasant-like, they horse me to my room.*
> *They let me down. I come to terms, assume a studied pose.*
> *Like backward dogs, they shower dirt. They fill me in on*
>   *doom.*

Dear Evelyn,

Well, as you can see from the salutation, I still haven't given up on the idea that we can be friends (even if you do seem insistent upon regarding me from the "height of an unwritten book"!). Actually, I never really thought about you as a suburban housewife at all: I just said that as a kind of test. Even if I hadn't been sure before, the phrase "so nothing manly shows" would have clued me in as to the true state of things.

Anyway, about the poem itself. I think it's fairly good. Your rhymes are a trifle sophomoric, but perhaps that is a good thing, given the subject with which the poem attempts to deal. I really object to two things: your use of puns, about which I cautioned you in my last letter, and which I really feel you would do well to avoid; and, second, the nebulous nature of what you like to call the "persona" of your work.

Expressions like "draw me out", "take it as it goes", "let me down", "come to terms" — all of these plays on words seem to me unfortunately chosen. You said in your letter that all your puns were deliberate, however, so this may just be one of those things we're going to have to agree to disagree about!

As for the "persona" — Beyond the fact that the speaker of the poem is a dead man, the reader knows nothing about him. Also, with the one possible exception of the phrase "padlock of my hands" (the meaning of which I'm afraid escapes me), I see little or no *traces* (turn about and all that!) of a truly poetic sensibility in your work. You are obviously intelligent, well-read, sensitive, etc. But it seems to me (and I cannot stress too strongly that this is a purely personal opinion — in fact, not even an opinion so much as a gut feeling, if you will) that you would do better in the medium of prose. I think the broader scope of a novel, or even a short story, would help you to develop your personae and your extremely interesting ideas. This is something one of my creative writing teachers told *me* once, and I've always been grateful to him for his honesty.

If you want to continue with the poetry, of course, that's your prerogative. If you do decide to stick with it, though, then my advice would be to choose something other than death to write about. Of all the subjects about which to write poetry, it seems to me, death is apt to produce the worst writing. If you want my honest opinion, I don't think anybody's been able to come up with even a half-way decent poem about the thing, including Donne and Thomas and whomever else you wish to include. Frankly, I look at it this way — death is just something that happens. We make a big deal out of it because it terrifies the hell out of us; when one looks at it objectively, though, one finds it is a good subject for a writer (particularly a poet) to steer away from.

As a matter of fact, I can't think of a more boring topic — unless it's daffodils!

Looking forward to hearing from you, I remain

Sincerely yours,
Prof. "Casey" Jedenacht

Dear Prof. Jedenacht:

As you will see from the enclosed, I took your advice about trying to express myself (much as I hate that phrase) in prose. I *tried* to take your other major piece of advice and write about something relatively positive, but the latter attempt, as you will soon discover, utterly failed. I find myself unable to write about anything except death.

And yet, I am not completely without hope that "Lucite" will strike some small spark of interest in you: after all, the *persona's* attitude toward the thing is very largely the same as I take yours to be.

Very truly yours,
Evelyn

Lucite

My father died when I was thirteen years old. I remember because that was my year for lucite.

Perhaps a little background information would be of use here before I proceed.

I am — and if I am, I undoubtedly always was — a genius. I am also extremely wealthy. I am also what I suppose you would call "a cold fish"; as far as I'm concerned, that's the only rational way to be.

Oh, I know most people believe in love and friendship and emotions and all that; in fact, one of my earliest maxim's was "The worse something is, the more people tend to believe in it."

I don't want to get into a discussion of Nazism or anything like that, not at this point. You want to hear about my father's death and I'm here to oblige you. About the love business, though: the two kinds of love which are most universally acclaimed are the parental-filial and the amorati. Allow me simply to point out that modern psychologists agree with me that the first is no more or less than a dependency bond. (As a person who could have survived by his own wits from an early age, I never really, or at least consciously, knew what it was to feel dependent.) As for romantic love, I shall exercise my well-known classical restraint and limit myself to pointing out that the concept of romantic love *qua* concept was invented as late as the thirteenth century by troubadours and minnesingers who probably dreamed it up as what we today would call "a promotion gimmick."

So much for love.

Now I know a lot of you are probably "feeling sorry" for me, and I can assure you there is no need. Perhaps you would not wish to grant me the right to use the term "happy." So be it. But I consider that my life is "blest," as a character in *Joseph Andrews* expressed it, since I continually "experience the falsehood of common assertions."

When my father died, I did not have any feelings of guilt or sadness. I hardly knew my father — as, indeed, I hardly knew, or know, anyone. He seemed pleasant enough, you understand, and I was glad (as opposed to grateful) not to have been born to a cruel or a stupid man. But that was all.

When mother came into my room, I was at work making a pair of lucite bookends. As most of my biographers have pointed out, my fame as an innovator in the field of crafts could have been predicted almost from the very beginning by anyone with a modicum of intelligence and sensitivity. Fortunately or unfortunately, I myself was the only such person then acquainted with my work.

I was always careful not to do *too* well in school, of course, since I knew all too well the resentment that would have stirred up in my peers and the annoying consequences I would have had to put up with.

Still, however, despite all my precautions on this score, I encountered a certain amount of residual hostility among my fellow students, particularly the boys.

It was partly in order to minimize this residual antipathy that I first began doing work with lucite. One boy of rather pronounced sadistic tendencies asked me to build him "a home for my guinea pig." The resulting cage was quite satisfactory. I built a number of cages for the pets (I privately referred to them as "the nameless horrors") of the other boys.

Then I began making book-ends. On the night my father died, I had just finished the well-known "Black-and-White Pony Book Ends" which I understand are the earliest pieces featured in the Smithsonian. It was the first time I had ever really carved the lucite, and the first time I had ever used a pictorial motif.

Anyway, when my mother told me my father had died — this may shock some of you — I was rather pleased. I had read all kinds of stories about children being made to kiss the lipsticked mouths of departed relatives and so on, and I suppose I hoped for something of the sort — anything, really, that would relieve the tedium of life in general.

Of course, nothing of the sort occurred. My father's casket was closed and the entire funeral service carried out in a quiet, dignified, and hence boring manner. To be sure, my mother cried a bit, but I had seen her cry as much when her mother's porcelain vegetable dish broke.

As it turned out, my father had left instructions that he be cremated: again, I had some expectations of drama — the casket sliding precipitously down into the roaring flames, and so on. Again, I was cheated. In fact, the family, at my mother's request, was not even present when the cremation took place.

A messenger brought us father's remains the following day. Mother didn't know what to do with them, she said, since father had left no instructions as to their disposal. She didn't want them walled up in some columbarium, with the other "cinery urns," she asserted. Nor did she "want the thing cluttering up the house and making people uncomfortable." I said I would be glad to keep the urn (it looked like a coffee can, I thought, for all that it had "R.I.P." engraved on the top). With only the slightest of hesitations, she agreed.

I think the rest is pretty well-known to you all. It took me only a few days to hit upon the idea of sifting the remains to get out the bone fragments and embedding a handful of the finest ash in a book-end. From there, it was only a small step to the whole line of "Loved Ones in Lucite" which first brought me fame and fortune.

Dear Evelyn,

To begin with, I'm delighted that you took my advice about trying out the short story form. I definitely feel that you're on the right track, although perhaps not quite yet at the station! *Calcite* seems to me very good for a first attempt. In fact, for a piece of its kind I think it's truly excellent; the only problem is, I think what you've written is not so much a story as it is a character portrait — the kind of thing Browning might have written if he'd written prose.

The main ingredient of a story is action, it seems to me, and not point-of-view, although, of course, point-of-view can be very important. What I'd suggest is that you try, in your next story, to develop a sequence of events — try to weave a narrative thread, as it were.

Also, if you must write about death, perhaps you could approach it from a more positive — at least a less morbid or offbeat — angle. If you could choose a more normal persona, I think you would appeal to a wider audience.

Keep up the good work.

> Very truly yours,
> Prof. K.C. Jedenacht

Dear Sir:

As usual, I agreed with the criticisms you made in your letter.

Enclosed please find my latest attempt to please you.

Sincerely yours,
evelyn trace

Catharsis

For purely personal reasons, I want to describe what she was like and how it happened.

She was so beautiful it almost hurt to look at her. She was very small and delicate, with skin so fair it seemed translucent. She had thick, dark hair that kind of swirled around, framing her little locket-face. I guess it was her high cheekbones and rather deep-set eyes that gave her a pathetically proud expression; she looked like a little girl facing her First Confession — not that that explains anything.

I suppose in her own way she was intelligent, but she got good grades mainly by virtue of her photographic memory. Being the kind of person who'd forget his head if it weren't attached, I really envied her that memory.

"God, school would be so much easier to take if I could only remember everything, like you do," I commented once. "It's not that I can remember," she said. "It's just that I can't forget."

Not only did she remember everything she read, heard or saw, however — unfortunately, she also tended to believe it. This uncritical acceptance of things prevented her from doing any real scholarship. Her papers always represented impressive but ultimately unsuccessful attempts to reconcile incompatible views.

Her term paper on Chamberlain was a perfect case in point. After skimming through it, I took her to task. "First, you side with those who think he was a schmuck, then you agree with the 'unsung hero' faction," I said. "Don't give me that 'hobgoblin of little minds' business, either. Just accept the fact that you can't have things both ways."

She mumbled something about black-and-white ponies and about light's being both a particle and a wave; I didn't pay too much attention. After a few minutes, she smiled ruefully and said: "Well, I've heard that most student papers tend to throw out the baby with the bath. At least I don't do that — I just try to diaper the water."

Naturally, her penchant for accepting things at face value stood

her in good stead socially. She came as close to being a real aristo-
crat as any midwestern Catholic can, but she never had that air of
inaccessibility most people of her class exhibit. Average people felt
at home with her.

There were widespread rumors to the effect that she was a little
too accessible, particularly when it came to men, but when I heard
things like that, I just shrugged them off. For one thing, she was
pretty religious. More importantly, though, it was hard for me to
imagine anyone's being promiscuous who was as uninterested in
sex as she was. I say uninterested because although she never put
me off or turned me down, not even during her periods, she never
initiated anything either.

Unfortunately, her doctor had advised her not to take the pill.
(Something to do with her having inherited a tendency to develop
embolisms — it seems they can prove fatal if they travel to the
heart — which meant birth control pills were dangerous for her.)

Anyway, what with her passivity and my having to wear a condom, sex wasn't all that satisfactory. . . .

It sounds funny, I guess, but the best times we had were spent in
discussing rather sad and serious things. I had her read my thesis
on the Aristotelian aspects of Euripides, since she had read most
of his plays. Although she had read them while quite young, she
remembered everything in them and more . . . . She started talking
about Medea's having cooked her children and served them up to
their father, for example; I'm afraid I teased her unmercifully
about that.

On the lighter side, she liked my collection of famous last words
("Puto deus fio") and treasured phrases from children's nursery
rhymes. Her favorite, which she claimed had something to do with
a battle, was typical of the kind of thing she liked. It started inno-
cently enough with reference to a garden full of seeds (weeds?).
But it went on to talk about a lion at the door and ended by saying,
"When your heart begins to bleed/ You're dead, and dead, and
dead, indeed."

She told me once her father used to feed her lines of gallows-
humor ("Why is dying like going to the bathroom?" — "When you
gotta go, you gotta go") while she drank her warm milk at bedtime.
With a father like that, I suppose it's no wonder she had a morbid
streak. For a time, in high school, she wanted to be a poet: she
wrote hundreds of strange little poems, all of them morbid:

> *Death moves toward me. I'm dancing — He cuts in*
> *The gay young blade — I'm now at his disposal.*
> *I get the point of Women's Lib,*
> *Accept his generous proposal.*

I don't really think I can tell you much more about her. I'll just try to describe what happened as near as I can recall it.

I remember I had trouble unlocking the door. (I'd had a key made for myself. I'm not sure whether she really liked that or not, but she spent a lot of time in bed, the covers pulled up over her head, and I was afraid one time she wouldn't hear the buzzer.) I was carrying a pizza in one hand, a 6-pack in the other.

I kicked the door shut behind me, turned off the t.v., and set out plates and napkins. I don't remember what was said, except that she called me "Ivan" (after her literary hero, Ivan Karamazov), which was usually a good sign.

I poured the beer too quickly and some of it foamed over on to the rug. I started dabbing at the wet spots with my napkin but she told me her mother, who had bought the rug for her, had said it was " 'a good rug and good rugs don't show stains.' " So I stopped dabbing.

After a while, I realized she wasn't eating. Usually, she ate whatever I put in front of her. I asked her about it, and she said she didn't want any more.

"How can you not want *more* when you haven't had *any?*" I wanted to know. She mumbled something about being a hunger artist, but bowed her head dutifully and began to eat.

She had told me a few weeks before that there was to be an important lecture-and-slide presentation on the Normandy invasion that evening, and I asked her what time it was supposed to start.

"8:00," she said. "But I don't think I'll go."

I was unpleasantly surprised: as far as I knew, she had never missed a single class or class-related event and now didn't seem the time to start.

"Why not?"

"I'm sick of having to brown-nose. Sick of educational insemination. Sick of being fed on the blood of gods. Sick of conceptual consumption, for Christ's sake!"

She rattled out the "k" sounds in a sort of rapid-fire machine-gun stutter and it struck me that I had never seen her show any sign of temper before.

In a way, I was encouraged. I had held off making love to her for a couple of weeks, hoping for once she'd be the one to make the overtures. I don't know — I suppose I connected temper with passion somehow. I'd had several beers by then, and the weeks of abstinence *had* left me sort of sexed-up.

At any rate, I remember thinking maybe she wanted to stay home so we could have a real night of it. I guess that was when I asked her if she'd been to confession. (The next day was the Feast of the Epiphany, a holy day of obligation.)

She said no, she hadn't, adding that she didn't want to take communion any more. Again, I asked her why. She said something about swallowing's being for the birds and gagging's not being a joke. I really didn't pay much attention; the fact she wasn't planning to take communion sort of cinched things in my mind.

I'm not sure what I said or did next. I do remember carrying her to bed and making rather short work of the situation.

I must have fallen asleep right away, because I woke up about an hour later and I was still on top of her and still attached, so to speak. She was wide-awake, apparently had been the whole time. Her eyes had a funny kind of glazed look. Her fists were clenched. Her whole body was rigid.

Needless to say, I immediately withdrew . . . .

I vaguely remember making a few comments about the way she'd been acting the last couple of weeks. I finished by saying something like, "I don't know what's gotten into you lately."

She didn't say anything for a few minutes. Then she asked me where I bought the "Trojans" I kept in her bathroom cabinet. I told her and she nodded. "I thought so," she said.

Naturally, I didn't let it go at that. I kept after her until she revealed the following facts:

1) The pharmacy where I bought condoms had recently fired one of their employees;

2) The guy they fired was mentally ill; among other things, he amused himself by opening packages of condoms and making pin-prick holes in some of the tips;

3) She thought I must have purchased a batch which included some of these "punctured prophylactics;"

4) She had missed her last period and although the rabbit-test

"hadn't taken" (and was thus inconclusive), she was pretty sure she was pregnant;

6) That's what had 'gotten into her' lately.

Well, I was pretty upset by what she'd said, mostly because it made our whole relationship sound like something out of daytime t.v. But I told myself it was no good sitting around thinking about it. If she were pregnant, there would be time enough in the days ahead to decide what to do, and if she weren't, so much the better. It occurred to me that getting out and going to the lecture might be just the ticket in getting our minds off things. "At any rate, it can't hurt," I thought.

It was sleeting out, apparently had been for some time; ice had glassed over large stretches of the sidewalks. The winds seemed to be of gale force — "things too fierce to mention." I was wearing boots and a hooded parka, though, so I didn't mind too much.

We were a little late. The elevator didn't seem to be in operation so we went up the fire-stairs. I guess others had been that way before us; in any event, the fire-door had been propped open.

As we walked down the corridor, I noticed that all the office doors were shut and the air in the corridor was unusually close. I thought of going back and opening the window at the far end of the hall, but decided there wasn't time.

We got to the office where the talk was being given, and she opened the door.

Out of nowhere, there was an ear-splitting explosion. Dagger-like shards of glass flew past her and into the hall. Someone began to scream.

Instinctively, I pulled her back into the corridor. She was dry-eyed, but making strangled, mewing sounds; she seemed to be having some sort of convulsions.

Someone later tried to explain to me just what had happened. It seems the fire door's being the only thing open had set up a kind of air-trap. I don't know — the explanation was too scientific to mean very much to me. What I do know is that at the instant she opened the door to the lecture-room, the window imploded. (I also learned later that, despite the screaming, no one had been seriously hurt.)

Well, all I could think of then was that I had to get her out of there. Whatever had happened in the room was not her fault, and nothing whatever would be achieved by our hanging around. Besides, she was obviously in a state of shock.

I led her back to the apartment. When we arrived, I got her to drink some warm milk while I finished the 6-pack. I gave her a tentative kiss, but there was a noticeable lack of response, so I turned in, advising her to do the same. ("Sleep knits up the ravelled sleeve of care" and all that.)

As I recall, she said she'd "be right there."

When I woke up the next morning, she wasn't in bed; one look at her pillow (in her sleep, she really mauled the thing) told me she hadn't been there at all.

I was heading for the study when I saw the note adhesive-taped to the bathroom door. In her curious, backhand scrawl, she had written: "I would be afraid of a less expressive death."

It's impossible to lock that door, but somehow she had managed to jam it shut. I forced it open, and peered in.

It was the most awful thing I've ever seen. (Luckily, I've pretty much managed to blot the sight out of my mind.) She had gotten into the bath tub — it was full — and cut her throat. There was blood everywhere. . . .

Being somewhat of a classicist, I don't think tragedies can be explained; I think they're to be felt rather than understood. . . . Describing what happened, reliving the pity and terror of it all, hasn't been easy, but I feel better for having done so.

Things have a way of working out.

Dear Evelyn,

Now you're really getting it together, as some of my other students like to say. I liked your story very much. I think this time you chose the right point-of-view and the subject is pretty much within the parameters of popular tastes. (What could be more normal than a guy getting his girl pregnant, right?)

The tissue of references and symbolic actions (spilling beer on the rug and all that) seems carefully, though perhaps a trifle too obtrusively (with an "r"!), elaborated. I haven't really had time to think about whether Euripides and the Latin ("I think I am making a god") and so on are truly *inevitable* in the story, but they sound good just on the surface of it, and I'm willing to take your word for the rest.

The only case which strikes me as a possible exception to the above is the girl's reference to a pony of some sort. Now I noticed horse references in a couple of your other things if I remember right, and I had trouble with the darn things then, too. . . . Probably ponies and horses and the like serve as some kind of private symbol for you — that's fine. But when you're writing a story, you have to make all your references at least potentially accessible to the reader. Not only that, but in this particular case, your private way of looking at horses — which I take to be almost completely asexual — directly conflicts with the standard (Freudian, neo-Freudian, psychoanalytic, whatever) way of looking at them. I suggest that you leave this particular warhorse (my puns are deliberate, too!) to the authorities and choose something else to be private about!

Enough of the harangue, already! Just one more point: although I think *Catharsis* is far and away the best thing you've written, it — like your other pieces — takes much too long to get going. Your beginning is more or less just deadwood, just straight exposition. I would suggest that the next time you do as Hemingway used to do: write your story, then go back and cut the first paragraph or two. (He used to cut the endings off as well, I believe, but I think your work is quite all right in that department.)

Incidentally, may I take this opportunity to remind you that additional coursework, according to the terms of that ad you liked so much, necessitates another financial remission on your part. How time does fly, eh?

Well, with that word to the wise, I remain

Yours truly,
"Casey" Jedenacht

Dear Sir:

Enclosed please find my latest and last submission. I am aware that it is not strictly covered by the terms of our agreement; I sent it to you as a kind of "thank you," in the hope you will find it enjoyable — or at least edifying.

Happy criticizing!
evelyn trace
N.B.   I am a woman.

Famous Last Words

She had not wanted a lingering death; she had wanted to "go out like a light," as her husband, a well-known journalist, had put it. That was how he had gone — a stroke in his sleep.

But turning misfortunes into their opposite had always been her strong point. This lingering death (her death), seen positively, represented a chance to get even, somehow. (With whom, for what, she didn't know.)

"Life imitates art," her husband had been fond of saying. She was experiencing the truth of that now.

As a girl, millenia ago, she had wanted to be a writer. She had written a story called "Famous Last Words" about an unbelievably old woman, lying on her deathbed, who was determined to go out with a flourish, if not a bang.

Now she herself was unbelievably old. . . . If she could just remember the story and follow it, she would be acting the lead in her own play. She could die in the service of her own creation. She could be the artist of her own destruction.

The trouble was, she couldn't remember how the story ended. . . . She remembered that her first thought had been to have the old woman choke to death in the middle of a tantalizing sentence: "The only thing that really matters is — " But even in her youth, she had had enough sense to reject that idea. "Dime-novel stuff," her husband would have called it.

Another possibility she'd considered was that of having the old woman be successful — say just what she wanted to say — and then die happy. The problem with that approach, apart from the fact that most people nowadays didn't believe one could 'die happy', was that it wasn't playing fair with the public not to tell them what those last words were. And if one elected to play it straight, what words could one put in the story-woman's mouth that would be meaningful but mysterious, etc., that would justify all the narrative build-up?

Of course, one could play the thing for laughs: have the old woman come out with a kind of vaudeville routine — "I'm goin' fast, but 'afore I go, I got one thing to say: 'I'm goin' fast.' "

But she had rejected that idea, too. It was too much like masturbating: (Her husband had said masturbation was "carried out in frustration, and concluded in defeat." "Even when it's good, it's bad," he had remarked.)

She had considered other endings and rejected them in turn: having the old bat's "famous last words" turn out to be gibberish ("The moon is an eagle") or something somebody else had already said ("More light") or a variation on it ("Less light," even "More life"), but all those endings were cheap, they were cop-outs, and she had never been one in favor of copping out.

A more attractive possibility had been having the old woman do something (give her grand-daughter a rose or a shiny new quarter) rather than trying to speak. But a story like that wouldn't be much more than a moralistic cliché (Her husband had called such pronouncements "profundisms"), like "Life must go on" or even (God forbid) "Actions speak louder than words."

She had also considered an epilogue-ending: the old woman would say something personally meaningful (like "Rosebud"), then there would be a significant space, then a sentence like "The doctor put away his stethoscope and, turning to the husband (son? father?), said: 'You can be thankful it was a stroke — she never knew what hit her.' "

All those endings and others had been rejected: she remembered that. But she couldn't remember, she simply could not remember, how she *had* ended the story. Maybe she hadn't finished it at all, in fact; maybe that was it.

Even if it had never been finished, though, she knew it had been a good story. Thinking too much about endings, after all, was a mistake: you have an idea; you write a story. The story ends whenever you stop writing.

Dear Evelyn:

Famous Lost Words was excellent. I'm only sorry you chose not to go on with me. As one of my sidelines, I publish a small journal. With a little polishing, your story might well have proved suitable for publication.

If you should change your mind, you know where I am! Until then, I remain,

Very truly yours,
Kathy Christine Jedenacht

ALICE MUNRO

Spelling

(FROM WEEKEND MAGAZINE)

ROSE DROVE OUT to the County Home. She was conducted through it. She tried to tell Flo about it when she came back.

"Whose home?" said Flo.

"No, the *County* Home."

Rose mentioned some people she had seen there. Flo would not admit to knowing any of them. Rose spoke of the view and the pleasant rooms. Flo looked angry; her face darkened and she stuck out her lip.

Rose handed her a mobile she had bought for 50 cents in the County Home crafts centre. Cut-out birds of blue and yellow paper were bobbing and dancing on undetectable currents of air.

"Stick it up your arse," said Flo.

Rose put the mobile up in the porch and said she had seen the trays coming up with supper on them.

"They go to the dining room if they're able, and if they're not they have trays in their rooms. I saw what they were having. Roast beef, well done, mashed potatoes and green beans, the frozen not the canned kind. Or an omelette. You could have a mushroom omelette or a chicken omelette or a plain omelette, if you liked."

"What was for dessert?"

"Ice cream. You could have sauce on it."

"What kind of sauce was there?"

"Chocolate. Butterscotch. Walnut."

"I can't eat walnuts."

"There was marshmallow too."

*

Out at the Home the old people were arranged in tiers. On the first floor were the bright and tidy ones. They walked around, usually with the help of canes. They visited each other, played cards. They had sing-songs and hobbies. In the crafts centre they painted pictures, hooked rugs, made quilts. If they were not able to do things like that they could make rag dolls, mobiles like the one Rose bought, poodles and snowmen that were constructed of Styrofoam balls with sequins for eyes; they also made silhouette pictures by placing thumb tacks on traced outlines: knights on horseback, battleships, airplanes, castles. They organized concerts; they held dances; they had checker tournaments.

"Some of them say they are the happiest here they have ever been in their lives."

Up one floor there was more television watching, there were more wheelchairs. There were those whose heads drooped, whose tongues lolled, whose limbs shook uncontrollably. Nevertheless, sociability was still flourishing, also rationality, with occasional blanks and absences.

On the third floor you might get some surprises. Some of them up there had given up speaking. Some had given up moving, except for odd jerks and tosses of the head, flailing of the arms, that seemed to be without purpose or control. Nearly all had given up worrying about whether they were wet or dry. Bodies were fed and wiped, taken up and tied in chairs, untied and put to bed. Taking in oxygen, giving out carbon dioxide, they continued to participate in the life of the world.

Crouched in her crib, diapered, dark as a nut, with three tufts of hair like dandelion floss sprouting from her head, an old woman was making loud shaky noises.

"Hello, Aunty," the nurse said. "You're spelling today. It's lovely weather outside." She bent to the old woman's ear. "Can you spell 'weather'?"

This nurse showed her gums when she smiled, which was all the time; she had an air of nearly demented hilarity.

"Weather," said the old woman. She strained forward, grunting, to get the word. Rose thought she was going to have a bowel movement. "W-e-a-t-h-e-r." That reminded her. "Whether. W-h-e-t-h-e-r."

So far so good.

"Now you say something to her," the nurse said to Rose.

The words in Rose's mind were for a moment all obscene or despairing. But without prompting came another. "Forest. F-o-r-e-s-t."

"Celebrate," said Rose suddenly.

"C-e-l-e-b-r-a-t-e."

You had to listen very hard to make out what the old woman was saying because she had lost much of the power to shape sounds. What she said seemed not to come from her mouth or her throat but from deep in her lungs and belly.

"Isn't she a wonder," the nurse said. "She can't see and that's the only way we can tell she can hear. Like if you say, 'Here's your dinner,' she won't pay any attention to it, but she might start spelling 'dinner.' "

"Dinner," she said, to illustrate, and the old woman picked it up. "D-i-n-n . . ." Sometimes a long wait, a long wait between letters. It seemed she had only the thinnest thread to follow, meandering through that emptiness or confusion that nobody on this side can do more than guess at. But she didn't lose it, she followed it through to the end, however tricky the word might be, or cumbersome. Finished. Then she was sitting waiting; waiting, in the middle of her sightless, eventless day, till up from somewhere popped another word. She would encompass it, bend all her energy to master it. Rose wondered what the words were like when the old woman held them in her mind. Did they carry their usual meaning, or any meaning at all? Were they like words in dreams or in the minds of young children, each one marvellous and distinct and alive as a new animal? This one limp and clear like a jellyfish, that one hard and mean and secretive like a horned snail. They could be austere and comical as top hats, or smooth and lively and flattering as ribbons. A parade of private visitors, not over yet.

Something woke Rose early the next morning. She was sleeping in the little porch, the only place in Flo's house where the smell was bearable. The sky was milky and brightening. The trees across the river — due to be cut down soon, to make room for a trailer park — were hunched against the dawn sky like shaggy dark animals, like buffalo. Rose had been dreaming. She had been having a dream obviously connected with her tour of the Home the day before.

Someone was taking her through a large building where there

were people in cages. Everything was dim and cobwebby at first, and Rose was protesting that this seemed a poor arrangement. But as she went on, the cages got larger and more elaborate, like enormous wicker bird cages, Victorian bird cages, fancifully shaped and decorated. Food was being offered to the people in the cages and Rose examined it, saw that it was choice: chocolate mousse, trifle, Black Forest cake. Then in one of the cages Rose spotted Flo, who was handsomely seated on a throne-like chair, spelling out words in a clear authoritative voice (what the words were Rose, wakening, could not remember) and looking pleased with herself for showing powers she had kept secret till now.

Rose listened to hear Flo breathing, stirring, in her rubble-lined room. She heard nothing. What if Flo had died? Suppose she had died at the very moment she was making her radiant, satisfied appearance in Rose's dream? Rose hurried out of bed, ran barefoot to Flo's room. The bed there was empty. She went into the kitchen and found Flo sitting at the table, dressed to go out, wearing the navy blue summer coat and matching turban hat she had worn to Brian's and Phoebe's wedding. The coat was rumpled and in need of cleaning, the turban was crooked.

"Now I'm ready to go," Flo said.

"Go where?"

"Out there," said Flo, jerking her head. "Out to the whattaya-callit. The Poorhouse."

"The Home," said Rose. "You don't have to go today."

"They hired you to take me, now you get a move on and take me," Flo said.

"I'm not hired. I'm Rose. I'll make you a cup of tea."

"You can make it. I won't drink it."

She made Rose think of a woman who had started in labor, such was her concentration, her determination, her urgency. Rose thought Flo felt her death moving in her like a child, getting ready to tear her. So she gave up arguing, she got dressed, hastily packed a bag for Flo, got her to the car and drove her out to the Home, but in the matter of Flo's quickly tearing and relieving death she was mistaken.

Some time before this, Rose had been in a play on national television. *The Trojan Women*. She had no lines, and in fact was in the play simply as a favor for a friend who had got a better part elsewhere. The director thought to liven all the weeping and mourning by having the Trojan women go bare-breasted. One breast apiece they showed, the right in the case of royal personages such as Hecuba and Helen, the left in the case of ordinary virgins or wives such as Rose. Rose didn't think herself enhanced by this exposure — she was getting on, after all, her bosom tended to flop — but she got used to the idea. She didn't count on the sensation they would create. She didn't think many people would be watching. She forgot about those parts of the country where people can't exercise their preference for quiz shows, police-car chases, American situation comedies, and are compelled to put up with talks on public affairs and tours of art galleries and ambitious offerings of drama. She did not think they would be so amazed, either, now that every magazine rack in every town was serving up slices and cutlets of bare flesh. How could such outrage fasten on the Trojan ladies' sad-eyed collection, puckered with cold then running with sweat under the lights, badly and chalkily made-up, all looking rather foolish without their mates, rather pitiful and unnatural, like tumors?

Flo took to pen and paper over that, forced her stiff swollen fingers, crippled almost out of use with arthritis, to write the word "shame." She wrote that if Rose's father had not been dead long ago he would now wish that he was. That was true. Rose read the letter, or part of it, out loud to some friends she was having for dinner. She read it for comic effect, and dramatic effect, to show the gulf that lay behind her, though she did realize, if she thought about it, that such a gulf was nothing special. Most of her friends, who seemed to her ordinarily hard-working, anxious and hopeful, could lay claim to being disowned or prayed for in some disappointed home.

Halfway through she had to stop reading. It wasn't that she thought how shabby it was to be exposing and making fun of Flo this way. She had done it often enough before; it was no news to her that it was shabby. What stopped her was, in fact, that gulf; she had a fresh and overwhelming realization of it, and it was nothing to laugh about. These reproaches of Flo's made as much sense as a protest about raising umbrellas, a warning against eating raisins. But they were painfully, truly, meant; they were all a hard life had to offer. Shame on a bare breast.

Another time Rose was getting an award. So were several other people. A reception was being held in a Toronto hotel. Flo had been sent an invitation, but Rose had never thought she would come. She had thought she should give someone's name when the organizers asked about relatives, and she could hardly name Brian and Phoebe. She had the idea her brother and his wife moved in a permanent cloud of disapproval of her. In Rose's presence Brian had said more than once that he had no use for people in her line of work. But he had no use for a good many people: actors, artists, journalists, rich people (he would never admit to being one himself), the entire arts faculty of universities. Whole classes and categories, down the drain. Of course it was possible that she did, secretly, want Flo to come, wanted to show Flo, intimidate her, finally remove herself from Flo's shade. That would be a natural thing to want to do.

Flo came down on the train, unannounced. She got to the hotel. She was arthritic then but still moving without a cane. She had always been decently, soberly, cheaply dressed, but now it seemed she had spent money and asked advice. She was wearing a mauve and purple checked pants suit, and beads like strings of white and yellow popcorn. Her hair was covered by a thick grey-blue wig, pulled low on her forehead like a woolen cap. From the vee of the jacket and its too-short sleeves her neck and wrists stuck out brown and warty as if covered with bark. When she saw Rose she stood still. She seemed to be waiting, not just for Rose to go over to her but for her feelings about the scene in front of her to crystallize. Soon they did.

"Look at the nigger!" said Flo in a loud voice before Rose was near her. Her tone was one of simple, gratified astonishment, as if she had been peering down the Grand Canyon or seen oranges growing on a tree.

She meant George, who was getting one of the awards. He turned to see if someone was feeding him a comic line. And Flo did look like a comic character, except that her bewilderment, her authenticity, were quite daunting. Did she note the stir she had caused? Possibly.

After that one outburst she clammed up, would not speak again except in the most grudging monosyllables, would not accept any food or drink offered her, would not sit down, but stood astonished and unflinching in the middle of that gathering of the bearded and beaded, the unisexual and the unshamedly un-

Anglo-Saxon, until it was time for her to be taken to her train and sent home.

Rose found that wig under the bed during the horrifying cleanup that followed Flo's removal. She took it out to the Home along with some clothes she had washed or had dry cleaned, and some stockings, talcum powder, cologne she had bought. Sometimes Flo seemed to think Rose was a doctor, and she said, "I don't want no woman doctor, you can just clear out." But when she saw Rose carrying the wig she said, "Rose! What is that you got in your hand, is it a dead grey squirrel?"

"No," said Rose. "It's a wig."

"What?"

"A wig," said Rose, and Flo began to laugh. Rose laughed too. The wig did look like a dead cat or squirrel, even though she had washed and brushed it; it was a disturbing-looking object.

"My God, Rose. I thought what is she doing bringing me a dead squirrel! If I put it on somebody's be sure to take a shot at me."

Rose stuck it on her own head to continue the comedy, and Flo laughed so that she rocked back and forth in her crib.

When she got her breath Flo said, "What am I doing with these damn sides up on my bed? Are you and Brian behaving yourselves? Don't fight, it gets on your father's nerves. Do you know how many gallstones they took out of me? Fifteen! One as big as a pullet's egg. I got them somewhere. I'm going to take them home." She pulled at the sheets, searching. "They were in a bottle."

"I've got them already," said Rose. "I took them home."

"Did you? Did you show your father?"

"Yes."

"Oh well, that's where they are then," said Flo, and she lay down and closed her eyes.

RUTH McLAUGHLIN

Seasons

(FROM CALIFORNIA QUARTERLY)

HE WAS TYPING a letter to his parents. Dear Mom: it said. His wife, Gail, was in the kitchen, it was raining. She was making medium loud sounds, cleaning out a cupboard or scouring a pan. The whole house smelled pregnant. A yeast, a slight decay, like the vitamins she took. He typed: a fallen womb. He retyped it: bomb, womb. He imagined his mother reading it, straining to read it at the mailbox on a slight rise in the prairie, a wind tore at the corners around where her fists framed it top and bottom. "Gail is what, what has happened . . ." the wind going to tear it away and pull it into the sky where it will disappear into holes she has not seen. He lined his typewriter carriage up on a faint *b*, to darken it; or, to place a *w* on top: behind it the shadow of a *b*, perhaps not clear but a suggestion of darkness and confusion and blood. Bomb, womb, he typed them both. He was no longer certain where terror lay, where a new birth began.

He stood on the concrete; a movement on the horizon became a car. He crossed to the island, clutching a letter; on both sides of him cars hurtled past. He stepped into the street; a car out of nowhere bore down on him, missed him by a breath, he felt it on his face, and was gone. He crossed to the mailbox. Looked down the street for as far as he could see, where it ended for him at the top of a hill. He stepped carefully off the sidewalk back into the street, walked toward home with care. Along the way dirt from a yard was piled against the sidewalk; something for someone had been broken or lost. He had not noticed, and his feet had slipped off the sidewalk, sunk into the dirt as easily as if taking root.

His mother wrote from Montana: how do you turn the soil for a garden. First, get the proper tools. Find the proper ground. Put your foot on the spade just behind the instep and press the spade into the earth to a depth of . . . no, believe me that a spade presses into the ground, dividing north from south, for example; earth boils over with a kind of smell, dark worms dig deeper, seasons change.

Their garden was small and shady. Sometimes, when Gail could not sleep, lay next to him on the bed hard and big and sweating like a melon, he rose to walk outside. There was no moon, the sky was deep and black. He walked carefully around the boundaries of the garden; the edges were straight with sharp corners he rounded as he walked. It was not yet planted: the earth was turned, it lay in broad uneven hills, shafts of straw here and there palely remembering the world this one had replaced.

Gail is doing what she pleases, he wrote. The garden is doing as well as it can. He lifted his hands from the typewriter to look at his garden through the window in front of him. Outside, the wind blew, plants moved slightly, but he heard nothing. Through the glass he was not certain what the plants he looked at were; from his distance they seemed a shifting fluid mass, like a body, an animal perhaps, moving along the boundaries of the garden.

At work the water cooler burst. It stood in the corner for as long as he could remember, like a patient dog or horse. It was about ten yards from his desk, in a corner between some file cabinets and the Xerox machine, making a little stall for it. He would get a drink of water from it every hour or so, using the tiny collapsible paper cup. You would hardly know it was alive, motionless, staring so blankly straight ahead as someone took a tiny drink. But sometimes, he could never calculate how often, it gave a kind of gulp or swallow, and all the water quivered. Then it seemed to be some one-celled animal, that you hardly know is alive it is so simple, it only moves once when it engulfs food, and when it expels it again. One morning it had burst. There were signs, it had been leaking. But nothing like this. Where the glass attached to the spigot, down where he couldn't see, something awful had happened and water rushed out, splattered like blood. Ran everywhere. There was so much water it covered the entire floor. People who thought the disaster was confined to one area were surprised to feel their shoes fill with blood. Wondering what had happened they would look down, it was only water, a broad sea of water had come under their desk, passed on as though it could not be stopped, filled the corners of the room. They were surprised: they mopped and mopped, thought they had it all up, but weeks later they still found tiny stagnant pools in odd corners, as though water sought some place, secret and dark, where it could start to form life, infinitely slow and almost unchanging; still, life would appear, would congeal in the water, make a brief movement all its own.

In eastern Montana, when it rains, it takes your breath away. It can be dry for months, the sun moves through the clear sky like a slow yawn, taking all day, returns again each day like it has forgotten something. The stalks of wheat that were green and moved fluid in the wind dry, turn white and rattle against each other. His mother stands on the front step and thinks of the children. One hand is balled into a fist in her apron pocket, holding her apron down against the wind. The other arm is flung onto her forehead as if in infinite sorrow, but she is shading her eyes to peer at the horizon. Far away beyond the blank of the wheat fields she sees something begin to move. It is grey and writhes. It is probably the dust of the mailman, but it could be the start of a cloud. She remembers when she had first come to Montana, it was just at the end of the war. The train had dropped her down from the mountains of the west coast onto the plains on the same day the bomb had fallen on Hiroshima. Weeks later, she had seen newsreels of it at the theater. That night, held in her new husband's arms, she had listened to her first thunderstorm in this new country; the sky crashed as though it would break and fall. She imagined the cows and horses in pasture beginning to move at the first sounds of thunder, pressing into a herd, running faster now for shelter . . . but there was no place to run to. There were no trees, no shelters, no mountains where the plain ended where one could lean against and wait it out. She learned later that though they knew there was no shelter they raced anyway, tried to escape, pressed on together in the dark barely sensing in time where they might stumble; leaving behind them all the space that was dangerous, moving into some promise that was slightly ahead of them.

If it rained early enough, the wheat would recover; if not the seeds fell into the ground, in their own tombs, which they would burst out of themselves the next spring. The next morning, there had been floods. She had not seen the differences in the land before, had not recognized the slight rises and dips, but water knew: flowed swiftly by them in a precise course, carrying things for them to watch, old wood and weeds, once a chicken. When it was over they had found a cow, lying on its side where there had been a pond for a few days, now disappeared. The cow, its belly bloated like the best meal it ever ate; its legs not curled but stuck stiffly in the air as though resisting.

Gail had always liked to cook. Since their marriage, four years ago, she had entered a recipe round robin. That meant you received a letter in the mail with a list of addresses; you made copies of a recipe and sent them to the last seven names on the list: you would get thousands in return. It was slow, because she had not yet got thousands; but they came: unexpectedly, pressed between a phone bill and a bank statement, a strange envelope with strange handwriting. Someone who has lived all her life in Oriole Point, Virginia, who has decided that she will join a round robin, that she will send in a recipe that is odd, but it is cheap and she has used it for years. She bravely writes: Mix 3 T cornstarch with 3 T oil . . .

Gail tried all the recipes, at least once. Some they could not eat. Someone in Illinois sent her directions for a dessert made of rutabagas. Someone must have stood outside as the sun set; listening, moving her nostrils slightly, trying to detect the disaster of frost. Something told her it would happen tonight: she gathered in the tomatoes, cucumbers, everything but the rutabagas. The tomatoes would lie under the bed in a box: some would ripen, redden and plump like an excited breast; others just like them would not, would shrivel in the dusty air heavy with the bed above. In the morning everything was gone: the vines were on the ground, and she could see past them the waste of the corral, deep pits where hooves had been, high barren mounds of manure. But the rutabagas survived. Held the horror of that night in their dumb, blind bodies; cooked, they lay on plates bitter and fouled. Someone, in Illinois, with a vision Gail could not imagine, someone out of her time, tried to make a dessert out of rutabagas. She had told her mother-in-law about it in a letter. The typewriter skipped; she wrote "imagine someone making a desert out of rutabagas."

She went to see her obstetrician monthly, then twice a month, and at the last weekly, to be measured and weighed and examined; her stomach like a globe. Everyone was drawn to it, doctors, nurses, placed all ten fingers on it, to hold the span of it in their hands, discovering by presses and probes what life lived here. She pulled on her clothes, left, explored; still it was only a ritual — like a map that was all ocean, there was no way for them to tell what land lay underneath; they could only guess at the secret changes beginning life. She had left the office unsteadily; she was eight and a half months' along. She must have taken a wrong door; every month she had gone out the right door, the one that took her to the main entrance that was only a step away from her car that would take her home. But she stepped out into a narrow hallway, dark, and she was not sure it smelled clean. It seemed to be deserted. She followed it along several turns. She knew she had never come down it before but it seemed familiar, even the turns she could anticipate. At the end it broke out into a green lush garden, grass growing thickly and cut close, beds of flowers sturdy and without weeds, the earth cultivated deeply around them. A kind of patio led to the garden, the sliding glass doors were open. She was drawn to it, she thought she could see a little bench beneath one of the trees. As she stepped towards the patio, slam! that whole world hit her in the face. She stepped back: the glass doors to the patio were closed. The baby in her stomach had been hit, too, and she felt nausea. Her face tingled as though she had been reached out and struck; she felt a slight bleeding from her nostrils. Behind the glass it was like another world that now she could not hope to reach. She watched it. She could not see any birds, the flowers and the grass grew, but there did not seem to be anything moving. As though it were an exhibit, or a model, or a world just outside this, waiting to replace it.

She finally found her way back through the hallway and out to her car. She pulled into the traffic, and felt herself begin to cry softly. Tears washed down her face, hung on her chin like raindrops before disappearing onto her stomach. She could not quit crying, each breath brought new moisture to the surface. The steering wheel pressed under her stomach; her stomach, the baby, resisting each movement of the wheel — she could swerve and hit the traffic island once, stabilize herself and be shaken — but the baby might lose the whole world. When she reached home, it was beginning to get dark; the grass beneath her feet was dark, and she could not make out individual plants or blades, she could tell you nothing about the grass — its color, how healthy it grew — it had lost all distinguishing features in the dark so that it was all grass, in pictures and in parks, wherever she had seen it all her life.

For Christmas he wanted to go home. Gail said no. She was already two months along. He looked at the map: Highway 80 lay like a long root between California and the northeastern corner of Montana, where he was born. The highway like a bindweed root he'd dug at in the garden as a kid; the root stretching in curves that spanned hundreds of miles, another branch reaching down into Colorado, New Mexico, into the gulf. He'd dug at the weeds in the garden till the dirt looked dark and clean, the hacked weeds lying limply along its edges. But underneath, the bindweed roots, making deep and secret links, beginning new life. His mother said there had been bindweed for as long as she could remember; they plowed the garden as deep as their biggest plow would go each spring, but it did no good. You could blast the garden; they never did, but he thought of it: the dirt would suddenly rear like an animal and only as it began its descent, a wave curling and falling, would he hear the huge boom. He might try to anticipate it, imagine it, the hugest sound of all, but it did no good. When it came it was more than he could imagine in his ears, a sound so complete that sound was filled and overflowed: so that it was not just sound, but sensation, something on his tongue and skin, and a feeling in the back of his mouth like a taste. Still the bindweed would live, would crawl to the surface a week later, the shoots white like shock against the bare earth. Instead they spent Christmas at their own home, the California rain rattling at their windows. In eastern Montana it would be silent; fresh snow an inch thick on everything: it seemed like overnight all the things familiar to them were destroyed and useless — the tools turned to something large and soft, so that only someone from another world could use them.

They had named their baby at Christmastime. They had thought to wait till he was born, that just by looking at him, he would somehow name itself. But by Christmastime they had waited two months, and they wanted to wait no more. They decided on Grace if it were a girl, but could not decide what to name it if it were a boy. She had said Justin, but he had argued that it did no good to pick out a name for a boy; he could not imagine what a boy named Justin would look like. In the end they drew names out of a hat — Christopher, Alexander, Gregory and Thrace — and rejected them all. They had sat dejected, their heads in their hands, facing their Christmas tree, growing more and more certain that their

baby would be a boy and unnameable. Gail tried to think of her
relatives: remembered tall, stiff men in suits, who had visited her
family in her childhood, dead now; she remembered her great-
uncle Isadore or Isaac, when he had died the relatives had stripped
the little room he lived in bare: She remembered boxes filled and
piled high at one side of the room; one had been full of letters. She
read one: "Dear Uncle," it read: "It is a devil of a time getting
something to grow in this country. It seems like you plant and then
before you know it the weather comes along and takes care of it
for you. We are all well. We wish you everything. It looks like it
won't be long and we will be seeing you." The letter was unsigned.
She had not been able to imagine why there was no name at the
bottom. The letter was written in a large masculine hand: when he
came to the signature was he suddenly rushed, or did a name seem
unnecessary.

He lay in bed beside his wife; there was something he wanted to
say. He lay with his arm encircling her; her head, turned away
from him, rested on his arm. Her breathing was becoming shal-
lower; she was nearly asleep, but there was something he wanted
to say. Their baby would be born sometime in the next two weeks.
What he had to say was something he had read somewhere, something so familiar it did not seem important. Oh, it had something
to do with pain. He imagined Gail would go through great pain to
have this baby. He was not even sure where he read it: he lay still,
his eyes searching out forms in the darkness that would give him
some clues. He was almost certain it was not in something that he
ordinarily read; not in a book or a good magazine, so that he read
it almost accidentally. What was it: Pain is a great equalizer. No, it
was something that Gail might want to hear. "Pain hates with a
passion that is profound." That was it, but he did not know why he
wanted Gail to hear it. She lay on his arm sleeping. Her belly under
her white nightgown taut and rounded; so that her form looked
like a mound of snow; of the kind he might find in the spring in
Montana: when the prairie was almost dry and new grass blew
busily in the wind, he might find hidden somewhere, under an
embankment where the sun did not yet reach, a sprawl of snow
such as this, silent and white; on the surface it looked like any
snow, yet he knew it was leaking, dying, water drawing into the
earth, finding tiny narrow chasms just for it to flow. Once as a child
he had been under the snow: the drifts that winter were so huge

he had dug tunnels. He remembered he had carefully planned turns and curves, but coming upon them again with no landmarks, the turns had always surprised him. The springtime had destroyed the tunnels, filling with water the dips inside that his knees had worn smooth. The melting soaked and chilled him; the warmer weather making him colder than he'd been all winter.

The night Gail had gone to the hospital they had had potato soup for supper. Potatoes from their own garden. She had made it carefully from scratch, brought it to the table in a steaming bowl, a teaspoon of pale butter in the center, sinking and disappearing. At the last minute Gail had not been able to eat. As far as she knew she was not ready to go to the hospital, but she could not eat any potato soup; it smelled funny, she said, as though something had gone bad. Outside, the garden was full of little craters where potato plants had been. It was a good year; the potatoes fat and heavy like cows, leaving large holes: some of the holes they had tried to cover in with dirt, but they'd sunk. She had left him to go to the bedroom. It was an odd, still night. Rain was predicted. He finished his soup and walked outdoors. He stood on his front porch and looked down the street. Back of him was the dark back yard and the garden he had worked in all day. He heard traffic from a long way off; sometimes seeing a car's light before he heard it; their lights a vague brightness on the other side of the hill, like a sun about to rise. The cars seemed to come slower now, or maybe the dark played tricks. A car creeping down the hill with a kind of shyness, a hesitation as though lost. One car, a dark and sleek one, had traveled particularly slowly down the hill, it was all alone on the street. It nearly stopped several times, then sped up again, weaving slightly, the lights reflecting off the mass of dark gleaming trees along the sidewalk. He had watched it, unable to move, feeling danger and anger; then it had pulled up right alongside him and stopped: It was not a stranger at all, it was a man who had visited next door for as long as they had lived in the neighborhood; a man, he could almost feel, that he had known all his life.

As he stands, it begins to rain softly. A drop strikes his face and is warm as a tear. Soon it comes faster, so that he can no longer count. He thinks of his garden behind him, the rain disappearing in the dark, soft earth. From the house, Gail cries out. Rain, he hears her say, it is raining. Pain, she cries. He finds her in the kitchen, one hand wrapped around a large spoon as if in defense.

She clutches the counter with one hand; she has a fearful stricken look and he does not dare go near her; it is like an animal trapped: everything is changed, it may be dangerous, it may act like it has never acted before. He goes around the table to get by her; upstairs finds on the bed her overnight bag. When he comes down she is gone; he imagines she is in the bathroom. He goes out to the street to find his car.

She stands in the pantry, clutching the shelves, looking at the food she has canned from the garden. It is so narrow she can hardly turn around; food waits on shelves on either side of her. It has always been dark in the pantry, now it seems light enough that she imagines she can see what is in the jars. In the corner of one of the shelves there is something damp; she imagines one of the jars has begun to leak. She feels tears in her eyes, run down her face; she holds on to a shelf that is as high as her chin; she feels like a child about to leave everything she has loved. Her stomach protrudes hugely, almost rests on a shelf; she knows she is getting dirty. Outside the car honks once, twice; at first it is a sound she cannot place, tries to imagine an animal the size and shape that would make that sound. She hears the motor race like a warning. She feels her way along the shelves out the door of the pantry, imagines the fingerprints she leaves in the dust.

He still believes the traffic is lighter than usual. Travels along the street at a faster and more dangerous speed than usual; the rain has turned the street dark and gleaming, the reflection of the streetlights white vague spots in front of him. Travels in the fastest inside lane, close to the island, sees out of the corner of his eye Gail pull back and away from him as he changes to the inside lane. She has said little. Stares out the window at the scenery going by; the trees are a dark blur on either side of them.

He turns into the hospital complex; the hospital huge and white, set back from the road, lit outside and in, emerging from the dark like an island. The roads are confused; they branch off. He thinks he has found the right one and it branches off again; finally only one road leads to the emergency entrance. When he has parked, someone rushes out to help Gail into a wheelchair. He sits in the car for a moment; Gail is disappearing ahead of him like a blur. He feels hungry; remembers with an ache of pleasure the potato soup he had for supper. Enters the hospital, follows the long corridors to find the cafeteria; he does not ask but searches it out like an animal might, makes sudden unthinking decisions to turn, and finds it at the end of a short hallway that has opened abruptly off another. He sits down at a table; he seems to be the only one there. He has nothing on the table in front of him; an empty coffee cup upside down, white and gleaming is in front of him. Across the room he hears a sudden loud noise: behind a serving counter is a woman leaning and laboring over something, holding something with her left hand, her right arm making large circular motions; she is scrubbing a huge pot, or she is working with all her might to pull something up from a sink or where it is trying to go down.

He has forgotten he is hungry, he thinks to notify his mother. At his hand is a large paper napkin. He finds his pen, clicks it to a point, holds it above the napkin for a moment. Drops his hand onto the soft white surface. Dear Mother, he writes. We are in difficult times. He wanted to cross it out, instead he continued: There is no way of knowing right now just how things are going to turn out with the baby. Gail is upstairs and I haven't seen her. Well, I am hoping everything will turn out okay, and I will get in touch with you as soon as I know anything. He unclicked his pen, fastened it to the edge of his pocket. Folded the napkin carefully, placed it in his breast pocket; only realized then that time had been lost to him, that mailing a letter to his mother would take days, and the baby would be here in hours.

His mother stands on the front step. She is thinking it will soon be time for the mailman. The sky is blank and it will be another hot day. She can see some of the garden has dried up without rain, the plants disappeared to the ground, the ground crazed by cracks, so that it is no longer solid ground, but pieces isolated, islanded by the deep, dark crevices. She hears a rumble; she doesn't know where it came from, it may even have been in her stomach, she has not yet eaten. She looks off across the fields, raises her arm and it falls back to her forehead, shades her eyes. Sees something familiar forming on the horizon.

ROBLEY WILSON, JR.

Living Alone

(FROM FICTION INTERNATIONAL)

THE CAT came home around midnight. I knew he'd been at the lumber yard again; he'd arranged some of those squiggly pine shavings around his head, trying to look like an African lion with a mane. It wasn't a very good mane. He's a black cat.

"What is it with you?" I said to him. "You look like a chimpanzee trying out for Goldilocks."

He shook himself — the shavings dropping to the floor and the rest of the movement shivering down his back and out to the tip of his tail.

"Get to bed," I told him. "Cut the funny stuff."

But at three a.m. he woke me. I was a mile deep in a dream about cows — miles and miles of cows on a green-brown meadow that stretched as far as the sea — when I felt his eyes. I snapped awake. His eyes were ocean green and big as the moon.

"What is it?" I said.

His eyes closed. I got up in the dark and let him out.

It is impossible not to be fond of him — his posturing, his imagined *éclat*, his gall.

One day just before dinner I watched him making his way home from across the street. He was proceeding backwards when I first noticed him, an enormous — half-again longer than himself — brown pheasant in tow. He had the pheasant's neck, that black ring with the greenness shimmering against the setting sunlight, in his jaws, and he was dragging and dragging. Every two or three feet he was obliged to stop, to rest. Once or twice he tried a different way — a way one might think to be "instinctive" — and straddled the dead bird; then he clamped his jaws at the neck and tried to walk, the carcass between his legs making him waddle and trip. Panther. Leopard. If there had been a low tree he would have climbed it, carrying this prey.

Of course it wouldn't work. The pheasant — male, beautiful, huge — defeated him. So backwards it was, graceless and clumsy.

He got it to the foot of the porch steps and left it there — for me to dispose of.

It turns out the pheasant blundered into town and flew against a neighbor's garage, breaking its own neck. It is a found object.

Later I tell the cat he ought to be ashamed, for faking it.

After breakfast, when I opened the screen door and brought in the milk, here was a dead rabbit — torn open, its fur scattered at the foot of the steps — and on the porch as many as a dozen pink fetuses, rabbits unborn, no one of them any larger than one joint of my thumb and seeming oddly as if made of human flesh. I had to turn away.

"Look," I said to the cat, "didn't you ever hear of propriety?"

He was lying on the porch rail, his front paws folded into his chest, a mandarin in a black silk robe. Now his eyes were yellowed, and he opened them only wide enough to show two arrogant slits of light leading back into perfect serenity.

"Oh, go to hell," I said to him.

I cleaned up the rabbit debris and hid it all in the garbage can. I know how he does it, have watched him more than once run down a surprised animal and break its neck. Death is sudden and soft.

My lord, I feed him all day long. Why does he do it? Kill.

Once a dog came into the yard — a boxer, large and tan and big-boned, carrying with it a kind of awesome muscular discipline. The cat was asleep under the yews.

Afterward, no one could explain it or provide a chronology, but when I looked out the door I saw that the boxer had the head of the cat in its jaws, and I saw it whip the cat — as one whips a rope to free it from a stump or a stone — and release him through the vivid air until he struck the base of the birch tree.

I ran out screaming, cursing. It was four weeks before the cat was physically recovered.

Naturally I had tried more than once to explain to him about dogs — how they really couldn't help their clumsiness, how it was just the way they were made, heavy-pawed and uncoordinated and victims of poor judgment. I told him dogs didn't see as well as cats, that they were color-blind and either near- or far-sighted — I couldn't remember which. I said it wasn't their fault they smelled funny when they were wet; I said it had to do with the chemistry of their fur. I admitted dogs had this *thing* about cats, but I reminded him of his *thing* for mice and sparrows. I told him he should keep his eyes peeled, that no self-respecting cat ever actually got caught by a big clumsy dog, and I said I imagined dogs were jealous of cats anyway, because cats had rough, useful tongues — nice for drinking and washing — while dogs had this oversized floppy thing good for not much more than simple-minded drooling on hot days. I told him What the hell, live and let live and keep your head tucked in.

One Sunday afternoon I fell asleep on the sofa under the window, dreaming. I dreamed of the blue ocean and an applause of dolphins over the white-seamed waves. I floated and arched. We played follow-the-leader; it was my turn to break into the clear sky, to fall out of the light. I splashed, I sank.

When I woke up, the cat was sprawled on my chest, his claws out to pierce my skin, then drawn in, then out to hurt, then in.

He can't bear me to be asleep if he is awake.

He can be almost tragic. One night a storm rolled over us at two in the morning — a horror, with near lightning and torrents of rain. I got out of bed and came to the front door; usually when I turn on the porch light he appears from under the yews or the junipers and streaks inside. This time the power was off. I opened the door into the darkness and whistled, lightning flashing all over, everything in the neighborhood suddenly coming into being and then, like magic, vanishing. No trace of him.

I lay awake, listening to the rain. Then I *knew* — perhaps the clock on the dresser had started its hum — knew the power was back on. I went downstairs and flicked on the porch light. When I opened the door the cat shot past me, drenched, his wet fur soaking my pajama leg.

The storm went on for another hour; there was nothing for it but to let him crawl under the covers with me, even though the

sheet and mattress pad got wet and I knew I'd have to change the
bed a week early.

One morning he didn't come home. The remains of a robin
were on the step — entrails and feathers strewn along the walk —
so I knew he'd been around earlier. Sometimes he stays out past
noon, if the hunting is good.

This time he didn't come home all day. I called him; never a
response. By dinnertime I'd resigned myself to this being one of
the long holidays he allows himself every so often. But I looked
out three or four times during the evening. No sign.

By the next day I was getting worried. When I went for groceries
that afternoon I saw the carcass of a black cat in the gutter. *Dear
God,* I thought. But when I looked closely — turned it over with
my foot — I saw it was wearing a red flea collar. Something for
someone else's trash can. A crazy coincidence. A relief.

You know how it is when you're worried. I wasted the rest of the
day, prowled around the house, cleaned up dishes I hadn't washed
since yesterday's breakfast. I did a little reading, watched television
for an hour or so.

On the third day I phoned my wife.

"Listen," I said to her, "he isn't home, and I'm starting to get
worried."

"Who isn't home?" she said. The phone had rung five or six
times; she sounded as if I'd waked her up.

"The cat," I said. "He's been gone — this is the third day."

"Oh, God, that damned screwy cat," she said.

"It's not like him."

"He's a cat. Everything's not like him."

"But what do you think?"

"Is this a serious phone call?" she said. "Are you honestly and
seriously asking me to *do* something about your cat?"

"Could you come over and help me look for him?"

"No."

"Really, please? He always used to come when you called for
him. You had that funny little whistle I can't do. Maybe he'd show
up if he heard that whistle again."

"He came because I fed him," she said. "He knew when he heard
that whistle that there was food in his dish; it wasn't that we had

this great rapport. Besides, it's been two years since I've called him."

"He'd remember you."

"Don't you feed him now?" I could hear her lighting a cigarette.

"Naturally I feed him."

"Then he wouldn't remember me. Cats remember what they *need* to remember; they don't clutter up their heads with extraneous and obsolete stuff. They aren't *people*, you know."

"You're getting impatient," I said.

"Of course I am. I'm busy. I have a life to lead."

"It's just that I think he might have gotten hurt. He had a run-in with a boxer not too long ago —"

"Look," she said. "Don't worry so much. Cats always come home. Always. It's what makes them spooky."

"I hope so," I said.

"Is that all you called about?" she said.

"Yes."

"Then I'm going to hang up now."

"All right."

"I'm hanging up. Goodbye."

"Goodbye."

"Please don't bother me about the cat. I'm hanging up."

We both hung up.

I stayed up late to write a letter. Around one in the morning — this was the beginning of the fourth day! — I heard him under the living room window.

I went to the front door, ready to be furious. He slunk in past me, looking wretched. His fur was matted, there was a glisten of dark blood behind one ear, bits and pieces of juniper twigs were caught all over his bedraggled coat. I knelt down and stroked him under the jaw.

"My God," I said, "you had me terrified. When are you ever going to stop all this and settle down?"

MARY HEDIN

The Middle Place

(FROM SOUTHWEST REVIEW)

THE TAN THERMOS is filled with iced tea and the battered green
gallon-sized thermos jug with cool tap water. Victoria carries them,
her straw sunhat, two terrycloth towels, and a bar of soap down to
the car, where Aaron is putting his tools in the trunk. As they drive
past the Ross Valley Savings and Loan, the electronic sign on the
building's face flashes 98°, 12:03 P.M. Yes, the middle of the day.
August. Hot. It is Aaron's "afternoon off," and they are going to
the vineyard.

On Highway 101 the concrete lanes shimmer under sheaths of
light. Flashes of chrome from speeding cars dart against the eye.
Air flowing through the open windows is warm, dry, dusty.

Aaron drives intently, his head thrust forward a little, his shoulders moving with the rhythms of long curves. He likes to drive. His
square strong hands hold the steering wheel firmly. His face appears both attentive and relaxed. But, of course, Aaron likes all
doing and demands of himself that he do all things well. He is so
easily graceful, it seems, having no awkwardness of body. And no
inefficiencies of mind, either, Victoria believes, perhaps because he
gives precise concentration to whatever task or problem faces
him.

A sigh drifts from her. She shifts a little on the sticky plastic
passenger's seat. She has always envied Aaron a little. She is erratic,
absent-minded, her head doing one thing, her hands another. And
so she falls into foolish error. Just this morning she had turned the
stove on high, intending a quick cup of coffee. Then she had gone
out to water the potted plants on the patio. Only when the dark
stench of burning dregs tainted the outside air did she remember.

She had burned the pot! Of course she irritates him, though he is accustomed to her.

She is just home after four months in England, where her daughter Elise has borne their first grandchild. And while there, she decided to travel the continent, see everything she could. Now, though they have been married forever, and Aaron was well cared for in her absence, she feels she has been gone too long. For the one traveling, time goes too fast, but for the one at home, it absurdly lengthens. Victoria feels a strangeness in Aaron, a growth of something new which she cannot identify. Of course, in new situations persons shove out newnesses, unobserved and unattended sproutings, that when discovered startle even themselves. And hasn't she also sent out strange tendrils, traveling alone, stretching herself, or restraining, to accommodate foreign ways? Yes, the four months apart have pushed them into difference, and Victoria watches Aaron, listens intently to what he says, studying him, trying to perceive how he is changed. She observes a darkness in his look, a shadow lying under his familiar broad smile. What unshared thought lies beyond his words? What does the change portend?

It has been a beautiful summer, he has said. *A perfect summer.* It is a statement he repeats, not realizing, she sees, that repetitiveness. He seems to be explaining something, or offering excuse. But the summer seems to her like all other California summers. The days since her return have been, like this one, identically clear of sky, warm of mornings, hot of afternoons. Each evening comes with suddenness and is cooled by the breath of fog sifting over the tanned hilltops. Yes, California summers are always equable — long, pleasant, and predictable. What then, in all this, is *especially* beautiful? What is the particular perfection Aaron marvels at?

She looks at the passing land, the tan flanks of long high hills. The grasses are dry now and the slopes no longer golden, but dun-colored, almost gray. The runnings of live oak in the folds of land look tarnished. In the brilliant sun the green crowns blackened by the deep shadow lying under leaf. This is not fertile land they are driving through, range country, and the scattered cows droop in the trees' aprons of shade.

Beautiful? England had been lush with summer green, the fields flowery and fruitful, the summer skies dappled with billowy cloud.

Ripeness, rich growing, summer bounty, blue and green, moist and fragrant. Yes, that was beautiful. But this, this time of long dusty sameness, the perennial stasis of California days — can this be called beautiful?

The car is slowing. On either side of the highway, orange and yellow machines roll along the great hills, moving in their toothed scoops great mounds of earth. The cut slopes are ragged with stone and dry soil. Clouds of dust rise from the machines' heavy treads, fly out in sheets with the hot wind. Aaron closes his window, Victoria hers. They stifle in the small closed space, and the construction project forces them to drive slowly.

Bernie found leafhoppers last week, Aaron is reporting. *He thinks we'll have to spray.*

Bernie is the farmer who tends the vineyard. He is a vigorous, positive man, but long experience gives his robust enthusiasm a cast of wisdom. Victoria wipes the sweat from her forehead, asks, *What are leafhoppers?*

As Aaron talks, she watches for clues, extends intuitions. Something deep in Aaron's primitive self, something unknown to him in his earlier years, comes with great joy to the tending of his land. A nature lover herself, she does not find it hard to pleasure in his weekly trips north to the small vineyard: the hour's drive through this countryside, the spread of prune orchards in the valley flatlands, the small cattle ranches in the sparser soiled, partially wooded hill-lands, the apple groves near Petaluma, the charming acres of orderly vineyards around Healdsburg. Yes, all these delight her, ring the closed circle of her daily living with a fine earthy connection. And she likes working in the vineyard with Aaron, tying vines to stakes and wires, pruning suckers from the ropy stalks, pulling the wiry tenacious morning-glory weeds from the powdery earth, exchanging slow talk as they move down the rows of fruit, sharing silence under a cover of nature's quietness. But she knows the vineyard does not signify to her what it does to Aaron. For her the connection is a loved finery; for him it is a root thrusting more deeply than he had known it would, "feeding" the very center of his existence. Yes, for him, it is a connection to a life source. The artery, the heartbeat, yes.

Where the large green highway sign reads DRY CREEK ROAD, Aaron takes the off-ramp, drives under the overpass and then along the two-lane macadam road bordered by small houses with fenced ungardened yards. Beyond the last pasty pink house he makes a sudden turn left and bumps along the unpaved roadway to the field's gate. Aaron stops, sets the brake, slides out. His faded blue workshirt sticks damply to his back. He pulls the key from his jeans pocket, opens the rusty lock, swings wide the long gate. He returns and drives through to the edge of the field.

Hot, Victoria murmurs. *It's going to be terribly hot.*

Wear your hat, Aaron cautions.

She climbs out, settles the cheap Mexican straw hat on her head. She stands in layers of heat, feeling suddenly and strangely small. The vineyard lies before her, the vines, Johannesburger Riesling, hanging voluptuously from the wires, their broad, flat, hand-shaped green leaves coated with a thin film of dust. The green looks slightly reddened under that dusting of earth, as if slowly rusting. Set precisely eight feet apart, the vines stretch in straight, green rows, and from where she stands at this end, it seems that the rows close together at the far end, making a great scalloped Oriental fan.

In the near rows Victoria sees the thickly crowded grapes hanging in pendant clusters under the shelter of leaves. They are silvery green, each globe round and tight, the skin's sheen milky and luminescent, like opals. On the left side of the narrow roadway, the neighbor's fields are also heaped with leaf and fruit. Those vines are spur-pruned, without wires, and at this time of year they seem a wild tangle of untended growth. To the eye moving the distances of the field, they look like round green huts crammed close together, hundreds of them, no space visible between one green hump and another. Victoria crosses the road, leans close to examine the grapes. These clusters of Pinot Noir are blue, a pearly deep sapphire blue, and they smell of sun and sweetness and must. She reaches out, pulls one perfect blue globe from its stem, puts it in her mouth. It lies warm and smooth on her tongue. When she crushes it between her front teeth, the liquid spurts out tart blue and sourly sweet. She shivers, grins.

Aaron has opened the trunk of the car and is hooking to his belt the yellow plastic pail which contains a pumpkin-sized ball of thick yellow twine. He pushes over his thumb a metal ring with a small protruding blade, a miniature scimitar. Victoria particularly delights in this small, fifty-cent tool, designed to meet so special a need: freeing the hands to hold vine and string while a motion of the ringed thumb cuts the needed length. Aaron lifts his shovel to his shoulder and moves along the edge of the field to a center row. He enters the green-edged aisle. Victoria follows after him, simply observing. It is so long since she has been here! She missed all the spring, the flowering of the valley's prune trees, the burgeoning of the lifeless-looking crooked vines, the first miraculous growth!

It's a good set. Aaron lifts a leafy branch to demonstrate. *It should be a good crop.*

Yes, there is so much fruit that the strong vines are strained to bear it. Aaron bends to chop a sucker from the base of one thick woody trunk, rises to tie a wind-loosened branch. Victoria watches his hands: the motions of winding the cord twice around branch and wire, the loopings for the knotting, are perfectly precise, without waste. Boy Scout, Navy man, surgeon. Order, deftness, economy, control. Gardener now, scrupulous farmer, he works with the vines with as much absorption and skill as he brings to a medical problem. Victoria laughs at him, admiring his absurd industry, loving him. But she continues to stroll the aisle like a tourist, makes no pretense of working.

Grapes! She remembers blue heaps in a blond wooden basket, a crimson border around its edge, a wire handle for carrying. Bought at the Farmers' Market Saturday morning, cool and dewy. Her tall father. Her mother ambling in slow pleasure along wooden platforms heaped with bushel baskets and crate boxes of corn and beans, tomatoes and apples, potatoes, and, yes, grapes. Overalled, sunburned Minnesota farmers, tightmouthed with shyness, eyes evasive with fear, their short-sleeved shirts showing the odd whiteness of their arms, making them seem peculiarly vulnerable. The 1930s. Those grapes in that place were purple, deeply fragrant, all you wanted to eat. The grapes slithering under the teeth, released from their thick, papery skins, the green-seeded pulp still round and whole. Tiny seeds spit out. Grapes crushed under the potato masher, hung in an old, thin flour sack to drip their red (how do purple skin and green fruit make *red*?) juice into the blue and white enameled pan. The boiling jelly, thick, lilac colored, chuckling hotly to the deep pot's very rim. The steaming glasses, wax whitening over the darkening sweet.

But these: Johannesburger Riesling and Pinot Chardonnay, wine grapes, will hang on the tough, sunbattered vines another two months, Bernie and Aaron checking the acid and sugar content, watching the ripening for the finest moment. Then amiable Mexican farm workers will move along the rows plucking the heavy clusters, carrying their boxfuls to the waiting bins. The bins will be lifted on the fork, the grapes dumped by the ton into the gondolas of large trucks and taken at dusk to the winery, where they will be crushed through large rolling cylinders, pumped into vats, coopered, and later bottled . . . the fermented fruit. Differences, yes. California and Minnesota, childhood and now.

How long ago. How far she has come. How changed. That child she remembered, who now seems in Victoria's mind innocent enough to pity, who read the Bobbsey Twins books and wept that she could not see oceans — could that child have dreamed that she would become a middle-aged woman walking a summer vineyard in California? Ah, no. What child ever imagines middle age or the ordinary lot that will be his?

Aaron has checked the thermometer hung from a stake. He reports that it reads 104°. He is pleased. The heat will raise the sugar content. He works now without his shirt, hatless. His body is lean and muscular and the skin browned by such hours in the sun. He is dark as any farm worker. He is extremely fit. *Fifty-five, I am fifty-five*, he has said several times since she arrived home. She thinks how he says those words. Is he teaching himself, trying to overcome disbelief? Or disappointment? How is she to interpret his low, tense tone?

It's taken me twenty years, he said last week, *to really love California. But how I love this place now!*

Twenty years? Twenty years to learn love of this place? And even then Victoria heard the timbre of sorrow in his voice, as if what he declared a gain robbed him of something. And had he been, then, discontent those long twenty years? He had never said so. Of course, California was not his home, and his family, unlike hers, was far away. Yet he had often declared that he could not live in his small hometown of terrible weathers and provincial interests. He needed freedom, newness, and change, the larger pond.

But now his avoval of finally achieved contentment throws all into question. And Victoria finds herself guilty and puzzled and a bit estranged. How much has he disguised, this willfully cheerful, practical, disciplined man? And has the disguise been kept up to benefit her? Has he secretly sacrificed for that, for what he believes she needs? But if that is so, she has not been allowed to perceive his sacrifices, nor to refuse them. And where was the justice in that?

How many desires bloom in his secret head which he weeds out from fantasy, even from dream? In the early hours of the night, when he sleeps most soundly and she lies awake, she hears him laugh, often, in his dreams. In the morning, curious because her dreams most often give life to her fears, she asks, *What did you dream last night?* He pauses in his reading of the news, frowns, but is not interested. He cannot remember. And he is honest; he does not recall. Why does he turn away from such knowledge? Even on those rare nights when he mutters aloud, begins to thrash, struggling in nightmare against some immense dream force, and she wakens him, crying, *What is it, Aaron? What is the matter?* Even at that moment he cannot recall his dream. Only the shake of breath and the beat of heart mark the edited message of the dark.

Love, Victoria thinks, stooping to drag up the long involved root of a morning-glory weed, ripping open the shallow skin of dry earth. Love becomes so complex. Suddenly she knows that she now pities this accomplished man, her husband. Pity? Yes, though it surprises her, it is pity that is shooting new growth out of the tough stalk of her love.

Why should *she* pity *him*? *He* is better in human exchange than she. He is more knowledgeable about the demands of living than she. He does more of import in the world, and governs more of it, than she. It is he who is needed by many people and also deeply loved. Why *should* she pity him?

Victoria tugs at other flat, gray persistent weeds, chastises her judgment. It does not shift. She is hot. Sweat drips from nose and chin, smarts in her eyes. She stands straight, hands on hips. She looks at Aaron, unpausing in his work under the blaring sun. He is far ahead of her now, pruning, tying, inspecting. It seems that from the act of work he takes in energy, rather than expends it. His vitality is everyone's marvel.

She thinks of his life: out of the house at seven A.M., home again at seven P.M., patients filling all the hours of his day; calls in the middle of the night from people who have been sick three days and choose to demand help — penicillin or flu shots, Nembutol or antihistamines — then, at that sleep-robbing time; the friends who dash over on Sundays for a quick, friendly consultation; the cranky aged, the anxious careless teen-aged girls, the impudent aggressive young jocks. Everything they put on him, he accepts. He refuses anger or impatience. For years it has seemed that he gains strength from the burdens the desperately ill or neurotic place on him. The paradoxes of getting and spending.

Yes, he has been strong, stronger than she, surely, stronger than most. Of course, gray hairs thread through the dark brown now, and the laughlines in his cheeks are permanent creases. But still it seems he will never tire. He continues the rhythm of work, the stride, bend, smooth rise. Clippers drawn, used, returned to his belt, a lean downward to lift a heavy sagging branch, a pull of twine, the neat tie: oh, he is full of grace and vitality. No, pity is out of place.

I am fifty-five, he has said, with sorrow. She laughs a little, appreciating absurdity.

Aaron, she calls out. *Would you like some tea?*

Great! he calls back and moves without pause to the next vine.

She walks the long way back to the car, conscious of the damp film all over her body. She gets the thermos of iced tea and returns. He stops when she reaches him, straightens, waits as she pours the amber liquid into the clumsy wide plastic cup. He has pulled the blue handkerchief from his pocket, wipes his wet face. He pulls off a glove, takes the cup, drains it without pause. He stops, grins, and she fills his cup again. He stands sipping, his eyes roaming the vineyard, lifting to the ringing hills. She perceives that his happiness is whole, without qualification. *It's beautiful here, isn't it, Tory?* he comments. *Look how the burn is almost grown over.* Yes, the hills were blackened last summer under a sweeping weeklong fire. But now the burned areas show a green scrub, and the eye must take special care to discern the blackened tree trunks thrusting upward in the green. *But it's coming again,* she says. *The dangerous season.*

She has always hated the threat of September and October. The dry earth crackles under the heat of the day and the cool of night. Over all the California hills, the dry grasses invite flame. In their town sirens ride the air daily, riding also the paths of wary nerves. Grass fires. Children playing. Spontaneous combustions. The rich, fruity, lush, dry, terrifying autumn. While the great valleys give up their grains and fruits, supplying the world from that richness, the mountains burn, the hills sear. Bounty and danger, hand in hand.

Paradox. Yes, we teeter on such razors' edges, chance, autumn, September, October. Still, it is only August.

We need a long, hot fall, Aaron says. *The sugar won't be up until October.* He hands her the empty cup, stretches, pulls his glove back on. *If it doesn't rain, we'll have a tremendous crop.* He begins again the bend and rise of his labor.

Victoria finishes her cup of tea. She decides to leave the thermos there beside a stake and pick it up on her way back. She leans down to set it in place. A momentary darkness flickers over her, a blink in the eye of the sun. She looks up. A falcon is taking the wind on spread wings, the wing-fingers distinct as printing against the blue. She watches its flight, the elegant veering, the sudden spring upward, the swift slide away toward the hills. And then, as if taking up a waning theme, a rabbit leaps over the field, small, gray, swift. Its ears are peaked, the hind legs pump a strong rhythm. It stops momentarily, looks back at her with wide eyes. Tenderness for the creatures' beauty springs up in her. But it is the rabbit, is it not, that commands pity, not the falcon? In any parable what pity is offered the strong, the untrammeled, the self-reliant?

She pulls weeds and ties vines, then, until she feels herself slowing with heat and tiredness. Far ahead of her, Aaron shows no sign of stopping. She pulls the hat from her head. Her skull is damp, her hair flat and wet against it. She runs her fingers through the wet strands, lifts them out to the drying air. She decides to stop, to wait for Aaron in the shade of the prune orchard to the west of the vineyard. There are old fruitboxes there. She will, as she has done before, set one of them against a tree trunk and rest till Aaron is ready to leave.

She has not brought a book or even a notebook. She will be idle then, letting sensation and thought move in will-less motions. Inexplicably, in the midst of the grove of tended prune trees, stands one old apple tree, twisted, unpruned, obviously too old for fine bearing. Nothing is done for it. But it still bears not altogether perfect but abundant fruit. The apples are ripening; some have already fallen. They lie on the earth, their redness growing golden and the soft bruises of their fall turning a mushy brown. The opulent lush fragrance of their ripeness mingles with the tang of those still green. She sits under the umbrella of green, gazing sometimes up through the cage of leaf, sometimes over the patterned fields fanning in all directions. She feels an immense stillness under the circular roofing. The winy air stirs with the beginning afternoon wind. The small motions of leaves cast wavering shades through the lemon light. Thrumming bees spin around the fallen, decaying fruit, their wings a dazzling blur. Such calm, such stasis: Victoria feels what has been coming to her the entire day. She is in the center, the middle place. Far from beginning, far from early ambitions and angers and desires, here there is no great threat, no awesome demand, only this nowness, this halt in moving, this balance. Sitting there, she understands her completeness and is happy. This is not ecstasy: this time in her life has neither such height nor such swiftness. But it is the fruit, ripened, guarded over through long early seasons, fruit grown full, round, ready. Has she not waited for such a time all her life, a time when she would say, *This is it, I am happy, I want nothing more?* Has she not nurtured her days to grow into this most perfect time? Smiling, she envisions herself: a woman of middle years under an old gnarled apple tree in the middle of ripe fields in the middle of a summer day, happy, contented — in the center, the heart of being.

The vine shadows grow long to the east of their stakes. The wind begins to pull strongly across the valley. Swallows fly in great numbers along the creek, over the fields. It is growing late. She sees Aaron making his way back to the car, still tending plants as he walks along the row. She watches him a little while, thinks of the falcon's shadow over her surprised face, thinks of the darkness in his eye, the shade behind his smile. The air is cooler now, and gooseflesh briefly runs along her arms. She rises, dusts off her hat and puts it on. She gathers a few apples, making the tails of her shirt into a bag for them. She enters again the golden sunlight and walks slowly toward the car.

Then in the dusty tan furrow at her feet a small object catches her eye. Curious, she leans over, sees that the thin, wee gray thing is an animal. A mouse? A field mouse. Stiff, two inches long, sundried, a mummy.

She leans down and takes one curled paw between thumb and forefinger, plucks up the corpse, looks at it closely. The large wee ear, closed delicate eye, wiry stiff brown tail. How tiny, how perfect. A week or two old, perhaps, just lying there, shriveled in the brutal sun. How had it died? Attacked? Poisoned? Or simply inadequate, too weak to survive? The baby mouse mesmerizes her. She feels peculiar grief and almost she cannot let it go.

Then Aaron whistles, and she sees that he is standing beside the car, beating dust from his jeans. She recalls the thermos. She still must pick it up. She lets drop the compelling insignificant corpse, moves quickly over the hillocks of earth between the rows of vines, retrieves the thermos, and hurries to the car. Aaron has stored his twine and tools in the trunk. She offers him the last of the tea, tepid now, but wet.

We'll stop for a beer, Aaron says, *I want the newspaper anyway.* They buy the beer and the paper at the cluttered roadside market and then agree to stop by the river. Already it is six-thirty and the chain is across the parking lot driveway, the bathing beach empty. There is a sign posted forbidding swimming after 6 P.M., but they strip in the shelter of shrubs and slip into the water.

The cold current shocks delightfully, sweeps away sweat and dust. Aaron ducks his head, rubs his scalp. He comes up spewing spray, laughing at the luxury of coolness. He reaches for her and holds her close. They look into one another's faces. Victoria sees no shadows beyond his pleasure. Yes, they are content, and very happy, this moment. Now. Weary and refreshed, comfortable and middle-aged and sensuous. Yes, they have everything. She thinks again of centers, fulfillments, perfections. Lucky, they are, happy and blessed.

That night in bed, they love one another and then calm and at ease in the cool evening dark, with the bedroom door opened to an angle of August stars, they murmur small declining thoughts. Bernie doubts he can sell to Couvaison this year . . . Your father's birthday next week . . . Must write Arnold . . . Invited to the Nashes . . . Surgery at seven-thirty . . .

She falls asleep and does not know how much time has passed when she wakens, feeling along the backs of her arms the shivers, knowing the startle in her mind. What has wakened her? She listens to the night: the crickets' wild chirrs, the cry of the small owl, the almost inaudible whirr of the electric clock, Aaron's long breaths. She finds nothing out of place, turns to her pillow, readies herself for return to sleep.

But in her mind shapes the image of the small dead field mouse, locked by curious process into the form of his living. She holds that tiny creature before her, compelled to attend it.

And yes, now in the dark she knows, knew all the time, perhaps, what it is that darkens Aaron's eye and quietens his smiling. He has gotten there just one step ahead of her. The perfect summer, the perfect center. It will turn her, of course, to another time. Oh, certainly the center is beautiful and may seem secure, but that is, of course, only illusion. There is no stasis ever. There is never that. She turns to Aaron, holds his warm body close to her own, wanting now to comfort him as well as herself for what he does not confess he knows.

HERBERT WILNER

The Quarterback Speaks to His God

(FROM ESQUIRE)

BOBBY KRAFT, the heroic old pro, lies in his bed in the grip of medicines relieving his ailing heart. Sometimes he tells his doctor your pills beat my ass, and the doctor says it's still Kraft's choice: medicine or open heart surgery. Kraft shuts up.

He wasn't five years out of pro football, retired at thirty-six after fourteen years, when he got the rare viral blood infection. Whatever they were, the damn things ate through his heart like termites, leaving him with pericarditis, valve dysfunction, murmurs, arrhythmia, and finally, congestive failure. The physiology has been explained to him, but he prefers not to understand it. Fascinated in the past by his strained ligaments, sprained ankles, torn cartilage, tendinitis, he now feels betrayed by his heart's disease.

"You want to hear it?" Dr. Felton once asked, offering the earpieces of the stethoscope.

Kraft recoiled.

"You don't want to hear the sound of your own heart?"

Sitting on the examining table, Kraft was as tall as the short doctor, whose mustache hid a crooked mouth.

"Why should I?" Kraft said. "Would you smile in the mirror after your teeth got knocked out?"

This morning in bed, as with almost every third morning of the past two years, Kraft begins to endure the therapeutic power of his drugs. He takes diuretics: Edecrin, or Lasix, or Dyazide, or combinations. They make him piss and piss, relieving for a day or two the worst effects of the congesting fluids that swamp his lungs and gut. He's been told the washout dumps potassium, an unfortunate consequence. The depletions cramp his muscles, give him headaches, sometimes trigger arrhythmias. They always drive him into depressions as deep as comas. He blames himself.

"It has nothing to do with will power," Dr. Felton explained. "If you ran five miles in Death Valley in August, you'd get about the same results as you do from a very successful diuresis."

To replenish some of his losses, Kraft stuffs himself with bananas, drinks orange juice by the pint, and takes two tablespoons a day of potassium chloride solution. To prevent and arrest the arrhythmia, he takes quinidine, eight pills a day, 200 mg per pill. To strengthen the enlarged and weakened muscle of his heart wall, he takes digoxin. Together they make him nauseous, gassy, and distressed. He takes anti-nausea pills and chews antacids as though they were Life Savers. Some nights he takes Valium to fall asleep. If one doesn't work, he takes two.

"I can't believe it's me," he protests to his wife, Elfi. "I never took pills, I wouldn't even touch aspirins. There were guys on coke, amphetamines, Novocain. I wouldn't touch anything. Now look at me. I'm living in a drugstore."

His blurred eyes sweep the squads of large and small dark labeled bottles massed on his chest of drawers. His wife offers little sympathy.

"Again and again the same thing with you," she'll answer in her German accent. "So go have the surgery already, you coward ox."

Coward? Him? Bobby Kraft?

"I have to keep recommending against surgery," said Dr. Felton, named by the team physician as the best cardiologist in the city for Kraft's problems. "I'm not certain it can provide the help worth the risk. Meanwhile, we buy time. Every month these hotshot surgeons get better at their work. Our equipment for telling us precisely what's wrong with your heart gets better. In the meantime, since you don't need to work for a living, wait it out. Sit in the sun. Read. Watch television. Talk about the old games. Wait."

What does coward have to do with it?

This morning, in his bed, three hours after the double dose of Lasix with a Dyazide thrown in, Kraft has been to the toilet bowl fourteen times. His breathing is easier, his gut is relieved; and now he has to survive the payments of his good results.

He's dry as a stone, exhausted, and has a headache. The base of his skull feels kicked. The muscles of his neck are wrenched and pulled, as if they'd been wound on a spindle. His hips ache. So do his shoulder joints. His calves are heavy. They're tightening into cramps. His ankles feel as though tissue is dissolving in them, flaking off into small crystals, eroding gradually by bumping each other in slight, swirling collisions before they dissolve altogether in a bath of serum. His ankles feel absent.

He's cold. Under the turned-up electric blanket, he has chills. His heart feels soaked.

He wants to stay awake, but he can't help sleeping. By the sixth of his returns from the bowl, he was collapsing into the bed. Falling asleep was more like fainting, like going under, like his knee surgery — some imperfect form of death. He needs to stay awake. His will is all that's left him for proving himself, but his will is shot by the depression he can't control.

By tomorrow he'll be mostly out of bed. He'll have reduced the Lasix to one pill, no Dyazide, piss just a little, and by the day after, with luck guarding against salt in his food, he'll have balanced out. He'll sit on the deck in his shorts when the sun starts to burn a little at noon. He'll squeeze the rubber ball in his right hand. He'll take a shower afterwards and oil himself down to rub the flaking off. He'll look at himself in the full-length mirror and stare at the part of his chest where the injured heart is supposed to be. He'll see little difference from what he saw five years ago, when he was still playing. The shoulders sloping and wide, a little less full but not bony, the chest a little less deep but still broad and tapered, the right arm still flat-muscled and whip-hanging, same as it was ten years ago, when he could throw a football sixty yards with better than fair accuracy. What he'll see in the mirror can infuriate him.

He once got angry enough to put on his sweat suit, go through the gate at the back fence and start to run in the foot-wide level dirt beside the creek bed in the shade of the laurels. After five cautious strides, he lengthened into ten hard ones. Then he was on his knees gasping for air, his heart arrhythmic, his throat congested. He couldn't move for five minutes. By the next day he'd gained six pounds. He told Elfi what he'd done.

"Imbecile!" She called the doctor. Kraft, his ankles swollen, was into heart failure. It was touch and go about sending him to the hospital for intravenous diuretics and relief oxygen.

It took a month to recover, he never made another effort to run, but he knew even today, that after all this pissing and depression, exhaustion and failure, when he balanced out the day after tomorrow and he was on the deck and the sun hit, nothing could keep the impulse out of his legs. He'd want to run. He'd feel the running in his legs. And he'd settle for a few belittling house chores, then all day imagine he'd have a go at screwing Elfi. But at night he didn't dare try.

When she gets home from her day with the retards, she fixes her Campari on ice, throws the dinner together, at which, as always, she pecks like a bird and he shovels what he can, making faces to advertise his nausea, rubbing his abdomen to soothe his distress and belching to release the gas. After dinner he'll report his day, shooting her combative looks to challenge the boredom glazing her face. They move to the living room. Standing, he towers over her. He's six foot two inches and she's tiny. His hand, large even for his size, would cover the top of her skull the way an ordinary man's might encapsulate an egg. She stretches full length on the couch; he slouches in the club chair. She wears a tweed skirt and buttoned blouse, he's in his pajamas and terry cloth robe. He still has a headache. His voice drones monotonously in his own ears, but he's obsessed with accounting for his symptoms as though they were football statistics. When he at last finishes, she sits up and nods.

"So all in all today is a little better. Nothing with the bad rhythm."

He gets sullen, then angry. No one has ever annoyed him as effectively as she. He'd married her six years ago, just before his retirement, as he'd always planned. He knew the stewardesses, models, second-rate actresses, and just plain hotel whores would no longer do. He'd need children, a son. And this tiny woman's German accent and malicious tongue had knocked him out. And sometimes he caught her reciting prayers in French (she said for religion it was the perfect language), which seemed to him — a man without religion — unexplainably peculiar and right.

Now, offended by her flint heart (calling *this* a better day!), he goes to the den for TV. He has another den with shelves full of his history — plaques, cups, trophies, photos (one with the President of the United States), footballs, medals, albums, video tapes — but he no longer enters this room. After an hour, she comes in after him. She wants to purr. He wants to be left alone. His headache is worse, his chest tingles. She recounts events of her day, one of the two during the week when she drives to the city and consults at a school for what she calls learning-problem children. He doesn't even pretend to listen. She sulks.

Words go back and forth. He didn't think he could do it, but he tells her. In roundabout fashion, the TV jabbering, he finally makes her understand his latest attack of anxiety: the feel of his not feeling it. His prick.

She looks amazed, as if she were still not understanding him, then her eyes widen and she taps herself on the temple.

"You I don't understand," she sputters. "To me your head is something for doctors. Every day I worry sick about your heart, and you give me this big soap opera about your prick. Coward. You should go for the surgery. Every week you get worse, whatever that Dr. Felton says. You let all those oxes fall on you and knock you black and blue, then a little cutting with a knife, and you shiver. When they took away your football, they broke your baby's heart. So now, sew it up again. Let a surgeon do it. You don't know how. You think your heart can get better by itself? In you, Bobby, never."

When it suits her, she exaggerates her mispronunciation of his name. "*Beaubee. Beaubee.* What kind of name is this for a grown man your size, Beaubee?"

He heads to the bedroom to slam the door behind him. After ten minutes, the door opens cautiously. She sits at the edge of the bed near his feet. She strokes the part of the blanket covering his feet, puts her cheek to it, then straightens, stands, says it to him.

"I love you better than my own life. I swear it. How else could I stay with you?"

He hardly hears her. His attention concentrates on the first signs of his arrhythmia. He tells her, "It's beginning." She says she'll fetch the quinidine. She carries his low sodium milk for him to drink it with. He glances at her woefully through what used to be ice-blue eyes fixed in his head like crystals. He stares at the pills before he swallows them. He can identify any of them by color, shape and size. He doesn't trust her. She can't nurse, she always panics.

His heart is fluttering, subsiding, fluttering. Finally it levels off at the irregularity of the slightly felt extra beat which Felton has told him is an auricular fibrillation. Elfi finds an excuse to leave the room. He sits up in bed, his eyes closed, his thick back rammed against the sliding pillows, his head arched over them, the crown drilling into the headboard.

The flurries have advanced to a continuously altering input of extra beats. They are light and rapid, like the scurryings under his breastbone of a tiny creature with scrawny limbs. After ten minutes, the superfluous beats intensify and ride over the regular heartbeats.

There's chaos in his heart. Following a wild will of its own, it has nothing to do with him, nor can he do anything with it. Moderate pain begins in his upper left arm, and though the doctor has assured him it's nothing significant, and he knows it will last only through the arrhythmia, Kraft begins to sweat.

The heart goes wilder. He rubs his chest, runs his hands across the protruding bones of his cheeks and jaw. Ten minutes later the heart begins to yank as well as thump. It feels as if the heart's apex is stitched into tissues near the bottom of his chest, and the yanking of the bulk of the heart will tear the threads loose. Again and again he tries to will himself into the cool accommodation he can't command. Then at last it seems that for a few minutes the force of the intrusive beats is diminishing. He dares to hope it's now the beginning of the end of the episode.

Immediately a new sequence of light and differently irregular flurries resumes. The thumpings are now also on his back. He turns to his right side, flicks the control for the television, tries to lose himself with it, hears Elfi come in. She whispers, "Still?" and leaves again.

The thumpings deepen. They are really pounding. The headache is drilled in his forehead. It throbs. He thinks the heart is making sounds that can be heard in the room. He claws his long fingers into the tough flesh over the heart. It goes on for another hour. He waits, and waits. Then, indeed, in moments, they fade into the flutter with which they began. After a while the flutter is hard to pick out, slips under the regular beating of his heart, and gives way at last to an occasional extra beat which pokes at his chest with the feel of a mild bubbling of thick pudding at a slow boil. Then that's gone.

His heart has had its day's event.

Kraft tells himself: nothing's worth this. He's told it to himself often. He tells himself he'll see Felton tomorrow. He'll insist on the surgery.

Afraid of surgery? Coward? She wasn't even in his life when he had his knee done after being blindsided in Chicago. He came out of the anesthesia on a cloud. The bandage on his leg went from thigh to ankle, but the girl who came to visit him — stewardess, model, the cocktail waitress — he couldn't remember now, she was the one whose eyes changed colors — she had to fight him off because he kept rubbing his hand under her skirt up the soft inside of her thigh. She ended on his bed on top of him. He was almost instantaneous. He had to throw her off, remembering his leg, his career. But was it really that Felton runt who was keeping him from surgery?

In despair now, could he really arrange for the surgery tomorrow? Not on a knee, but on his opened heart?

Bobby Kraft's heart?

"That's crap," he once said to a young reporter. "Any quarterback can throw. We all start from there. Some of us do it a little better. That's not what it's all about. Throwing ain't passing, sonny, and passing ain't all of quarterbacking anyway."

"You mean picking your plays. Using your head. Reading defenses?"

"That's important. It's not all of it."

"What's the mystique?" the youth asked shyly, fearful of ignorance. "Not in your arm, not in your head. I know you all have guts or wouldn't play in such a violent game. If it's a special gift, where do you keep it?"

"In your goddamn chest, sonny. Where the blood comes." He smiled and stared icily at the reporter until the young man turned away.

Actually, Kraft worked hard mastering the technical side of his skills. If he needed to, for instance, if the wind wasn't strong against him, he could hang the ball out fifty yards without putting too much arc in it. It should've been a heavy ball to catch for a receiver running better than ten yards to the second. But Kraft, in any practice, could get it out there inches ahead of the outstretched arms and have the forward end of the ball, as it was coming down, begin to point up slightly over its spiralling axis. That way it fell with almost no weight at all. The streaking receiver could palm it in one hand, as if he were snatching a fruit from a tree he ran by. It took Kraft years to get it right and do it in games.

There were ways of taking the ball from the center, places on it for each of his fingers, ways of wrist-cradling the ball before he threw if he had to break his pocket, and there was the rhythm set up between his right arm and the planting of his feet before he released the ball through the picket of huge, upraised arms.

He watched the films. He studied the game book. He worked with the coaches and his receivers for any coming Sunday. What the other team did every other time they played you, and what they did all season was something you had to remember. You also had to be free of it. You had to yield to the life of the particular game, build it, master it, improvise. And always you not only had to stand up to their cries of "Kill Kraft," you had to make them eat it. The sonsabitches!

That's what Kraft did most of the week waiting for his Sunday game. He worked the "sonsabitches" into a heat. Then he slid outside himself and watched it. It was like looking at a fire he'd taken out of his chest to hold before eyes. Tense all week, his eyes grew colder and colder as they gazed at the flame. By game time he was thoroughly impersonal.

Sunday on the field in the game, though he weighed 203, he looked between plays somewhat on the slender side, like someone who could get busted like a stick by most of those he played among. He stood out of the huddle a long time before he entered it through the horseshoe's slot to call the play. Outside the huddle, except in the last minutes when they might be fighting the clock, his pose was invariable. His right foot was anchored with the toe toward the opening for him in his huddle about nine feet away, the left angled toward where the referee had placed the ball. It threw his torso on a rakish slant toward the enormous opposing linemen, as though he'd tight-rigged himself against a headland. He kept the knuckles of his right hand high on his right ass, the fingers limp. His left hand hung motionless on his left side. Under his helmet, his head turned slowly and his eyes darted. He wasn't seeing anything that would matter. They'd change it all around when he got behind the center. He was emptying himself for his concentration. It was on the three strides back to the huddle that he picked his play and barked it to them in a toneless, commanding fierceness just short of rage.

Then the glory began for Kraft. What happened, what he lived for never got into the papers; it wasn't seen on television. What he saw was only part of what he knew. He would watch the free safety or the outside linebackers for giveaway cues on the blitz. He might detect from jumping linemen some of the signs of looping. The split second before he had the ball he might spot assignment against his receivers and automatically register the little habits and capacities of the defending sonsabitches. He could "feel" the defenses.

But none of it really began until, after barking the cadence of his signals, he actually did have the ball in his hand. Then, for the fraction of a second before he gave it away to a runner, or for the maximum three seconds in the pocket before he passed, there was nothing but grunting and roaring and cursing, the crashing of helmets and pads, the oofs of air going out of brutish men and the whisk of legs in tight pants cutting air like a scythe in tall grass and the soft suck of cleats in the grassy sod, and the actual vibration of the earth itself stampeded by that tonnage of sometimes gigantic, always fast, cruel, lethal bodies. And if Kraft kept the ball, if he dropped his three paces back into his protective pocket, he'd inch forward before he released it and turn his shoulders or his hips to slip past the bodies clashing at his sides. He would always sense and sometimes never see the spot to which he had to throw the ball through the nests of the raised arms of men two to five inches taller than himself and twice as broad and sixty, eighty pounds heavier. One of their swinging arms could, if he didn't see it coming, knock him off his feet as though he were a matchstick. He was often on his back or side, a pile of the sonsabitches taking every gouge and kick and swipe at him they could get away with. That was the sweetness for him.

To have his ass beaten and not even know it. To have that rush inside him mounting all through the game, and getting himself more and more under control as he heated up, regarding himself without awareness of it, his heart given to the fury, and his mind to a sly and joyous watching of his heart, storing up images that went beyond the choral roaring of any huge crowd and that he would feed on through the week waiting for the next game, aching through the week but never knowing in the game any particular blow that would make him hurt. Not after the first time he got belted. They said he had rubber in his joints, springs in his ass, and a whip for an arm.

The combination of his fierce combativeness and laid back de-

tachment infuriated the sonsabitches he played against. They
hated him; it made them lose their heads. It was all the advantage
Kraft ever needed. His own teammates, of course, went crazy with
the game. They wound themselves up for it in the hours before it,
and some of them didn't come down until the day after, regardless
of who won.

Kraft depended on their lunacy. He loved them for needing it.
And he loved them most during the game because no one ever
thought of him as being like them. He was too distant. Too cun-
ning. Too cold. But on the sideline, among them, waiting for his
defensive team to get him back into the game, he might run his
tongue over his lips, taste the salty blood he didn't know was there,
and swallow. Then he'd rub his tongue across his gums and over
the inside of a cheek, and an expression of wonder might flicker
across his face, as if he were a boy with his first lick at the new
candy, tasting the sweetness of his gratified desires, not on his
tongue but in his own heart.

Three more months passed with Kraft delivered up to the cycles
of his illness and medicines and waiting and brooding. Then he
was sitting in his sweat socks and trunks at the side of the pool one
late afternoon. He gazed vacantly at the water. His chest had caved
a little; and his long head seemed larger, his wide neck thicker. Elfi
had been reading on a mat near the fence under the shade of a
laurel.

"So how long are you going to live like this?" she asked. Immediately he thought she was talking sex. "Two more years? Five?
Ten?" She crossed her arms over her slender, fragile chest. "Maybe
even fifteen, hah? But sooner or later you'll beg them for the
surgery. On your knees. So why do you wait? Look how you lose
all the time you could be better in."

His answer was pat.

"I told you. They can cut up my gut. They can monkey with my
head. They can cut off my right arm even, how's that? But they're
not going to cut up my heart. That's all. They're not putting plastic
valves in my heart."

"Again with this plastic. Listen, I am reading a lot about it. There
are times they can put in a valve from a sheep, or a pig."

He looked at her in amazement. He stood up. She came to his
collarbone; he cast a shade over all of her.

"Sheep and pig!"

He looked like he might slam her, then he turned away and headed for the glass door to the bedroom.

"Your heart," she said. "You have such a special heart?"

When he turned she looked up at him and backed off a step.

"Yeah, it's special. My heart's me." He stabbed his chest with the long thumb of his right hand.

"You think I don't understand that? With my own heart I understand that. But this is the country where surgeons make miracles. You are lucky. It happens to you here, where you are such a famous ox. And here they have the surgeon who's also so famous. For him, what you have is a — is a — a blister."

He glared. She backed off another step. He turned and dove suddenly into the pool, touched bottom, came up slowly and thought he could live a long time in a chilly, blue, chlorinated water in which he would, suspended, always hold his breath. He rose slowly, broke the water at the nearer wall, hoisted himself at the coping and emerged from the water, with his back and shoulders glistening. He was breathless, but he moved on to the bedroom. He didn't double over until he had closed the glass door behind him. While he waited for his throat to empty and his chest to fill, he hurt. He got dizzy. Bent, he moved to the bed and fell on it. He stretched out.

He napped, or thought he did. When he woke, or his mind cleared, words filled him. He clasped his hands behind his neck, closed his eyes and tried to shut the words out. He got off the bed and stood before the full-length mirror. He put his hands to his thighs, bent his weight forward, clamped the heels of his hands together, dropped his left palm to make a nest for the ball the center would snap. Numbers barked in his head. When he heard the hup-hup he moved back the two swift steps, planted his feet, brought his right arm high behind his head, the elbow at his ear, then released the shoulder and snapped the wrist. He did it twice more. He was grinning. When he started it the fourth time, he was into arrhythmia.

Kraft consults Dr. Felton. Felton examines him, sits, glances at him, gazes at the ceiling, puts the tips of his index fingers to a pyramid point on his mustache, and says, "I'm still opposed, but I'll call him." He means the heart surgeon, Dr. Gottfried. They arrange for Kraft to take preliminary tests. He has already had some of them, but the heart catheterization will be new. A week later Kraft enters the hospital.

An hour after he's in his room, a parade of doctors begin the listening and thumping on Kraft's chest and back. A bearded doctor in his early thirties who will assist in the morning's catheterization briefs him on what to expect. He speaks rapidly.

"You'll be awake of course. You'll find it a painless procedure. We'll use a local on your arm where we insert the catheter. When it touches a wall of the heart, you might have a little flurry of heartbeats. Don't worry about it. Somewhere in the process we'll ask you to exercise a little. We need some measurements of the heart under physical stress. You won't have to do more than you can. Toward the end we'll inject a purple dye. We get very precise films that way. You'll probably get some burning sensations while the dye circulates. A couple of minutes or so. Otherwise you'll be quite comfortable. Do you have any questions?"

Kraft has a hundred and asks none.

The doctor starts out of the room, stops, comes back a little haltingly. He has his pen in his hand and his prescription pad out.

"Mr. Kraft, I have a nephew. He'd get a big kick out of . . ."

Kraft takes the extended pad and pen. "What's his name?"

"Oh, just sign yours."

He writes: "For the doc and his nephew for good luck from Bobby Kraft." He returns the items. He feels dead.

In the morning they move him on a gurney to a thick-walled room in the basement. He's asked to slide onto an X-ray table. They cover him with a sheet. He raises himself on his elbows to see people busy at tasks he can't understand. There are two women and two men. All of them wear white. One of the women sits before a console full of knobs and meters on a table near his feet. Above and behind his head is a machine he'll know later is a fluoroscope. In a corner of the room there's a concrete alcove, the kind X-ray technicians hide behind. One of the men keeps popping in and out of its opening on his way to and from the fluoroscope. The ceiling is full of beams and grids on which X-ray equipment slides back and forth and is lowered and raised. The other man plays with it, and with film plates he slides under the table. A nurse attaches EKG bands to his ankles.

The two doctors come in. They are already masked, rubber-gloved, and dressed in green. The bearded one introduces the other, who has graying hair and brown eyes. A nurse fits Kraft's right arm into a metal rest draped with towels. "I'm going to tie your wrist," she says. She ties it and tucks the towels over his hand and wrist and over his shoulder and biceps. She washes the inside of his shaved arm with alcohol, rubbing hard at the crook of his elbow. The bearded doctor ties his arm tightly with a rubber strap, just above the elbow, then feels with his fingers in the crook of the elbow for the raised vessels. He swabs the skin with the yellow Xylocaine and waits. The other doctor asks the nurse at the console if she is ready. She says, "Not yet." He looks at Kraft, and Kraft looks up at the rails and grids.

In a few minutes the bearded doctor injects the anesthetic into several spots high on the inside of Kraft's forearm. It takes ten more minutes before the woman at the console is ready. She gets up twice to check with the man in the alcove. The older doctor goes there once. When the woman finally signals she's ready, Dr. Kahl says, "OK." Kraft looks. The older doctor stands alongside Kahl. The scalpel goes quickly into Kraft's flesh in a short cut. He doesn't feel it. Kahl removes the scalpel, and a little blood seeps. The doctor switches instruments and goes quickly into the small wound. Blood spurts. It comes in a few pumps about six inches over Kraft's arm, a thick, rich red blood. Kraft is astonished. Then the blood stops. The towels are soaked with it.

"I'm putting the cath in."

The older doctor nods. He turns toward the fluoroscope. Kraft watches again. The catheter is black and silky and no thicker than a cocktail straw. Still Kraft feels nothing. Kahl's brow creases. He's manipulating the black, slender thing with his rubbered fingers. He rolls his thumb along it as he moves it. Kraft waits to feel something. There is no feeling. He can't see where the loose end of the catheter is coming from. He turns his head away and takes a deep breath. He takes another deep one. He wants to relax. He wants to know how the hell he got into all this. What really happened to him? When? What for?

"You're in," the older doctor says.

The thing is in his heart.

It couldn't have taken more than ten seconds. They are in his heart with a black silky tube and he can't feel it.

"Hold it," the nurse at the console says. She begins calling out numbers.

"How are you feeling?" Dr. Kahl asks. Kraft nods.

"You feeling all right?" the older doctor repeats, walking toward the fluoroscope.

"Yeah."

They go on and on. He feels nothing. He hears the older doctor instructing the younger one: "Try the ventricle . . . Hold it . . . What's your reading now . . . There's the flutter . . . Don't worry about that, Mr. Kraft . . . Watch the pulmonary artery . . . He's irritable in there . . . Withdraw! . . . Fine, you're through the cusps . . . Try the mitral . . . You're on the wall again . . . How are you feeling, Mr. Kraft?"

Kraft nods. He licks his lips. He tries not to listen to them. When the flutter goes off in his chest, he thinks it will start an arrhythmia. It doesn't. It feels like a hummingbird hovering in his chest for a second. Something catches it. Occasionally the other doctor comes beside Kahl and plays for a moment with the catheter while he watches the fluoroscope. The bearded doctor chats sometimes, saying he's sorry Kraft has to lie so flat for so long, it must be uncomfortable. Does he use many pillows at home? Would he like to raise up for a while?

The arm hurts where the catheter enters it. Kraft feels a firm growing lump under the flesh, as if a golf ball is being forced into the wound. Kraft concentrates on the pain. He thinks of grass.

"How much longer?" he asks.

"We're more than half way."

In a while the nurse tells him they are going to have him do the exercises now. Something presses against his feet. The brown-eyed doctor talks.

"We have an apparatus here with bicycle pedals. Just push on them as you would on a bike. We'll adjust the pedals to keep making you push with more force. If it gets to be too much work, tell us. We want you to exert yourself, but not tire yourself."

What's he talking about, Kraft asks himself. He begins to pump. There's no resistance. He pumps faster, harder.

"That's fine. Keep it going. You're doing real fine."

He gets a rhythm to it quickly, thrusting his legs as rapidly as he can. He expects to get winded, but he doesn't. He's doing fine. He almost enjoys it. He concentrates. He feels the pain in his arm and pumps harder, faster. He imagines he's racing. For a moment it gets more difficult to pump. He presses harder, feels his calves stretch and harden. He gets his rhythm back. They encourage him. He licks his lips and clasps the edge of the table with his left hand and drives his legs. He forgets about any race. He knows he's doing well with this exercise. It will show on their computation. They'll tell him his heart is getting better. The resistance to his pumping gets stronger. He pumps harder.

"That was very good. We're taking the apparatus away now. You feel all right?"

"Fine."

Kraft closes his eyes. There's the pain in his arm again. His forearm is going to pop. It's too strong a pain now. They are moving in the room. He grinds his teeth.

"We're going to inject the dye now," the older doctor says.

Kraft turns his head and sees the metal cylinder of the syringe catch glinting light for a moment in Kahl's raised hand. He sees the rubbered thumb move; a blackish fluid spurts from the needle's tip. The needle goes toward his arm — into the wound or the catheter, he can't tell. He turns away.

"You'll feel some heat in your head very soon. That's just the effect of the dye. It'll wear off. You'll feel heat at the sphincter too. Are you all right?"

Kraft nods. He turns away. Why do they keep asking him? He sees the man from the alcove hurrying with X-ray plates that he slides into the slot under the table just below Kraft's shoulder blades. He hurries back to the alcove. The doctors call instructions. The voice from the alcove calls some words back and numbers. Kraft closes his eyes and tries to think of something to think of. He thinks if Elfi could — then Kraft feels the rush. It comes in way over the pain in his arm. It raises him off the table. He feels the heat racing through him. A terrific pounding at his forehead. It doesn't go away. He tries to think of the pain in his arm, but he feels the heat rushing through him in a rising fever. Then it hits his asshole and he rises off the table again. It burns tremendously. They have lit a candle in his asshole and the burned flesh is going to drop through.

"Wow!"

"That's all right. It'll go away soon."

It does, but not the headache. It burns and throbs in his fore-head. He hears metal dropping under the table. The man runs out and removes film plates. Someone else inserts others. They call numbers. The plates fall again. They repeat the process. He closes his eyes. The rush is fading, but the headache remains, throbbing.

"How you doing?"

"All right. My head aches."

"It'll pass."

"How was the exercise part?"

"You did fine. We'll be through soon. How's the arm?"

"Hurts."

"No problem. More Novocain."

"No. Leave it."

They hurry again. Words are exchanged about the films. Some-one leaves the room. Someone enters it later. Kraft keeps his eyes closed. The ache is still in his forehead, but he thinks he might sleep.

"Well, that's it," the bearded Kahl says. Kraft looks toward him, then down at his arm. The wound is stitched. He hasn't felt it. The doctor covers it with a gauze pad and two strips of tape. The catheter's gone. Kraft sees no sign of it. They wash his arm of blood and get him onto the gurney. He hears someone say, "I think we got good results." The older doctor tells Kraft they'll know some things tomorrow. "It looks good."

Back in his room Elfi is waiting for him. He gets into bed, and they leave. She throws herself on him. She's breathless. Her cheeks are streaked, her eyes are red. She's been crying. She's almost crying now.

"I don't want to talk about it now," he says when she begins to speak.

"I don't want to hear it. That's the truth. Listen, I'm going home. Beaubee, I'm not good here."

She rushes from the room. He contemplates the increasing pain in his arm. It reaches into his biceps now. He keeps thinking about his heart. They had their black tube in *his* heart. The sonsabitches.

On the next day, just before lunch, reading a magazine in the chair in his room, he sees Dr. Gottfried for the first time. With him, in his white coat, is the gray-haired doctor from the catheter-ization. Dr. Gottfried is in the short-sleeved green shirt and the green baggy cotton trousers of the operating room. He has scuffed sneakers, and the stethoscope — like a metal and rubber noose — hangs from his neck. He looks tired. He has the sad eyes of a spaniel. And yet the man — in build neither here nor there, just a man — introduced by his colleague, stares and stares at Kraft before he moves or speaks, like a man before a fight. He keeps looking into Kraft's eyes, as if through his patient's eyes he could find the as yet untested condition of his true heart. He keeps on staring; Kraft stares back. Then the great famous doctor nods; a corner of his mouth flickers. He has apparently seen what he has needed to — and judged. He leans over Kraft and listens with the stethoscope to Kraft's chest. He could not have heard more than three heartbeats when he removes the earpieces, steps back, and speaks.

"Under it all, you've got a strong heart. I can tell by the snap."

Kraft, the heroic old pro, begins to smile. He beams. The doctor speaks in a slow, subdued voice; Kraft's smile fades.

"There's no real rush with your situation. However, the sooner the better, and there's a cancelled procedure two weeks from today. We can do you then. I'll operate. Right now I want to study more of the material in your folder. We've got several base lines. I'll be back soon. Dr. Pritchett will fill you in and answer any questions you have. He knows more than anyone in the world about pulmonary valve disease."

Leaving, Dr. Gottfried moves without a sound, his head tilted and the shoulder on that side sagging. When he closes the door, Kraft turns on Dr. Pritchett.

"What operation? He said my heart's good. You said you got good results on that catheter. The fat one yesterday said he got good results on his machine."

The doctor explains. The "good" results meant they were finding what they needed to know. They are all agreed now the linings of the heart should be removed. A simple procedure for Dr. Gottfried — "he's the best you could find" — even if the endocardium is scarred enough to be adhesive. They are also agreed about the pulmonary valve. It will be removed and replaced by an artificial device made of a flexible steel alloy. "Dr. Gottfried will just pop it right in." We're not, however, certain of the aortic valve. "Dr. Gottfried will make that decision during surgery." Positive results are expected. There's the strong probability of the heart restored to ninety-percent efficiency and a good possibility of total cure. Of course, you'll be on daily anti-coagulant medicines for the rest of your life. No big affair. The important point, as Dr. Gottfried said, is the heart is essentially strong. Surgery, done now, while Kraft is young and before the heart is irreparably weakened, is the determining factor. Of course, as in any surgery, there's risk.

"Have I made it clear? Can I answer any questions, Mr. Kraft? I know we get too technical at times."

"I'm not stupid."

"No one implied you were."

Emptying with dread, Kraft slips his hands under the blanket to hide their trembling. "Will I still need pissing pills after the operation?"

"Diuretics? No. I wouldn't think so."

"No more arrhythmia?"

"We can't be sure of that. Sometimes the —"

"Then what kind of total cure, man?"

"I can't explain all the physics and chemistry of the heart rhythm, Mr. Kraft. If you'd continue to have the arrhythmia, it would be benign. A mechanical thing. We have medicine to control it."

"You said I did great with the exercises."

"Yes. We got the results we needed."

Dr. Gottfried returns, still in his operating clothes, holding the manila folder, looking now a little bored as well as fatigued, his voice slow, quiet.

"Any questions for me?"

"The risk? Dr. What'shisname here said . . ."

"There's ten-percent mortality risk. That covers all open heart surgery. A lot of it relates to heart disease more advanced than yours, where general health isn't as good as yours. There's risk however, for you too. You know that."

Kraft nods. He suddenly detests this man he needs, who'll have the power of life over him. He closes his eyes.

"As I said, there's no emergency. But I can fit you in two weeks from now. You could have it over with. Decide in a day or two. I'd appreciate that. Talk it over with your wife. With Dr. Felton. Let us know through him."

Home again, Kraft, on his medicines, pissed, grew depressed, endured his headaches and lassitude, the arrhythmias, the miscellaneous pains, his sense of dissolution, the nausea; and, as before, continued to blame himself as well as feel betrayed. He submitted, and he waited. He never looked in the mirror anymore. While he shaved, he never saw himself. Sometimes he felt tearful. On the few days that he came around, he no longer went out to the sun and the pool but stayed indoors. He called no one, but answered the phone on his better days and kept up his end of the bullshit with old buddies and some writers who still remembered. No one but Elfi knew his despair.

When he passed the closed door to the den of his heroic history, his trophy room, he wasn't even aware that he kept himself from going in. The door might as well have been the wall. What he kept seeing now was behind his eyes: The face of Dr. Gottfried. It flashed like a blurred, tired, boneless, powerful shape, producing a quality before which Kraft felt weak. He began to exalt the quality and despise the man and groped for a way by which he could begin to tell Elfi.

One night, in bed with her, a week after he'd made the decision to go for the surgery, which was now less than a week away, with the lights out and her figure illumined only by a small glow of clouded moonlight entering through the cracked drapes, he thought her asleep and ventured to loop his hand over her head where he could easily reach her outside shoulder. He touched it gently. It was the first time since his discovery of his impotence that he'd touched her in bed.

Immediately she moved across the space, nestled her head in his armpit, and pressed against his side. He resisted his desire to pull away. He was truly pleased by the way she fit.

"Every day now I pray," she said. "Oh, not for you, don't worry. You are going to be fine. I swear it, how much I believe that. You don't need me to pray for you. I need it. I do it for myself. Selfishly. Entirely."

He spoke of what was on his mind. "That surgeon's freaking me."

"You couldn't find anyone better. I have the utmost confidence. To me that is what you call a man. You should see in his clinic. What the patients say about him. The eyes they have when they look at him. He walks through like a god. And I tell you something else. He has a vast understanding."

He moved his hand from her arm. "It's *my* heart, not yours." His voice fell to despair. "It's a man thing. You can't understand. A sonofabitch puts his hand in Bobby Kraft's heart. He pops in some goddamned metal valve. He's flaky. He freaks me."

"I tell you. I feel sorry for you. Too bad. For any man I feel sorry who doesn't know who are his real enemies. Not to know that, that's your freak. That's the terrible thing can happen to a man in his life. Not to know who his enemies are."

"That's what *he* is," Kraft declaimed in the darkness. "He's my enemy. If there's one thing I've always known, that's it. The sonsabitches. Now Gottfried is. And there ain't no game. I don't even get to play."

"You baby. Play. Play. It's because all your life you played a game for a boy. That's why you can't know. Precisely. I always knew that."

He pulled away from her. He got out of bed and loomed over her threateningly.

"Go on back home, Kraut. I don't need you for the operation. To hell with the operation. I'll call it off. How's that?"

"Here is home, with you. Try and make me leave. I am not a man. I don't need enemies."

He got out of bed to get away. The bitch. She'd caught him at a time when there was nothing left of him.

Kraft enters the hospital trying to imagine it's a stadium. The act lasts as long as his first smell of the antiseptics and the rubbery sound of a wheeled gurney. He tastes old metal in his mouth. He refuses the tranquilizers they keep pushing at him. He wants wakefulness. Elfi keeps visiting and fleeing.

He has nothing to say to her. She wants his buddies to come, she says he needs them. He says if one of them comes, that's it. He clears out of the hospital, period. He wants to talk, but he can't imagine a proper listener. For two years he endured what he never could have believed would've befallen him. There was no way to understand it, and this has left him now with loose ends. He can't think of any arrangement of his mind that could gather them. They simply fall out.

It occurs to him he doesn't know enough people who are dead.

It occurs to him he isn't sick enough.

He thinks he will be all right. He thinks he will be able to brag about it afterwards. Then he sees his heart and Gottfried's hand,

and he wants the man there at once to ask him what right he thinks he has.

It occurs to him he never really liked football. It was just an excuse for something else.

It occurs to him he just made that up. It can't be so.

He wonders if he has ever really slept *with* Elfi. With any woman. He laments his development of a double chin.

Sleep is a measure of defeat. Before games he never slept well.

Here, even at night, he keeps trying not to sleep. Most of the time he doesn't. He asks one of the doctors if it will matter in the outcome that he isn't sleeping now. The doctor says, Nope.

On the morning of the surgery, a nurse comes in. She sneaks up on him. She jabs a needle in his arm before he can say: What are you doing? She leaves before he can say: What the hell'd you do? I told you I ain't taking anything will make me sleep. He begins to fight the fuzzy flaking in his head. He thinks he will talk to himself to keep awake and get it said. Say what?

Say it's only me here to go alone if there's no one going with me when he comes down like that from my apple to my gut to open where my heart is with a band of blood just before the saw goes off and rips from the apple to the gut down the middle of the bone while they pull the ribs wide the way mine under the center's balls when I made the signals to my blood and was from the time it ever was until they saw the goddamned Bobby Kraft slip a shoulder and fake it once and fade back and let it go uncorked up there the way it spirals against the blue of it, the point of it, leather brown spiralling on the jolted blue to the banging on me that was no use to them. You sonsabitches. Cause the ball's gone and hearing the roar of them with Jeffer getting it on his tips on the zig and in and streak that was going all the way cause I read the free safe blitz and called it on the line and faded against his looping where Copper picked him up and I let it go before the rest caved me with their hands pulling my ribs now and cranking on some ratchet bar to keep me spread and oh my God his rubbered hand on. Gottfried down with his knife in my heart's like a jelly sack the way he cuts through it with my blood in a plastic tube with the flow of it into some machine that cleans it for going back into me with blades like wipers on cars in the rain when I played in mud to my ankles and in the snows and over ninety in the Coliseum like in hell before the roar my God. Keep this my heart or let me die you sonsabitches.

Pray for me again Elfi that I didn't love you the way such a little thing you are, and it was to do and I couldn't, but what could you know of me and what I had to and what it was for me, born to be a thing in the lot and the park, and in the school too with all of them calling me cold as ice bastard, and I wasn't any of that or how would I come to them in the pros out of a dink pussey college and be as good as any of them and better than most of all those that run the show on the field that are Quarterbacks. Godbacks goddammit. The way he's supposed to, this Gottfried with that stare and not any loser. Me? A loser? Because I cry in the dread I feel now of the what?

ANNETTE SANFORD

Trip in a Summer Dress

(FROM PRAIRIE SCHOONER)

MOTHS ARE ALREADY dying under the street lamps 'when I board the bus. I have said goodbye to my mother and to Matthew, who is crying because he's almost six and knows I won't be back in time for his birthday. I won't be back for the next one either, but who's going to tell him that?

I spread myself out on two seats. I have a brown plastic purse, a tan makeup case, and a paperback book. I could be anybody starting a trip.

The driver is putting the rest of my things in the luggage compartment. His name is E. E. Davis, and the sign at the front of the bus says not to talk to him. He can count on me.

The bus is coughing gray smoke into the loading lanes. I can see my mother and Matthew moving back into the station, out of sight. I fan myself with the paperback and smooth the skirt of my dress. Blue. Cotton. No sleeves.

"It's too late for a summer dress," my mother said while we waited. Before that, she said October is a cold month in Arkansas. She said that Matthew needs vitamins, that the man who sells tickets looks like Uncle Harry. Some things she said twice without even noticing.

We're moving finally.

E. E. Davis is making announcements in a voice like a spoon scraping a cooking pot. *We rest twenty minutes in Huntsville, we stay in our seats while the coach is in motion.* All the time he's talking I'm watching my mother and Matthew on the corner waiting for the light to change. Matthew is sucking two fingers and searching the bus windows for me. I could wave, but I don't.

I'm riding off into the night because two days from now in Eureka Springs, Arkansas, I'm going to be married. Bill Richards is his name. He has brown hair and a gentle touch and a barber shop. He thinks marriages are made in heaven. He thinks Matthew is my mother's son.

She's young enough. She married and had her first child when she was fifteen. So did I, but I wasn't married.

Matthew was born on Uncle Harry's tree farm in East Texas where I went with my mother after she told all her friends she was pregnant again. She needed fresh air and a brother's sympathy, she said, and me to look after her.

Knowing me, maybe some of them believed her.

I was skinny and flat-chested and worked after school in the aviary at the zoo mixing up peanut butter and sunflower seeds and feeding fuzzy orphans with an eye dropper. Most nights I studied. What happened was just a mistake I made because I'd never given much thought to that kind of thing and when the time came it caught me without my mind made up one way or the other.

So we went to the tree farm.

Every day while we waited my mother preached me a sermon: you didn't pass around a child like a piece of cake, and you didn't own him like a house or a refrigerator, and you didn't tell him one thing was true one day and something else was true the next. You took a child and set him down in the safest place you could find. Then you taught him the rules and let him grow. One thing for sure: you didn't come along later just when he was thinking he was a rose and tell him he was a lily instead, just because it suited you to.

What you did was you gave him to your mother and father and you called him your brother and that was that.

Except for one thing. They let you name him.

I picked Matthew because of the dream.

All through that night I'd been Moses' sister tending to the reed basket when the queen found him. All night I was Moses' sister running up and down that river bank hollering till my throat about burst. When the pain was over, there he was — with my mother taking care of him just like the Bible story says. Only you can't name a little pink baby Moses because Moses was mostly an old man. So I settled on Matthew.

It made him mine.

There are four people on this bus. There's a black boy in the second seat blowing bubbles with his gum. Across from him are a couple of ladies just out of the beauty parlor with hair too blue, and a child one seat up across from me. A little girl. Scared probably. She's pretty young for traveling in the dark.

I'm not going to look at them anymore. Everything you do in this life gets mixed up with something else, so you better watch out, even just looking at people. Landscapes are safer.

Pine trees, rice fields, oil rigs. I got my fill of them coming back from Uncle Harry's. I didn't look once at Matthew, but I felt him, even when he wasn't crying. He had hold of me way down deep and wouldn't let go for love nor money.

I sat on the back seat. My father drove and my mother cooed at her brand new son, the first one in four girls. If she said that one time, she said it a hundred.

Finally *I* said — so loud my father ran off the road, "He's not your child! I birthed him. I'm his mother, and I'm going to raise him up to know I am! Now what's the matter with that?"

My mother said, "Count the *I's,* and you'll know." She didn't even turn around.

I got used to it, the way you do a thorn that won't come out or chronic appendicitis. But it's hard to pretend all the time that something's true when it isn't.

So I didn't.

I talked to Matthew about it. I fed him cereal on the back porch by the banana tree, and I told him just how it was he came about. I took him to the park in his red-striped stroller and showed him pansies and tulips and iris blooming. I told him they were beautiful and that's the way it is with love.

Only I hadn't loved his father, I said, and that's where I was wrong. A person ought never to give his body if his soul can't come along.

I told him I'd never leave him because he was me and I was him, and no matter what his mother — who was really his grandmother — said, I had a plan that would save us.

Then he learned to talk, and I had to quit all that.

It's just as well 'cause look at me now. Leaving. Going away from him as hard and fast as ever I can. Me and E. E. Davis burning up the pavement to Huntsville so we can rest twenty minutes and start up again.

Now here's a town.

That little girl across the aisle is rising up and squirming around. Maybe she lives here. Maybe one of those houses going by with lights on and people eating supper inside is hers. But I'm not going to ask. You get a child started talking, you can't stop them sometimes.

Like Matthew.

The day I said yes to Bill Richards I set my plan a-going. I took Matthew to the park like I always had. We sat under a tree where I knew something was likely to happen because lately it always did, and when it started, I said: "Looka there, Matthew. See that redbird feeding her baby?"

"That's not her baby," he said when he finally found the limb. "She's littler than it."

"That's right. The baby's a cowbird, but it *thinks* it's a redbird."

He was real interested. "Does the redbird know it's not her baby?"

"Yes, but she keeps on taking care of it because it hatched in her nest and she loves it."

"How did it get in her nest?"

"Its mama left it there." I'm taking it slow by then, being mighty careful. "She gave it to the redbirds, but just for a little while."

Matthew looked at me. "Mamas don't do that."

"Sometimes they do. If they have to."

"Why would they have to?"

"If they can't take care of the babies, it's better that way."

"Why can't they take care of them?"

"Well. For one thing, cowbirds are too lazy to build nests. Or won't. Or can't." I saw right away I'd said it all wrong.

Matthew stuck out his bottom lip. "I don't like cowbirds."

"They aren't really bad birds," I said quick as I could. "They just got started on the wrong foot — *wing*." Nothing went right with that conversation.

"They're ugly too."

"The mama comes back, Matthew. She always comes back. She whistles and the baby hears and they fly away together."

"I wouldn't go. I'd peck her with my nose."

"Let's go look at the swans," I said.

"I'd tell her to go away and never come back."

"Maybe you'd like some popcorn."

"I would be a redbird forever!"

"Or peanuts. How about a nice big bag?"

When we got home he crawled up in my mother's lap and kissed her a million times. He told her cowbirds are awful. He told her he was mighty glad he belonged to her and not to a cowbird. She was mighty glad too, she said.

I told her now was the time to set things straight and she could be a plenty big help if she wanted to.

She told me little pitchers have big ears.

Eureka Springs is about the size of this town we're going through. In Eureka Springs the barber shop of Bill Richards is set on a mountain corner, he says, and the streets drop off like shelves around it. Eureka Springs is a tourist place. Christ stands on a hill there and sees the goings-on. In Eureka Springs, Bill Richards has a house with window boxes in the front and geraniums growing out, just waiting for someone to pick them.

I can see people in these houses in this town hanging up coats and opening doors and kissing each other. Women are washing dishes, and kids are getting lessons.

Next year Matthew is going to school in Houston. My mother will walk with him to the corner where he'll catch the bus. He'll have on short pants and a red shirt because red's his favorite color, and he won't want to let go of her hand. In Eureka Springs it will be too cool for a boy to start school wearing short pants.

In Eureka Springs, a boy won't have to.

I can see I was wrong about that little girl. She's not scared. She's been up and down the aisle twice and pestered E. E. Davis. She's gotten chewing gum from the boy and candy from the ladies. It's my turn now, I guess.

"Hello." I know better, but I can't help it.

She puts a sticky hand on my arm. "How come you're crying?"

"Dirt in my eye."

"From the chemical plant," she says, pretty smarty. "They're p'luters. They make plastic bags and umber-ellas."

I open my purse and take out a Kleenex. "How do you know?"

"I know everything on this road."

"You live on it?"

She throws back her head like a TV star. "Prac'ly. Fridays I go that way." She points toward the back window. "Sundays I come back. My daddy's got week-in custardy."

She hangs on the seat in front of me and breathes through her mouth. She smells like corn chips. "They had a big fight, but Mama won most of me. You got any kids?"

"No — yes."

"Don't you know?" A tooth is missing under those pouty lips.

"I have a boy, a little younger than you." I never said it out loud before to anybody but Matthew, and him when he was just a baby.

"Where is he?"

"At home. With his grandmother."

"Whyn't you bring him?"

"I'm going a far piece. He's better off there."

She pops her gum and swings a couple of times on one heel. "You got a boyfriend?"

"Yes." It's out before I can stop it. I ought to bite my tongue off or shake her good. A child with no manners is an abomination before the Lord, my mother says. That's one thing about my mother. She won't let Matthew get away with a thing.

The child turns up her mouth corners, but it's not a smile. "My mama's got one too. Name's Rex. He'g got three gold teeth and a Cadillac."

"How far is it to Huntsville?"

"Two more towns and a dance hall."

"You run on. I'm going to take a nap."

She wanders off up the aisle and plops in a seat. In a second her feet are up in it, her skirt sky-high. Somebody ought to care that she does that. Somebody ought to be here to tell her to sit up like a lady. Especially on a bus. All kinds of people ride buses.

I met Bill Richards on a bus. Going to Galveston for Splash Day. He helped us off and carried my tote bag and bought us hot dogs. He bought Matthew a snow cone. He built him a castle. He gave him a shoulder ride right into the waves. A girl married to Bill Richards wouldn't have to do a thing but love him.

A girl married to Bill Richards wouldn't tell him she had a son with no father, my mother said. And she wouldn't tell her son he was her son. Or a redbird either. She would forget it and love her brother.

We're stopping at a filling station sort of place. The blue-haired ladies are tying nets around their heads and stuffing things in paper sacks. They get out and a lot of hot air comes in. The door pops shut and E. E. Davis gives it the gas. "Ten more miles to Huntsville."

"My mama better be there this time!" the child says, loud and quivery. I had it right in the first place, I guess. Her scare is just all slicked over with chewing gum and smart talk. Inside she's powerful shaky.

"Your mama'll be there, don't you worry." Before I can close my mouth she's on me like a plaster cast. I should have been a missionary.

"She's always late. Last time I waited all night. The bus station man bought me a cheese sandwich and covered me up with his coat."

"Something kept her, I guess."

"Yeah." She slides down in the seat beside me. "Rex."

I don't want to talk to her. I want to think about things. I want to figure out how it's going to be in Eureka Springs with Christ looking right into the kitchen window when I'm kissing Bill Richards, and Him knowing all the time about Moses' sister. I want to think about Matthew growing up and getting married himself and even dying without ever knowing I'm his mother.

Most of all I want to get off this bus and go and get my baby.

"Huntsville!" yells E. E.

"I told you! I told you she wouldn't be here." That child's got a grip on my left hand so tight the blood's quit running. We're standing in the waiting room with lots of faces, but none of them is the right one. It's pitch dark outside and hot as a devil's poker.

"Just sit down," I say. "She'll come."

"I have to go to the bathroom."

"Go ahead. I'll watch for her."

I go in the phone booth. No matter what my mother says, Matthew is a big boy. He can take it. So can Bill Richards. I put two quarters and seven nickels on the shelf by the receiver. I get the dial tone. I spin the numbers out, eleven of them, and drop my money in the slot.

I see the woman coming in out of the dark. She's holding hands with a gold-toothed man and her mouth's all pouty like the child's. My mother's voice shouts hello in my ear.

"Wait," I tell her.

I open the door of the phone booth. "Wait! She's in the restroom. Your child. There, she's coming yonder."

I can see they wish she wasn't. I can see how they hate Sundays.

"Talk if you're going to," my mother says. She only calls long distance when somebody dies.

"Mama, I wanted to tell you —"

"That you wish you had your coat. I knew it! The air's too still and sticky not to be breeding a blizzard."

"It's *hot* here, for goodness sakes!"

"Won't be for long. Thirty by morning the TV says. Twenty where you're going. Look in the makeup case. I stuck in your blue wool sweater."

"Matthew —"

"In bed and finally dropping off. I told him an hour ago, the sooner you shed today, the quicker tomorrow'll come, but he's something else to convince, that boy."

"Comes by it naturally," I say, and plenty loud, but she doesn't hear.

"Have a good trip," she's yelling, "and wrap up warm in the wind."

When I step outside, it's blowing all right, just like she said. Hard from the north and sharp as a scissors.

By the time E. E. Davis swings open the door and bellows, "All aboard for Eureka Springs," that wind is tossing up newspapers and bus drivers' caps and hems of summer dresses. It's whipping through door cracks and rippling puddles and freezing my arms where the sleeves ought to be.

If I was my mother, I'd get mighty tired of always being right.

PAUL BOWLES

The Eye

(FROM THE MISSOURI REVIEW)

TEN OR TWELVE YEARS AGO there came to live in Tangier a man
who would have done better to stay away. What happened to him
was in no way his fault, notwithstanding the whispered innuendos
of the English-speaking residents. These people often have reac-
tions similar to those of certain primitive groups: when misfortune
overtakes one of their number, the others by mutual consent refrain from offering him aid, and merely sit back to watch, certain
that he has called his suffering down upon himself. He has become
taboo, and is incapable of receiving help. In the case of this particular man, I suppose no one could have been of much comfort; still,
the tacit disapproval called forth by his bad luck must have made
the last months of his life harder to bear.

His name was Duncan Marsh, and he was said to have come
from Vancouver. I never saw him, nor do I know anyone who
claims to have seen him. By the time his story reached the cock-
tail-party circuit he was dead, and the more irresponsible residents
felt at liberty to indulge their taste for myth-making.

He came alone to Tangier, rented a furnished house on the
slopes of Djamaa el Mokra — they were easy enough to find in
those days, and correspondingly inexpensive — and presently in-
stalled a teen-age Moroccan on the premises to act as night-watchman. The house provided a resident cook and gardener, but both
of these were discharged from their duties, the cook being replaced
by a woman brought in at the suggestion of the watchman. It was
not long after this that Marsh felt the first symptoms of a digestive
illness which over the months grew steadily worse. The doctors in
Tangier advised him to go to London. Two months in hospital

there helped him somewhat. No clear diagnosis was made, however, and he returned here only to become bedridden. Eventually he was flown back to Canada on a stretcher, and succumbed there shortly after his arrival.

In all this there was nothing extraordinary; it was assumed that Marsh had been one more victim of slow poisoning by native employees. There have been several such cases during my five decades in Tangier. On each occasion it has been said that the European victim had only himself (or herself) to blame, having encouraged familiarity on the part of a servant. What strikes the outsider as strange is that no one ever takes the matter in hand and inaugurates a search for the culprit, but in the total absence of proof there is no point in attempting an investigation.

Two details complete the story. At some point during his illness Marsh told an acquaintance of the arrangements he had made to provide financial aid for his night-watchman in the event that he himself should be obliged to leave Morocco; he had given him a notarized letter to that effect, but apparently the boy never tried to press his claim. The other report came from Dr. Halsey, the physician who arranged for Marsh's removal from the house to the airport. It was this last bit of information which, for me at least, made the story take on life. According to the doctor, the soles of Marsh's feet had been systematically marked with deep incisions in the form of crude patterns; the cuts were recent, but there was some infection. Dr. Halsey called in the cook and the watchman: they showed astonishment and dismay at the sight of their employer's feet, but were unable to account for the mutilations. Within a few days after Marsh's departure, the original cook and gardener returned to take up residence, the other two having already left the house.

The slow poisoning was classical enough, particularly in the light of Marsh's remark about his provision for the boy's well-being, but the knife-drawn designs on the feet somehow got in the way of whatever combinations of motive one could invent. I thought about it. There could be little doubt that the boy was guilty. He had persuaded Marsh to get rid of the cook that came with the house, even though her wages had to continue to be paid, and to hire another woman (very likely from his own family) to do the cooking. The poisoning process lasts many months if it is to be undetectable, and no one is in a better position to take charge of it than the cook herself. Clearly she knew about the financial arrangement that had been made for the boy, and expected to share in it. At the same time the crosses and circles slashed in the feet were inexplicable. The slow poisoner is patient, careful, methodical; his principal concerns are to keep the dosage effective and to avoid leaving any visible marks. Bravado is unknown to him.

The time came when people no longer told the story of Duncan Marsh. I myself thought of it less often, having no more feasible hypotheses to supply. One evening perhaps five years ago, an American resident here came to me with the news that he had discovered a Moroccan who claimed to have been Marsh's night-watchman. The man's name was Larbi; he was a waiter at Le Fin Bec, a small back-street restaurant. Apparently he spoke poor English, but understood it without difficulty. This information was handed me for what it was worth, said the American, in the event that I felt inclined to make use of it.

I turned it over in my mind, and one night a few weeks later I went down to the restaurant to see Larbi for myself. The place was dimly lit and full of Europeans. I studied the three waiters. They were interchangeable, with wide black moustaches, blue jeans and sport shirts. A menu was handed me; I could scarcely read it, even directly under the glow of the little table lamp. When the man who had brought it returned, I asked for Larbi.

He pulled the menu from my hand and left the table. A moment later another of the triumvirate came up beside me and handed me the menu he carried under his arm. I ordered in Spanish. When he brought the soup I murmured that I was surprised to find him working there. This brought him up short; I could see him trying to remember me.

"Why wouldn't I be working here?" His voice was level, without inflection.

"Of course! Why not? It was just that I thought by now you'd have a bazaar or some sort of shop."

His laugh was a snort. "Bazaar!"

When he arrived with the next course, I begged his pardon for meddling in his affairs. But I was interested, I said, because for several years I had been under the impression that he had received a legacy from an English gentleman.

"You mean Señor Marsh?" His eyes were at last wide open.

"Yes, that was his name. Didn't he give you a letter? He told his friends he had."

He looked over my head as he said: "He gave me a letter."

"Have you ever showed it to anyone?" This was tactless, but sometimes it is better to drive straight at the target.

"Why? What good is it? Señor Marsh is dead." He shook his head with an air of finality, and moved off to another table. By the time I had finished my crème caramel, most of the diners had left, and the place seemed even darker. He came over to the table to see if I wanted coffee. I asked for the check. When he brought it I told him I should like very much to see the letter if he still had it.

"You can come tomorrow night or any night, and I'll show it to you. I have it at home."

I thanked him and promised to return in two or three days. I was confused as I left the restaurant. It seemed clear that the waiter did not consider himself to be incriminated in Duncan Marsh's troubles. When, a few nights later, I saw the document, I no longer understood anything.

It was not a letter; it was a *papier timbré* of the kind on sale at tobacconists. It read, simply: *To Whom It May Concern: I, Duncan Whitelow Marsh, do hereby agree to deposit the sum of One Hundred Pounds to the account of Larbi Lairini, on the first of each month, for as long as I live.* It was signed and notarized in the presence of two Moroccan witnesses, and bore the date June 11, 1966. As I handed it back to him I said: "And it never did you any good."

He shrugged and slipped the paper into his wallet. "How was it going to? The man died."

"It's too bad."

"*Suerte.*" In the Moroccan usage of the word, it means *fate*, rather than simple luck.

At that moment I could have pressed on, and asked him if he had any idea as to the cause of Marsh's illness, but I wanted time for considering what I had just learned. As I rose to leave I said: "I'm sorry it turned out that way. I'll be back in a few days." He held out his hand and I shook it. I had no intentions then. I might return soon or I might never go back.

For as long as I live. The phrase echoed in my mind for several weeks. Possibly Marsh had worded it that way so it would be readily understandable to the *adoul* of Tangier who had affixed their florid signatures to the sheet; yet I could not help interpreting the words in a more melodramatic fashion. To me the document represented the officializing of a covenant already in existence between master and servant: Marsh wanted the watchman's help, and the watchman had agreed to give it. There was nothing upon which to base such an assumption; nevertheless I thought I was on the right track. Slowly I came to believe that if only I could talk to the watchman, in Arabic, and inside the house itself, I might be in a position to see things more clearly.

One evening I walked to Le Fin Bec and without taking a seat motioned to Larbi to step outside for a moment. There I asked him if he could find out whether the house Señor Marsh had lived in was occupied at the moment or not.

"There's nobody living there now." He paused and added: "It's empty. I know the guardian."

I had decided, in spite of my deficient Arabic, to speak to him in his own language, so I said: "Look. I'd like to go with you to the house and see where everything happened. I'll give you fifteen thousand francs for your trouble."

He was startled to hear the Arabic; then his expression shifted to one of satisfaction. "He's not supposed to let anyone in," he said.

I handed him three thousand francs. "You arrange that with him. And fifteen for you when we leave the house. Could we do it Thursday?"

The house had been built, I should say, in the Fifties, when good construction was still possible. It was solidly embedded in the hillside, with the forest towering behind it. We had to climb three flights of stairs through the garden to get to the entrance. The guardian, a squinting Djibli in a brown djellaba, followed close on our footsteps, eyeing me with mistrust.

There was a wide terrace above, with a view to the southeast over the town and the mountains. Behind the terrace a shadowed lawn ended where the forest began. The living room was large and bright, with French doors giving on to the lawn. Odors of damp walls and mildew weighted the air. The absurd conviction that I was about to understand everything had taken possession of me; I noticed that I was breathing more quickly. We wandered into the dining room. There was a corridor beyond, and the room where Marsh had slept, shuttered and dark. A wide curving stairway led down to a level where there were two more bedrooms, and continued its spiral to the kitchen and servants' rooms below. The kitchen door opened on to a small flagstoned patio where high philodendron covered the walls.

Larbi looked out and shook his head. "That's the place where all the trouble began," he said glumly.

I pushed through the doorway and sat down on a wrought-iron bench in the sun. "It's damp inside. Why don't we stay out here?"

The guardian left us and locked up the house. Larbi squatted comfortably on his heels near the bench.

There would have been no trouble at all, he said, if only Marsh had been satisfied with Yasmina, the cook whose wages were included in the rent. But she was a careless worker and the food was bad. He asked Larbi to find him another cook.

"I told him ahead of time that this woman Meriam had a little girl, and some days she could leave her with friends and some days she would have to bring her with her when she came to work. He said it didn't matter, but he wanted her to be quiet."

The woman was hired. Two or three days a week she came accompanied by the child, who would play in the patio, where she could watch her. From the beginning Marsh complained that she was noisy. Repeatedly he sent messages down to Meriam, asking her to make the child be still. And one day he went quietly around the outside of the house and down to the patio. He got on all fours, put his face close to the little girl's face, and frowned at her so fiercely that she began to scream. When Meriam rushed out of the kitchen he stood up smiling and walked off. The little girl continued to scream and wail in a corner of the kitchen, until Meriam took her home. That night, still sobbing, she came down with a high fever. For several weeks she hovered between life and death, and when she was finally out of danger she could no longer walk.

Meriam, who was earning relatively high wages, consulted one fqih after another. They agreed that "the eye" had been put on the child; it was equally clear that the Nazarene for whom she worked had done it. What they told her she must do, Larbi explained, was to administer certain substances to Marsh which eventually would make it possible to counteract the spell. This was absolutely necessary, he said, staring at me gravely. Even if the señor had agreed to remove it (and of course she never would have mentioned it to him) he would not have been able to. What she gave him could not harm him; it was merely medicine to relax him so that when the time came to undo the spell he would not make any objections.

At some point Marsh confided to Larbi that he suspected Meriam of slipping soporifics into his food, and begged him to be vigilant. The provision for Larbi's well-being was signed as an inducement to enlisting his active support. Since to Larbi the mixtures Meriam was feeding her master were relatively harmless, he reassured him and let her continue to dose him with her concoctions.

Tired of squatting, Larbi suddenly stood up and began to walk back and forth, stepping carefully in the center of each flagstone. "When he had to go to the hospital in London, I told her, 'Now you've made him sick. Suppose he doesn't come back? You'll never break it.' She was worried about it. 'I've done what I could,' she said. 'It's in the hands of Allah.'"

When Marsh did return to Tangier, Larbi urged her to be quick about bringing things to a head, now that she had been fortunate enough to get him back. He was thinking, he said, that it might be better for the señor's health if her treatment were not continued for too long a time.

I asked no questions while he talked; I made a point of keeping my face entirely expressionless, thinking that if he noticed the least flicker of disapproval he might stop. The sun had gone behind the trees and the patio was chilly. I had a strong desire to get up and walk back and forth as he was doing, but I thought even that might interrupt him. Once stopped, the flow might not resume.

Soon Marsh was worse than ever, with racking pains in his abdomen and kidneys. He remained in bed then, and Larbi brought him his food. When Meriam saw that he was no longer able to leave the bed, even to go into the bathroom, she decided that the time had come to get rid of the spell. On the same night that a fqih held a ceremony at her house in the presence of the crippled child, four men from Meriam's family came up to Djamaa el Mokra.

"When I saw them coming, I got onto my motorcycle and went into the city. I didn't want to be here when they did it. It had nothing to do with me."

He stood still and rubbed his hands together. I heard the southwest wind beginning to sound in the trees; it was that time of afternoon. "Come. I'll show you something," he said.

We climbed steps around the back of the house and came out onto a terrace with a pergola over it. Beyond this lay the lawn and the wall of trees.

"He was very sick for the next two days. He kept asking me to telephone the English doctor."

"Didn't you do it?"

Larbi stopped walking and looked at me. "I had to clean everything up first. Meriam wouldn't touch him. It was during the rains.

He had mud and blood all over him when I got back here and found him. The next day I gave him a bath and changed the sheets and blankets. And I cleaned the house, because they got mud everywhere when they brought him back in. Come on. You'll see where they had to take him."

We had crossed the lawn and were walking in the long grass that skirted the edge of the woods. A path led off to the right through the tangle of undergrowth, and we followed it, climbing across boulders and fallen tree trunks until we came to an old stone well. I leaned over the wall of rocks around it and saw the small circle of sky far below.

"They had to drag him all the way here, you see, and hold him steady right over the well while they made the signs on his feet, so the blood would fall into the water. It's no good if it falls on the side of the well. And they had to make the same signs the fqih drew on paper for the little girl. That's hard to do in the dark and in the rain. But they did it. I saw the cuts when I bathed him."

Cautiously I asked him if he saw any connection between all this and Marsh's death. He ceased staring into the well and turned around. We started to walk back toward the house.

"He died because his hour had come."

And had the spell been broken? I asked him. Could the child walk afterward? But he had never heard, for Meriam had gone to Kenitra not much later to live with her sister.

When we were in the car, driving back down to the city, I handed him the money. He stared at it for several seconds before slipping it into his pocket.

I let him off in town with a vague sense of disappointment, and I saw that I had not only expected, but actually hoped, to find someone on whom the guilt might be fixed. What constitutes a crime? There was no criminal intent — only a mother moving in the darkness of ancient ignorance. I thought about it on my way home in the taxi.

JEAN THOMPSON

Paper Covers Rock

(FROM MADEMOISELLE)

IT SEEMED she didn't know what she was doing. All that winter her mind was as blank and enclosed as a bubble of glass. At the time, of course, she thought the bubble was full of opinions, plans, disappointments, and so on. But those were just reflexes. Really thinking about what she was doing would have been intolerable. It was an odd way to have a love affair.

Or maybe it was the only way. She felt the drone of blood, the heat of skin and nothing else — like a cat. The winter sky streamed with rain which refused to crystallize into snow. Dripping trees ambushed her and she never arrived anywhere with dry feet. Like a cat, she tended scrupulously to her own comfort at the end of the day. She bought good sherry and expensive bath salts and lolled in hot water up to her neck, sometimes falling asleep in the tub.

Sometimes her lover arrived at that point. She'd open her eyes to see him standing over her, the blurred light behind him making it difficult to read his face. She'd missed something, she thought, by not being able to see him clearly at that moment, some clue to the future. The scented water made her feel languid, drugged. Her body seemed to undulate like a ribbon beneath it, more naked than if she were surrounded by air. He always waited until she was wrapped in towels, her skin shrinking a little from the sudden chill, then he'd lead her by the hand into another room.

Later, still without speaking a word, they might find their fingers curling towards their palms, and one of them would start the game. The fist beating one, two, then three, forming one of the simple shapes. Rock, scissors or paper. She didn't remember playing it as a child, but now the game delighted her. The awful restraint of preserving the fist, the impulse of the open hand, the more precise maneuver of the fingers. He allowed her this foolishness, and she gloried in his indulgence. It pleased her to be able to ask something of him, even a small thing. They tapped each other lightly for forfeits, and when one tired of playing the taps turned into caresses.

Sooner or later he always had to leave. They made a tradition of being brisk and cheerful about it. Time I put some clothes on, he'd say, and the answer to that was, Only if you're going outside. She watched him from the window, wishing he had something as uncomplicated as a wife. A married lover was, after all, a situation easily defined, with its own set of precedents, its own literature.

Instead there was mutable anarchy. He was not married to the woman he lived with, that she knew. It seemed to make her own status and expectations terribly unclear. As she picked her way through the sullen water in the gutters, as the wind blew wet leaves against her ankles, she imagined encountering the two of them together. Would her lover pass without acknowledging her, in the classic manner of adulterers? Would there be accusations and speeches? That all seemed incongruous, as if they should be wearing nineteenth-century costumes.

I just wanted to get things straight, she said once. We're crazy in bed — it's wonderful — we shouldn't expect more than that. She saw him frown and said hurriedly, I can live with it. I just want to make sure we understand each other.

He stroked her cheek with one finger, which always made her skin feel as if it would ring, like fine porcelain. Why do you sell yourself short, girl? Don't cheapen things.

Maybe nobody understands how to behave anymore, she said, struggling against the lulling finger. Nobody understands what they need.

You need a good man. Someone better than me.

She thought, but did not say, A lot of good men have told me that, and pressed his full hand against her face.

Once or twice she slept with other men when her lover was not around. She wasn't sure if she should feel guilty. Similarly, she felt hesitant to label her curiosity about his mistress (his *other* mistress, she reminded herself) as jealousy. She felt like a stray particle moving outside the laws of physics.

Perhaps her lover had several mistresses, she considered, and each mistress in turn had other lovers. It was like the nursery rhyme. As I was going to St. Ives, I met a man with seven wives and every wife had seven sacks and every sack had seven cats and so on. When she reached this point, it seemed to her that everyone in the world must be connected by hidden, erotic currents, everyone shared the same sly secret, and she gave up trying to make sense of it.

It didn't help to remind herself she'd wanted things this way. The first time she saw him it was the burnt end of summer. She'd been driven out of her apartment by airless heat and boredom. The sidewalks were a baked, dazzling white as she drifted past shop windows, trying to interest herself in the premature tweeds worn by slim, ecstatic mannequins. At the end of the block a figure was approaching. There was no one between them, and she felt her body stiffen in preparation for the inevitable awkward moment of passing. The figure changed from a dark spot edged by glare into a tall young man with black hair and beard. She wondered briefly whether to smile or not.

They were no more than a dozen yards apart when her face turned unaccountably brittle, flushed. Was it because he was staring at her? But then (how slow the heat made everything!), she was staring at him also. They passed without speaking or smiling, and she continued down the white street, wondering if she had imagined that odd moment.

The very next day she saw him drinking coffee in a restaurant. She was out of his sight and could examine him at length. Under the cool lights he looked paler, the contrast between hair and skin more pronounced. He had a newspaper spread out before him and his face was absorbed, almost stern. This time she identified her agitation as sexual. Yet she felt much more deliberate, more calculating. She left without speaking to him, sure that she'd see him again.

When she did she was surprised by how simple it was. The simplest thing in the world! She had a power she never suspected, maybe all women did. Hi, may I join you? she'd said. It was that easy. They sat in a bar, on opposite sides of a red vinyl booth. The seat beneath her was badly sprung and contributed to her sensation that she was about to topple over. Now the light was late-afternoon, green-tinged gold sliding through the narrow windows.

She said, I imagine you're used to strange women accosting you in public. And smiled.

Matter of fact, I'm not. But I could get used to it. His voice was lighter than she'd expected, but pleasant. And she liked the way he controlled his own surprise, not allowing her to unsettle him.

I'm sure most ladies are more subtle about it. Maybe they're afraid of you.

This seemed to startle him more than her intrusion had. Afraid? Good God, I'm the most inoffensive fellow I know. I'm even polite to those evangelists who knock on my door in the morning and get me out of bed. He spread his hands. Harmless, see?

Oh, but you look wicked, she said recklessly, trying to keep her momentum. You look like a pirate. Somebody who opens bottles with his teeth.

He shook his head. Maybe I should start carrying a briefcase and wearing ties.

They must have spent some time talking about neutral, informational things. She learned he worked for a radio station. He enjoyed reading novels. All the while she was at the mercy of her sense of sight: the sunburnt ridge of his collarbone disappearing beneath a shadowy fold of cloth, pointing towards the heart. The lean, anatomical beauty of his hands. And his eyes, which could not have been more startling, blue, large-pupilled, with a dark rim around the iris. Later he would tell her about a Cherokee great-grandmother.

Finally she said, I wish I could tell you how attractive I find you. Will you let me show you?

He neither smiled nor looked abashed. There's someone — he began, but she interrupted.

I don't want to hear about it. Not now, at least. He nodded and they left together. After all, she had not really given him much choice.

She supposed they were both nervous; she was ready to make allowances. But there was no need to. Perhaps she had already entered that blank glass bubble where sensation replaced thought. Their nakedness pleased them both. If it had not been their first time together, they might have lingered a bit beforehand. Her apartment had a window which showed nothing but sky. They watched it pass through all the exaggerations of sunset, then turn

sedate blue, then a little polished moon and one star appeared. He
had to go.

Don't say anything, she told him. What could we say that would
make any sense? She wanted to avoid the obligatory discussion of
whether or not either of them had done this sort of thing before.
The truth was she hadn't, but for the moment she wanted to
pretend she had. Her new daring elated her.

You're the pirate you know, not me.

An apprentice pirate. A mere cabin boy. Good-bye now.

So she had adopted violence, impulse, anarchy, at the expense
of safety. Even now she could not say she was entirely sorry. But
impulse did not sustain one over a matter of months. As the
interminable rains began, she found herself growing melancholy,
wondering what she had gotten herself into. It was mortifying to
cast yourself in the role of a seductress, a woman of grand, careless
passions, then find yourself yearning after something more predictable. If she'd been looking for the limits of her unorthodoxy,
she'd found them.

Some evenings she fixed him a meal, or hot whiskey with lemon
to guard against the dampness. At such times she was especially
bright and talkative, clattering dishes in the sink, fussing over
sugar bowls and napkins. This was to disguise the pleasure she
took in it, and also the irony of knowing that for them this was just
a parody of domestic intimacy. It was on one such occasion, sitting
on the rug as he ate toasted cheese, that she asked about his girl
friend.

He looked surprised, then rather grim. Oh come on, she said.
You're not going to hurt my feelings. I'm not trying to scheme or
plot, I'm just curious.

Still he hesitated. She had to prod him. How long have you
known her?

Three years. We met at a party. She'd come with this loudmouth
fellow who hangs around the bars. Well, he wanted her to go
upstairs with him. Turns out she hardly even knew the guy. And
he was shit-faced drunk. Tried to get her clothes off right in the
kitchen. A real charmer.

She was fascinated, apprehensive of what she'd hear next. And
then?

He shrugged. Well, I told him to lay off and when he didn't, I
got him bloody. Then she and I got together. He finished his
sandwich; it was obvious he didn't want to say more.

She was shaken, pulled in so many different directions, she didn't trust herself to look at him. First, his terseness disappointed her; she wanted to picture the incident in all its intolerable detail. The thought of him fighting, of that strength she knew so well in love erupting into violence, gave her a sharp erotic ache. It was no wonder that he and the girl had become lovers. What excited and dismayed her most of all was the evidence that he was not always the mild, obliging creature he made himself out to be. She knew that some of that was mere disclaimer, a self-effacement he felt comfortable with. But the thought that parts of him were hidden, that she could not elicit them, was intolerable.

After a moment she looked up, smiled, and extended her fist towards him. He smiled also and the game began. She was intent, almost desperate in her concentration, as if by anticipating his gestures she could read the rest of his mind. Rock, the smasher, she thought of as unadorned fact, unthinking force. Scissors were contrived, a tool, a sly edge. Paper she liked: it was harmless; it only covered rather than destroyed. Holding her breath she formed paper.

He had scissors. He tapped her wrist, then kissed her and said, I have to go.

She retrieved his coat and told him to be careful driving. When he was gone she began to weep, the first tears she had ever shed over him.

The tears reached their usual anticlimactic end. She felt hot-eyed and weak. Now, she told herself, is the time to think things out. That statement had a calming effect on her until she realized she couldn't just stop there.

Again she rallied herself. She supposed her choice was either to go on as they had or to stop seeing him. What did she really want? She wanted what the other woman had, his legitimate presence. Then she had to retreat from that, for what was legitimate about simple cohabitation, and did she want a lover who was unfaithful?

It was hopeless. She sat on the floor, back to the wall, legs bent crookedly beneath her. The perfect silence and the glossy black of the windows told her it was very late, that motionless hour sometime before dawn when the clock's hands point to zero. She conjured up her lover, imagined his weight against her taut legs, imagined his startling pallor threaded with milky blue veins. Of course they weren't really blue at all but red, a peculiar stream branching to every part of the skin. Blood, she thought, was something she could understand, its submerged, secret channeling, its frantic movement to and from the heart . . .

Her head ached. She realized she was smashing it against the wall behind her, but the realization was so gradual she did not immediately stop, but observed herself idly for a moment. Thud. Thud. Thud. A pause, and the rhythm was repeated. She simply didn't know whether to laugh or cry. Apparently it was impossible to make your head into anything but a head. The sky was still dark when she fell asleep, sagged against the baseboard.

It rained steadily through Christmas, smearing the colored lights and making the evergreens droop. In January the rain gave way to sleet. She skimmed across the treacherous pavement and when she fell, she abandoned herself to gravity, landing heavily. Often she told herself she was crazy, or going crazy, and that notion served to explain everything.

When she finally met the woman he lived with, she made another attempt at understanding it all. The circumstances were entirely innocent: she entered a bar with a man she knew casually, and someone called his name. Three people sat at a corner table — her lover, a woman, and the man who knew her friend. So without the slightest manipulation on her part, she found herself sitting down with them in the neutral role of a stranger, able to watch everything.

Her first glance at the woman startled her. She was, she thought, much plainer than herself, her clothes showing only the most ineffectual attempts at vanity, her light brown hair gathered at the neck. It made her face look too round, almost bland. She stored this impression and looked away, for her lover was trying to catch her eye. At first she thought he was anxious and she tried to reassure him with a glance. Don't worry, I won't blow it.

But that wasn't it. Then she knew, he was wondering about the man she was with. Oh *him,* she tried to convey, silently, lifting her shoulders to indicate a shrug, he's nothing, really, nothing at all. Though why she should apologize or justify being with another man, she didn't know.

Watching her lover's distraction and abrupt gestures, she became aware of something else. He was self-conscious about being on display; he knew she was watching the two of them with ferocious curiosity and it made him nervous. Good, she thought. This mild sadism was a novelty she enjoyed.

The woman he lived with — there was no doubt it was she — was filling the ashtray in front of her with cigarette after cigarette, dangling them between her fingers with an utter lack of interest. In fact, she seemed bored with everything. She looked like the sort of woman who would use her boredom and silence as a weapon, a kind of damp club. She had pale blue eyes, very pretty, her best feature. They reminded her of the pastel flowers painted on china. Once, in the middle of a conversation about politics, she tapped him on the arm and said, I've got to call Dinah. Don't let me forget. He acknowledged this and turned back to the discussion with a curtness which, watching, she felt only she understood.

She was a little sorry for him. The woman was showing such deadly low vitality, it must be painful. In such a situation one wanted to present the most invulnerable front possible. She felt sorry for the woman herself, slouching in her chair, one hand rumpling her cheek, mouth slack and pouting. Surely if she knew she were being judged, she'd make more of an effort. She felt a convoluted and misplaced helpfulness, imagining how she would coach the woman, tell her to comb out her hair, use more make-up, project herself. Then she realized how hysterical she herself must be, pretending to give fashion magazine advice to her rival.

Afterwards she hardly remembered the conversation, perhaps because the silence occupied her whole attention. But one part of it stuck in her mind. The man she came with said, I'm so tired of this town. Not to mention the weather. I wish we could all get drunk enough to pile in a car and drive to Mexico.

Why Mexico? asked the man she didn't know.

Because it's just far enough away to be impossible, I guess. My favorite fantasy cliché.

Oh, but it's not impossible, she heard herself saying. She leaned on her forearms so she was inclined towards the center of the table. We could surely get as far as Arkansas before we sobered up. We'd drive all night and by seven o'clock in the morning we'd be scroungy and god-awful hung-over and pissed off at each other. When was the last time you let yourself do something thoroughly stupid? It's the only way you can recapture your youth.

The others laughed, except of course the woman, who only lifted one corner of her mouth. The smile disappeared into the crease of her palm. *Screw her,* she thought, and continued, encouraged by the laughter and her own image glowing in the dim tabletop. We'd have breakfast in some terrible, fake franchise restaurant, you know, the Farmer's Daughter or something, where the waitresses all wear pinafores, and half of us would decide to go back on the bus.

And the other half? It was her lover, and his voice managed to sound both wistful and ironic.

We'd buy a gallon of foul red wine and pledge eternal friendship and start driving again. And when we got to the border — her hands moved in a wide circle to indicate the multitude of possibilities. The guards at the border will make us paranoid. None of us will know how to say *bathroom* in Spanish. The town will look like a running sore and we'll drive another four hours for some place to stay. Then the car will start hemorrhaging —

Stop, said her friend. It all sounds so enchanting, I have to restrain myself from leaping behind the wheel.

Maybe we should aim for Disneyland instead, said the strange man. More our speed. How about you, Catherine, want to break a bottle of champagne over the fender? Get us off to a proper start?

So she had a name after all. It seemed to shrink her further into manageable dimensions, like knowing the name of the disease you were suffering from. Catherine removed her hand from her cheek and spoke in a small, matter-of-fact voice: No, I can't take any vacation time before June. Besides, I don't like champagne.

Said like a true party-pooper, she thought. Again she felt her own power; at that moment it was dizzying, and she had to rein it in. But first she allowed herself one smile at her lover, open and challenging, as if forcing him to acknowledge that power, her smooth hair catching the light, the grace of her moving hands. He smiled back, though he couldn't help looking a little furtive. She felt a touch of scorn for him then.

Of course, neither that nor her confidence lasted very long. She and her friend had to leave, and as they stood exchanging good-byes, Catherine bent towards her lover, about to tell him something. That soft, placid face might have its own appeal, she realized, a wistful and sedate beauty. She arrived home depressed and with hiccups she couldn't get rid of.

The next time she saw her lover she said, I hope you weren't too uncomfortable the other day. I guess it was inevitable we'd have to suffer through that scene sometime.

He shrugged. I thought you almost enjoyed it.

Maybe I did, she admitted. I could pretend we'd come there together.

He crossed the room and examined the objects on her dresser. From the way he picked them up and replaced them — pencil, ball of yarn, nail file — she could tell he had no idea what they were, what he was doing. The room was dim and his nakedness looked nearly blue.

Of course she had not acknowledged his real meaning: she enjoyed confronting Catherine, however indirectly. She only wished she were a stage villainess, able to resort to outlandish weapons. Anything, she thought, was easier than putting things into words, asking him to choose between them. So she lay back on the pillows, her silence a demand and a reproach.

Would he speak? The issues between them seemed to have congealed. He sat on the edge of the bed and, without looking at her, rested one hand on her stomach. She shuddered a little at its careless weight, the ticking of nerves he evoked so easily. It's hard, he began, to get yourself out of certain situations. Even when there are good reasons to.

She stared, but his face was still averted. It was the most general of openings. Who was he talking about? What situation?

You see, Catherine and I — he stammered a bit over the name, and her own tongue seemed to go dead in her mouth — it's not that things are always that great for us. Of course you don't know her, but she can be entirely unreasonable. Sometimes she gets into these states . . . temper tantrums, I don't know what else to call them. She'll come after me with both hands. He smiled briefly. I know that's hard to imagine, looking at her.

No, she thought, not really. It made absolute sense, put her picture of Catherine into perspective. All that sullenness catalyzed. Fighting was their metaphor, had been right from the start.

He was waiting for her response; when she made none it seemed to disconcert him. Maybe I'm getting old, he said. I mean, maybe you realize that everything is imperfect, a compromise, you're willing to settle for less.

She wanted to scream, What are you trying to say? But the pressure of his hand kept her silent.

But anybody you've been with that long . . . he was floundering, apologizing for his weakness, begging her to finish things for him.

Had she waited all this time to hear something so commonplace as this? That he found it impossible to leave Catherine? She was answered by the cold, judgmental voice she'd stifled for so long, saying, What else did you expect? What else did you ever think would happen? She was gripped by such a fury of revulsion, for him, for herself, surely he must feel it through her skin. But his eyes showed only shame and anxiety.

I understand how things have to be, she said, speaking slowly, trying to buy herself time to think. She was afraid that his next words would be, We can't keep seeing each other, it's too risky, too sad, too painful. She had avoided words because they cut you loose so easily. One more breath and she'd be entirely adrift. So she said, Anyway, I've been thinking of leaving town. As she spoke it became true.

He looked genuinely startled. Why? Where are you going?

Mexico, she couldn't resist saying. No. Actually — and she detailed the standing offer of a friend in California. Come out any time, there was a spare bedroom, fine weather, a terrace with lemon trees, an offer she'd never seriously considered until now. She finished speaking and waited for him to talk her out of it or say he was coming with her. Of course he wouldn't and she wouldn't beg him. It occurred to her she had entirely the wrong sort of pride.

What he said was, I should know better than to try and change your mind about anything. You're the strongest woman I know.

Musclebound, she heard herself saying, wondering where her terrible flippancy came from. Musclebound between the ears. She was thinking, Strong? Would either of them ever see what the other did?

I'll miss you, he said. How easily they seemed to be letting each other go! Now he embraced her; he was hot and blind, she felt herself pushed to the very edges of the bed. This, their love-making, was something he would never let go or refuse; that was why it was all she offered to him. His breath rasped across her ear; he was saying — Love — I love you. What was that, she thought, a word, another word? She tried to maintain her anger, even turn it to contempt, telling herself she had expected some braver decision from him, some victory of passion over habit. But in the end she whispered back to him, Love. Yes, she loved him, using the word extravagantly. And maybe this was love and she had gone about it all wrong.

You're beautiful, she said afterwards. You look like those paintings of Christ after he's been taken down from the cross.

He opened his eyes. You do say the oddest things.

Do I? She tugged at a thick lock of his hair. Let's not make this the last time.

Oh no. Definitely not the last. When are you going to California?

Not right away. I haven't made any definite plans. She felt lightheaded, echoing with irony. Kits, cats, sacks, wives, how many were going to St. Ives? The answer, which had always eluded her: One.

This time it was he who began the game. They sat cross-legged on the mattress, resting their fists on their knees. She seemed to win without effort — rock to his scissors, paper to his rock, scissors to his paper — and he exclaimed in mock annoyance. Perhaps she really could read his mind now. Or perhaps, she thought, she was seeing the laws by which those shapes moved. Perhaps they were she, her lover, and Catherine, each able to damage the other, each combination causing loss. Though who stood for what? Nothing was ever that precise.

It was raining, of course, when he had to go, a thin black rain in the early winter darkness. She allowed herself to imagine the heat and brilliance of California skies. She allowed herself to imagine some perfect balance of love, some working anatomical model where blood looped smoothly between head and heart.

He was lingering at the door, hesitant, mournful, beautiful as a wound in perfect flesh can be beautiful. Perhaps, in spite of what they'd said, this was indeed their last time. Instead of embracing him she smiled and pressed her open hand against his, palm to palm, paper kissing paper.

MAXINE KUMIN

The Missing Person

(FROM TRIQUARTERLY)

THEY LEAVE the car at one of those park-and-lock lots; "No Attendant After 9 P.M.," the signs warn. But Alan says it is senseless to try to drive into center city at this hour and she agrees with him. She tucks her purse out of sight under the front seat, unwilling to carry it in the predictable crowd.

"You have to take something, Ellie. Your wallet at least; you can't walk around the city like an orphan."

Because it is a very small fold-over wallet she argues only briefly, then thrusts it deep in her coat pocket. They trudge through blackened slush to the subway entrance.

Years ago Alan lived here, a student at the university. He knows intersections, sirens, one-way streets; he is a confident, serious man. She has ridden the subway four times in her life. She is terrified but says nothing. Her terror, she knows, is banal. They are sucked into the tube; the sound presses against her ears. Alan's lips move. She nods, pretending to understand. At home it is so quiet she can hear the dog sneeze in the night. They are expelled at the correct stop.

Downtown is cluttered with Christmas lights and after-work pedestrians pushing in and out of shops. The corner taverns give off enough surplus heat to melt the sidewalks in rough arcs around their entrances. She comments on this, thinking of the sullen, now-empty wood stoves at home and their acres of forested, uninhabited land now locked under this new all-day snow.

They have driven 370 miles for this evening. They know no one in the city anymore, except Kathleen, their daughter-in-law, who has a part in the repertory production they have come to see. It is a substantial part, she has assured them by mail, the letter containing a pair of tickets. Kathleen still writes dutifully every six or eight months. She is living with an older man, a lighting technician. When the theater is dark she waits on tables in a nearby bistro. Words like *co-vivant* and *psyche*, *life style* and *energy* bedeck her letters. Reading them, Alan snorts like a choosy horse picking through weeds for the timothy.

They are the parents of an MIA who married this girl six years ago on brief acquaintance. They feel wary about her still. Her grief was shallow and impossible to sustain. Theirs is eternal.

James Alan, the son — Jay, they had always called him — toyed with Canada, Sweden, and jail, but in the end inanition prevailed. He was drafted. He put on his country's uniform, he was written up in the *Argus County Gazette* under his high school graduation photo, and he came home on furlough that summer. Ellie remembers that his hands shook as if with cold. They were both ashamed of their fears, mother and son, sharing an aversion to Ferris wheels, observation towers, and diving boards, and they did not speak of his condition. Toward the end of the fourteen days he sent for Kathleen. They had been secretly married three months ago; he hoped his parents would love her as much as he did, his earnest face cracking with the desire to make an amalgam of his people, to consolidate his loyalties.

Kathleen wears her long hair parted in the middle. Whenever she leans forward, it sweeps across her eyes, the corners of her mouth — an impediment, Ellie thinks. Kathleen loves bathrobes and long-sleeved shirts. When Jay's furlough ends, she takes with her his flannel, his chamois, and his royal-blue corduroy shirts to keep her warm all winter. Only two months later, before the weather has turned properly cold, he disappears in a helicopter, this child who dreaded heights.

Every year thousands of Americans die accidental deaths. Bizarre deaths, drownings, freak electrocutions, mushroom poisonings. A man chokes to death on a piece of steak in an expensive restaurant. A young woman falls from her loved and trusted horse and breaks her neck. Jay vanishes over hostile territory; neither he nor his eleven companions are ever found. When an only child leaves you — she cannot yet say dies — the air comes out of the basketball, the tire flattens, your own lungs threaten to crumple.

She is reclusive. She grows things; she preserves and freezes and dries them; she knows all the local wild mushrooms, all the local nuts. In the winter in her greenhouse she harvests cherry tomatoes and actual curly lettuce. Her project this year is to make Belgian endive sprout under layers of well-manured sawdust in boxes in the cellar. When she is not forced away from the farm, she is peeking under the sawdust to see if the roots have sprouted yet.

This is the way Ellie's mind skips and bumbles as they gruel through the wet, halfhearted snowfall toward Liberty Street. They walk a little apart, husband and wife of twenty-eight years, not at all like two people who imagine they are holding one another. Ellie examines oncoming pedestrians. She notes what they are wearing, how they walk. A city stride is tight, she is thinking; at the same time she is thinking her winter coat is years behind the style. People walk angrily with tense buttock muscles, probably from the hard sidewalk.

The light changes. She stands obediently on the curb, watching, mooning. When the green goes on, she starts across. Alan is not at her side. She stops, waiting for him to catch up; she steps out of the human flow and waits next to a building. The texture of the rough brick makes itself felt against her back as she tries to relax, to lean into and imprison the moment.

In perhaps ten seconds she is flooded with panic. He has been struck by a car, he has been mugged and dragged into an alley, he has suffered a stroke, a heart attack. She rushes back across the street, darting this way and that, like a dog separated from its master. Everything around her is normal. People press forward in both directions; they know what they are doing. Her ears are ringing, her eyes are filling with brilliant asterisks, her peripheral vision is fading.

A policeman was directing traffic at a major intersection two blocks behind her; she remembers passing him, remembers noting his cheeks inflated like birthday balloons around the whistle. He does not stop shrilling air through the whistle. Nor can she now attract his attention, even standing at his side, even tugging his sleeve. She is out of breath; it requires a great effort to remain coherent.

When finally he allots her a sentence — expecting, undoubtedly, to be asked directions — he shakes his head decisively. He is Traffic, he shouts, and points where she must go. At the precinct house, two blocks west, three south, a patrol car is drawn up to the sidewalk. An altercation is taking place on the steps. There are raised nightsticks, grunts, a scuffle, arms pinned behind backs. She waits as long as she dares, watching the gray snowflakes melt as they strike pavement, enlarging the puddles like a late spring snow in the sugar bush.

Alan sells debarkers and wood chippers and other mechanical wood-harvesting aids. He can tell every species of tree from its bark, and he can do this even with his eyes closed, just from the texture and aroma of the bark. Now he is getting into machinery that mills wood flour. "Do you know about wood flour?" she asks the sergeant. "It's an expanding market. They add it to plastic as a low-grade reinforcement. It's dangerous, it's explosive, a spark will set it off. I always thought if something happened to Alan it would be with wood flour."

She realizes she is babbling; the sergeant scribbles as she talks. Probably he thinks she is part of an underground cell, part of a plot to blow up the city's water supply. Meanwhile in the back room she is aware of a methodical thumping, muffled voices. A suspect. is being beaten? Someone is cranking a mimeo machine? It is hard to concentrate; she feels scattered. She feels as though the top of her head might come off and her brains ooze out, all gray and clayey.

Her husband might have stepped out to visit a friend, the sergeant suggests. Or he might have stepped in somewhere to answer a call of nature. Has she continued on to the theater where, after their accidental separation, he is possibly now anxiously waiting for her to catch up with him?

She has not. In any case, he has the tickets.

Has she thought of returning to the parking lot to see if he is waiting at the car for her, having become accidentally separated from her and realizing that she might grow confused about the location of the theater but would remember where they have parked the car?

No, she has not thought of that. Besides, he has the car keys. Hers are in her purse. Which is locked in the car.

Any history of mental disorder?

Wordlessly she shakes her head.

Maybe — this hangs on the air although it is not actually voiced — maybe he has grown tired of her and has elected this admittedly uncommon method of deserting her. Does she remember any unusual incident that transpired between them today?

She resolves not to mention the incident of the wallet. After all, Alan is practical. She ought not to wander around a big city without her name and address and a few dollars. This is not Argus County, where the doors of households are left open and only stall latches are shut. No, nothing. Nothing!

Hundreds of people are reported missing every day, it is explained to her patiently, but with an air of lassitude. Of every hundred persons who are reported missing by their loved ones, 99 and 99/100ths of them are deliberately missing. They have dropped out, taken a powder, vamoosed, they don't want to be found. And 99 percent of the 99 and 99/100ths undergo a change of heart within the first twenty-four hours. They get over their bad feeling, they experience remorse, they return. This is the reason for the Police Department's regulation: a missing persons bulletin cannot be issued on her husband until approximately this time tomorrow.

No, he is genuinely sorry, he is not empowered to take down a description of the, ah, possibly missing person until tomorrow evening at approximately . . .

She gets up finally, fumbling, realizing that she is not carrying the pocketbook a woman may fumble to retrieve from her lap as she rises. She has no will. She is directionless. She cannot see beyond the passage of twenty-four hours so that she may return to this varnished brown office and describe her vanished husband to an officer of the law. For surely if they know what he looks like, they can find him?

Gradually her mind refocuses on the theater. It is all up to Kathleen now. It soothes her to imagine that Alan and Kathleen have been in secret communication all along. There is a word for it, it will come to her, right now she must just concentrate on walking in the right direction. Back, back past the traffic cop, his whistle now dangling on his chest. Alan knows how she feels about Kathleen. She pretends she is indifferent to her, but in truth she has resented her from the beginning. Back down Liberty Street in the direction of the theater, which actually is housed in a former church. That much she remembers from Kathleen's letter . . . The word is *collusion*.

The church is shabby inside. It smells of mildew and low-grade heating oil. Footpaths are worn in the maroon carpet. The lobby is deserted except for a slender young man in a blue jump suit. The ebb and flow of conversation comes through the double doors; stagey laughter follows. The play is in progress. She and the young man converse in hushed tones. He has a pale goatee that points at her as he talks. Everything is haloed in her sight. Her words have little halos around them, too, little sunbursts of Indian decoration.

She does not have the tickets, she is explaining; they are complimentary tickets sent to her and her husband. Who is. She does not know. By Kathleen Blakeslee. She is proud to have remembered Kathleen's other name. Their daughter-in-law.

What a shame, murmurs narrow beard, because Kathleen was called out of town just this morning. It seems her father had a heart attack in Cincinnati. Her part for this performance is being played by Angela Rountree.

They stand silently side by side, equally passive, although he is imparting information and she is absorbing it, her mind racing, seizing on and discarding possibilities. There's the scattered affirmative sound of applause. Lights go up; the double doors open.

"Excuse me," her companion says, distracted. He has his duties to perform. She stands for a moment watching the audience file past as if magically Alan and Kathleen might appear among them. Finally she joins the last little cluster of people moving out into the night. As if she too had a sense of purpose, trailing behind a young couple, walking east again through the still intermittent snow to the mouth of the subway.

She is absorbed once again into the tunnel. Fishing out change for a token, she thinks to count her money: $21.89. Strange, that extra ten — she has no memory of it. Somewhere Alan asked her to make change, somewhere in a turnpike Howard Johnson's handed her a ten-dollar bill and asked . . . ? She has no memory. Terrible at figures, at maps, at mechanical devices. Intuitive. Adept with hammer and saw, nonmotorized tools, calm with animals. That's who I am, she tells herself over and over as the subway lights slap past, riffling like cards in a deck, and the clatter of a train passing in the other direction assaults her ears. Who I am Iam miam. She gets off at the correct stop; she is followed. Deliberately she slows down, listening. She waits to be mugged. They are her own footsteps. She finds herself on the correct street. At the next corner looms the park-and-lock, lights around the perimeter feebly gleaming.

Somewhere toward the third section over, she thinks. Just below the middle strip. Here and there a set of headlights goes on, a motor makes that reassuring cough as it turns over. Others too are wholesomely bent on retrieving their cars. She does not tell herself that Alan waits inside theirs, she is beyond such fantasies now. There is a spare key attached by magnet under the left rocker panel; if only she can get inside! They took this step a year ago when Alan absentmindedly locked the keys in the car at the Eastern States Exposition. They are anomalies, both of them, unused to locks.

But the car is not where she remembers it. Not in the next row or the next. Frantic now, reversing sides, she prowls up and down the rows. Two figures are sitting on the hood of an old Edsel watching her. There is the glint of a bottle being passed between them and by its glint, as it were, she spots her car, it is *her* car now, parked right next to the Edsel.

They face each other, she and the two men. Boys, really. One is reed-thin with a shaved head the shape of a football. A religious sect? she thinks. An escaped convict? The other, heavier, bobs around. He is less clear, wrapped in an oversized coat — no, a blanket. They are black.

She cannot require herself to kneel down, feel under the car for the key. She cannot take possession of her car in their presence. The menace is so direct that someone, she thinks, has told them where to wait. Her plan is known. She will not invite a blow on the head with a blunt instrument; she will not so easily become another victim of the city. She moves away, giving no sign, as if still in search of a car, walks farther and farther, does not turn until she knows she is out of sight. And watches the two forms asprawl on the hood of the Edsel in the snow and the bottle tilting up.

Somehow she has no recollection of the entrance or the stairwell or even of the station platform; she is in the subway again. In motion, this time she leans her head back against the metal frame of the car, letting the pulse of the underground rock her. The shrieks of the rails, the protests of metal on metal blur into a kind of dangerous music. It is the music of the sea. Washed overboard, she bobs on the surface, determined not to drown. She does not even know which direction she is going in. She has not looked at any of her traveling companions to sort out the indigent, the malicious, and the crazy. At the end of the line only one other person is left in the car, a tired-looking middle-aged woman dressed in men's sneakers and wearing a bandanna knotted under her chin. When they get out, Ellie walks as close to this woman as she dares. Although they do not speak, there is something hovering between them. They are allies.

Suddenly she realizes how tenuous is the thread that ties her to the parking lot, the car, her pocketbook within, her identity. The subway has become her connector; she turns and hurries back down the dank stairs. Conveniently, at the end of the line there is no choice to make. Conveniently, a car yawns in the station. A guard lounges alongside the empty conveyance. He blows his nose onto the tracks and she is grateful to him. She enters the car and goes immediately to the map to find her stop. Luckily, it is the name also of a famous painter and she has no difficulty locating it. Fourteen stops, though. She has come a long way. She sits down opposite the map so she can keep an eye on it. The car starts up.

It is after midnight now, the streets on the outskirts deserted, the sidewalks coated with a thin grease of city snow. Approaching the parking lot she has to fight her terror; suppose those two men are still there? She has to fight an impulse to fall to her knees, to wriggle along unseen like a guerrilla between the rows.

The Edsel is gone. Snow is beginning to stick to the wet lozenge of asphalt it covered. She can hear her heart. It makes explosive thumps of relief in her ears. Now she falls to her knees, groping under the car for the little magnetic cup. Her hand fastens on it immediately. What luck! She withdraws the key.

She opens the door and drops onto the front seat, has barely the presence of mind to pull the door closed and press down the lock before great waves of trembling overtake her. It is a shivering fit, the kind she endured during frequent childhood bouts of fever. Her body trembles, chattering like aspen leaves in a light wind. From time to time the quaking subsides. She takes a cautious calming breath as one does after the hiccups. Two breaths, three; then some subliminal thought racks her anew with tremors.

Little by little she sleeps, shakes, sleeps again. When she comes fully awake there is a line of light in the sky and her purse lies heavy in her lap like a cold animal. Somehow she has pulled it out from under the seat. She recognizes that she has been hugging it.

As soon as it is light enough to navigate without headlights, she takes out her own set of car keys and eases out of the lot. Except for the trucks, there is no traffic on the main artery into center city. Despite her normal panic at the multiple signs full of proscriptions, she has no trouble finding Liberty Street. After Liberty Street, the precinct house.

A new sergeant is on duty. It has not occurred to her that last night's man is off duty, has gone home for breakfast, is already safely asleep. She is surprised by her anger. This morning's sergeant respects her account of the night that has passed. He notes down carefully a description of Alan. She gives him a snapshot from her wallet, four years old now, but accurate enough. In it Alan stands by the barn, stiffly posed, squinting into the sun. The head of one horse, the rump of another are visible on the left. Alan is holding a sledge. He looks boyish and capable. And most of all, he looks startlingly like Jay.

Finally she begins the long drive home. Oddly peaceful, she ascribes the serenity to her extreme fatigue. Also to shock. You're in shock, she tells herself sternly, waiting to grieve. Think how you miss him. Think how you love, loved him.

But she cannot. The main thing now, the thing that is flooding her with euphoria, is how she has survived her ordeal. How she has coped. She has conquered the subway. She has forced the city to declare Alan a missing person twelve hours ahead of schedule. She knows now that Jay has been dead all these years. When will she need to know about Alan? She reviews the extreme and contradictory emotions the sight of Alan's dead, well-known body will arouse in her.

Resolutely, holding to fifty-five mph on the hypnotic turnpike, she pulls the lumpy brown leather pocketbook onto her lap and rests her free hand, palm down, on its surface.

LOUIS D. RUBIN, JR.

Finisterre

(FROM THE SOUTHERN REVIEW)

Although more and more people are coming to refer to boats with the neuter pronoun "it," the traditional "she" remains fully correct in speaking or writing about any size of vessel.

— CHAPMAN, *Piloting, Seamanship and Small Boat Handling*

THE CITY OF CHARLESTON, South Carolina, is bounded on three sides by rivers and the harbor. In such a place, with ships and tugboats and small craft always moving about, I was very much aware of the water and wanted to go out on it. But except on very rare occasions when my uncle would take me sailing, I never got the opportunity. No one else that I knew owned a boat of any kind. My father was not an outdoorsman and was utterly uninterested in boats or in fishing. For me to have proposed that we acquire a rowboat would have been as far-fetched as to have suggested the purchase of an airplane or a railroad locomotive. Moreover, I had been declared by my mother to be ineligible for going out on boats except under the most reliable of adult supervision, such as my uncle's, because of my failure to learn how to swim.

When we had lived downtown on Rutledge Avenue I was only a few blocks from the Ashley River, and it was a walk of ten blocks down Tradd Street to Adger's Wharf and the Cooper River waterfront, but I seldom thought to go there. Not until we moved far up to the northwest end of town did I begin to get interested in the waterfront.

I was fourteen years old that fall, and on Saturday mornings after the movies I would set off down King Street for the waterfront, pausing to examine the postage stamps, Confederate army buttons, insignias, and belt buckles, and the swords and pistols on display in the window of Bruchner's Antique Store. In the center of the window was a framed picture that fascinated me. It was an old engraving depicting the body of Stonewall Jackson lying in state at the Confederate capitol rotunda in Richmond. Standing behind the coffin were Robert E. Lee, Jefferson Davis, J. E. B. Stuart, and other Confederate heroes, all looking very gloomy. Sometimes I wondered whether any of the various antique pistols and sabers displayed in the window had belonged to soldiers killed in the war, and might actually have been taken from the hands of dead men.

After looking at the window display I would walk on to Broad Street and then eastward toward the Cooper River. Usually I would stop in at the law office where my aunt Ellen was employed as a secretary, spend a little while there, and then proceed across East Bay Street and along Exchange to the shore. The *Cherokee*, one of the coastal passenger ships of the Clyde-Mallory Line, would usually be tied up alongside the pier just upstream, in full sight.

Compared to the transatlantic liners that put in at ports such as New York and Boston, I knew, the *Cherokee* was no doubt a very small ship, but she seemed enormous to me. Her great black hull took up the entire length of the pier from close to the shore all the way to the end, where her stern protruded out into the ship channel, while her cabins and superstructure, painted white and gold, towered above the two-story warehouse on the dock. The *Cherokee* arrived early in the morning, lay alongside the dock while her passengers were off touring the city, and departed in mid-afternoon. While in port the ship was festooned with pennants and flags, and appeared altogether glamorous.

I would remain there for a while to watch, then I would walk southward along the shore. Just downstream, next to a marine railway, there were the remains of several old wooden boats partly buried in the mud and marsh grass, with the weathered ribs and timbers protruding up like arms and legs. At high tide the harbor water would wash about the old hulks, but when the tide was out they were imbedded in the mud, with fiddler crabs scurrying about the surface of the black, viscous tidal flat. There was a salty fragrance in the air that seemed to be part of the scene. No doubt the old craft had been towed there years ago and left to disintegrate gradually in the heat and moisture of the marsh. Once my aunt Ellen walked down to the waterfront with me, and referred to the place as a "ship's graveyard."

I would pause there briefly, then proceed along the shoreline to Adger's Wharf. It was actually two wharves, and was home port for a variety of shrimp boats and small working craft, several of which were in freight service between Charleston and the various sea islands up and down the coast. There was a packing house, situated on the land side of the north pier, with a tin-covered roof beneath which black women worked at sorting and packing shrimp brought in from off the various boats. Meanwhile the crews of the shrimp boats were working aboard their craft, hosing down the decks and the hold, repairing nets and adjusting lines. The shrimp boats were of all shapes and sizes. Some were painted in bright blues, reds, and greens; others were unpainted and drab. But all held their attractions for me, for they were seagoing boats, and went out beyond the jetties at the harbor mouth and into the ocean.

By far the most interesting craft berthed at Adger's Wharf, however, were the tugboats of the White Stack Towboat Company, which occupied the far end of the south pier. There were three of them, the *Cecilia,* the *Robert H. Lockwood,* and the *James P. Congdon.* They were painted brick red, with glossy black hulls and white trimming, and their smokestacks were white with black rings. They were kept in prime condition, and when not at work somewhere about the harbor lay waiting alongside the pier, their boilers always kept fired, with wisps of smoke trailing from their stacks. It was always my hope to see one of them departing or returning, for it was a formidable sight to view the sturdy craft in action, their powerful propellers churning the harbor water at the stern into foamy little hills, as they maneuvered confidently alongside the dock, while crewmen waited to tend the lines. They were owned by the Lockwood brothers, the eldest of whom, Captain Tunker Lockwood, was mayor *pro tem* of the City of Charleston and had lived next to us on Rutledge Avenue. My father had told me once that the two Lockwood boys, Henry and Edward, would one day succeed to command of the tugboats, and I always viewed them with awe and envy. They were several years older than I, and hardly knew me, but I watched them from afar, as among the more fortunate of the earth.

Berthed at Adger's Wharf along with the shrimp boats, cargo

launches, pilot boats, and the White Stack towboats were a few small open boats with make-and-break gasoline engines and several rowboats. They were used for fishing or for work about the waterfront, and sometimes while I was watching, the owner of one of them might show up, climb down to where his boat was moored alongside the dock, and after a time cast loose the lines and proceed out into the harbor. I was deeply envious, for I could envision myself as someday being able actually to own a boat of that size, and the idea of heading out into the harbor in a boat of my own, rowing along the waterfront past the Clyde Line docks and up toward the Cooper River Bridge, or else downstream past the Carolina Yacht Club and along the sea wall of the High Battery, was marvelous to contemplate. Even better, if more remote, was the hope of possessing one of the larger craft with gasoline engines. With such a boat I could go out to the center of the harbor, explore the wooded shoreline along the southern rim of the harbor up to Fort Johnson and beyond, or even head upstream on the Ashley River, rounding the point of the Battery and up along the Boulevard past the lighthouse station at the head of Tradd Street, to where the river widened and the Intracoastal Waterway entered it at Wappoo Creek across the river.

But if that was beyond any hope of fulfillment for years to come, at least I might someday own a rowboat and keep it at Adger's Wharf. Not any time soon, to be sure — for even if it were somehow possible for me to buy a rowboat, the fact that I could not swim would be an insurmountable barrier to any such hope, since my mother had made it quite clear that until or unless I learned how to swim, I could go out in no boat not supervised by an adult.

Logically I knew that the first step in persuading my parents to acquire a rowboat, or in abetting me in getting one, would be to learn how to swim. But that I had proved unable to do. The summer before, when we still lived downtown, I had tried. I had been sent to the YMCA to take swimming lessons, but had failed miserably. I could not force myself to let go of the railing around the pool or to keep my head under water. I was not afraid of the water as such; when not in it I would vow to do what I was supposed to do. But once I felt myself unsupported, I lost all control over my actions, and came raging back to the surface and to the side of the pool, where I hung on for dear life, oblivious to encouragement or expostulation by the instructor. My will power was simply not strong enough to overcome my fear. Where the other boys in the swimming class were soon splashing across the pool and learning to dive deep and come up, breathing hard and blinking water from their eyes, yards distant from where they had gone under, I remained clinging to the side.

"See how easy it is?" the instructor, a pleasant-voiced man named Mr. Fudge, would say to me. "There's nothing to be afraid of." But I could not do it.

When my parents realized that I was not learning how to swim, they were exasperated. My mother telephoned the swimming instructor, to my considerable embarrassment, to discuss my failure. "He says you won't try," she reported. "The others have all been swimming for a week now, but you won't let go of the railing." I was informed in no uncertain terms that I was to obey the instructor.

After the next lesson, during which I kept unhappily to the side of the pool, unable to force myself to push loose from the side with my feet and dive under the water, the instructor told me to remain when the others had gone. He got down into the water himself, and took hold of my body by the waist. "Now just let yourself go," he said. "Don't worry, I've got hold of you." Feeling his hands supporting me I did as he asked, and tried to move my arms and kick out with my feet, while he held me up and walked across the pool with me.

"This time I'm going to let go and let you swim," Mr. Fudge said. "I'll have my arms right under you to hold you up if you begin to sink. Now just have confidence in yourself, and you can do it." But when he let go and I felt myself unsupported in the water, I thrust my legs down, groping for the bottom of the pool with my feet, and when I could not touch it I lost all control of myself, grabbed hold of the instructor's arms, pulled myself partly out of the water, and clung to his shoulders and chest, panting and half-sobbing in embarrassment and anger at myself.

After a few minutes, Mr. Fudge climbed out of the pool and told me to do the same. "I can't teach you to swim if you won't try to relax and let go," he said. My lips were tight and my teeth chattering, as if the water were frigid. I felt humiliated and exhausted.

When I returned home I knew he had telephoned my mother to report my failure, for, while my mother said nothing about it, her silence was so studiedly casual that I knew she was very disappointed at my cowardice. At dinnertime my father also made no reference to it, and only told me that there was a new *S. S. Glencairn* story, which he knew I liked, in that week's number of *Collier's.* That evening my mother said that it would not be necessary for me to return to the YMCA swimming classes any more. Though ashamed at my failure, I felt relieved.

So now, a summer afterward, I remained a nonswimmer, and could not hope to own a rowboat. In June school ended, and there was no longer anything to prevent me from sometimes riding my bicycle downtown to the waterfront and spending all morning there, returning only in time for two o'clock dinner. I would take along a pair of inexpensive binoculars that my father had bought for me to observe the occasional ships that moved up the Ashley River past our house. I would ride all the way to the High Battery at the very tip of the city. From there I could see all the way across to where the low form of Fort Sumter lay near the harbor entrance, so that most of the activity in the lower harbor was visible to me. When a ship came into view, she was first a smudge of smoke and a dot of superstructure far out beyond Sumter.

With the binoculars I could observe her all the way in until she disappeared behind Sumter, and afterwards reemerged, much larger in visible size, along the Fort Moultrie side of the fort.

The next minutes were crucial. For if she were a ship from a foreign port she would anchor out in the Roadstead for customs inspection and come no closer that morning, while if she were bound up the Cooper River she would move along the Rebellion Reach channel on the far side of the harbor, pass out of sight beyond Castle Pinckney, which was on an island in the harbor, and at no time come closer than three or four miles from where I stood. But if when the ship rounded Sumter and moved toward the inner harbor she neither anchored nor swung northward, then I knew that I would soon be able to observe her from close by, for the destination would be either the downtown waterfront or else up the Ashley River, and in either event she would pass within less than a half-mile of the High Battery. What I most hoped was that the ship was headed for the Cooper River waterfront, for then she would move right across my line of vision, in front of me, no more than a few hundred yards away, and I should not only be able to observe her every detail but also get a long look at the White Stack tugboat that had gone out to meet her and guide her in.

The tug designated to receive the ship would make its rendezvous with the visitor well out in the harbor. The ship would have stopped her engines to await her escort. There would be a ceremonial (as I thought) exchange of whistled salutes, the tug's high-pitched whistle signal answered by the deep-voiced note of the ship. I would watch through the binoculars and try to catch sight of the passing of the towline from tug to ship, but it was too far out to see. Eventually, however, the tug would take up its position in front and the procession would head for port, the tug in the lead, followed by the much larger ship. As they neared the point at which the Cooper River waterfront channel veered from the Ashley River channel there would be more whistle signals, and then first the tug and then the ship would make the turn, and come slowly, massively toward the waterfront. Past where I stood watching they would steam, the sturdy red tugboat in the lead, the huge freighter or tanker following obediently behind, still under her own power but linked to the tug by the manila towline that was to be used in the docking operation. The White Stack tugboats never looked more capable and confident than at such times. As they churned their way past the Battery they seemed to be aware of their own importance as worthy stewards of the port, and without ostentation but in entire self-possession and pride they would lead the visitor to the wharf and the waiting slip.

Meanwhile a second White Stack tugboat would by then have cast off its lines from its berth at Adger's Wharf and be waiting off at the far side of the channel, ready to follow along upstream and assist in the docking. As the first tug and its tow moved by, it would take up its station abeam and proceed upstream too, and I would watch until finally the ship and her escorts passed out of view, and only the tall masts of the ship were now visible above the low roofs of the warehouses along the shore.

What I would have liked to be able to do was to own a small boat, so that I could row upstream to where the freighter was being docked, take up a position safely out of the way, and observe the entire operation. As it was, I could only look enviously at the occasional small craft that did come moving along the waterfront. If, as sometimes happened, the occupants of such craft were not adults but boys seemingly only a little older than myself, then my envy was almost beyond bounds. To have to stand there on the Battery, looking out at the harbor, while some fortunate boy was out on the water in a boat, rowing along in splendor past me, perhaps even glancing up, as I imagined, in momentary pity for such as myself, but for the most part too satisfyingly engaged in rowing his boat to have time for mere landlubbers — it was a mournful business.

Our new house was located far up at the northwest end of the city, on a bluff that overlooked the Ashley River. We moved there in the spring of 1935, after my father had recovered from a severe illness and had spent a number of months in the hospital. Twice during those months he had been expected to die. He was much better now, however, and part of the reason for building the new house was that he would be able to plant flowers and shrubs and work in the yard. There were only two other houses within a mile of us, one of them owned by Mr. Herbert Simons, my father's closest friend and Saturday night poker-playing companion, who was in the real estate business and had bought and renovated an old plantation house, Versailles, and was now preparing to develop the surrounding area. Our house was situated across from an avenue of huge water oaks on Mr. Simons' grounds, and beyond the oaks and Mr. Simons' house the land sloped abruptly down some thirty feet or more to the edge of the salt marsh, which was spread out along the shore in either direction as far as the eye could see.

From the edge of the marsh to the river itself was a distance of a quarter-mile or so. A creek led from the river through the marsh to a small dock behind Mr. Simons' house, though doubtless it had been many years since a boat had been moored there. On summer mornings sometimes my mother and I would go crabbing off the dock, tying hunks of old meat to strings, with weights attached, dropping them into the creek, then waiting for blue crabs to come in with the tide, take hold of the meat, and allow themselves to be netted. Though the creek was narrow, there was a steady procession of crabs, and in a morning's crabbing we could fill half a washtub with them.

Sometimes while we sat there crabbing a freighter might come up the river, bound for the fertilizer docks a mile upstream, preceded by a White Stack tugboat. The river channel led so close to the edge of the marshland that from where we watched the freighter seemed to be floating upon a sea of reed grass as she moved by. Much later the tugboat would come heading back, having completed its task of docking the freighter, en route downstream to the harbor.

At low tide there was only a trickle of water in the creek. Occasionally I would sit down on the dock then and watch the fiddler crabs sunning themselves on the banks of black mud. There were also oyster shells on the sides, and little pools of inky rainbow-hued oil formed by the marsh gases. Sometimes I could hear birds and small animals, swamp rats probably, stirring about off in the marsh grass. There was a continual popping and cracking sound on hot days, caused I supposed by the heat of the sun on the decaying surfaces of the mud and grass.

When the tide was very high, not only the creek but much of the marshland between the shore and the river's edge was also covered by water. It did not take very long for me to come up with the idea that, even if my inability to swim meant that I could not hope to go out on the river in a boat, I might possibly be able to persuade my parents to let me paddle a boat about the marshland at high tide, since there could be little danger involved in going on water that was only a couple of feet deep in most places.

If, that is, I had a rowboat. But where was I to get a rowboat? One of my parents' friends was a woodworking contractor, and I asked him what it would cost to have a small rowboat built. "Oh, about fifteen dollars," he said. Since my weekly allowance was fifty cents, the prospect of my saving enough to buy a boat seemed somewhat remote. If I could bring myself to set aside a dime a week, which was unlikely, it would take three years before I had enough to afford the boat.

In late June my cousin Charles, from Atlanta, came to visit us for two weeks, and one day we went to the waterfront. Since he had no bicycle we rode down on the trolley car. A freighter was coming in along the south channel when we arrived at the Battery, and after we watched her swing by us, preceded by the escorting tug, my cousin was eager to follow them up the waterfront and see the docking take place. I explained to him that the slip where the freighter would be docking was entirely hidden from view from the shore, but he insisted upon seeing for himself, so we headed up Concord Street, which fronted the docks, in pursuit of the ship and tug. It turned out that they were bound for the Bull Line wharf, beyond Market Street, which was not only completely screened from view by several large corrugated tin warehouses but surrounded by a high wire fence as well.

We tried to walk out past the Bull Line dock to find a place from

which to observe the operation. There was a swampy field, partly
under water, beyond the extremity of the fence, and we picked our
way through it, past the ruins of an old brick building. When we
reached the edge of the marsh, however, the downstream view was
blocked off by the farthest warehouse, which protruded some distance out into the ship channel.

As we were making our way back to solid ground, I noticed,
piled near the brick ruins, what appeared to be some boxes. I went
over to examine them, jumping from one spot of dry ground to
another across the boggy ground, with my cousin following. Lying
there in the marsh, exposed to the rain and the tidal water, was a
mass of deteriorated cartons, filled with papers. Most were waterlogged and soggy, but when I pulled away some of the papers on
the exterior of one carton we found beneath them, in quite satisfactory shape, great quantities of postcards, letters, and envelopes.
They were all handwritten, were addressed to a firm called F. W.
Wagener Company, and consisted of orders and correspondence.

It was the postage stamps that interested me. For the papers
were all dated in the 1880s and 1890s, and on the envelopes were
stamps that for the most part I had never seen before, older than
any in my own stamp collection.

"I bet some of these are worth money," my cousin said.

"I bet they are, too."

And suddenly the thought came to me that I might be able to
sell the stamps for enough money to buy a rowboat.

For the next several hours my cousin and I combed through
some of the boxes of old correspondence. It was a hot, moist day,
and the water lying about us in the marsh and covering some of
the cartons of papers had a powerful, cloying odor of decaying
sweetness. Beetles and other insects infested the material, but we
worked away excitedly. A majority of the stamps, to be sure, were
identical two-cent red George Washingtons, but there were numer-
ous other kinds as well. We assembled stacks of postcards and
envelopes, with all manner of stamps on them, until finally we had
as many as we could possibly carry, even though we stuffed them
inside our shirts until we bulged out on all sides.

By now it was early afternoon, and we set out across the field,
bound for King Street and Bruchner's Antique Store, which
bought and sold stamps. As we walked we speculated on the worth
of our find. If each envelope was worth a dime and each postcard

a nickel, my cousin declared, we ought to receive at least twenty dollars apiece in payment for them. More than enough to buy a rowboat! "Now don't tell where we found them," my cousin whispered as we opened the door of the store.

Into Bruchner's we walked, down a long aisle between showcases of silverware and old coins, past a glass-front case with a complete Confederate uniform including polished black boots, gauntlets, sash, military belt, grey coat, and trousers with gold buttons, gold epaulets, and a wide-brimmed hat, displayed on a mannequin of some sort that looked almost like a ghost. At a desk at the rear of the dark, cavernous showroom the proprietor, an angular, bony-faced man, sat working at some papers. The desk was illumined by a single gooseneck lamp, which cast a yellow glow on the papers. At first, the man seemed not to notice us in the gloom, but after a moment he looked up.

"We want to know if you want to buy some stamps," I told him.

"Let's see them."

My cousin and I began extracting stamps and postcards from inside our shirts. It took us several minutes to assemble them all. While we were doing so the man did not so much as reach out to examine a single one of the envelopes and cards, but only waited for us to be done. When finally we had placed them all on the counter in a heap, he began to leaf through our cache, while we waited tensely.

"They aren't worth anything," he said after a minute.

The gloom of the dark store now matched my hopes.

"They're all very common," he added.

We stood there, waiting.

The man turned over a few more envelopes. "You go through them," he said after a minute, "and pick out two of each kind for yourself, and I'll take the rest of them off your hands for a dollar."

I looked at my cousin, who looked back at me. My cousin shrugged.

"Okay," I said.

It was some time before we had sorted through all the envelopes and cards and put aside two each of each kind. The man did not seem particularly interested. He went back to what he had been working on, while we sorted stamps. I had not realized just how many envelopes and cards we had collected. Though most were duplicates, and these would be what the man was taking off our hands, there remained a considerable variety in the pile that we were to keep for ourselves.

When we were done the man handed me a paper sack. "Put all those in there," he said, gesturing with his bony hand toward the discards. We complied, and placed the sack full of stamps on the desk.

Then the man reached out for the stack of two each that we were to keep, and took them from me. "Now I'll take these," he said, "and you can keep those in the sack."

He opened the drawer of the desk, extracted a dollar bill, and handed it to me.

It was not until my cousin and I were outside the store and walking up King Street that we could begin to think about what had happened.

"Why did you let him get away with that?" my cousin asked.

"I don't know," I said. And I didn't. I had been so ill at ease that when he had reached out for and taken the stack of envelopes and cards from me I had been unable to do anything except relinquish them. There was something about his thin bony hand, with its yellow fingers, that had frozen me into inaction.

"You shouldn't have given them to him. You should have said No," my cousin declared.

"Why didn't you, then?" I retorted. "They were just as much yours as mine." We had both been afraid of the man.

By the time we boarded the Rutledge Avenue trolley car and were headed uptown, most of the fifty cents apiece that we had been paid for the stamps had been spent. We still had the sack of discards, but the best ones were gone. I sought to rationalize my failure by reminding myself that even if the stamps had been marketable for enough money to buy a rowboat, it was unlikely that my parents would have permitted me to have one, anyway.

My cousin, after thinking the matter over, decided that while the man had clearly tricked us, it was unlikely that any of the stamps or postcards were really rare, because in that case the man would have wanted all of them, and not just two of each variety. They might have been worth, say, five or six dollars in all, he said, instead of the single dollar we had been paid. His idea was that since Bruchner's was the only stamp dealer in Charleston, what we would do would be to go back down to the waterfront tomorrow, assemble another cache of stamps, and he would take them along

when he went home to Atlanta that weekend, and see whether a
stamp dealer there would buy them.

We reckoned, however, without my parents, or more particularly, my mother. For when we related what had happened, my
mother was not at all impressed by the possible value of the stamps.
Instead she was quite angry at the notion of our foraging about in
the marsh for old papers. We might have fallen and cut ourselves
on broken glass, or contracted Lord knows what manner of disease,
she declared, or been bitten by snakes or rats, or otherwise placed
our lives in peril. Under no circumstances were we to return for
more stamps the next day, nor was I ever again to go poking about
in trash or junk or anything of the sort, as if I were no more than
some poor white trash myself, on pain of being forbidden absolutely ever to go down to the waterfront again.

She had a good mind, she said, to deduct the dollar from the
next several installments of my allowance, and return it to Mr.
Bruchner. But the last was an idle threat, as even I recognized, for
my mother was no admirer of the sharp practices of shopkeepers.
So I made no reply and let the storm blow over, which it did, but
only after she ordered us to go into the bathroom at once and run
a hot bath, and wash away every trace of the stamps and postcards
from our bodies. I sent my cousin in to run the bath, while I went
down to the basement where we had left the sackful of discards
and hid it in the woodpile. In a few days' time, I knew, I could
safely take the stamps up to my room, for she would have ceased
to worry about the matter.

My cousin left for home that weekend, and though several times
in subsequent weeks I disobeyed instructions, went back to the
cache of papers in the marsh on the waterfront, and collected
additional varieties of stamps and postcards, I made no further
attempt to sell them. Without in any way intimating to my father
that I had acquired more envelopes and postcards, I asked him
about the F. W. Wagener Company, to which all the envelopes had
been addressed. He said that F. W. Wagener had been a very
wealthy and prominent wholesale grocery dealer in Charleston at
one time, when he was a boy. His own father, my grandfather, had
done business with Wagener while operating a grocery store in
Florence, South Carolina. I had never known my grandfather, for
he had died many years before I was born, when my father was
about my present age. Afterwards I looked through the letters and

postcards that I had found in the marsh, to see whether any of them might have been from my grandfather, but did not find any.

That September there was a hurricane, which though it did not strike Charleston itself came ashore near enough along the coast to cause extremely high tides and heavy rains. When several weeks afterward I went back to collect more stamps I found that the marsh where they had been located had been thoroughly flooded, and where the boxes of papers had once been were now only standing water and mud.

Any further thoughts about acquiring a rowboat remained only very general and passive during the autumn and winter months that followed. From time to time I went down to the waterfront and observed the goings-on in the harbor, but it was not until the late spring that I began again to meditate ways of getting a boat. My uncle Edward, my father's brother, who was city editor of the afternoon newspaper and owned a sailboat, invited me to go sailing with him one Sunday in late April. His plan was to sail his boat up the Ashley River from where he kept it, at the foot of Beaufain Street downtown, all the way to where we lived, and to come ashore by way of the creek through the quarter-mile of tidal marsh, and tie up at the dock behind Mr. Simons' house. By leaving in mid-morning he would arrive when the tide was scheduled to be close to high, have Sunday dinner with us, and return downstream on the outgoing tide. "Now be careful and don't jump around in the boat," my mother told me as my father prepared to drive me downtown to join my uncle. "You know you can't swim."

It was a trip of several hours upstream, though the distance by water was only some three miles, for though the incoming tide was with us we had to do considerable tacking and reaching to make progress against the northwest wind. It was past one o'clock when we reached the mouth of the creek. The tide was very high — a spring tide, my uncle called it — so that the water covered all but the tips of the marsh grass alongside the creek. With the centerboard halfway up we were able to sail right along the winding creek with almost no rowing or poling. I found it tremendously exciting to sail up to the dock, where my parents and Mr. and Mrs. Simons stood waiting, and step over the side of the wooden sailboat onto the dock.

Walking up the slope of the bluff toward our house, on dry land once again, I felt most important, and after dinner when we went back down to the dock and my uncle and I prepared to leave on the return journey, I imagined that my uncle Edward and I were two veteran mariners about to set off from Adger's Wharf for the high seas. The tide had ebbed sufficiently to make it necessary to raise the centerboard all the way to get out of the marsh creek and into the river, and since the wind was against us my uncle had to row, but once we gained the open river we had wind and current with us, and we sailed rapidly down the Ashley, the mainsail swung wide to take the wind, and with no tacking necessary at all.

"I wish I had a boat," I told my parents at supper that evening.

"We haven't any use for one," my mother said.

"I'd like to use it in the marsh."

"You're too young for a boat," my mother replied, "and you can't swim. You might fall overboard and you'd drown."

"Not in the marsh," I said. "I wouldn't go out in the river. I just want to row around in the marsh."

"Well, we don't have a boat and we're not going to get one," my mother declared.

That night, as I lay in bed thinking back on the day's excitement, I told myself that while I was no closer to being able to afford to buy a boat than before, my remark about wanting to row around in the marsh had not been vetoed as such. My mother had said only that they were not going to buy a boat. My argument about not being in danger of drowning so long as I stayed in the marsh had not been refuted. If my mother thought differently about it, she had not said so. Silence, I had read somewhere, gives consent.

Though I could foresee no likelihood of acquiring a boat, I knew that if ever I were somehow to manage to get one, it would be through my father, not my mother, that I should proceed so as to gain consent. He had said nothing during the suppertime discussion. There was no chance whatever that he could ever be coaxed into buying a boat, or even into helping me to buy one, but if a boat were in some undreamed-of way to materialize, I felt, he at any rate would not use the grounds of my inability to swim to forbid my using it. So that was something, anyway.

For several days following the end of school there was a very high spring tide, with the water converting the salt marsh into what seemed almost a lake, and with only the tips of the reed grass along the edge of the shore and the channel visible. The tide rose so high that it even covered the wooden planks of the dock behind Mr. Simons' house. John Carmody, a friend from up Versailles Street, and I went down to the water's edge to investigate, then decided to climb out on a huge water oak on the shoreline, to a point at which we were suspended in the air some twenty feet up, and well over the edge of the marsh. If I fell, I knew, I would get myself thoroughly ducked, so I clung carefully to the tree.

From our perch we watched the marsh and the river, and I told of how I hoped someday to acquire a rowboat to go out in the marsh.

"Why don't we build one?" John Carmody asked.

The thought had never occurred to me. It seemed an obvious solution. Within minutes we were scrambling down the tree and headed for my house. We went up to my room, I got out pencil and paper, and we began designing a boat. That night, as soon as it was sufficiently dark, we took a wagon and went up Pendleton Street to the site of a house under construction, and selected an assortment of boards from the scrap lumber pile. From a keg that had been conveniently left open on the uncompleted second floor of the house we collected several pounds of nails. We were careful to take only boards of which a portion had been sawed away, so that we could assure ourselves that we were only using scrap lumber, even though some of the scraps were ten feet or more in length. As for the nails, no such rationale was needed. Once a nail keg had been opened and left exposed it was fair game. My father observed us as we carted our materiel back into the yard and set up operations under the side porch, but he made no objection, for on more than one occasion he had paid nighttime visits to the scrap lumber pile himself.

Since we would be using the boat in the marsh, we decided it was not necessary to give it a pointed bow. Instead we planned a bateau, with blunt ends and uniform width. It was to be some eight feet long and three feet wide, with sides made of two eight-inch-wide planks, giving us ample freeboard. The bow and stern did not come straight down all the way but were tucked in on an angle about halfway down, to give the boat somewhat greater mobility in the water than a mere box would have.

The next day we built the sides, then the ends, and were preparing to add the planking by nightfall. While we were at work my father came by several times to observe. I knew that he recognized exactly what was being undertaken, even though he made no comment on it, contenting himself by reminding us to be sure to put the tools away when done and to pick up all the scraps of boards lying about and put them in the kindling wood box. If my mother was aware of the project she said nothing about it, and I was careful to avoid making any reference to the boat myself, for if I brought the matter out into the open she would feel obliged, if only for the sake of consistency, to object, and my father would then be equally obliged to support her objections.

The next morning we cut the planks, nailed them into place, then turned the boat rightside up and nailed planks across the top at each end and in the middle for seats. In lieu of oars, we built paddles, nailing flat pieces of board to both ends of two-by-twos so that they would be double bladed. Our boat was now ready for launching. While we were loading it onto the wagon, my father came by again. "If you're going to paddle around in that," he said, "you'd better take a can along to bail it out."

"Yes, sir," I agreed, "we sure better," and I hurried off happily to find a coffee can, for now I had formal acknowledgment of and consent for the boat.

We rolled the boat out of the yard, across Mr. Simons' grounds through the oak grove, and down the bluff to the wharf. I tied a length of manila rope to a bolt I had placed at one end, and then we eased the boat out onto the dock, slid it over the end, and into the creek. It rode high, and rocked a little as the current pushed against it.

"It floats good!" John said.

"Let's get in," I proposed. "You hold the rope and I'll climb in, then you can get in."

"How about the paddles?"

"That's right." We had forgotten to load them into the boat. John retrieved them from where we had left them on the shore, and we dropped them into the boat. "Okay, I'll get in the stern," I said, "and you get in the middle."

"How do we know which end's the stern?"

"It doesn't matter. I'll sit in the back, and you sit in the middle facing the same way, and the end we're facing will have to be the bow."

"All right."

I climbed into the boat, scrambled back to the far end, and sat down. John followed, took his seat amidships, and we took up the paddles and prepared to move out.

"It leaks!" John said.

The water was jetting in through the seams in little fountains.

"Give me the coffee can," I said. "I'll bail and you paddle."

I began scooping water out, while John used his paddle to turn the boat around. We moved off down the creek, with John paddling while I bailed away.

"This is great!" John said.

I looked back at the dock. It was twenty-five feet away. "You bail while I paddle," I proposed. I handed him the can and began paddling. The boat moved sluggishly through the water, but it made steady progress.

Though the water kept coming in steadily through the seams, we found that it was not necessary to keep bailing at all times. We could paddle for a while, until the water rose a couple of inches into the bottom, and then one of us could bail while the other paddled. We proceeded along the creek for some distance, until we came into an opening in the wall of marsh grass along the creek and could move out into the wider area of flooded marsh. We paddled through it until I could see our house, back through the oak trees. My parents were standing on the front porch watching. I waved to them. My father waved back.

"Boy, isn't this fine?" John asked.

I agreed. "We're going to have to do something about these leaks, though." The water kept coming in.

"Let's take it back to the dock," John said.

We paddled back through the marsh and along the creek to the dock, with considerable bailing of water en route. We climbed out, tied the rope to the dock, and stood there for a while, watching our boat swaying in the current. There were several inches of water in it, but now that we were no longer in it, it seemed not to be taking any more water. Meanwhile, there it was, a genuine boat, crude to be sure and given much too much to leaking, perhaps more of a long wooden box than a boat and resembling a crude coffin, but I had gone out into the marsh aboard it, and hereafter could do so whenever I wanted.

We discussed ways whereby our boat might be kept from leaking. My idea was that we might cover the entire bottom with a sheet of tarpaper, but John was dubious. The water would only seep in between the tarpaper and the planks and come in through the seams just as before, he said. We considered getting some lath boards and nailing them over the seams, but decided that the uneven bottom would make it more difficult to paddle the boat, and would also only solve the problem partially, for water would still get in around the lath boards. It was suppertime, so we decided to think upon the problem overnight.

Now that my parents had seen us paddling out in the marsh in the boat, it could be mentioned openly, and at supper I described its performance in glowing terms.

"Did your boat leak much?" my father asked.

I told of our troubles along that line. "You need to caulk the seams," my father said.

"We don't have any cork."

"Not cork, caulk — c-a-u-l-k. It's like string."

"Does it cost much?"

"I doubt it. You have to wedge it into the seams."

My mother was not especially pleased with developments. "You'd better be careful," she repeated several times. "If you fell in you couldn't swim."

I assured her that there was no danger of my falling in, and that even if I did I would be safe enough in the marsh, because I could always stand up in the reed grass.

"You might cut yourself on oyster shells or old pieces of glass," she said. "You don't know what's out there in that mud."

I thought it best to argue no more. She had accepted the fact of my going out in the boat. That was what mattered.

It turned out that when the tide came in the next afternoon and we were able to go out in the boat again, the leaking had diminished considerably. Water still came in, to be sure, but at nothing like the rate of the previous day, so that it was necessary to bail out the boat only every quarter-hour or so. We decided that the wood must have swelled in the water overnight. We also discovered that the boat leaked even less when only one of us was in it.

After a few days my friend John Carmody's interest in paddling around in the marsh creeks subsided, but mine did not. Almost every day, when the tide permitted, I would go out for a trip. I explored up and down the marsh, along all the little creeks leading off the main creek, sometimes venturing along channels so narrow that I could not paddle but had to pole along by pushing from the stern. There were neap tide days when the tide rose much less than at other times and when, standing in the boat, I could scarcely see over the top of the reed grass and went traveling down creeks that seemed like high-walled tunnels through the marsh. At such times, if there was no wind, the marsh was very hot and sticky, with the reed grass screening off any slight breeze. Sometimes, as I threaded my way through the maze of narrow channels, there would be a sudden splash and a flurry of wings up ahead, as a heron or a marsh hen, alarmed at my unexpected appearance, would take to the air and go speeding off across the marsh grass. Sometimes, too, I would come upon hordes of little white insects which swarmed hotly around me, and I would have to pole frantically to get the boat out of range.

The days I liked best were those when there were very high tides, for then I did not have to confine my explorations to the creeks, but could paddle across the expanses of submerged marsh in whichever direction I wished. Though the reed grass just beneath the surface slowed the boat somewhat, at such times there was almost nowhere in the marshland that I could not go, and at times I ventured near the edge of the river itself. But it was a while before I dared to take my boat all the way along the creek to where it emptied into the river. For one thing, it was a long way to paddle — for though the river's edge was only a quarter-mile from the shore, the creek was winding and contained a series of bends and curves. Several times I reached the place at which the creek executed its last turn before opening directly upon the river some seventy-five feet away, but I always stopped there. I was afraid that if I moved any closer, my boat might somehow get caught in the river current and be carried out into the channel. So I held up just beyond the final turn, not venturing to take my boat into the delta-shaped creek mouth, even though the water seemed calm enough, and looked at the river flowing past.

Finally, late one afternoon, I resolved that I was going to go all the way to the river itself. I was under strict orders from my parents to remain in the marsh, to be sure, but the mouth of the creek was hidden from view from our front porch by the Simons' house and the oak trees. I paddled along the creek, rounded the final bend, and moved forward, paddling vigorously with the perceptibly stronger current that pushed against the blunt stern of the boat, until I was actually within the deltalike creek mouth itself, and could look over the reed grass about the sides and see the edge of the river upstream and down. For an instant I held there, the channel flowing by in front of me, the low shoreline of the farther side of the river clearly visible across the water, until the current propelled the boat sideways toward the marsh grass. I let it drift into the edge of the grass. The tide was going out. I could feel the river current moving across the creek and pushing against the boat, which rocked in the flow. I could see the long curving edge of the marsh downstream, and the Seaboard railroad trestle more than a mile distant. Upstream I had a clear view of the fertilizer docks, and could see a freighter tied up alongside one wharf.

It was exciting, but I also felt very uneasy, and after a minute I pushed away from the marsh. Once I did I yielded to panic and began desperately paddling the boat back into the creek, and did not stop until I was safely back at the bend of the creek. There I let the boat swing around and then guided it into the marsh grass, and watched the river from a distance. I breathed easy again. I had taken my boat to the very edge of the river, but had then lost my nerve. And it was silly, I realized, for I had had no trouble paddling the boat back up the creek.

That night, after I had gone to bed, I thought of how exciting it had been to be there at the river's edge, holding my boat in place at the creek mouth, with the current pushing vigorously against the side of the boat, and with the entire panorama of the Ashley River open before me, upstream and downstream. If only I could make myself bold enough to paddle out beyond the marsh, I could swing around the point of reed grass that marked the entrance, and move down the edge. I could take my boat up and down the side of the river, and provided I stayed close to the marsh there could be no danger, for the current had not really been too strong. My panic had been needless. There was nothing to be afraid of; the boat handled well. It was not like the swimming lessons, for I was in a boat, and knew how to handle the boat. Yet I had been afraid, and I had lost control of myself. I had wanted to go out in a boat, and now I had the boat, and I had failed.

It seemed to me — however much I recoiled at the thought — that I *must* take the boat out into the river the next day, no matter what. I was not sure why it was necessary. After all, there would be other days, and besides, the boat had not been built to be taken out into the river. If that had been the intention we would have tried to build it with a pointed bow to handle the current better. But now that I had the boat, I knew that I had to do it. To think about what I was going to do made me tremble. My mother, if she knew what I planned, would forbid it emphatically. If she caught sight of me out there, it would be the end to my boating in the marsh or anywhere else, for she would order me never to go out in the boat again.

I told myself that in any event I could not do it tomorrow, because the tide would be high too late in the day. I felt relieved. But then I thought that I could go early in the morning, when the tide would also be high. So that excuse was invalid.

I tried to think about something else, but my thoughts kept returning to the boat. It occurred to me that now that I had won the right to have a boat in the marsh, I might be able to get a full-fledged boat, one with a pointed bow and a curved design, that would be much better for going on the river. True, I had no money, but I could take my entire stamp collection, which I had been assembling for years and which was worth at least twenty dollars by book value in the Scott catalog, and sell it to Mr. Bruchner. He could not possibly offer me less than that. But I found the idea of going back into Bruchner's Antique Store and dealing with the man disturbing. Besides, my mother would not let me sell the stamps that way.

I was a long time going to sleep, and when I did, I had a dream in which I was being taken by my nurse to play in Hampton Park. I recognized it at once, because when I was a small child I had been taken there every afternoon to play. When we got to the park there was another nurse seated on a bench, and she too was overseeing the play of a child, whom I recognized at once as a girl named Janet Dennis, who was in my seventh-grade class at school. Janet suggested that we play hide-and-go-seek, and she went off to hide, while I kept my hands over my eyes and counted up to a hundred. But I had secretly peeked through my fingers, and I knew she had gone down the path to a large stand of bamboo canebrake about seventy-five feet away, so when I was done counting, I ran straight to the canebrake. There was a path in the canebrake, and I hurried along it. The bamboo was so thick that it was almost like nighttime, and several times I had to pass through swarms of insects, while off in the underbrush I could hear animals scurrying about.

I groped my way along until I found her, deep inside the thick canebrake. "This is my hideaway," she told me. She reached down and turned on a single gooseneck electric lamp which was there, and in the darkness it illuminated a white and gold colored box which was lying on the ground under a rosebush. Printed on the box were the words SALT WATER DIVINITY FUDGE, MANUFACTURED BY THE F. W. WAGENER COMPANY. "Do your parents let you eat candy?" Janet Dennis asked. I nodded. She opened the box, but instead of fudge candy inside there were some Confederate army buckles and insignia.

I could hear the nurses calling us, and wanted to leave, but Janet refused. "I'm going to stay here and not go back to my nurse," she insisted, laughing. At that point I saw a length of manila rope lying on the ground, so I picked it up, made a lariat, and dropped the noose over her shoulders. She laughed again, and I began towing her back along the path. She resisted, but not too vigorously, and I had the feeling that she really wanted to come back to the nurses, whom I could hear calling, but her pride dictated that she struggle. After much tugging we were near the edge of the canebrake, but we had taken a different path and a dense thicket blocked our escape. Though it was dark in the canebrake I could see that beyond, outside, it was broad daylight, and I saw a man who was busily pruning an arbor of Cherokee roses. It was my uncle, and I wondered why he was there. Meanwhile I kept trying to pull Janet Dennis through the thicket, and she continued to resist. "Watch out!" she said, laughing, "you'll fall on those thorns and cut yourself!" I laughed, and then as I gave another tug on the rope I lost my footing suddenly and fell in the thicket, and the momentum tumbled Janet toward me. "Watch out! Watch out!" she cried. And at that instant I woke up. The dream seemed very real, and it took me a minute or so to realize fully that I was lying in my bed, and it had been only a dream.

The next morning I went right out to my boat after breakfast. The tide, though ebbing, was still quite high. I set out down the creek, rounded the last bend, and paddled straight for the mouth. The current was with me; I went swinging out past the fringes of marsh grass into the river itself.

At once the current swung my boat about, and took it in tow. The bow turned downstream. I tried to steer the boat toward the edge of the marsh. The current took me along, but finally I managed to get the bow up into the marsh grass, grabbed hold of a fistful of reeds to hold the boat in position while the stern swung downstream, and with the paddle I was able to nose it farther into the marsh so that the current would not dislodge it. For the moment I was safe.

I sat there, breathing hard. The river was flowing powerfully by, no more than a few feet from where I clung to the marsh. It was, I thought helplessly, a bright clear day, in no way ominous or threatening in itself, and yet here I was. The current was much stronger than I had guessed. If I let the boat get caught in it I might well be swept out to sea, or — worse still — be taken into the rougher water of the lower river, and the boat might capsize. And I had no life preserver.

To get back into the protection of the creek, I had two possible courses of action. One would be to pull the boat all the way through the marsh grass, and get to the creek from the side. But that seemed impossible, for except along the very edge of the marsh up by the creek mouth the reed grass was much too tall and dense.

The other choice was to go back out into the river. What I would have to do, I realized, was to let loose of the marsh grass along the side, push off with the paddle so that the stern of the boat would swing parallel with the current, and the bow point upstream, and then work along the edge, against the current, until I could shove the bow up into the thin grass just at the edge of the creek mouth, from where I could push the boat over into the creek mouth itself.

The thing to do was to remain calm and not to panic. If I failed to make sufficient headway against the current, I thought, I could always slip back into the marsh again, and I would be no worse off. So long as I kept my head and did not let the boat swing broadside to the current, where it would be carried rapidly offshore, I would be safe. The very worst that could happen would be that I should have to stay there alongside the marsh all day until the tide rose that evening.

I wanted to delay, but I knew that the longer I did, the stronger the tide would be running and the more difficult it would be to paddle the boat against it.

Trembling, I let go the reed grass and pushed the paddle against the bank. The boat slid back into the current, was taken by it, began to swing about. I dug the paddle into the water, pulling furiously. The boat straightened out, drifted back a few yards but remained parallel to the marsh, then began moving ahead. I could feel the current throbbing as it pushed against the blunt bow. Slowly, with much effort, I was able to work the boat ahead along the marshside. I paddled steadily, forcing myself to take my time and make each thrust count.

Then after several minutes I realized that I was now in somewhat slacker water, screened from the full force of the river current by the protruding marsh grass at the creek entrance. I paddled ahead, made more progress, nosed the bow into the reed grass, paddled in as far as I could go, then, before the current could shove the boat back, jumped up into the bow and dug the paddle into the mud, pushed, until the boat was up into the fringe of the marsh, balanced there, and then, as I stepped to the stern and pushed again with the paddle, it eased over the point and into the mouth of the creek. Now the current turned it broadside, but it was all right, for the marsh was there to hold it. I pushed against the marsh, paddled, and the boat moved up into the creek. I kept paddling all the way until I had reached the bend of the creek, seventy-five feet distant. There I moved the boat up into the marsh, where it held, secure.

I sat in the boat, panting for breath, exhausted. My arms were shaking from the exertion they had made. My face felt as if it were on fire.

After a few minutes I realized that there were four inches or more of water in the bottom of the boat. I had been too caught up in my efforts to think to bail it. I picked up the coffee can and began dipping water from the boat.

Yet the boat had performed well enough. I had simply not realized how powerful the river current could be. When I ventured out into the river again I must be careful to do so while the tide was right. The thing to do was not to work against the current but to go with it. If I wanted to go upstream I could go at slack tide, or while the tide was still coming in, not when it was ebbing. If I wanted to go downstream I could keep to the side of the marsh and nose in to rest when I grew tired, and when I got ready to return I would need only to swing the boat about and go back with the tide, using my paddle to steer.

While I was waiting there, preparatory to returning up the creek to the dock, I heard a ship's whistle off toward town. I stood up in the boat and looked over the marsh grass. A half-mile or so downstream, a freighter was coming up the channel, preceded by a tugboat, bound for the fertilizer docks upstream. They would soon be passing right beyond the mouth of the creek.

I knew there would be wake, so I pushed my boat out of the marsh and paddled across the creek to where there would be a belt of reed grass between me and the creek mouth. I pushed up into the grass to wait, next to an old waterlogged tree trunk, or perhaps a piling — it was so decayed that I could not tell for sure — that was lying in the marsh, studded with barnacles and oyster shells.

Toward me they came, the tugboat first, then behind it, the towline slack in the water but ready, linking them, the freighter, many times the size of the tugboat, moving slowly and under control. They passed no more than several hundred feet off the creek mouth. The tugboat was the *Robert H. Lockwood.* I could see the crew of the tugboat, and even the captain in the wheelhouse. I waved my hand, and one of the crew on the deck saw me and waved back. Then the freighter eased by, stately and high-sided, with crewmen standing along the railings watching over the sides. I saw the cargo booms, the wheelhouse, the lifeboats attached to the davits, the air ports, the companionway ladders, the portholes, the deck machinery. At the stern a French tricolor was flying. Beneath the raised stern the blades of a propeller thumped slowly, half out of the water. I read the name and the home port on the stern as the freighter moved upstream: *FINISTERRE:* BORDEAUX.

The wake came surging toward the shoreline, and as it broke along the marsh there was a low, churning sound of water, rolling steadily upstream. Into the delta of the creek mouth the hills of water flooded, to beat against the marsh bank and be contained by the reed grass. Even through the expanse of marsh separating me from the open water I could feel the surge. My little boat rocked as it lifted above the water and dropped back. It bumped against the tree trunk, which momentarily was almost covered by the flowing water. Then it was calm again in the marsh.

The creek was well down as I paddled up to the dock behind Mr. Simons' house. I had simply arrived at the water's edge too late, when the tide was already moving out. In a couple of days' time the tide would be high late enough in the morning so that I could get out in my boat while it was still coming in, I thought. Then there would be no trouble. I would go upstream with the tide a little while, and paddle back to the creek when the current slacked off.

I tied my boat up to the dock, and walked on back up the bluff and across the oak grove toward our house. As I entered the gate my father was working in the garden.

"Where've you been for so long?" he asked.

"Just paddling around in the marsh," I said.

SILVIA TENNENBAUM

A Lingering Death

(FROM THE MASSACHUSETTS REVIEW)

HER FIRST BLACKOUT came on quite naturally. It was like a cloud passing across the sun. It *was* a cloud passing across the sun, she thought, and did not find it at all unusual. Clouds frequently pass across the sun. But this time, after the cloud had gone on and the sun shone again, Amalie found herself on the floor. She had been standing beside the armchair, watering the plants in front of the long French windows and then the cloud came and she was on the floor, water from the watering can all over the carpet. Amalie was too startled to think there was anything wrong. She got up and fetched a dishtowel to dry the carpet and set the long spouted brass watering can back on its saucer. She did not, however, think about continuing to water the plants. She sat down on the couch and thought that she ought to read Rilke again. Had she been thinking of him before the cloud passed? (She now remembered it, quite resolutely, as a cloud.) It had been many years since she read Rilke. Amalie saw that there was a run in her stocking and some blood on her knee. The telephone rang but she would not answer, it was imperative that she try to reconstruct what happened before she spoke to anyone. It would be impossible to explain the cloud unless she was certain of her own interpretation. Another person might see it differently, might read it as an omen. Amalie felt her heart beating. The light of winter danced into her livingroom on yellow-gray drops. She had chosen the apartment for its light. In the morning it flooded her bedroom and in the afternoon it moved into the livingroom on long, graceful beams. There were plants at all the windows and paintings on every wall. Amalie liked the pictures as much now as she had in her youth. They never seemed emptied of life; she could always rephrase her perception of them. The apartment was spacious, the furniture good. Amalie had lived in a number of cities in her time, she had finally chosen to settle in this one (it was her birthplace) because it was benign and gray. Cities began for her directly outside her window; her comfortable apartment was the center of her life and was rendered most carefully. Amalie felt that arrangement mattered and details were important. She knew exactly what shelf the Rilke was on, and had monograms stitched on her linens. The city was cool and often slick with rain. The sky retained the gray cast of the rain clouds on the nicest of days and spread it like a dingy sheet above the squat stone houses (many of them painted pale gray) and the river, but the distant rolling hills were always raked by sunlight. Everything in the city had changed in the years Amalie had been away and nothing had changed. The streets were buzzing with vacant-eyed strangers and oddly colored cars but the numbers and destinations of the trolley cars were just as Amalie remembered them. The town council enacted laws regulating the height of buildings and the thickness of masonry; an old-age home stood on the Fuseli estate where once the deer had grazed. It was named after a poet who had lived to be ninety-six. The city was a reasonable place, the river had not flooded since 1736. One never saw beggars or whores. After dark the streets were empty and the great white street lights illumined a desert of gray boxes; in spring the scent of lilacs stole over the courtyard walls. Amalie noticed that the phone had stopped ringing. She belched and saw that there was now also a pink bruise on her elbow. The great clouds in the sky moved slowly, dragged down by the weight of their gray bellies. When they rolled over the sun the afternoon became dreary, but it remained the color of day. Amalie felt diminished, as though she had walked through an unfamiliar alley and seen something not meant for her eyes. A couple engaged in an obscene act. She sat on the couch for a long time. Her thoughts would fasten on one thing or another until fear brought them back into the room. Amalie waited for a pain that never came and when she bent over to rearrange the dried gourds she thought once more of Rilke. It grew dark slowly. At one moment the light inside was exactly the color of the light outside, then the sky paled and the room closed in on the emerging darkness. It became necessary to turn on a lamp even though it was not yet night. The blackness, Amalie saw, had been behind her own eyes — a moment of death. The paintings on the opposite wall were illumined from above by the chandelier and from below by the lamp on the table. Amalie could not remember having turned on the light a minute after she had pressed the switch. It was difficult to follow a single thought to its conclusion. Amalie sometimes went back to the beginning and found that there was no end. The rhythm of the paintings had changed in the light. They looked like ikons and there was still a yellow glow on the rim of the sky. The Beckmann was Amalie's largest picture; she owned several drawings by Saul Steinberg, whom she had also known, two early Chagalls and three Klees. Klee had died the year she had gone hiking in the Alps near Zermatt. She had met Kandinsky in Weimar. Amalie saw her life as a series of connections to history. She often thought her reminiscences had value and tried to write them down. But when she read back what she had written, the words she had used conveyed only a small and obscure portion of the event. It was different with her letters. Observations made in the heat of vision did not break apart as easily as her reconstituted memories. Her friends and relations were amused by her lively transcriptions of what took place at the next table or in the railway station. She hoped Evelyn had kept her letters as promised. Evelyn, the daughter of her oldest friend, was also her godchild. Amalie felt closer to her than to any of her blood relatives. Evelyn was a professor of art history and travelled to Italy every summer. Her Italian was impeccable. Her papers were models of scholarship. Amalie did not like her friend's cluttered apartment and rarely went there. It had a lovely view of the river but was depressing in all other aspects. Evelyn never arranged her belongings, she simply stacked them up or set them in a row against the wall. On Wednesday evenings Amalie and Evelyn met for dinner at a local Italian restaurant. They always shared the large antipasto. "I made my will today," Amalie said one evening, right after they had ordered. "You'll get all my paintings and furniture." This had been about ten years before. "I want you to keep it all intact. Throw your own stuff out, it's junk anyway." Evelyn was flattered and pleased. The gift carried with it a desire for a small monument and was in keeping with Amalie's only talent: to create order out of chaos. Amalie quarreled with most people. She liked to rearrange people's furniture and as a result quarreled with most of her friends, but Evelyn was, at heart, lethargic and selfish. She never responded to criticism. Amalie spent a considerable portion of her time shopping; she enjoyed the act of unwrapping a package and put away its contents with proud care. She saved string and paper; she had a long list of people to whom she sent gifts and birthday greetings. Amalie had outlived many of her friends and frequently visited the cemetery. Her only surviving brother lived across the river in an eighteenth-century house whose garden grew wild to the water's edge, but they met only on New Year's Day and for dinner on his birthday. Amalie had not noticed her life slowly shrinking around her until the afternoon of the cloud. Then, sitting very still on the sofa, watching as everything around her grew indistinct in the fading light, she traced her movements for the past several years and found that her days no longer followed the sequences of old. There were places she no longer visited, foods she no longer tasted, choices she no longer made or made only after foolish deliberations. Her very language had dried up, she used fewer words and those she did use had a worn sound to them. Amalie felt herself oozing into the soft cushions of the couch, she was happy that the view from that place was pleasant. When she heard the doorbell ring she would not get up; she had made no plans to entertain a visitor; her mind was cleared of small talk. She sensed that only a spontaneous gesture would allow her to rise. How she had laughed with Max Beckmann and Quappi! Their photos stood on her desk, inscribed in German. In one of its drawers, tied with grosgrain ribbon, were packets of letters, all of them written by hand. They included a number of gossipy letters from Nolde's wife; Amalie had bought several of his watercolors. When the chimes of the Church of St. Anthony of Padua struck six, Amalie got up (without thinking about it) and poured herself a sherry. She felt much better, everything was fine again and she smiled broadly when she passed the mirror in the hall. There was nothing the matter after all. The bruise did remain for a while but the cloud was put in its place (the only surrealist painting Amalie owned was a Magritte) and referred to once or twice, but not in such a way as to encourage a response.

It happened again a month later, just as she finished brushing her teeth at bedtime. Amalie saw the lightbulb flicker and go out as she reached for the lavender hand towel. The pain on her forehead reached her consciousness first, then the fact that she was sitting awkwardly on the floor. Amalie got up and looked in the mirror; there was a purple bruise on her cheek. She thought, absurdly, that she must wear a veil. Amalie went to bed and tried to read Rilke's "Letters to a Young Poet" but it was difficult for her to keep in mind what she had read. She went over the same sentence again and again, until it made sense and then quickly destroyed it with the memory of her drained old face. Perhaps Rilke had been a mistake. It was a Saturday night and she took a novel by Colette from the night table and read that until very late, she felt the need to keep a light burning and not chance the dreams of sleep. She kept fingering the bruise and the pain warded off irrelevant speculation. It was 4:00 A.M. before Amalie fell asleep. Outside, an inch or two of snow had fallen and the city turned dark. Snowflakes tumbled through the light from the street lamps. The bruise was still painful in the morning and had grown larger. Amalie remembered Colette's story with pleasure but she was tired and stiff. She thought she ought to have a big breakfast but there were no eggs and the rolls were stale. On Sunday it was impossible to buy fresh rolls. Snow was no longer falling, yet the sky remained overcast. After breakfast (Amalie buttered two stale rolls and toasted them in the oven) she made some telephone calls to see how others were faring in the snow. Her conversations were abrupt, as though she were only checking to see who was left in the devastated city. "The roads are already cleared," said Evelyn. Amalie tried to drive away the buzzing worry with chatter. She wondered what the black cloudbursts signified, and thought that "cloudburst" sounded well, divorced from water. She said "black cloudburst" in the middle of her conversation with her oldest friend. "What?" said Dora, who was not easily startled. "My mind took a sudden turn," Amalie told her and Dora was satisfied. Amalie had lived alone so long she knew how to dole out her allotment of fear; there was no one to catch her cheating or to let on, by some wayward startled glance, what horrors she saw. Some years before, she had had an operation to remove a cancerous growth. She had known of its existence for some time and taught herself not to probe it. (The initial discovery had been the only shock.) Not until the swelling seemed about to break open like a rotten fruit did Amalie go to the doctor. It was one thing not to hold her life very dear, she thought, quite another to mess with the putrefaction of death. The operation had been relatively easy to take. All visible signs of malignancy were removed, the wound soon healed, the scar grew white. Amalie continued on her daily rounds in her VW. She did errands for neighbors and visited the old-age home named for a poet. On Sundays she drove up the river to drink hot chocolate and eat buttery croissants at an inn whose terrace was in the shade of a giant oak tree. The gray city welcomed her back in the misty light of early evening (Mark Tobey had once told her it was his favorite hour) when she would sometimes stroll to the Roman Catholic church to watch an Italian wedding. In order to maintain her distance, Amalie always took a back seat and never knelt. The days when she had talked with artists seemed very distant now. Amalie had been good at flattery. She had been pretty as well, though without faith in her beauty — the family had taken no notice of it in days when it might have mattered. All her life, looking into a succession of mirrors, Amalie saw a startled spinster; she played out the role whenever one of the artists drew her to him for a kiss. She remembered sitting with groups of young bohemians in the cafes and posing with them for photographs she never got to see. She always stood to the side, without smiling. None of the artists later remembered who she was. Amalie drifted out of their circle and found companions, most of them women, who made her less self-conscious. In subsequent years she came to know artists whose reputations had already been made; the paintings on her walls dated from that period. She travelled a great deal and became more querulous; she refused to explain who she was and paid close attention to appearances and signs of good breeding. She became a simplified person, laced into one comprehensible whole with leather gloves to match her shoes. She stopped buying paintings when her walls could take no more; the new art appalled her. She sent out peals of laughter when she saw it in the museum and Evelyn could not explain its logic to her, hard as she tried.

The black cloud came upon Amalie a third time, without warning and outside her apartment. Amalie was standing in line at the bank and the next thing she knew a soundless earthquake had folded the room down upon her. Amalie tried to keep her eyes open but the ceiling blanked them out and when she looked again, there were people bending over her. "I'm all right," she said. The faces were puffed like those of spectators peering over a balustrade. "We are calling an ambulance," said the guard. "No!" said Amalie, as firmly as she could, from the floor. The guard was an

African and spoke in a high voice. His lips swelled with blood. "Please don't bother," said Amalie, "just let me sit for a minute and I'll be fine." One leg was folded under her, she thought she was a piece of sculpture and wondered if the floor was dirty. Her hat was just beyond the reach of her fingers. A young woman (probably a secretary on her lunch hour) picked it up and reached for the (far-flung) handbag at the same time. "Leave it!" Amalie cried. She was helped into a leather chair in a vice-president's office. The guard had picked up her bag; Amalie realized she would have to tip him later. The vice-president seemed to know her and spoke to her in a smooth, low voice. He told her that an elderly lady had been run over by a trolley car only a few days before, directly across the street from the bank. She had tried to cross behind a stationary tram and walked directly into another, coming from the opposite direction. "She disregarded the 'don't walk' sign," the vice-president said. "Maybe she was a foreigner," said Amalie. "Oh no! She was an old customer," said the vice-president. Amalie noticed that she had bitten her tongue, the blood tasted like metal. Amalie thanked the vice-president and put on her hat (it had been an unpleasantly cold spring) and walked quite steadily back into the bank. The guard led her out the revolving door and she pressed a folded bill into his hand; he slipped it into his pocket with a gesture that was completely natural. When she was back in the VW Amalie allowed herself to think about the consequences of her public collapse. She drove directly home and called Dr. Freundlich for an appointment. When she sat across the desk from him after the examination (his position reminded her of the bank vice-president) and saw that he was having some difficulty articulating his remarks she quickly said to him, "Signs of old age, eh?" Dr. Freundlich looked puzzled and (Amalie thought) a little guilty. He withdrew into the clean white thicket of his own language. Medical terms meant nothing to Amalie. "I see," she said, and knew only that he was trying to tell her something impossible to talk about. "Mother had the same thing," she said. "You know all about it then," Dr. Freundlich said. He seemed willing to sit and chat for a while. "I would like to take some x-rays," he said. "No," said Amalie. "Be reasonable, my dear," said the doctor and looked rather down at the mouth, Amalie thought. "We must begin treatment," he said. "Some pills and I'll be as good as new?" Amalie laughed like a young girl. There was an arrangement of dried flowers on the doctor's desk and photos of young couples, smiling before a snow-covered mountain and clowning on a veranda before a lake. None had been taken in recent years. "I would prefer treating you in the hospital," Dr. Freundlich said, "a massive assault might halt the spread . . ." Amalie got up, she thought his attentions uncouth. "You have other patients to see," she said. "I will let you know. Is there any urgency?" "You ask me that now?" he answered and shook his head. Amalie felt some sadness. "At my age, what's the use?" she said. "Please call me," said Dr. Freundlich. It was almost as though he had invited her to a concert and she had refused him. At home Amalie drank a glass of sherry, which went directly to her head. She had not eaten since breakfast. For a few minutes the feeling was very pleasant but it was followed by nausea and a terrible headache. Amalie stretched out on the couch and held a cool vase to her forehead. Her oldest friend, Dora, called to ask about her visit to the doctor. "I am quite well, thank you," said Amalie, "just growing old. You will too." Dora recommended a homeopathic physician. "No thanks," said Amalie, "they're good only for hypochondriacs." Amalie often hurt Dora's feelings with her brusque manner. Her oldest friend was good-natured on the whole, but a little silly. She sometimes didn't know that she had been insulted. She considered herself more worldly than Amalie and when she was angry, punished her by talking about parties to which Amalie had not been invited. Amalie's brother also called and told her that his chauffeur had driven the Mercedes into an abutment. Amalie didn't understand the word "abutment"; it was like a term the doctor had used. Her brother became angry. "You don't listen!" he said. Amalie felt abandoned. "Why don't you lose some weight?" she asked him. "I saw you walking down by Edward Garcia's office the other day and almost didn't recognize you, you were so fat." "What were you doing in that part of town?" said Paul. "Going to the museum," Amalie told him. "I always drive the back way in order to avoid that left turn at the bridge." "What did the doctor say?" "Nothing very much," said Amalie and hung up, saying there was someone at the door. "A botched life," Amalie's brother Paul said to his law partner as they left for their club. Amalie told Mrs. Forster, the cleaning lady, that Dr. Freundlich wanted her to go to the hospital for treatment. "If I was you, I wouldn't go," said Mrs. Forster, "you'll never get out of there alive. My sister had this pain in her side and when it persisted she went to see Dr. Aram at the clinic. He put her in the hospital, wanting to operate. They stirred around in her a little bit and said it didn't look so good and they couldn't help her. Four days later she was dead." (Mrs. Forster had told the story before.) "She was lucky," said Amalie, "she suffered very little." Mrs. Forster did not respond. She thought Amalie presumptuous, like all the rich. Mrs. Forster was well served by a handful of words; she spoke in phrases she had learned through constant repetition. They never led her astray; they were like the #5 trolley that took her home. Amalie sometimes rattled her by talking about things Mrs. Forster deemed foreign and out of place among the well-rubbed homely sentences that encased all her thoughts and bore them gently into a world spiked with insults and disasters. Mrs. Forster had never got used to the Beckmann. After twelve years she despised it as much as the first day she came to work for Amalie. It made her sick to look at it. If Amalie hadn't been such a good employer (she always had extra coffee for her and fresh Danish) Mrs. Forster might well have quit and all on account of that evil picture. The others weren't any too hot either, but that one was the worst. "You really *like* it?" she asked Amalie. "Very much," Amalie answered, but did not know how to go on. Once, when Mrs. Forster felt particularly well-disposed toward Amalie she said, "You know I almost didn't come to work for you on account of that thing." "Imagine that," said Amalie. She wanted Mrs. Forster to like the picture; she wanted Mrs. Forster to understand her, yet she seemed always to be describing a set of objects so odd they might have evolved out of her private fantasy. (Amalie no longer bothered with fantasies, it was enough to sift through the past.) The Beckmann represented everything that stood between the two women, however much they talked. Mrs. Forster's only daughter had not turned out well and was married to a crook. Amalie kept asking her what did he do. "He must do something," she insisted. Mrs. Forster wondered why Amalie should doubt her. Possibly she had never known a crook. Amalie called Dr. Freundlich and told him she had decided against being treated in the hospital. "Your discomfort will increase," the doctor said. "I can always change my mind," Amalie said. Dr. Freundlich ordered some medication and it was not until midsummer that Amalie had any further trouble. Driving out of the garage one day she found that she could not turn her head to the right to see if something was coming down the road. Fortunately the way was clear and Amalie drove about her business looking straight ahead. She stopped at Dr. Freundlich's office but he was on vacation. The nurse asked her if she wanted to see Dr. Brill, the assistant, but Amalie declined, saying it was not an emergency. She went home and took a steaming bath, even though it was quite hot outside. Evelyn was in Italy, Dora was at a mountain resort and her brother Paul had prostate trouble. Amalie drank sherry and asked Mrs. Forster to come an extra day. She did not drive her car and did her best to keep unpleasant thoughts from taking over her mind. As a result she talked a great deal and Mrs. Forster grew irritable. "Why pick on me?" she said to her daughter, "don't she have her own kin?" When the pains began where there had only been stiffness, Amalie took aspirin and switched from sherry to brandy. She ordered a television set for the livingroom and this pleased Mrs. Forster; the brilliant burst of light from its flickering screen triumphed over the Beckmann (too bad Amalie had been too cheap to buy one in color). Amalie began sorting her letters and pasting loose photographs into albums. "She's been giving me a lot of junk lately," Mrs. Forster told her daughter, who was glad for it and sold what she couldn't use to her husband's friends. "See if you can get me some silver," he said, but Mrs. Forster was afraid. When Dr. Freundlich came back, tanned and fit, with large splotches of sunburn on his bald head, Amalie took a cab to see him. He looked troubled and said, "I can only tell you again that you should be hospitalized." Amalie shook her head as best she could. "I will take treatment as an out-patient," she said, "nothing more." Amalie knew she had the upper hand. As long as she never asked a direct question nor gave an entirely truthful answer she forced the doctor to be her accomplice. When Evelyn came back from Italy, Amalie said, quite casually, "I gave up driving my car." Evelyn's mind was on Mantegna. "Let's meet for lunch instead of dinner," Amalie said, "I'll take a cab." Shortly after they hung up, Evelyn called back. "I'll pick you up," she said. From then on they went to the Italian restaurant for lunch every Wednesday. It was possible to see a long way down the river from the restaurant terrace and the sunlight fell like a shower of gold through the leaves of the chestnut trees. Evelyn said something about Danae and Zeus but her mouth was full and Amalie did not answer. The green of the trees obscured the gray stone houses and seemed to cast its color on the languid river. "I must say I prefer winter," said Amalie, and Evelyn saw, for the first time, that her friend was in pain and took no pleasure in the taste of ripe fruit. The full sweet roses were an affront; Amalie wanted them dead in the wintry ground. Before long it was autumn and the leaves turned brown and yellow and a cool wind blew them down the wet streets. The treatments had relieved Amalie's pain but the stiffness persisted. It was hard for her to turn her head in either direction and the tires on the VW had all gone flat. "Could your son-in-law use the car?" Amalie asked Mrs. Forster, who came three times a week and did the laundry and folded the sheets and marketed. "I bet he could, that good-for-nothing!" said Mrs. Forster, "but I think he ought to pay for it." She told her daughter, who said, "with all the work it'll need, she ought to pay us." "You're terrible," said Mrs. Forster. She never mentioned paying for the car again and one day her son-in-law appeared and drove it off. He had had to use a hand pump on the tires but otherwise the car ran well.

In November, Amalie fell again, in the livingroom, almost exactly in the spot where she had seen the first black cloud. There was no watering can in her hand this time, but when she came to she was in great pain and it took her a long time to get into bed. Amalie was frightened. It was Saturday and raining and the children upstairs were especially noisy. Amalie felt as though her head were improperly attached to her body; she had to lie very still and in an awkward position to ease the pain. She stayed in bed, taking as many pills as she needed and sleeping as best she could. She dreamt of many different places, each one familiar but not exactly the way it really was. When she awoke she felt tired and it seemed as if she had indeed been travelling. Lying as still as she could Amalie reviewed her dreams and tried to keep their images intact. She did not answer the telephone when it rang and wondered if anyone would think to look in on her. She summoned all her acquaintances to walk behind her closed eyes and saw that they were like actors at a rehearsal, learning their lines one moment but joking and laughing when they were off-stage and free of the rote speeches and constraint of the inanimate play. On Sunday Amalie felt a little better and heated some soup. Her brother called (he always phoned on Sunday) and said, "You sound strange today." Amalie grew very angry. She had never shouted at him but now she shrieked some incomprehensible words into the receiver; when she hung up she was glad she had spoken nonsense. She wrote down a whole list of words without meaning and used them when she was in pain or angry on the telephone. In the middle of the day Evelyn called. She thought Amalie was hallucinating and rang up her mother. "I don't feel well myself. You go to her," Dora said, "you're the one who gets the pictures." Evelyn drove across town and stood for a long while, waiting for Amalie to let her in. She was drenched by the time she got upstairs. Amalie opened the door after another wait. Evelyn was not prepared for the sight of her. Amalie could barely stand. Her entire face was out of joint, as though it had been made up of parts of other people's faces. But she was perfectly lucid. Evelyn helped her back into bed and sat beside her for a while. She noticed that the face of the apartment had changed as well; there was no longer any order in it. Amalie fell asleep and Evelyn quietly got up and fixed herself a drink. She studied the paintings for a while and heard Amalie thrash her thin arms about in painful sleep. Uncertain of what to do, Evelyn kept on drinking and finally dozed off in the armchair next to Amalie's bed. Amalie awoke and saw her — like the dream landscapes — subtly altered, distorted. How could she have liked her so well all these years? Amalie wondered. She was repulsive. Evelyn had hairs on her chin and unkempt hair. Amalie made a loud sound to awaken the girl, but it was no use. She fell asleep again herself and the next time she opened her eyes Evelyn was reading her Rilke. The "Duino Elegies," of course, Amalie thought. "I fixed you some tea," said Evelyn and brought her a cup, spilled in its saucer. "I can't drink this," said Amalie, but when Evelyn had left she drank it up thirstily. The next day was Monday and Mrs. Forster would be in. She was always punctual and full of weekend complaints about her daughter. Amalie looked forward to Mondays; the weekends were tedious, as they had been in childhood, but on Monday the pace quickened and vendors cried in the streets. Mrs. Forster pretended not to notice how awful Amalie looked. She switched on the TV as soon as she had taken off her coat. Amalie asked her if she could spare yet another day. Mrs. Forster was firm. "I have to keep two days for Mrs. Angstrom," she said, "who is good to me too and always asking if I have extra time."

Dr. Freundlich paid a call and did not mention the hospital. He prescribed shots and asked Mrs. Forster if she could give them. "Not on your life," Mrs. Forster said, "that's not my job." A nurse was found, boarding illegally in another apartment; she agreed to give them, morning and evening, every day. Dr. Freundlich came regularly now and Amalie looked forward to his visits. They talked in whispers when Mrs. Forster was there. After Christmas Amalie's condition took a turn for the better. She seemed almost euphoric. She talked loud and long on the telephone and laughed with the doctor. She almost never used her gibberish. She spent a good part of each day sitting up, answering letters and watching the finches and sparrows come to her feeder. The plants blossomed and grew, Evelyn gave her oldest dresses away and got a haircut, and Paul came to visit every Sunday with something his cook had made. He told Amalie about his daughter's latest book. "It is positively pornographic," he said. "Is she as fat as ever?" Amalie asked. Easter came very early. It snowed on Good Friday and Amalie felt tired. On Easter Sunday the sun rose pale over the city and the fog would not lift. Amalie could see neither the street nor the buildings across the courtyard. The trees were flattened darkly against the gray clouds. Drops of water clung to the screens. The river sent up the bellowing sounds of foghorns. Amalie stayed in bed. A dull pain had settled down the length of her back; she could hardly lift her arms to lay them on top of the quilt. In the course of the afternoon she remembered that she had given Mrs. Forster Easter Monday off. "How stupid," thought Amalie. The afternoon sun spread a pale light through the livingroom; the Beckmann took well to that cool glow. Amalie called Mrs. Forster. The phone rang a few times and then was answered by Lola, her daughter. "Mother isn't home," she said, "she had a little accident and we had to take her to the hospital." "I hope it isn't serious," Amalie whispered, "will she be there long?" "I don't know, they never tell you those things." "Why didn't you call me?" Amalie asked. "I was planning to," said Lola. "Did she say anything about coming to work?" Amalie didn't care that she sounded shrill. "Mother had other things to think about, to tell the truth," Lola said, taking offense, "Could *you* come in?" Amalie was aware that her voice skittered toward the breaking point. She hadn't cried in over sixty years. "I don't do that kind of work," said Lola. "Just tomorrow?" "But tomorrow is Easter Monday." "I'll pay you double!" "All right, all right," said Lola. Amalie felt a sigh of grateful relief escape through a sob. She fell asleep. She woke at 4:00 A.M. and again at seven. At ten o'clock she called Lola. There was no answer. The pain was terrible and the nurse had not yet returned from a visit to the country. Paul was away for the races and Evelyn was attending a conference. Amalie's oldest friend had invited a young poet to spend the week and Dr. Freundlich's answering service did not understand her. She had lapsed into her masked language. Amalie saw that there was nothing to be gained by waiting but she did not know how to beckon death. She remembered her father, whistling for the dog. She remembered a summer meadow. Amalie tried to get up. Her memory stopped. Where the meadow had been, there hung only a white sheet. Amalie wanted to vomit; the words would not come. In the bathroom her head struck the edge of the basin. The pain was new, a blessing. A song of praise escaped from her mouth. Black paint welled over the sheet.

BERNARD MALAMUD

Home Is the Hero

(FROM THE ATLANTIC MONTHLY)

> *On the road he saw a jogger moving toward him, a*
> *man with a blue band tied around his head.*
> *The man slowed down as Dubin halted.*
> *"What are you running for?" the biographer asked.*
> *"All I can't stand to do. What about you?"*
> *"Broken heart, I think."*
> *"Ah, too bad for that."*
> *They trotted away from each other.*

DUBIN WAS FIFTY-SEVEN on the twenty-ninth of December, 1973, and the last thing he wanted was to celebrate the dismal occasion, but Kitty had urged, insisted. "For Pete's sake, let's get out of the rut we're in. We haven't had a dinner party since before you left for Italy." He was born in a cold season, a season he disliked, yet he liked to think he had been conceived in spring. Dubin dragged his feet because he had forgotten Kitty's last birthday, in April, and wanted her to forget his.

But she roasted two ducks, produced some bottles of Cabernet Sauvignon and five of champagne, and arranged masses of red and lavender anemones and bronze chrysanthemum daisies in white vases. He decided her favorite color was white.

Kitty, for the occasion, had invited the Greenfelds, Ondyks, Habershams, and, of course, Myra Wilson. The Habershams were new guests: Kitty had met them often at Myra's and at last invited them. Fred Habersham was an activist civil rights attorney, and his wife, Ursula, a Vermont state senator, one of three women in the legislature. The Ondyks were present, Evan and his wife, Marisa, a lady with thin cheeks, high nose, lips down at the corners. When you kissed her on the cheek she said "mmmuh," meaning a passionate kiss in return. Her passion was a play-reading group she had formed which Kitty sometimes attended.

Kitty and Flora Greenfeld were currently amiable and though they were never really at ease with each other — one coveted "more," one "less" — greeted one another cordially. It was, through the years, an ambivalent relationship. Flora was an animated woman of regal bearing, a violinist without career or children. Kitty pitied her for not having children, not because she hadn't had them, but because she had wanted children and Oscar hadn't. Dubin had always responded to Flora; they kissed on meeting. Kitty called her "born dissatisfied."

"She pretends, hides so much. When you talk to her you can feel the weight of all she's holding back."

"We all hide," Dubin confessed.

"Obviously," she said sadly.

"Then why blame her?"

"She pretends not to."

He let it go at that.

Myra Wilson, at eighty, was a still vital self-reliant white-haired farmer's widow. Widowhood had not frightened or soured her. She lived alone and competently with her arthritic pains. "So long as I have my aspirins." Kitty admired her and invited the old woman to her dinner parties; she almost daily attended her. They talked often on the phone. Kitty was genuinely fond of old people, perhaps women more than men; she had been brought up, she often said, by a loving grandmother. Dubin, for this birthday and this mood, would have preferred a few young people around, but only Flora was younger than fifty. Not that much younger. But she was feminine and attractive in a low-cut dramatic black dress. She was the one woman Dubin was drawn to that night.

"We hardly ever see you, William," Flora said. "Oscar says he meets you on his walk once in a while. I hear you're into a new biography."

"Deeply," said Dubin.

Oscar Greenfeld and the biographer embraced after skirting each other during drinks.

"Give us at least half a smile," Oscar said. "Anything wrong?"

"Does it show?"

"A strained swimming against the stream."

"My work, I guess."

"Not going well?"

"No."

"Too bad I didn't bring my flute to cheer you up."

"Too bad," said Dubin.

He went through the evening with a show of having a good time. Knowing he wasn't, he ate too much too quickly, tasted little, shoveled down more food, grew irritated with himself. He hurried upstairs to brush his teeth.

Dubin slogged through the night in a saddened mood. Kitty, taken in by his pretense, seemed to assume the party was working for him. For dessert she sailed in with a birthday cake she had baked, lit with a flickering candle; and the guests toasted the biographer with champagne as he smiled with his head bowed.

Kitty would not play the harp when Flora asked her to, amid the applause of her dinner guests. "No, no," she laughed and almost cried, "I'd spoil the fun."

"Oh come on," said Flora.

"Let her alone," said Greenfeld to his wife.

Afterward Maud called. Dubin, sitting in the downstairs bathroom that morning, had heard Kitty dial Maud and quietly ask her to remember to telephone her father that night. He assumed Kitty had also called Gerald but doubted she had been able to persuade him to put in a collect call.

"Hi, Papa," Maud said. "Happy Birthday!"

"Thanks. How are you, Maud?"

"No kicks."

Dubin said he missed her and was counting on her coming home for the winter vacation.

"I miss you, too. I will if I can."

As he sat at the phone in the hallway he was watching Kitty in the kitchen by the sink. Both faucets were running, and she was talking seriously with Ondyk.

If she's consulting him about me I'll break her ass, Dubin thought.

Maud said she'd be back in early February.

"I thought the intersession began in mid-January?"

"I'd like to rest up a few days after exams. I hate to leave the sun."

"It would help me to see you," Dubin said.

Her voice grew serious. "Is something the matter?"

"I like to look at you," he said. "I like you around."

"Please don't put any more pressure on me, Papa. I'll be taking five exams."

He said there was no pressure and felt low. She had changed. If a man needs his daughter so much, he thought, maybe he needs someone else more.

Maud's voice was tender when she said goodbye.

In their bedroom later he thanked Kitty for the party.

She was sitting in a chair, her skirt hiked up over her knees, legs raised, looking long at them.

"I have pretty good legs," she said. "Not bad for my age."

Dubin agreed.

"Did you like the evening?"

"Yes. Thanks for going to the trouble."

She got up to undress. "I don't think of it as trouble. You don't look very happy."

"I don't pretend to be," he said, though he had pretended.

Kitty asked whether he might want to talk to Evan Ondyk. She said it doubtfully.

"Were you talking to him about me?"

"No, about myself."

"What would you like me to say to him?"

"Stop being ironic. He might be able to help you pinpoint things — to figure out where you stand."

"I know where I stand," Dubin said huffily. "He doesn't know. I doubt he knows where he stands."

"I know people he's helped. He's an excellent therapist."

"I don't need his advice. His view of life is reductive. With him more is determined than with me. I know how free I am. I've picked the horse I ride."

"Never mind the horse. How free do you feel?"

"I asked him his interpretation of Thoreau and he came up with the usual can of Oedipal worms. There's that but there's a lot more."

"He's not a literary critic."

"He's not wise."

"Neither are you," said Kitty.

"That's true," Dubin said after a pause, "but I think I know as much about life as he does. Once I didn't, now I do."

"No, you don't," she said. "Maybe you do about the careers of

certain accomplished literary figures, but not necessarily about
yourself and not necessarily about the unconscious."

"Biography teaches you the conduct of life. The unconscious is
mirrored in a man's acts and words. If he watches and listens to
himself sooner or later he begins to know the contours of his
unconscious self. If you know your defenses you pretty much know
what it's about. In my work I've discovered how to discover. You
see in others who you are."

"Mirrored is right. You ought to hear yourself talking in the
bathroom."

"I hear, I listen. That's the point I'm making. I've lived fifty-
eight years."

"Fifty-seven."

"Fifty-seven. I think I know myself reasonably well. No one
knows himself totally. There's a great mystery in knowing. The big
thing is what you do with what you know."

"You exercise? You lose weight?"

"Right now I'm saying to myself that I *can* exercise and lose
weight."

"Where does that get you?" Kitty asked. "You're still a depressed
man who has trouble working. William, I feel there's more to this
than either you know or have said."

She's clever, Dubin thought, but this is still not the time to tell
her about Fanny. He thought he would wait till the worst blew
over. What's past and in perspective will hurt less than what's
bothering her now. I won't clobber her with honesty, hers or mine.

He said he had real literary problems with his book.

"It's dry, a compilation of facts rather than a living life — more
like De La Grange's *Mahler,* or Blotner's *Faulkner.* I want life in it
that I haven't got so far. My reaction is not, simply, neurosis."

She never said it was. "I feel in the dark," Kitty said, her voice
strained. "In the dark I'm afraid. I feel you can't work for a reason,
William. If you know what it is, please tell me. Don't keep me in
the dark."

Dubin told her that he would tell her when he knew.

"Losing weight won't do it," Kitty went on, looking at him with
moist dark eyes. "Nor what you think you know about life because
you write biographies. Working it out with someone usually helps.
If you don't want to talk to Evan, why don't you go see Dr. Lecroix
in Salem? I hear he's very good."

"I haven't got that kind of time. Salem is seventy miles one way and another seventy back. It'll kill a day to go there."

"Go once to talk to him instead of frittering the morning away getting nothing done."

"Once leads to twice, then twice a week. I haven't got that kind of time."

"Stop yakking about time, for Christ's sake. You're not doing much with it."

"Life is what I'm thinking of," Dubin said. "I know its structure and spin and many of the ways of surprise if not the whole pattern or order. I know enough, in other words, to take my chances. I want to run my own life my own way, not like yours or Nathanael's. I don't want to go on sharing with you to my dying day the benefits of your previous marriage."

"That's cruel."

Kitty drew her dress over her head. He looked away from the mark on her buttock through her white underpants. When he looked again she was slipping on a white nightgown.

"Don't be so fucking proud," Kitty said in bed.

My pain is tolerable, Dubin thought. All I can not do is work.

He fought winter as if it were the true enemy: if he tore into it the freeze would vanish, his ills be gone, his life, his work, fall into place. He would overcome belly, mood, joyless labor — lust for Fanny, the burden of his unhappy experience with her. Dubin fought the winter by daily testing himself: running through its icy womb to demonstrate he was not afraid of the dead season. Not fearing it he would fear less the dysfunctioning self — what was happening, or not happening. He ran in rain, slush, in end-of-December fog — to show weather, winter, staring at him as he ran, the quality of Dubin's self, his premise, the thought he ran by. As a youth he would hold a burning match till the flame touched his fingertips: if you held onto the glowing matchstick to the very end the girl you loved would love you.

It was as hard a winter as he had feared it would be. He had to force himself, after breakfast, to open the back door and step into the frozen morning, facing his icy breath. The cold struck him like a blow from a fist. His face tightened, he could tell every stroke he had shaved. Dubin walked two steps and broke into a run, his spine touched by chill; across the inert grass, through light snow, along the solitary path of the icy-damp morning wood. Thoreau had called winter a resonant instrument that twanged its own music. Dubin, as he ran, heard branches creaking in the cold; once on an icy day a dead tree exploded. The listening wood, animistic, druid-ical, recalled Stonehenge. Occasionally he saw a small animal stirring, rat or woodchuck scuttering across the brush; or a dark bird in flight, unrecognizable. Dubin thumped alone along the path in the wood.

He left Kitty's Wood — she had named it her wood, years ago, when they had moved to the country — trotting on the dirt road to the bridge, the stream misting by his side, his breath flowing behind him. If a car appeared this early in the morning, neither jogger nor driver dared look at the other. Dubin slowed down at the bridge, limped through the booming snow-covered edifice, crossed the highway, and at the fork relentlessly ran into the long route. There were times he turned back at the wooden bridge: temporary cure: he felt he could get into his work if he tried. He turned back rarely. Dubin went on if when he thought of himself it touched pain. The trick was to get into the winter world and out of within, shift the weight of inner conflict to outside. The cock's tail turns to where the cock's head had been. His thoughts there-fore were images of gnarled broken-fingered oaks, naked white birches, delicate leafless ash — there were more winter birds than he had guessed — and the frozen circular road.

It took him a half-hour to turn the shivery clinging cold in his clothes to warmth gained in running. He then slowed to a fast walk, past farmhouses with monumental barns resembling forever; cows in the winter pasture as still as statues, their breaths flags in motion; hard frozen fields undulating up the mist-streaked hills. He pushed on in winter silence, every step striding against the force of nothing, aware of roadside rows of mustard-yellow willows, their long yellow strings dancing in the cutting wind. He plodded breathlessly up the road, conscious of the weight of ascent, dismal cold, the unhappy task he had set himself. Walking uphill, Dubin stared at his feet lest the hike to the top slay him. Trotting down, he kept his eyes in the beckoning distance. The ascents were endless. Segments of the road he had thought level were, he now realized, graded up from ten to twenty degrees. He tried not to stop on the walk up; it was hard to get started again. Ravenous for summer, for an end to the barren season, he hurried on, thinking of the next bend or rise. He felt with each step the resistance of the long long walk-run, monotony of self-inflicted cure. Climbing is not ascending. My will is my enemy. It restoreth not my soul. Yet he stayed with it: if he overslept he ran faster.

The flutist remembered him at this time as a strained, almost haggard, man in motion, heavily bundled up, a grim-faced man who had lost weight, or might, without knowing it, be ill. He wore a red wool hat his wife had knitted, a long striped scarf his wife had knitted, galoshes with unbuckled buckles that clinked as he ran, and a poplin fleece-lined coat with synthetic fur collar. He ran slowly, heavily, in snow or slush, as if his boots were lead and each step an ordeal, his sober inward grayish-blue eyes set dimly in the distance. What he saw there Greenfeld hesitated to guess.

When they met, although the biographer appeared to be drowning in all there was to say, he was mute. Sometimes in passing he would stammer half a sentence, break off and hurry on.

William, Oscar cried, let's not forget each other. Let's keep our friendship alive. William, it's a lonely world!

Greenfeld was haunted by the expression of Dubin's eyes as he looked back — almost embittered — as though the fault were the flutist's that he did not then know what his friend was living through.

When Dubin was back in the house, after resting he tried to work. He never did not work, though he stayed at it less time now, down to an hour and a half each morning. He wrote long swirling sentences on sheets of yellow foolscap and reflected on each. Kitty, one Saturday morning, brought up a cup of consommé. He took a grateful sip and thanked her but did not finish it.

"Don't you like it?"

"Warming — after that long haul."

"Why don't you finish it?"

He did not want to eat between meals.

"You're mad," she said.

After Kitty had left he went back to his long tortuous sentences. It was a bright sunny day shortly after the New Year. Later she brought up the mail. Kitty bent to kiss him as she handed him an airmail letter.

*

Fanny hoped to hear from him.

"It isn't easy to write to someone who hasn't much use for you and won't answer you. I know you're there, William, because my letters aren't returned to me here, yet you aren't there because you haven't answered me.

"At least your first letter I had the pleasure of opening before it hit me in the face like a bucket of ice. It's not exactly a joy to put a letter in the mailbox to somebody who isn't going to answer it. Or if he does, will tell you what a bitch you are. *I said I was sorry.*

"As you can tell by the postmark, I have left Murano. Arnaldo was not like my idea of an easy guy to get along with. He was good in bed though no finger ever touches you, but there's not much more than that. Whatever we did, the next thing we did was fuck. When I told him I was leaving he begged me to stay. He said he would marry me but I said I didn't want to marry anybody yet. He got awfully sore, he beat his long cock on the table. I felt depressed.

"I am in Rome now, staying in an apartment on the Via Nomentana with this old friend of mine I mentioned to you when we broke up that day, and who is very generous about money, seeing I am broke. Harvey says I am a genuine person, whatever mistakes I make. He says I'm the only woman he knows who can still be relaxed with him when he's impotent and it isn't going to work. He's sixty-two and was once a singer. He knew my father in L.A. and doesn't like him either. My father said I was oversexed and I used to think he was right until I realized what a fool he is. Harvey says I am independent and enjoy life. Part of that is right.

"Recently when we were standing in a movie line I passed out. I thought I was pregnant — that Arnaldo had knocked me up — but in the hospital it turned out I had developed a cyst in one of my tubes because of the IUD I had changed to. I hate the Pill because it makes me bleed. Anyway, I had to be operated on and lost a fallopian tube. I felt depressed until the doctor said I still could have children. Harvey has been kind and faithful.

"Lately I've been thinking of going back to the States to find some sort of steady work — don't ask me what. I've always had a hard time deciding what to do with myself. Sometimes I feel I have a lot to give, sometimes I feel I have little. I have ideas about what I ought to be doing but am afraid of the next move. I don't want to get myself into something I can't get out of if I make the wrong choice. Or into something that won't come to much and will make me feel again that I am up Shit Creek in a leaky rowboat. William, please advise me about my life. I like the way you talked to me about myself.

"I wish you would write me a long letter with things in it I could think about. What happened at the hotel between us wasn't all my fault, if you have stopped to think of it. You were kind in your way but your mind wasn't really on me. Besides, not everybody can be lovers — I'm sure you'll agree with that. Could you specifically say what I ought to be thinking about in the way of a job or career, or recommend books that might help? Or give me the names of some courses I could take when I get back to New York? Why did you say that time we first met that I ought to be kind to myself? How did I give it away? I have a feeling we could have been true friends.

"I'd like to get better organized and enjoy my life more but Harvey here is not that well put together and has had personal problems all his life that remind me of my own, so I don't think I want to stay around. I don't think I am so good for him, either. I am afraid of my day-to-day life. A day scares me more than a week or month.

"But the truth of it is I want to be responsible, to work out my life in some decent way. Couldn't we at least talk about that?

Affectionately,
Fanny B.

"P.S. If you don't want me to write anymore, I won't. This is my last letter unless you answer it — gently."

Dubin burned the letter.

Fanny wrote once after that, "I am not writing to humiliate myself, but to show you I have respect for you though you don't seem to have much for me.

F."

He kept this letter, her last. She had enclosed a snapshot of herself in jeans, sneakers, and blouse, her long hair stringy, her sad face plain. She was not an ideal woman. Why was he so drawn to her? In the woods later, he thought if he had had her in Venice he might not have wanted her afterward. He also thought he had wanted more than just wanting her.

Dubin awoke in moonlight, unhappy to wake. He'd gone to bed after supper, too intent on sleep to draw the window shades. It was

late January and the ground was covered with snow. Kitty had
been sleeping in Maud's bed so as not to disturb him with her
restlessness. With moonlight spilling on his face, he thought he
ought to get up to pull down the shades. Dubin lay there, trying to
rouse himself. At last he flung the blanket aside. At the window the
moon was full and the somber hills bathed in a bronze glow. He
stared at his wristwatch on the night table: it wasn't yet ten. He
looked again in disbelief. He had slept a few hours and now it felt
as though today were tomorrow. He felt a sadness of waste. Dubin
dressed and went down the stairs.

Kitty, reading in bed, called to him through Maud's closed door.
"Is there something you need, William?"

"I waked up and can't sleep. I'm going out for a short walk. It's
a full moon."

After a moment she asked, "Would you want company?"

He didn't think so.

Dubin drew on his overcoat and wool hat and buckled on his
galoshes. He took along a short thick stick that had once belonged
to Gerald. He might walk to the bridge.

"It's a cold night," she said through the door, "don't go far."

He didn't think he would.

He was at first afraid to enter the wood. Then he walked through
it, the lit trees casting shadows on the dimly moonlit snow.

At the road he turned left, instead of right toward the bridge. A
few fleecy clouds floated in the lit night-blue winter sky. After some
minutes of careful walking on and off the snowy road he passed
the Wilson farmhouse, a narrow two-story white frame house with
a sloping addition on the left side. It lay off the road about two
hundred feet. An orange light burned in the upstairs darkened
bedroom. It was Myra's night-light. An old woman alone in a farmhouse in the dead of winter.

He imagined her sleeping alone in a bed she had lain in with her
husband for fifty years. Ben, the dog, growled as Dubin went by.
He held his stick tightly.

Oscar Greenfeld's house was a half-mile farther up the road, a
two-story spacious red clapboard with a large lawn. Dubin thought
of their friendship with regret. He had enjoyed coming to Oscar's
in the past — walking along this road in summer, driving the front
way through town streets in winter. They played cards and chess
and talked and drank. The flutist had come less often to Dubin's

house. He never came with Flora. "If you're not alone with a friend there's no friendship." In his company Dubin drank more than he was accustomed to, and Kitty worried when he got into the car at one or two A.M. to take Oscar home. The flutist didn't drive. Flora drove him there but wouldn't call for him that late at night, though she stayed up waiting. That was one of the things about her that antagonized Kitty: Kitty would go for Dubin when she had to. Both women didn't care for the drinking, and driving on the icy streets. Oscar Greenfeld stopped coming to Dubin's house; then Dubin stopped going to his. After an evening together hitting the brandy bottle, Oscar when he woke in the morning would reach for his flute and move to Mozart on the music stand. With Mozart flipping out the notes Oscar could toot away most of his hangover. Dubin, working with words, felt he was pushing rocks with his nose, so he stopped visiting the flutist though they sometimes talked on the phone. But a phone conversation wasn't good enough.

He drank, Oscar had told Dubin, because he was not a better flutist.

"You're one of the best, Oscar."

"Not in my own ears."

"Rampal thinks so."

"Not in my ears."

As Dubin entered the driveway he heard Oscar's flute clearly from within the house. He listened: Schubert's "Serenade." Lately Oscar had been transcribing lieder into flute songs. The song was like a lit candle in the night. In his "Short Life of Schubert" the biographer had written that the composer, on hearing the song sung at a concert, was supposed to have said, "You know, I never remembered it was so beautiful." How moving a simple song is, Dubin thought. How often they go to sadness. It's as though the sad song is the natural one, the primal song. Someone sings without knowing why, and it's a song expressing hunger for love, regret for life unlived, sorrow for the shortness of life. Even some of the joyful songs evoke memories of something lost yet enduring.

The moon bathed the birch trees on the lawn in liquid light. There were white trees in an irregular circle, bent in different directions, looking like dancers in the snow. Oscar had written a flute song called "The Birch Dancers."

Listening to the serenade, this lied of yearning, the biographer reflected that Schubert had often intertwined themes of love and death. At a certain time of his life the two experiences had become one. He had died of typhus at thirty-one. A few years before, at twenty-six or -seven, he had been infected with syphilis. "Each night," he wrote to a friend, "when I go to sleep I hope I won't wake again; and each morning reminds me of yesterday's misery." Love, he told his friend, could offer only pain. The doppelgänger sees the mystical fusion of love and death.

Dubin did not go into the house. When the song had ended he left the driveway and walked toward town.

> *in diesem Haus wohnte mein Schatz;*
> *sie hat schon längst die Stadt verlassen,*
> *doch steht noch das Haus auf demselben Platz.*

It looked in the garish moonlight like a piece of stark statuary, or an old painting of an old house. Ah, Fanny, what if you had found me in the Gansevoort that night in the city, would a different beginning have made a decent ending?

A window went up with a rasp on the top floor of the house under the high-gabled roof and Dubin was too surprised to duck into the shadow of a tree. A naked large-shouldered man with a hairy chest leaned out into the wintry night and stared down at the astonished biographer. This was not the Eve of St. Agnes nor was Dubin Porphyrio, so he could not have expected to be gazing at Fanny, naked or clothed; but it was a strange surprise, and not unrelated to his mood, to behold Roger Foster's bare, curly-haired chest and moonlit handsome face.

"Good God, Mr. Dubin, is that you down there?" the librarian said in surprise.

On a freezing January night he talks to you naked from his window without a shiver.

"I'm afraid so."

"Anybody in particular you're looking for?"

Dubin calmly replied, "No one in particular. I couldn't sleep and am out for a walk."

"Sorry about that. Anything I can do for you? Would you care to come in for a drink or maybe a cup of hot coffee?"

"Thank you, no."

He wanted to ask about Fanny but dared not.

"How are things going, Roger?"

"Pretty good. All's well at the library. What with the help of your kind wife."

"Wonderful," said Dubin.

"Has anybody heard anything from Fanny?" Roger asked. He had once lived with Fanny and still wanted to.

"She's in Rome, I believe. Haven't you heard from her?"

"Just a postcard, a couple of weeks ago, that she was in Venice having herself a ball."

"You don't say," said Dubin.

"She sure gets around."

"She seems to."

"You know, Mr. Dubin," Roger then said, "someday I hope we get to understand each other better. We have things in common — bookwise, I mean to say. We keep your biographies, every one of them, on our shelves. I know you've never liked me all that much but I'm not such a bad guy, if you ask around, and I hope to accomplish more than you might think."

"You put it well, Roger, I wish you luck."

"And I wish *you* luck, Mr. Dubin."

He breathed in the cold air and exhaled a steamy breath.

"Well, good night now, it's getting chilly."

Roger shut the window and pulled down the shade.

Dubin waited a minute for Fanny to peek out through a slit in the drawn shade. She did not.

After walking home, he listened to a recording of "Death and the Maiden." It was after midnight. Kitty came down in her robe and had a drink as she listened.

They went to sleep in the same bed, Kitty wearing a black chiffon nightgown. She offered herself, and he accepted. Afterward she changed into a white flannel nightgown and got back into their double bed.

"I want to travel again soon," Kitty said. "There's so much of the world we haven't seen, so much that's varied and beautiful. Let's have more fun than we've been having. When do you think we'll travel again?"

Dubin didn't know.

It seemed to him he'd been sleeping profoundly when he heard a shrill ring and sat stiffly up in bed. At first he thought the doorbell had sounded and was about to run down the stairs when it shot through him that the phone had rung piercingly once and stopped.

No one answered his insistent hellos.

"Maybe it was Maud," Kitty said. "Or Gerald."

If it was Fanny calling from Rome he was glad she had rung off.

Kitty was soon asleep. She had snuggled close, and fallen asleep. Dubin lay awake.

Middle age, he thought, is when you pay for what you didn't know, or have, when you were young.

The man trudged diagonally across the snowy field to the slushy road. Dubin watched him as he came, listing to the left. He seemed insufficiently dressed for the cold — had on a ragged jacket, denim pants, wet field boots. He wore no hat, his thin hair black, eyes expressionless. He was a burly man with small ears and heavy features, face unshaven. He waited in the road till Dubin had caught up with him and then walked at the biographer's side.

"Good morning," Dubin said.

The man grunted. Once he hawked up a gob of phlegm and spat at the snow. Every so often, as they went on, he lifted his arms as if he were pointing a shotgun at a sparrow flying overhead. "Bang bang." The bird flew off. The man lowered his arms and trudged on with Dubin.

Who is he? Does he think he knows me because he's seen me walking here? They were alone on the road and he was uneasy with the stranger.

"You live nearby?"

The man barely nodded.

They walked on, saying nothing. Dubin, after a while, would point at something in the distance and say what it was: "Frost's farmhouse, one summer — the poet. His daughter Irma went mad that year."

The man trudged along with him, scanning the sky. Is he an escaped convict? Dubin worried, or some poor bastard looking for company?

Suppose he knifes me? He saw himself lying dead in a pool of blood in the frozen snow. There's Dubin lying in the road with a gaping wound in his chest, both gray-blue eyes staring at the gray-blue sky. It's a long hard winter.

The man hung close, their arms occasionally bumping as they walked. Dubin reconciled himself to his company. It's a public road. He's picked me to walk with, though who he is he's not saying.

"Neither am I," he said aloud.

The stranger scanned the sky.

Suppose a man like this hangs close to you forever? You try to shake him but he follows you home. You have him arrested and he convinces the judge he's your uncle and moves in. Suppose by one means or another he stays forever. Who is he to you then? The biographer talked to himself sub voce.

As he was thinking these thoughts two crows flew overhead in the white sky. The man dropped to his knee with a grunt and raised his arms as though sighting up a gun barrel.

"Boom boom." To Dubin's astonishment one of the black birds wavered in flight and plummeted to the ground. The stranger let out a hoarse shout and plunged into the white field to retrieve the bird. Holding it up for Dubin to see, he pressed the dead crow to his chest and awkwardly ran, kicking up snow, diagonally across the field in the direction he had come.

Can a crow have a heart attack?

One of us is crazy, the biographer thought.

He must not tell Kitty.

Dubin ran in his wide circle.

He remembered, when he was twelve, one day walking home from school with his teacher, a broken-nosed, knowing, nasally talkative young man. As they were walking, a strange reddish-haired woman wearing a green hat trimmed with bright red felt flowers approached in excitement from down the block, and when William saw his insane mother coming at them he said goodbye in the middle of somebody's sentence and ran across the street. When he looked back she was standing alone on the sidewalk, sobbing crazily, waving her fist.

> *"In diesen Wetter, in diesen Braus,*
> *nie hatt ich gesendet die Kinder hinaus,"*

Kitty sang at her harp.

Q. Why don't you keep a journal?
A. I'm afraid what it might say.

At night they sat in opposite armchairs, hers a wing-back against possible drafts, reading in separate pools of light. He had offered to build a fire but she felt too hot.

"This is one of those nights I keep sweating, then getting cold."

"Don't open the window," Dubin advised.

"I will if I want to."

When they were reading, Kitty, a day behind with the papers, read him humorous snippets of yesterday's news.

"Don't," Dubin said. "I find it hard to concentrate."

"Why bother?" She said afterward, "We used to talk about everything in the world. We talk about nothing now."

He got up to put on a record, not because he wanted to listen to music but because he had to think of Fanny. His thoughts of her were a gluey collage, representing an immovable desire to be with the girl.

Why don't I tell Kitty about her and maybe the misery will yield?

It seemed to him he hadn't told her because Fanny was still possible. If he wrote her a note they would meet again.

Mad, he thought, after the treatment she had dished out in Venice. What can I anticipate, despite her recent letters, but more of the same? What imbecility am I living in? I'm making of her more than she is. Or I flirt with the future — see her as she may one day be. In any case, it's fantasy.

After the record had ended Kitty asked him if he would like her to play the harp. He said no, did not want to pretend he was listening to his wife as he lay with the girl.

He was in his thoughts with Fanny, living it as they hadn't lived it. Dubin was in Rome, in her room, eating what she cooked, sleeping with her, enjoying life. They strolled through the Pincio in winter sunlight; wherever he turned he felt her embrace. They talked about themselves for hours at a time. Before his eyes the girl had changed, become loyal, loving, protective, kind. She loved Dubin and he, in his right mind, loved her.

"Tell me about Lawrence," Kitty sometimes said as they sat alone in the room, and he would make the effort to relate episodes of the man's life.

"You tell it so interestingly, why is it so hard to write?"

"It resists my pen."

"Why don't you try dictating?"

"That's not for me."

"Why not?"

"I've tried it," Dubin said.

"I feel cold. Is there a draft?" Kitty asked, looking around.

"It's you, the house is warm."

Shivering, she tried to read. She glanced at the book she had opened, took in a few sentences, then stole a look at him, or looked away. She read slowly, every word of every sentence. She wanted to know totally what each sentence said. He knew the book she was reading.

She had suggested chess and Dubin had declined. He had never felt, he thought, this much apart from her. Kitty sat huddled in the Queen Anne chair, wearing pants and two sweaters, a rose cardigan over a black pullover. She's hurt by what she doesn't know.

From behind his book he reflected on his silence. He had nothing to say because he hadn't said what he had to say. What you don't say makes more not to say. A locked house is full of locked rooms.

He was, in his silence, elsewhere. He was not who she thought he was. Whoever he was, wearied by his sticky fantasies, he wanted escape from his dream-drugged existence. He did not forever want to go on dreaming of Fanny Bick as she wasn't now and never would be. Dubin waited for this drawn-out hot reverie at last to come to an end. He waited for it to wither, die in the mind. Until it did he was separate, alone, a fog in a chair pretending to read. He chilled the room with his presence. Kitty hugged herself against the cold.

At ten she glanced at her wristwatch, yawning, and shut the fat book.

"You've been whispering to yourself all night, William. Why don't you let me in on it?"

"What was I saying?"

"I wish I knew. Would it help," she asked, her long hands clasped between her knees, "if I were to stay home mornings — I mean quit the library?"

God, no, he thought.

He didn't think so, Dubin said. He wanted not to say it, to say he needed her here; but the truth was he felt no need of her.

"Is there something I can do for you? Some other way I can help?"

He was grateful for her patience, he said.

"Patience is minimal. I'd like to do more for you if you'll let me."

Only patience, he urged. The misery would not last forever.

She spoke firmly: "You're splendid with your gymnastics, William. You take brave long walks in every weather. You diet as planned — I give you credit, though I'd go mad if I had to do it if I were feeling like you. You do what you've set yourself to, although I don't know what it comes to except that you've lost weight, your clothes droop on you, your face is strained. I almost don't know what to say to you anymore. You're out on your private little sailboat in the rough sea and here I am alone on a dreary shore. I don't know how to comfort you. I've never seen you so low so long. It has me frightened."

He asked her not to be.

"I can't help it," Kitty said, her voice wavering.

He spoke these words: "I've lost weight and move more easily. I feel lighter, a change at least. Something good may be happening. One day you wake up and whatever it was that was sitting on your head has flown off. You feel yourself again."

"I hope so." She seemed doubtful. "Nathanael wasn't a psychiatrist — he almost became one but wouldn't because he enjoyed physical medicine. But he read a lot in psychotherapy, possibly because of me. I remember his saying that a sudden depression usually had a specific cause — you lost a job or love object — a specific disappointment or loss would set it off. William, did anything unusual happen to you while you were abroad?"

Dubin thought: Right here I could get off the train. I could walk out from under the pile of rocks I wear as a hat.

"I saw Gerald," he said. "It wasn't a happy time."

The train chugged on. There was no station. He had not got off.

"I don't mean that. I mean something in Italy?"

He did not meet her eyes. "Why Italy?" he asked, irritated, not wanting her to guess what was his to say.

"Just a feeling I have."

He said, believing it, the trouble was his work. If he solved that he'd solve everything.

She vehemently denied it. "It isn't your work that's doing this to you. It's you doing something to your work. I know your doubts about Lawrence as subject but you had similar doubts about Thoreau. You always have doubt at the beginning. Please don't put it ass-backward. It's not your work that hurts your work, it's you."

"Why would I need Ondyk if I have you?"

"I'm not trying to sell you anything," Kitty said with hauteur. "But I think you need help."

"I'm not a kid anymore," Dubin said. "I don't doubt I could have been helped by analysis once but I've lived my life without it. Now I have to go on what I know."

"I've been reading about depression and I think you've had it more often than you think, sometimes simply as lack of joie de vivre —"

"Does the book explain why you sometimes lack joie de vivre?"

"Not as much as you. Sometimes I think you've never felt young in your life; you've almost always interpreted it as obligation or lost opportunity. I'm basically a more carefree, happier person than you."

He hoarsely denied it.

"There are times your nature dampens mine," she said.

"That works both ways."

"Let's drop it," Kitty said emphatically. "Forget the joie de vivre. I know you know a lot about people, William, because of the way you contemplate lives, but I'm saying you could cut out a lot of unnecessary suffering if you consulted with someone. The will isn't everything."

"It keeps me going," the biographer shouted.

"If you know what's wrong with you," she said, her voice thickening, "for Christ's sake, tell me."

He said he needed time, things would change in time.

"But what about me while you're dieting and exercising for wisdom? I feel like shit when you want nothing."

"I want everything," he shouted, waving his arms.

"You seem to want nothing I have to give. You hide your life, whispering what I can't hear. You're not affectionate. We never really talk."

"What the hell are we doing now?"

"We aren't talking. You're yelling, we are not talking."

"You have no confidence in me. You insult me by giving me psychiatric advice. Spare me Nathanael's textbooks. I don't want to be his posthumous patient. I don't want to be yours."

Grabbing her *Handbook of Psychiatry,* Kitty ran up the stairs.

To quiet his self-disgust for renewing, replenishing, the deceit, Dubin sniffed the gas burners for her.

He found the brandy bottle and poured himself a glassful.

He drank with his hat on in the cold house, his coat draped on his shoulders. The wind clattered down from the mountains. He drank, listening to the roaring wind blowing snowflakes through the straining, groaning, crackling branches of the trees. After midnight he felt himself go to bed in a blizzard. Dubin wound the clock gloomily, unable to look at it. The wind wailing around the house seeped in through storm windows. He felt it like a live presence in the room. Undressing, he got into the lonely bed, compounded by two. Kitty slept soundly, her breathing heavy. Dubin lay awake listening to the storm; primordial blast, blowing from the beginning of the world. If it could only change a man's life. He slept and woke heavily, resisting waking. The drinking had added to the weight of the heaviness. It was a black heaviness, iron on the soul. Or you were drowning in nothing and this stone arm forced your head under. The arm was your own.

He rose in the live morning dark and stumbled groggily, step by step, through the brutal routine of the day. I must go through it. It is to show the depression that it is not all. It is to show I fear it only so much, only so far. It is depression, an entity, it is not all. I know its black heaviness. I must be detached. I will not lock hands with it so that it becomes an adversary, another self; an ax to hit me with. I will wait for it to go its way. If I daily do what I have to, go through the motions, it will leave the house. It wants me to be its love, fuck it, marry it, but I won't. I welcome the white blizzard. It is a thing to think of, to be in other than depression. Thoreau was wrong in saying nature doesn't sympathize with sorrow. It does because it interrupts; it flings its frozen self at you; presses against the plots and conjurations of my bleak brain.

He was old in the bathroom mirror. Dubin was afraid not to shave. He told himself not to but didn't know what else to do. This was the wrong day not to shave. He had rarely not shaved when he wasn't sick.

In the lusterless mirror his left eye was distant, cold; contemplating his right eye, fixed, frightened.

Dubin felt himself groan.

"Hush," said Kitty, impatiently, from the bedroom.

"Horse's ass," he groaned.

"Who?" she asked.

He groaned silently.

"Be silent," Carlyle writes in his journal, "be calm, be not mad."

Dubin tried to get a religious thought going.

"Love," Lawrence wrote, "is a thing to be learned through centuries of patient effort."

Who has time?

"Please come out of the bathroom," Kitty said.

She was up early, dressed, studying herself in the mirror. A night's decent sleep had helped her mood, looks; had brightened her eyes, vitalized last night's lank hair.

"I wouldn't go on the long walk if I were you," Kitty said. "It's going to blizzard."

"I thought it already was."

"So far it's been the wind, with snow flurries. The radio says a storm's coming."

"I thought it had begun."

"That was the wind," Kitty said.

If it snowed he'd come back to the house, Dubin said.

"No more than to the bridge," she cautioned. "And put on long johns and your wool socks or you'll catch cold."

He looked away from her. They ate breakfast in silence. He listened to her chew her crisp toast.

Kitty left for the library. She returned to sniff the burners. "Ta ta," she called as she left.

He tried to work; not think how he felt. He held the misery off, kept it at bay with a stiletto as he wrote out his long yellow page of snaky sentences, reflecting on each, trying to connect them; by some act of grace to weave a tapestry, a life, a biography. Then on a white page he wrote a dozen new sentences and read them carefully to see what they said; to find out if they were taking him seriously. He read them with dignity to show the sentences he had written and respected them, and must himself be respected. They were not to crawl or slither or flop around. They must go somewhere seriously into the life of D. H. Lawrence, revive, re-create, illuminate it. But the last sentence, when he read it, said, "I am trapped." Dubin with a cry flung his pen against the wall. Disgust rose to his gorge and he fought the approach of panic. I've got to get out of here. I've got to get away from my fucking mind.

*

He left by the kitchen door and ran through the trees into the field. Here the wind leapt at him, struck him, clawed his face. He gasped, choked, stood immobilized by the wind. His eyes teared, breath ached, as he tried to push on. The wind was a gorgon with an armlock round his stone head.

He retreated to the house, waited, shivering, in the kitchen, to recover his strength. He wanted not to go anywhere, to stand there till the weather abated, winter disappeared, the world changed. But he was afraid, if he stayed, of nothing, heavy, painted black. He was afraid of the silence ticking. After endless minutes he went out the front door, stumbled down the steps, hurried along the street. The heavy wind tore through the moaning trees. He made his way downtown, icy snowflakes stinging his face.

Dubin hurried to the library. If he bought a newspaper he could read it there; he dared not return to the empty house. Could he sit in the library reading the paper? Not with Kitty around, disturbed to see him there. It was best not to buy a paper. He'd be better off in his routine, better part of it than none. Not doing what he had to do added to the misery. He would walk in the weather rather than do nothing.

He went slowly in the falling snow to the outskirts of town, past the thermometer assembly plant, the auto graveyard, two gas stations; then a motel and a tourist house. Along the wet highway he trod, approaching the long route by the back way. A circle, once you're in it, is a circle whichever way. He had never walked it this way before. If Kitty asked why he had taken the long walk after all, he would say he had never done it this backward way before.

Whatever diverts the mind from its pain may help. What else is there to do? The wind-driven snow was now falling heavily. Dubin tramped on a quarter of a mile in a world growing white, then had to tell himself it was no use, to turn back. For a while the wind had been shoving him forward and it was no great trouble plodding on. Now it shifted, blew at him from the east. The wailing wind blew the coarse snow in blasts across the open field, assailing him like a cluster of arrows, as though he were its only target. His field of vision was luminously white. He had turned tail but had trouble walking back to the highway. Dubin inched on, stopping every several steps to see if he knew where he was. When the blustery, freezing wind died down and the snow thinned he was able to stride along. Once he beheld in the distance winter fields growing white, a wall of whitening black trees, and beyond that the rising mist-white fields flanking the snow-topped hills. Extraordinary sight: he felt a minute of elation before it vanished in the snow. Dubin peered around for a house but saw none. Most of them were behind him, toward the middle of the long road. He expected he would soon reach the highway. The wind came at him again. He wavered, staggered forward, then realized the ground had roughened and he was no longer on the road. The snow, blowing in veiled gusty waves across the fields, had wiped out every sign of it.

He felt fright, an old fear: his mother frightened by weather; himself, city boy, out where he oughtn't to be. Dubin felt himself moving on a slope, propelled downward. With fear in his gut he diagonally ascended the incline, following his tracks disappearing as he sought them. The snow came down momentarily slowly, the flakes hanging in the air before touching earth. He was standing in a hollow in an unknown field. As he tried to think which way to go he saw a rabbit skittering through the snow, pursued, he thought, by a dog, then realized it was a fox. The rabbit slid up against a rock. The fox pounced on it and in a moment tore the screeching creature apart. The snow was covered with blood. Dubin stumbled away. The "wild" begins where you least expect it, one step from your daily course. A foot off the road and you're flirting with death. He had changed the black inner world for the white outer, equally perilous — man's fate, to varying degrees; though some were more fated than others. Those who were concerned with fate were fated. He struck his boot against the inhumanly white ground to get a fix on where he was but could not tell one part of the frozen earth from another. He could see nothing in the distance, had no awareness of direction. Then he kicked up some threads of dead grass and knew he was still far from the road.

He waited for the wind to die down so he could see more than snow whirling around him. But the blustery wind continued to blow strongly. Pushing into it, assuming it was coming from the east and that he had probably gone off the western side of the road, because he had not been walking facing traffic, he wandered amid ridges that rose at last to a level surface. Dubin, with relief, stumbled onto the road. He chose what he thought was the direction to the highway and walked on, holding his arm above his eyes, trying to see ahead. Now and then he could make out a utility pole streaked with snow, and occasionally, overhead, the snow-coated thick utility wire. Lowering his head against the wind he pushed on, stopping often to peer around through his snow-encrusted eyes. He brushed the snow off his face with his wet mittens. He had gone perhaps an eighth of a mile farther when he felt his galoshes sinking into the soft snow as a grove of trees opened before him. Disheartened, Dubin knew he had lost the road once more.

Panic shot through him. He saw himself running in circles, then managed to bring himself under control. For a while he stood motionless, breathing heavily, trying to puzzle out where he was. No tracks of his own could he see beyond ten feet. Probably the road had turned, though not he with it. He must be near it and surely not far from the highway? Backtracking, he was once more in the open. He thought he knew where he was: the road had curved to the right as he had walked on level ground straight ahead, gone into the trees. If he had turned with the road and stayed with it he'd soon have got to the highway. After a mile, possibly via a ride he might hitch in a passing truck — if there was a truck in this wild weather — he would be safely into Center Campobello.

To find his way he had to make the right next move. Dubin trudged along in the direction he had taken, stopping at intervals to listen for traffic in the distance; or perhaps a car on the road he'd been walking. Sooner or later a clanking snowplow would come by; sooner on the highway, later on this country road. He heard only the soughing wind. The storm was increasing in intensity. He heard a shrieking bird but could not see it. He wanted to run but dared not — break his leg if he ran into a hole. A moment later it became strangely light. He looked up at the sky; there was no sky. He beheld an oceanic whiteness. Why haven't I learned more about nature? Which is north? He had seen moss on all sides of a tree. How can I keep from going in circles? You can't if you live in them. He felt fear again; he felt an icy trickle on his head, his brain pierced by cold. With a cry Dubin tore off his wool hat and slapped it savagely on his arm, beating off the wet snow. The red hat in his hand startled him. Nature was not the only thing present — a good sign.

He was growing tired. Coming to a low stone wall — would it be bounding the road or dividing a field? — Dubin climbed over it, following until it ended in a spill of rocks amidst trees; then he slowly traced it back the other way. The wind had decreased in force, coarse wet snowflakes falling so rapidly he could barely see five feet ahead. He thought he might follow the wall, touching it with his hand; but it was not there to be touched. He was into the trees once more. The woods were gusty, terrible when the wind blew through them. Now I am really lost. Should he cry out for help? Who would hear him in the wailing wind? If a car came by, its windows would be shut. No one would hear his shouts.

Was there a shelter somewhere? He pictured an abandoned house. He pictured the kind of hut children built and left in the fields. After walking up the long flank of a ridge and then down, Dubin was again at a gray lichen-covered stone wall — the same? — another? It made no difference; he must stay with it, go where it led. The wall crumbled as he climbed it. Dubin, after a while, got himself up, brushed off his clothes, limped on. He went through a grove of high pines. For a minute he was sure he knew where these trees were — close to the road before the bend to the highway where the road sloped down on the right. But there was no downward slope he could feel, let alone see. Are these the pines I think they are? Am I where I think I am? What a stupid thing not to have stayed home with my small, stationary miseries. Now I risk my life. He thought he ought not move until he could think of something sensible to do. How few choices there are when the weather is white, wind fierce, and snow thick. I'm mad to be here. There was a man in his mind wandering in the snow.

Exhausted, Dubin sank to the ground and crawled under the branches of a large spruce. Here was room to sit. Above, the drooping branches were heavy with snow, the lower ones dry tufts of green. The beige spruce needles that covered the ground between trees were dusted with patches of white. He sat with his back to the spruce, waiting for fatigue to ease, trying to hold down his fears, to stay alert.

It was quiet where Dubin sat, though he could hear the wind groaning in the swaying trees, and once in a while a pile of snow fell, sifting like mist through the spruce. He would wait till he had recovered his strength to get up and go on being lost. His lungs ached, burned. He could feel a trembling of the mouth. Despite the cold he felt sweaty; he felt his age. It was easy enough to sit under a tree but he feared the woods filling with snow. He saw himself trapped amid trees, in snow up to his neck. Embarrassing to die so close to the road; like drowning in a bathtub. Dubin let out a shout for help but the strange cry frightened him, so he sat with hard-pounding heart, silent in the still spruce grove.

What a mad thing to happen. What a fool I am. It was the having I wanted more than the girl. She doesn't deserve the feeling I give her. See what I've done to myself. I'm like a broken clockworks, time mangled. What is life trying to teach me?

The woods grew dark. He sat unable to decide whether to stay longer under the trees, wait the storm out. Suppose it snowed till nightfall and throughout the night until morning: Dubin, frozen stiff, snowman? Death's scarecrow? He heard a sudden plop in the branches overhead and cried out as lumps of snow showered over him. His first wild fear was that a bobcat had seen him and had leapt for his throat; but when the powdery mist settled, he beheld a hook-nosed white owl, perched on a swaying branch above his head, staring at him through the slits of its cold blinking eyes. But the owl, as though frightened by Dubin, flew off into the wind-driven snow with a hoot and great flapping of its long wings. Dubin rose to his knees, crawled out from under the spruce, moved into an open field.

The wind had quietened; the snow was still falling silently. It was now more than a half-foot deep, deeper in drifts. He floundered around the fringe of a stand of thin bleak trees, two of which were down. Dubin picked his way over the fallen trees. Through the brush ahead he made out a snow-covered stone wall at least a foot higher than the others he had encountered. Separating him from what fate? He was dully fatigued, could barely keep his eyes open. With difficulty he lifted himself up on the wall, trying not to hope. He climbed because it was the next thing to do. It was next because it presented itself at this moment. He lifted himself up and over the rock wall. For once his guess, if it was that, was a good one: the biographer again found himself on the recognizable road. He assumed he had in his wandering crossed and recrossed it.

The narrow road had been plowed, plowed narrowly, though he hadn't heard the truck go by. Since then another two inches of snow had fallen, but there were earth-streaked mounds of plowed-up snow banking both sides of the road, and he felt with relief that he could easily follow it. Yet snowflakes continued to come down thickly, so that he still could not tell direction; was still not sure which was the way to go. It begins again: which is the nearest way to the highway? What side of the road did I go off? Where did I come out of the field? Did I cross the road without knowing it? Why is it I don't remember the high stone wall I just climbed? Has it always been there and have I never noticed; or have I noticed but am now too scared to remember? Is this the long hard-topped road I usually walk, or have I gone somewhere I have never been before? It must be more than a secondary road or they wouldn't have plowed it so soon. Unless some farmer plowed his own access road and I'm on it.

That should mean there would be a barn or farmhouse nearby. Dubin gazed around but saw no lights. Now which way shall I go? Am I already into the turn of the road, therefore head west for a short distance, then south and I should soon hit the highway? But if I go the other way, north — if I'm lucky and there's a light — I may sight a house in twenty minutes if I can keep going that long.

Dubin turned left where he had been standing at the wall and after some tedious and, at moments, forgetful walking, as dusk grew darker, he was convinced he was on the right road plodding the long but wrong way back. He stopped, deathly wearied, trying again to decide whether to go the other, possibly shorter way. He was cold, his clothes wet, face stiff, hands and feet freezing. The wind had died down and it was beginning to rain as well as snow. He could feel the icy rain and see it snowing. Dubin trudged on.

After a white wet timeless time it seemed to him something was approaching, a truck, or car, its wheels churning in the slush, lights on, wipers flapping as it loomed up like a locomotive out of the raining snow. The biographer flailed both arms, frantically waved his red hat as he stumbled toward the slowly moving vehicle. It then went through his frozen head that the white-faced woman, her head wrapped in a black shawl, who sat tensely behind the wheel, peering nearsightedly through the fogged windshield, frightened, perhaps already in mourning, was his wife.

Kitty held the door open as Dubin numbly got in beside her.

"I saw a white owl."

Crying silently, she drove him home.

DONALD BARTHELME

The New Music

(FROM THE NEW YORKER)

— WHAT did you do today?

— Went to the grocery store and Xeroxed a box of English muffins, two pounds of ground veal and an apple. In flagrant violation of the Copyright Act.

— You had your nap, I remember that —

— I had my nap.

— Lunch, I remember that, there was lunch, slept with Susie after lunch, then your nap, woke up, right?, went Xeroxing, right?, read a book not a whole book but part of a book —

— Talked to Happy on the telephone saw the seven o'clock news did not wash the dishes want to clean up some of this mess?

— If one does nothing but listen to the new music, everything else drifts, goes away, frays. Did Odysseus feel this way when he and Diomedes decided to steal Athene's statue from the Trojans, so that they would become dejected and lose the war? I don't think so, but who is to know what effect the new music of that remote time had on its hearers?

— Or how it compares to the new music of this time?

— One can only conjecture.

— Ah well. I was talking to a girl, talking to her mother actually but the daughter was very much present, on the street. The daughter was absolutely someone you'd like to take to bed and hug and kiss, if you weren't too old. If she weren't too young. She was a wonderful-looking young woman and she was looking at me quite seductively, very seductively, *smoldering* a bit, and I was thinking quite well of myself, very well indeed, thinking myself quite the — Until I realized she was just practicing.

— Yes, I still think of myself as a young man.

— Yes.

— A slightly old young man.

— That's not unusual.

— A slightly old young man still advertising in the trees and rivers for a mate.

— Yes.

— Being clean.

— You're very clean.

— Cleaner than most.

— It's not escaped me. Your cleanness.

— Some of these people aren't clean. People you meet.

— What can you do?

— Set an example. Be clean.

— Dig it, dig it.

— I got three different shower heads. Different degrees of sting.

— Dynamite.

— I got one of these Finnish pads that slip over the hand.

— *Numero uno.*

— Pedicare. That's another thing.

— Think you're the mule's eyebrows don't you?

— No. I feel like Insufficient Funds.

— Feel like a busted-up car by the side of the road stripped of value.

— Feel like *I don't like this!*

— You're just a little down, man, down, that's what they call it, down.

— Well how come they didn't bring us no ring of roses with a purple silk sash with gold lettering on that mother? How come that?

— Dunno baby. Maybe we lost?

— How could we lose? How could we? We!

— We were standing tall. Ready to hand them their asses, clean their clocks. Yet maybe —

— I remember the old days when we almost automatically —

— Yes. Almost without effort —

— Right. Come in, Commander. Put it right there, anywhere will do, let me move that for you. Just put that sucker down right there. An eleven-foot-high silver cup!

— Beautifully engraved, with dates.

— Beautifully engraved, with dates. That was then.

— Well. Is there help coming?

— I called the number for help and they said there was no more help.

— I'm taking you to Pool.

— I've been there.

— I'm taking you to Pool, city of new life.

— Maybe tomorrow or another day.

— Pool, the revivifier.

— Oh man I'm not up for it.

— Where one can taste the essences, get swindled into health.

— I got things to do.

— That lonesome road. It ends in Pool.

— Got to chop a little cotton, go by the drugstore.

— Ever been to Pool?

— Yes I've been there.

— Pool, city of new hope.

— Get my ocarina tuned, sew a button on my shirt.

— Have you traveled much? Have you traveled enough?

— I've traveled a bit.

— Got to go away 'fore you can get back, that's fundamental.

— The joy of return is my joy. Satisfied by a walk around the block.

— Pool. Have you seen the new barracks? For the State Police? They used that red rock they have around there, quite a handsome structure, dim and red.

— Do the cops like it?

— No one has asked them. But they could hardly . . . I mean it's new.

— Got to air my sleeping bag, scrub up my canteen.

— Have you seen the new amphitheater? Made out of red rock. They play all the tragedies.

— Yeah I've seen it that's over by the train station right?

— No it's closer to the Great Lyceum. The Great Lyceum glowing like an ember against the hubris of the city.

— I could certainly use some home fries 'long about now. Home fries and ketchup.

— Pool. The idea was that it be one of those new towns. Where everyone would be happier. The regulations are quite strict. They don't let people have cars.

— Yes, I was in on the beginning. I remember the charette, I was asked to prepare a paper. But I couldn't think of anything. I stood there wearing this blue smock stenciled with the Pool emblem, looked rather like a maternity gown. I couldn't think of anything to say. Finally I said I would go along with the group.

— The only thing old there is the monastery, dates from 1720 or thereabouts. Has the Dark Virgin, the Virgin is black, as is the Child. Dates from 1720 or around in there.

— I've seen it. Rich fare, extraordinarily rich, makes you want to cry.

— And in the fall the circus comes. Plays the red rock gardens where the carved red asters, carved red phlox, are set off by borders of yellow beryl.

— I've seen it. Extraordinarily rich.

— So it's settled, we'll go to Pool, there'll be routs and revels, maybe a sock hop, maybe a nuzzle or two on the terrace with one of the dazzling Pool beauties —

— Not much for nuzzling, now. I mostly kneel at their feet, knit for them or parse for them —

— And the Pool buffalo herd. Six thousand beasts. All still alive.

— Each house has its grand lawns and grounds, brass candlesticks, thrice-daily mail delivery. Elegant widowed women living alone in large houses, watering lawns with whirling yellow sprinklers, studying the patterns of the grass, searching out brown patches to be sprinkled. Sometimes there is a grown child in the house, or an almost-grown one, working for a school or hospital in a teaching or counseling position. Frequently there are family photographs on the walls of the house, about which you are encouraged to ask questions. At dusk medals are awarded those who have made it through the day, the Cross of St. Jaime, the Cross of St. Em.

— Meant to be one of those new towns where everyone would be happier, much happier, that was the idea.

— Serenity. Peace. The dead are shown in art galleries, framed. Or sometimes, put on pedestals. Not much different from the practice elsewhere except that in Pool they display the actual —

— Person.

— Yes.

— And they play a tape of the guy or woman talking, right next to his or her —

— Frame or pedestal.

— Prerecorded.

— Naturally.

— Shocked white faces talking.

— Killed a few flowers and put them in pots under the faces, everybody does that.

— Something keeps drawing you back like a magnet.

— Watching the buffalo graze. It can't be this that I've waited for, I've waited too long. I find it intolerable, all this putter. Yet in the end, wouldn't mind doing a little grazing myself, it would look a little funny.

— Is there bluegrass in heaven? Make inquiries. I saw the streets of Pool, a few curs broiling on spits.

— And on another corner, a man spinning a goat into gold.

— Pool projects positive images of itself through the great medium of film.

— Cinemas filled with industrious product.

— Real films. Sent everywhere.

— Film is the great medium of this century — hearty, giggling film.

— So even if one does not go there, one may assimilate the meaning of Pool.

— I'd just like to rest and laze around.

— Soundtracks in Burmese, Italian, Twi, and other tongues.

— One film is worth a thousand words. At least a thousand.

— There's a film about the new barracks, and a film about the new amphitheater.

— Good. Excellent.

— In the one about the new barracks we see Squadron A at morning roll call, tense and efficient. "Mattingly!" calls the sergeant. "Yo!" says Mattingly. "Morgan!" calls the sergeant. "Yo!" says Morgan.

— A fine bunch of men. Nervous, but fine.

— In the one about the amphitheater, an eight-day dramatization of Eckermann's *Conversations with Goethe*.

— What does Goethe say?

— Goethe says: "I have devoted my whole life to the people and their improvement."

— Goethe said that?

— And is quoted in the very superior Pool production which is enlustering the perception of Pool worldwide.

— Rich, very rich.

— And there is a film chronicling the fabulous Pool garage sales, where one finds solid-silver plates in neglected bags.

— People sighing and leaning against each other, holding their silver plates. Think I'll just whittle a bit, whittle and spit.

— Lots of accommodations in Pool, all of the hotels are empty.

— See if I have any benefits left under the G.I. Bill.

— Pool is new, can make you new too.

— I have not the heart.

— I can get us a plane or a train, they've cut all the fares.

— People sighing and leaning against one another, holding their silver plates.

— So you just want to stay here? Stay here and be yourself?

— Drop by the shoe store, pick up a pair of shoes.

— Blackberries, buttercups, and wild red clover. I find the latest music terrific, although I don't generally speaking care much for the new, qua new. But this new music! It has won from our group the steadiest attention.

— Momma didn't 'low no clarinet played in here. Unfortunately.

— Momma.

— Momma didn't 'low no clarinet played in here. Made me sad.

— Momma was outside.

— Momma was *very* outside.

— Sitting there 'lowing and not-'lowing. In her old rocking chair.

— 'Lowing this, not-'lowing that.

— Didn't 'low oboe.

— Didn't 'low gitfiddle. Vibes.

— Rock over your damn foot and bust it, you didn't pop to when she was 'lowing and not-'lowing.

— Right. 'Course, she had all the grease.

— True.

— You wanted a little grease, like to buy a damn comic book or something, you had to go to Momma.

— Sometimes yes, sometimes no. Her variously colored moods.

— Mauve. Warm gold. Citizen's blue.

— Mauve mood that got her thrown in the jug that time.

— Concealed weapons. Well, what can you do?

— Carried a .357 daytimes and a .22 for evenings. Well, what can you do?

— Momma didn't let nobody work her over, nobody.

— She just didn't give a hang. She didn't care.

— I thought she cared. There were moments.

— She never cared. Didn't give pig shit.

— You could even cry, she wouldn't come.

— I tried that, I remember. Cried and cried. Didn't do a damn bit of good.

— Lost as she was in the Eleusinian mysteries and the art of love.

— Cried my little eyes out. The sheet was sopping.

— Momma was not to be swayed. Unswayable.

— Staring out into the thermostat.

— She had a lot on her mind. The chants. And Daddy, of course.

— Let's not do Daddy today.

— Yes, I remember Momma, jerking the old nervous system about with her electric *diktats*.

— Could Christ have performed the work of the Redemption had He come into the world in the shape of a pea? That was one she'd drop on you.

— Then she'd grade your paper.

— I got a C, once.

— She dyed my beard blue, on the eve of my seventh marriage. I was sleeping on the sun porch.

— Not one to withhold comment, Momma.

— Got pretty damned tired of that old woman, pretty damned tired of that old woman. Gangs of ecstatics hanging about beating on pots and pans, trash-can lids —

— Trying for a ticket to the mysteries.

— You wanted a little grease, like to go to the brothel or something, you had to say, Momma can I have a little grease to go to the brothel?

— She was often underly generous.

— Give you eight when she knew it was ten.

— She had her up days and her down days. Like most.

— Out for a long walk one early evening I noticed in the bare brown cut fields to the right of me and to the left of me the following items of interest: in the field to the right of me, couple copulating in the shade of a car, tan Studebaker as I remember, a thing I had seen previously only in old sepia-toned photographs taken from the air by playful barnstormers capable of flying with their knees, I don't know if that's difficult or not —

— And in the field to your left?

— Momma. Rocking.

— She'd lugged the old rocking chair all that way. In a mauve mood.

— I tipped my hat. She did not return the greeting.

— She was pondering. "The goddess Demeter's anguish for all her children's mortality."

— Said my discourse was sickening. That was the word she used. Said it repeatedly.

— I asked myself: Do I give a bag of beans?

— This bird that fell into the back yard?

— The south lawn.

— The back yard. I wanted to give it a Frito?

— Yeah?

— Thought it might be hungry. Sumbitch couldn't fly you understand. It had crashed. Couldn't fly. So I went into the house to get it a Frito. So I was trying to get it to eat the Frito. I had the damn bird in one hand, and in the other, the Frito.

— She saw you and whopped you.

— She did.

— She gave you that "the bird is our friend and we never touch the bird because it hurts the bird" number.

— She did.

— Then she threw the bird away.

— Into the gutter.

— Anticipating no doubt handling of the matter by the proper authorities.

— Momma. You'd ask her how she was and she'd say, "Fine." Like a little kid.

— That's what they say. "Fine."

— That's all you can get out of 'em. "Fine."

— Boy or girl, don't make a penny's worth of difference. "Fine."

— Fending you off. Similarly, Momma.

— Momma 'lowed lute.

— Yes. She had a thing for lute.

— I remember the hours we spent. Banging away at our lutes.

— Momma sitting there rocking away. Dosing herself with strange intoxicants.

— Lime Rickeys.

— Orange Blossoms.

— Rob Roys.

— Cuba Libres.

— Brandy Alexanders and Bronxes. How could she drink that stuff?

— An iron gut. And divinity, of course.

— Well. Want to clean up some of this mess?

— Some monster with claws, maybe velvet-covered claws or Teflon-covered claws, inhabits my dreams. Whistling, whistling. I say, Monster, how goes it with you? And he says, Quite happily, dreammate, there are certain criticisms, the Curator of Archetypes thinks I don't quite cut it, thinks I'm shuckin' and jivin' when what I should be doing is attacking, attacking, attacking —

— Ah, my bawcock, what a fine fellow thou art.

— *But on the whole,* the monster says, I feel fine. Then he says, Gimme that corn flake back. I say, What? He says, Gimme that corn flake back. I say, You gave me that corn flake it's my corn flake. He says, Gimme that corn flake back or I'll claw you to thread. I say, I can't man you gave it to me I already ate it. He says, C'mon man gimme the corn flake back did you butter it first? I say, C'mon man be reasonable, you don't butter a corn flake —

— How does it end?

— It doesn't end.

— Is there help coming?

— I called that number and they said whom the Lord loveth He chasteneth.

— Where is succor?

— In the new music.

— Yes, it isn't often you hear a disco version of *Un Coup de Dés.* It's strengthening.

— The new music is drumless, which is brave. To make up for the absence of drums the musicians pray nightly to the Virgin, kneeling in their suits of lights in damp chapels provided for the purpose off the corridors of the great arenas —

— Momma wouldn't have 'lowed it.

— As with much else. Momma didn't 'low Patrice.

— I remember. You still see her?

— Once in a way. Saw her Saturday. I hugged her and her body leaped. That was odd.

— How did that feel?

— Odd. Wonderful.

— The body knows.

— The body is perspicacious.

— The body ain't dumb.

— Words can't say what the body knows.

— Sometimes I hear them howling from the hospital.

— The detox ward.

— Tied to the bed with beige cloths.

— We've avoided it.

— So far.

— Knock wood.

— I did.

— Well, it's a bitch.

— Like when she played Scrabble. She played to kill. Used the filthiest words insisting on their legitimacy. I was shocked.

— In her robes of deep purple.

— Seeking the ecstatic vision. That which would lift people four feet off the floor.

— Six feet.

— Four feet or six feet off the floor. Persephone herself appearing.

— The chanting in the darkened telesterion.

— Persephone herself appearing, hovering. Accepting offerings, balls of salt, solid gold serpents, fig branches, figs.

— Hallucinatory dancing. All the women drunk.

— Dancing with jugs on their heads, mixtures of barley, water, mint —

— Knowledge of things unspeakable —

— Still, all I wanted to do was a little krummhorn. A little krummhorn once in a while.

— Can open graves, properly played.

— I was never good. Never really good.

— Who could practice?

— And your clavier.

— Momma didn't 'low clavier.

— Thought it would unleash in her impulses better leashed? I don't know.

— Her dark side. They all have them, mommas.

— I mean they've seen it all, felt it all. Spilled their damn blood and then spooned out buckets of mushy squash meanwhile telling the old husband that he wasn't number three on the scale of all husbands . . .

— Tossed him a little bombita now and then just to keep him on his toes.

— He was always on his toes, spent his whole life on his toes, the poor fuck. Piling up the grease.

— We said we weren't going to do Daddy.

— I forgot.

— Old Momma.

— Well, it's not easy, conducting the mysteries. It's not easy, making the corn grow.

— Asparagus too.

— I couldn't do it.

— I couldn't do it.

— Momma could do it.

— Momma.

— Luckily we have the new music now. To give us aid and comfort.

— And Susie.

— Our Susie.

— Our darling.

— Our pride.

— Our passion.

— I have to tell you something. Susie's been reading the Hite Report. She says other women have more orgasms than she does. Wanted to know why.

— Where does one go to complain? Where does one go to complain, when fiends have worsened your life?

— I told her about the Great Septuagesimal Orgasm, implying she could have one, if she was good. But it is growing late, very late indeed, for such as we.

— But perhaps one ought *not* to complain, when fiends have worsened your life. But rather, emulating the great Stoics, Epictetus and so on, just zip into a bar and lift a few, whilst listening to the new, incorrigible, great-white-shark, knife, music.

— I handed the tall cool Shirley Temple to the silent priest. The new music, I said, is not specifically anticlerical. Only in its deepest effects.

— I know the guy who plays washboard. Wears thimbles on all his fingers.

— The new music burns things together, like a welder. The new music says, life becomes more and more exciting as there is less and less time.

— Momma wouldn't have 'lowed it. But Momma's gone.

— To the curious: A man who was a Communist heard the new music, and now is not. Fernando the fish-seller was taught to read and write by the new music, and is now a leper, white as snow. William Friend was caught trying to sneak into the new music with a set of bongos concealed under his cloak, but was garroted with his own bicycle chain, just in time. Propp the philosopher, having dinner with the Holy Ghost, was told of the coming of the new music but also informed that he would not live to hear it.

— The new, down-to-earth, think-I'm-gonna-kill-myself music, which unwraps the sky.

— Succeed! It has been done, and with a stupidity that can astound the most experienced.

— The rest of the trip presents no real difficulties.

— The rest of the trip presents no real difficulties. The thing to keep your eye on is less time, more exciting. Remember that.

— As if it were late, late, and we were ready to pull on our red-and-gold-striped nightshirts.

— Cup of tea before retiring.

— Cup of tea before retiring.

— Dreams next.

— We can deal with that.

— Remembering that the new music will be there tomorrow and tomorrow and tomorrow.

— There is always a new music.

— Thank God.

— Pull a few hairs out of your nose poised before the mirror.

— Routine maintenance, nothing to write home about.

JAYNE ANNE PHILLIPS

Something That Happened

(FROM GALLIMAUFRY)

I AM in the basement sorting clothes, whites with whites, colors with colors, delicates with delicates — it's a segregated world — when my youngest child yells down the steps. She yells when I'm in the basement, always, angrily, as if I've slipped below the surface and though she's twenty-one years old she can't believe it.

"Do you know what day it is? I mean do you KNOW what day it is, Kay?" It's this new thing of calling me by my first name. She stands groggy eyed, surveying her mother.

I say, "No, Angela, so what does that make me?" Now my daughter shifts into second, narrows those baby blues I once surveyed in such wonder and prayed *Lord, lord, This is the last.*

"Well never mind," she says. "I've made you breakfast." And she had, eggs and toast and juice and flowers on the porch. Then she sat and watched me eat it, twirling her fine gold hair.

Halfway through the eggs it dawns on me, my ex–wedding anniversary. Angela, under the eye-liner and blue jeans you're a haunted and ancient presence. When most children can't remember an anniversary, Angela can't forget it. Every year for five years she has pushed me to the brink of remembrance.

"The trouble with you," she finally speaks, "is that you don't care enough about yourself to remember what's been important in your life."

"Angela," I say, "in the first place I haven't been married for five years, so I no longer have a wedding anniversary to remember."

"That doesn't matter" [twirling her hair, not scowling]. "It's still something that happened."

*

Two years ago I had part of an ulcerated stomach removed and said to the kids, "Look, I can't worry for you anymore. If you get into trouble, don't call me. If you want someone to take care of you, take care of each other." So the three older girls packed Angela off to college and her brother drove her there. Since then I've gradually reassumed my duties. Except that I was inconspicuously absent from my daughters' weddings. I say inconspicuously because, thank God, all of them are hippies who got married in fields without benefit of aunts and uncles. Or mothers. But Angela reads *Glamour,* and she'll ask me to her wedding. Though Mr. Charm has yet to appear in any permanent guise, she's already gearing up to it. Pleadings. Remonstrations. Perhaps a few tears near the end. But I shall hold firm, I hate sacrificial offerings of my own flesh. "I can't help it," I'll joke, "I have a weak stomach, only half of it is there."

Angela sighs, perhaps foreseeing it all. The phone is ringing. And slowly, there she goes. By the time she picks it up, cradles the receiver to her brown neck, her voice is normal. Penny bright, and she spends it fast. I look out the screened porch on the alley and the clean garbage cans. It seems to me that I remembered everything before the kids were born. I say kids as though they appeared collectively in a giant egg, my stomach. When actually there were two years, then one year, then two, then three between them. The Child Bearing Years, as though you stand there like a blossomed pear tree and the fruit plops off. Eaten or rotted to seed to start the whole thing all over again.

Angela has fixed too much food for me. She often does. I don't digest large amounts so I eat small portions six times a day. The dog drags his basset ears to my feet, waits for the plate. And I give it to him, urging him on so he'll gobble it fast and silent before Angela comes back.

Dear children, I always confused my stomach with my womb. Lulled into confusion by nearly four pregnant years I heard them say, "Oh, you're eating for two," as if the two organs were directly connected by a small tube. In the hospital I was convinced they had removed my uterus along with half of my stomach. The doctors, at an end of patience, labeled my decision an anxiety reaction. And I reacted anxiously by demanding an X-ray so I could see that my womb was still there.

Angela returns, looks at the plate which I have forgotten to pick up, looks at the dog, puts her hand on my shoulder.

"I'm sorry," she says.

"Well," I say.

Angela twists her long fingers, her fine thin fingers with their smooth knuckles, twists the diamond ring her father gave her when she was sixteen.

"Richard," I'd said to my husband, "she's your daughter, not your fiancée."

"Kay," intoned the husband, the insurance agent, the successful adjuster of claims, "she's only sixteen once. This ring is a gift, our love for Angela. She's beautiful, she's blossoming."

"Richard," I said, shuffling Maalox bottles and planning my bland lunch, "Diamonds are not for blossoms. They're for those who need a piece of the rock." At which Richard laughed heartily, always amused at my cynicism regarding the business which principally buttered my bread. Buttered his bread, because by then I couldn't eat butter.

"What is it you're afraid to face?" asked Richard. "What is it in your life you can't control; you're eating yourself alive. You're dissolving your own stomach."

"Richard," I said, "it's a tired old story. I have this husband who wants to marry his daughter."

"I want you to see a psychiatrist," said Richard, tightening his expertly knotted tie. "That's what you need, Kay, a chance to talk it over with someone who's objective."

"I'm not interested in objectives," I said. "I'm interested in shrimp and butter sauce, Tabasco, hot chiles and an end of pain."

"Pain never ends," said Richard.

"Oh, Richard," I said, "no wonder you're the King of the Southeast Division."

"Look," he said, "I'm trying to put four kids through college and one wife through graduate school. I'm starting five investment plans now so when our kids get married no one has to wait twenty-five years to finish a dissertation on George Eliot like you did. Really, am I such a bad guy? I don't remember forcing you into any of this. And your goddamn stomach has to quit digesting itself. I want you to see a psychiatrist."

"Richard," I said, "if our daughters have five children in eight years [which most of them won't, being members of Zero Population Growth who quote the foreword of *Diet for a Small Planet* every Thanksgiving] they may still be slow with Ph.D.'s despite your investment plans."

Richard untied his tie and tied it again. "Listen," he said. "Plenty of women with five children have Ph.D.'s."

"Really," I said. "I'd like to see those statistics."

"I suppose you resent your children's births," he said, straightening his collar. "Well, just remember, the last one was your miscalculation."

"And the first one was yours," I said.

It's true. We got pregnant, as Richard affectionately referred to it, in a borrowed bunk bed at Myrtle Beach. It was the eighth time we'd slept together. Richard gasped that of course he'd take care of things, had he ever failed me? But I had my first orgasm and no one remembered anything.

After the fourth pregnancy and first son, Richard was satisfied. Angela, you were born in a bad year. You were expensive, your father was starting in insurance after five years as a high school principal. He wanted the rock, all of it. I had a rock in my belly we thought three times was dead. So he swore his love to you, with that ring he thee guiltily wed. Sweet Sixteen, does she remember? She never forgets.

Angela pasted sugar cubes to pink ribbons for a week, Sweet Sixteen party favors she read about in *Seventeen*, while the older girls shook their sad heads. Home from colleges in Ann Arbor, Boston, Berkeley, they stared aghast at their golden-haired baby sister, her Villager suits, the ladybug stickpin in her blouses. Angela owned no blue jeans; her boyfriend opened the car door for her and carried her books home. They weren't heavy, he was a halfback. Older sister no. 3: "Don't you have arms?" Older sister no. 2: "He'll take it out of your hide, wait and see." Older sister no. 1: "The nuclear family lives in women's guts. Your mother has ulcers, Angela, she can't eat gravy with your daddy."

At which point Richard slapped oldest sister, his miscalculation, and she flew back to Berkeley, having cried in my hands and begged me to come with her. She missed the Sweet Sixteen party. She missed Thanksgiving and Christmas for the next two years.

Angela's jaw set hard. I saw her reject politics, feminism, and everyone's miscalculations. I hung sugar cubes from the ceiling for her party until the room looked like the picture in the magazine. I ironed sixteen pink satin ribbons she twisted in her hair. I applauded with everyone else, including the smiling halfback, when her father slipped the diamond on her finger. Then I filed for divorce.

The day Richard moved out of the house, my son switched his major to premed at the state university. He said it was the only way to get out of selling insurance. The last sound of the marriage was Richard being nervously sick in the kitchen sink. Angela gave him a cold wash cloth and took me out to dinner at Senor Miguel's while he stacked up his boxes and drove them away. I ate chiles rellenos, guacamole chips in sour cream, cheese enchiladas, Mexican fried bread and three green chile burritos. Then I ate tranquilizers and bouillon for two weeks.

Angela was frightened.

"Mother," she said, "I wish you could be happy."

"Angela," I answered, "I'm glad you married your father, I couldn't do it any more."

Angela finished high school that year and twelve copies each of *Ingenue, Cosmopolitan, Mademoiselle.* She also read the Bible alone at night in her room.

"Because I'm nervous," she said, "and it helps me sleep. All the trees and fruit, the figs, begat and begat going down like the multiplication tables."

"Angela," I said, "are you thinking of making love to someone?"

"No Mother," she said, "I think I'll wait. I think I'll wait a long time."

Angela quit eating meat and blinked her mascaraed eyes at the glistening fried liver I slid onto her plate.

"It's so brown," she said. "It's just something's guts."

"You've always loved it," I said, and she tried to eat it, glancing at my midriff, glancing at my milk and cottage cheese.

When her father took over the Midwest and married a widow, Angela declined to go with him. When I went to the hospital to have my stomach reduced by half, Angela declined my invitations to visit and went on a fast. She grew wan and romantic, said she wished I taught at her college instead of City, she'd read about Sylvia Plath in *Mademoiselle.* We talked on the telephone while I watched the hospital grounds go dark in my square window. It was summer and the trees were so heavy.

I thought about Angela, I thought about my miscalculations. I thought about milk products and white mucous coatings. About Richard's face the night of the first baby, skinny in his turned-up coat. About his mother sending roses every birth, American Beauties. And babies slipping in the wash basin, tiny wriggling arms, the blue veins in their translucent heads. And starting oranges for ten years, piercing thick skins with a fingernail so the kids could peel them. After a while, I didn't want to watch the skin give way to the white ragged coat beneath.

Angela comes home in the summers, halfway through business, elementary education or home ec. She doesn't want to climb the Rockies or go to India. She wants to show houses to wives, real estate, and feed me mashed potatoes, cherry pie, avocados and artichokes. Today she not only fixes breakfast for my ex-anniversary, she fixes lunch and dinner. She wants to pile up my plate and see me eat everything. If I eat, surely something good will happen. She won't remember what's been important enough in my life to make me forget everything. She is spooning breaded clams, french fries, nuts and anchovy salad onto my plate.

"Angela, it's too much."

"That's OK, we'll save what you don't want."

"Angela, save it for who?"

She puts down her fork. "For anyone," she says. "For any time they want it."

In a moment, she slides my plate onto her empty one and begins to eat.

Biographical Notes

Biographical Notes

Donald Barthelme was born in Philadelphia and raised in Houston. His stories have appeared in *The New Yorker, New American Review, Paris Review,* and other publications. Some of these stories were collected in *Come Back, Dr. Caligari,* published in 1964, and in two later collections, *Unspeakable Practices, Unnatural Acts* (1968) and *City Life,* which the *New York Times Book Review* called one of the twelve outstanding books of 1970. Mr. Barthelme's other books include a novel, *Snow White* (1967), *Sadness* (1972), *The Slightly Irregular Fire Engine,* a book for children that was awarded the 1972 National Book Award, and *Guilty Pleasures,* nominated for a National Book Award in the category of fiction in 1974. His most recent novel, *The Dead Father,* was published in 1975. *Amateurs,* a collection of short stories was published in 1976, and *Great Days,* Mr. Barthelme's most recent collection of stories, was published in 1979.

Saul Bellow, born in Canada of Russian immigrant parents, grew up in Chicago and has lived there for most of his life. He is the author of *Henderson the Rain King, Herzog, Seize the Day, Humboldt's Gift* and other books. The recipient of many awards, he received the Nobel Prize in 1976.

Paul Bowles has published four novels, of which three — *Let It Come Down, The Spider's House,* and *Up Above the World* — are out of print. The fourth, *The Sheltering Sky,* was reissued in 1978 by Ecco Press. *The Collected Short Stories* (1939–1977), published by Black Sparrow Press, appeared in 1979. Mr. Bowles lives in Morocco.

ROSELLEN BROWN has had stories included in an earlier volume of *The Best American Short Stories* (1975) and in three volumes of the *O'Henry Prize Stories.* She has published two books of poetry, *Cora Fry* and *Some Deaths in the Delta;* a book of stories, *Street Games;* and two novels, *The Autobiography of My Mother* and *Tender Mercies.* The recipient of Guggenheim, National Endowment for the Arts, and Radcliffe Institute grants, she lives in Peterborough, New Hampshire, with her husband and two daughters, Elana and Adina.

LYN COFFIN's first book of poems, *Human Trappings,* will be published by Abattoir Editions in 1980. The University of Michigan's Department of Slavic Languages will bring out a collection of her translations of the modern Czech poet Jiri Orten this year.

MARY HEDIN grew up in Minnesota and now lives in Marin County, California. Her poetry and fiction have appeared in many literary journals, among them *Southwest Review, South Dakota Review, Perspective, Shenandoah, Southern Poetry Review,* and *South.* She is the recipient of the 1979 University of Iowa School of Letters Award for Short Fiction for her collection of stories, *Ladybird, Fly Away Home.* Her stories have been included in the *O'Henry Prize Stories* (1977) and in *The Best American Short Stories 1966.* Ms. Hedin teaches full-time at College of Marin, Kentfield, California.

KAATJE HURLBUT was born in Manhattan and attended Columbia University and the College of William and Mary. Her short stories have appeared in literary and popular magazines here and abroad and in a number of anthologies including *The Best American Short Stories 1961, 21 Great Stories, 40 Best from Mademoiselle, Modern Stories from Many Lands,* and the seventh annual *Year's Best SF.* At present, she is working on a collection of her stories. She and her husband, John Schoolfield, live in Albany, New York. They have three children.

MAXINE KUMIN has published four novels; most recently, *The Designated Heir.* A collection of her poems, *Up Country,* won the Pulitzer Prize in 1973, and her sixth collection of poems, *The Retrieval System,* has been recently published. A previous story, "Opening the Door on Sixty-Second Street," was chosen by Mar-

tha Foley for inclusion in *The Best American Short Stories 1974.* Ms.
Kumin lives on a farm in New Hampshire.

PETER LASALLE, born in 1947, grew up in Rhode Island and studied at Harvard College and the University of Chicago. He has
worked as a newspaper reporter, lived in Europe, and, more
recently, taught creative writing at colleges in Vermont, Texas,
and Iowa. His work (mostly fiction and some poetry) has appeared in many magazines, including *Esquire, North American
Review, Fiction International, Epoch,* and *The Georgia Review.* He
has contributed literary and political journalism to *The Nation,
The New Republic, The Progressive, America,* and *Africa Today.* In
1979, he traveled in West Africa investigating the region's writing under a research grant from Iowa State University.

BERNARD MALAMUD is the author of seven novels and three collections of short stories. His last novel, was *Dubin's Lives,* published
in 1979. Mr. Malamud has been awarded two National Book
Awards and the Pulitzer Prize. He teaches at Bennington College
and is at present writing short stories.

RUTH MCLAUGHLIN was born and raised in northeastern Montana
where her grandparents homesteaded. She attended the universities of Montana and Arizona and has held odd jobs, including five summers as a fire lookout for the U.S. Forest Service.
"Seasons" is her first published story.

ALICE MUNRO was born and grew up in Ontario, Canada, where
she now lives with her second husband. "Spelling" appears in
her most recent book, *The Beggar Maid* (1979). This book, published in Canada in 1978 under the title *Who Do You Think You
Are,* won Canada's highest literary prize, the Governor-General's
Literary Award. Her other books are *Dance of the Happy Shades*
(which also won the Governor-General's Award), *Lives of Girls
and Women,* and *Something I've Been Meaning to Tell You.* Her short
fiction has been published in *The New Yorker, McCall's, Redbook,
Toronto Life, Weekend,* and many other magazines.

FLANNERY O'CONNOR was born in Savannah, Georgia, in 1925. She
and her parents moved to Milledgeville, Georgia, when she was
twelve. There she attended both high school and college (Geor-

gia State College for Women, now Georgia College). After college, she attended the School for Writers, conducted by Paul Engle, at the State University of Iowa. In 1951, she returned to Milledgeville where she lived until her death in 1964. Her first collection of stories, *A Good Man Is Hard to Find,* was to have included the story "An Exile in the East," but it was pulled at the last minute to make room for another story. The story, reprinted here, went unpublished until twenty-three years later when it appeared in the November 1978 issue of *The South Carolina Review.*

JAYNE ANNE PHILLIPS was born in 1952 in West Virginia and grew up in a small town there. Her stories have appeared in *Fiction, Iowa Review, North American Review, Ploughshares,* and other magazines and were selected for inclusion in *Pushcart Prize II* and *IV.* Two short collections of her work, *Sweethearts* and *Counting,* were published in limited editions, and a first book of stories, *Black Tickets,* will be published in 1979 by Seymour Lawrence/Delacourt. Ms. Phillips is a recipient of a National Endowment for the Arts Fellowship and the St. Lawrence Award for Fiction. She lives at the Fine Arts Work Center in Provincetown, Massachusetts.

LOUIS D. RUBIN, JR., is a native of Charleston, South Carolina, and was educated at the College of Charleston, the University of Richmond, and the Johns Hopkins University. For a number of years he was chairman of the English Department at Hollins College in Virginia, and since 1967 he has taught at the University of North Carolina at Chapel Hill, where he is University Distinguished Professor of English. He is author and editor of thirty books, mostly on the literature and history of the South.

ANNETTE SANFORD's first story, "A Child's Game," published by *St. Anthony Messenger* in 1968, won a first-place award from the Catholic Press Association that year. Since then her fiction has appeared in a variety of publications, including *Prairie Schooner, Ohio Review, Redbook,* and *Yankee.* Mrs. Sanford, who has worked under a Creative Writing Fellowship Grant from the National Endowment for the Arts, is a former teacher and lives in Ganado, Texas.

ISAAC BASHEVIS SINGER, the son and grandson of rabbis, was born in Radzymin, Poland, in 1904. He came to the United States in 1935 and his writing has appeared in the *Jewish Daily Forward* for many years. Although he originally wrote in Hebrew, Mr. Singer long ago adopted Yiddish as his medium of expression. Dozens of Mr. Singer's novels and story collections are available in English — as many for children as for adults — and three new books are due from his publishers, Farrar, Straus & Giroux, their year. Mr. Singer has been the recipient of many literary awards, including two National Book Awards, the Louis Lamed Prize, and a grant from the Academy and National Institute of Arts and Letters, of which he is a member. In 1978 the Swedish Academy of Letters awarded him the Nobel Prize for literature. Mr. Singer lives in New York with his wife, Alma.

LYNNE SHARON SCHWARTZ, whose story "Rough Strife" appeared in *The Best American Short Stories 1978*, was born and educated in New York City, where she still lives. Her fiction, criticism, and translations from Italian have appeared in a wide range of magazines. Her collection of stories, *Rough Strife,* and her novel, *Balancing Acts,* are soon to be published by Harper & Row.

WILLIAM STYRON was born in Newport News, Virginia, and graduated from Duke University in 1947. He is the author of the novels *Lie Down in Darkness, The Long March, Set This House on Fire, The Confessions of Nat Turner* (which won the Pulitzer Prize in 1968), and *Sophie's Choice.* Also the author of many essays and reviews in American periodicals, Mr. Styron was elected to membership in the American Academy and Institute of Arts and Letters in 1966. Married and the father of four children, he lives in Roxbury, Connecticut, and on Martha's Vineyard.

SILVIA TENNENBAUM was born in Frankfurt am Main, Germany, in 1928. She emigrated to America with her family in 1938 and graduated from Barnard College in 1950. She has been married since 1951 to Lloyd Tennenbaum, has three grown sons, and has been writing all her life. Her first novel, *Rachel the Rabbi's Wife,* was published in 1978 and she is currently at work on a second novel that traces the history of three generations of a German-Jewish family. Mrs. Tennenbaum lives in East Hampton, New York, in a shingled farmhouse near the bay.

JEAN THOMPSON was born in 1950 in Chicago. Her fiction has appeared in *Mademoiselle, Ploughshares, Ascent, Carolina Quarterly, Fiction International,* and other magazines. Her first collection of stories, *The Gasoline Wars,* will be published in the University of Illinois Press's short fiction series. She is the recipient of a National Endowment for the Arts Fellowship.

HERBERT WILNER was educated at Brooklyn College, Columbia University, and received his Ph.D. at the University of Iowa's writers workshop with the help of a Rockefeller Grant in Creative Writing. He taught at Yale University and directed the Creative Writing Program at San Francisco State University. His stories have appeared in several *O'Henry Prize Stories* collections and other *Best American Short Stories* volumes. His novel, *All the Little Heroes,* won the California Commonwealth Club Gold Medal Award for best fiction in 1966 and "Dovisch in the Wilderness," the title story of a collection published in 1968, has been anthologized many times. "The Quarterback Speaks to His God" is the title story of a collection completed just before he died in 1977.

SEÁN VIRGO has lived in Canada since 1966. His fourth book of poetry, *Death Watch on Skidegate Narrows,* has just appeared and a collection of short stories, *White Lies and Other Fictions,* is forthcoming.

ROBLEY WILSON, JR., is returning to his teaching duties at the University of Northern Iowa after a year spent in Canada, where he completed a novel, *Firework.* His fiction has appeared in *Antæus, Esquire, Fiction International, Story Quarterly,* and a number of recent anthologies. "Living Alone" is the title story of his second collection of short fiction; his first, *The Pleasures of Manhood,* was published in 1977 by the University of Illinois Press. Since 1969 he has been editor of the *North American Review.*

ROLF YNGVE is a native of Minnesota, has lived in Utah, and is now home-ported in Norfolk, Virginia. He has been in the Navy for eight years. He holds a B.S. in Meteorology from the University of Utah, obtained through the Navy Enlisted Scientific Education Program. While at Utah, he bootlegged English courses and wrote. "The Quail" is his second published story. At sea, he stands watch on the ship's bridge, tries very hard to be good to the people who work so hard for him, and writes as well as he can to make himself feel better. He is twenty-eight and married to Gail Fowers.

The Yearbook of the American Short Story

January 1 to December 31, 1978

100 Other Distinguished
Short Stories of the Year 1978

ADAMS, ALICE
    The Last Unmarried Man. The Virginia Quarterly Review, Spring.
    Related Histories. The Atlantic Monthly, May.

BANKS, RUSSELL
    The Caul. Mississippi Review, Spring.
BAUER, WILLIAM
    What Is Interred with Their Bones. The Fiddlehead, Winter.
BAUMBACH, JONATHAN
    Passion? The North American Review, Spring.
BAXTER, CHARLES
    Xavier Speaking. The Antioch Review, Winter.
BEATTIE, ANN
    Octascope. New England Review, Autumn.
BENNETT, JAMES GORDON
    In the Grass. The Antioch Review, Spring.
BOYLE, T. CORAGHESSAN
    The Second Swimming. The Paris Review, No. 72.
BREWSTER, ELIZABETH
    Essence of Marigolds. The Fiddlehead, Winter.
BROUGHTON, T. ALAN
    The Pursuit. Soundings, Spring.

BRUBAKER, BILL
    There Goes the Rose (I Used to Know). Cimarron Review, No. 42.
BUSCH, FREDERICK
    My Father, Cont. Harper's, February.

CARUS, A. ROSS
    Notebook of the Night Janitor. Story Quarterly, Vol. 7, No. 8.
CORRINGTON, JOHN WILLIAM
    Every Act Whatever of Man. The Southern Review, Summer.

DEMPTSTER, BARRY
    Story That Saw Defeat. The University of Windsor Review, Spring/Summer.
DIBBLE, BRIAN
    Fliers. Colorado Quarterly, Summer.
DILLARD, ANNIE
    The Living. Harper's, November.
DWORZAN, HÉLÈNE
    The Healer. Prairie Schooner, Fall.

ELKIN, STANLEY
    The Bottom Line. Antæus, Winter.

GALLANT, JAMES
    Preludes and Evolutions. The North American Review, Spring.

GALLANT, MAVIS
With A Capital T. Canadian Fiction Magazine, No. 28.

GARBER, EUGENE K.
The Poets. The Sewanee Review, Winter.
The Rememberers. Four Quarters, Winter.

GARDINER, JOHN ROLFE
A Crossing. The New Yorker, February 6.

GORDON, MARY
Delia. The Atlantic Monthly, June.

GROVES, DAVID
Forms (Some Things That Happened While Emilia Was in Arizona). North American Review, Spring.

HALEY, ALBERT
Down on the Farm. The New Yorker, April 10.

HARRIS, MARK
Touching Idamae Low. Esquire Fortnightly, April 25.

HECHT, JULIE
I Want You, I Need You, I Love You. Harper's, May.

HEMENWAY, ROBERT
The Border. The New Yorker, January 23.

HERMANN, JOHN
Notes on a Horse Worth Four Marks. The Antioch Review, Winter.

HIGGINS, JUDITH
Missing. Texas Quarterly, Spring.

JHABVALA, RUTH PRAWER
Parasites. The New Yorker, March 13.

KATZ, STEVE
The Stolen Stories. The Cornell Review, Spring.

KENNEDY, RAYMOND
A Private Station. The Massachusetts Review, Autumn.

KINSELLA, W. P.
Black Wampum. Descant, XX–XXI.

Mr. Whitey. The University of Windsor Review, Spring/Summer.
Scars. Shadows, April.

KOCH, CLAUDE
Uncle. Four Quarters, Spring.

LINDNER, VICKI
Comayagua. Mississippi Review, Spring.

LUND, ROSALIND ROSEN
The Cardinal in the Garage. Ascent, Vol. 3, No. 3.

LYNCH, GERALD
When It Rains. The Fiddlehead, Spring.

MACMILLAN, IAN
At Flood's End. Yankee, April.

MADDEN, DAVID
On the Big Wind. New Letters, Winter.

MARSHALL, JACK
Hurrying Ends. The Hudson Review, Vol. XXXI, No. 2, Summer.

MILLER, ARTHUR
The White Puppies. Esquire Fortnightly, July 4.

MILLER, WARREN C.
Like It Was. Mississippi Review, Winter.

MILTON, EDITH
Codes of Honor. The Yale Review, Vol. LXVIII, No. 2.

MINOT, STEPHEN
Surviving the Flood. Ploughshares, Vol. 4, No. 4.

MORGAN, BERRY
Arthuree. The New Yorker, March 27.

MORRIS, MARY
The Joggers. Kansas Quarterly, Vol. 10, No. 1.

MUNRO, ALICE
Characters. Ploughshares, Vol. 4, No. 3.

MYERS, LOU
Birdsong. The New Yorker, May 15.

NEUGEBOREN, JAY
  Uncle Nathan. Ploughshares, Vol. 4, No. 4.
NORDAN, LEWIS
  Rat Song. Harper's, January.
  Welcome to the Arrow Catchers' Fair. Harper's, September.

OSBORN, CAROLYN
  Running Around America. The Antioch Review, Winter.

PANCAKE, B. D'J.
  In the Dry. The Atlantic Monthly, August.
PHILLIPS, JAYNE ANNE
  Home. The Iowa Review, Spring.

ROGIN, GILBERT
  The Hard Parts. The New Yorker, November 20.
ROSE, DANIEL ASA
  The Goodbye Present. Partisan Review, No. 4.

SCHOTT, MAX
  The Drowning. Ascent, Vol. 4, No. 1.
  Early Winter. The Massachusetts Review, Spring.
SCHWARTZ, LYNNE SHARON
  Acquainted with the Night. The Literary Review, Fall.
SHAPIRO, GERALD
  Vital Signs. Kansas Quarterly, Vol. 10, No. 2.
SHAW, IRWIN
  Full Many a Flower. Playboy, January.
SHELNUTT, EVE
  Obligato. Ploughshares, Vol. 4, No. 3.
SINGER, ISAAC BASHEVIS
  The Bus. The New Yorker, August 28.
SKILLINGS, R. D.
  The Unforeseen. Cornell Review, Fall.
SMILEY, JANE
  Mama in Her Kerchief, and I in My Cap. Redbook, January.

New Poems. Fiction, Vol. 5, Nos. 2 and 3.
SMITH, LEE
  Mrs. Darcy Meets the Blue-Eyed Stranger. Carolina Quarterly, Spring/Summer.
STEADMAN, MARK
  Cast on the Waters and Raised on High. The South Carolina Review, Vol. 10, No. 2.
STEWARD, D. E.
  Down the Hill. Mississippi Review, Winter.
SULLIVAN, WALTER
  The Brief Detention of Charles Weems. The Southern Review, Fall.

TARGAN, BARRY
  Kingdoms. The Sewanee Review, Summer.
TEITELMAN, JILL
  Missing Mao. Chicago Review, Vol. 29, No. 4.
THALER, SUSAN
  Postscript to a Wedding. Colorado Quarterly, Winter.

VAUGHN, STEPHANIE
  Able, Baker, Charlie, Dog. The New Yorker, June 5.
VIVANTE, AUTURO
  Crossroads. The New Yorker, April 17.
VOGAN, SARA
  Miss Buick of 1942. Quarterly West, Winter.
VREULS, DIANE
  Boys and Music. The New Yorker, December 4.

WARD, ANDREW
  At an Inn. The Atlantic Monthly, April.
WETHERELL, W. D.
  The Lob. Colorado Quarterly, Summer.
  Past-things. The Carolina Quarterly, Fall.

Editorial Addresses of American and Canadian Magazines Publishing Short Stories

Adena, Kentucky Metroversity, Garden Court, Alta Vista Road, Louisville, Kentucky 40205

Agni Review, P.O. Box 349, Cambridge, Massachusetts 02138

Americas, Organization of American States, Washington, D.C. 20006

Antæus, 1 West 30th Street, New York, New York 10001

Antioch Review, P.O. Box 148, Yellow Springs, Ohio 45387

Apalachee Quarterly, P.O. Box 20106, Tallahassee, Florida 32304

Aphra, RFD, Box 355, Springtown, Pennsylvania 18081

Ararat, 628 Second Avenue, New York, New York 10016

Argosy, 420 Lexington Avenue, New York, New York 10017

Arizona Quarterly, University of Arizona, Tucson, Arizona 85721

Ark River Review, English Department, Wichita State University, Wichita, Kansas 67208

Arlington Quarterly, Box 366, University Station, Arlington, Texas 76010

Ascent, English Department, University of Illinois, Urbana, Illinois 61801

Aspen Anthology, The Aspen Leaves Literary Foundation, Box 3185, Aspen, Colorado 81611

Atlantic Monthly, 8 Arlington Street, Boston, Massachusetts 02116

Aura, Box 348 NBSB, University Station, Birmingham, Alabama 35294

Bachy, 11317 Santa Monica Boulevard, Los Angeles, California 90025

Back Bay View, 52 East Border Road, Malden, Massachusetts 02148

Bennington Review, Bennington College, Bennington, Vermont 05201

California Quarterly, 100 Sproul Hall, University of California, Davis California 95616

Canadian Fiction, Box 46422, Station G, Vancouver, British Columbia V6R 4G7, Canada

Canadian Forum, 3 Church Street, Suite 401, Toronto, Ontario M5E 1M2, Canada

Canto, Realforms Company, Inc., 11 Bartlett Street, Andover, Massachusetts 01810

Capilano Review, Capilano College, 2055 Purcell Way, North Vancouver, British Columbia, Canada

Carleton Miscellany, Carleton College, Northfield, Minnesota 55057

Carolina Quarterly, P.O. Box 1117, Chapel Hill, North Carolina 27514

Chariton Review, Division of Language & Literature, Northeast Missouri State University, Kirksville, Missouri 63501

Chelsea, P.O. Box 5880, Grand Central Station, New York, New York 10017

Chicago Review, Faculty Exchange, Box C, University of Chicago, Chicago, Illinois 60637

Cimarron Review, 208 Life Sciences East, Oklahoma Sate University, Stillwater, Oklahoma 74074

Colorado Quarterly, Hellems 134, University of Colorado, Boulder, Colorado 80309

Commentary, 165 East 56th Street, New York, New York 10022

Confrontation, English Department, Brooklyn Center for Long Island University, Brooklyn, New York 11201

Connecticut Fireside, Box 5293, Hamden, Connecticut 06518

Cornell Review, 108 North Plain Street, Ithaca, New York 14850

Cosmopolitan, 224 West 57th Street, New York, New York 10019

Cumberlands (formerly Twigs), Pikeville College Press, Pikeville College, Pikeville, New York 41501

Cutbank, Department of English, University of Montana, Bainville, Montana 59812

Dark Horse, % Barnes, 47A Dana Street, Cambridge, Massachusetts 02138

December, 4343 North Clarendon, Apartment 615, Chicago, Illinois 60613

Denver Quarterly, University of Denver, Denver, Colorado 80210

Descant, P.O. Box 314, Station P, Toronto, Ontario M5S 2S5, Canada

Ellery Queen's Mystery Magazine, 229 Park Avenue South, New York, New York 10022

Epoch, 245 Goldwin Smith Hall, Cornell University, Ithaca, New York 14853

Esquire, 2 Park Avenue, New York, New York 10016

Event, Douglas College, P.O. Box 2503, New Westminster, British Columbia V3L 5B2, Canada

Falcon, Mansfield State College, Mansfield, Pennsylvania 16933

Fault, 331515 Sixth Street, Union City, California 94587

Fiction, Department of English, The City College of New York, New York, New York 10031

Fiction International, Department of English, Saint Lawrence University, Canton, New York 13617

Fiction-Texas, College of the Mainland, Texas City, Texas 77590

Fiddlehead, The Observatory, University of New Brunswick, Fredericton, New Brunswick E3B 5A3, Canada

Forum, Ball State University, Muncie, Indiana 47306

Four Quarters, LaSalle College, 20th and Olney Avenues, Philadelphia, Pennsylvania 19141

Gallimaufry, Gallimaufry Press, P.O. Box 32364, Calvert Street Station, Washington, D.C. 20007

Georgia Review, University of Georgia, Athens, Georgia 30602

Good Housekeeping, 959 Eighth Avenue, New York, New York 10019

GPU News, % The Farwell Center, 1568 North Farwell, Milwaukee, Wisconsin 53202

Graffiti, Box 418, Lenoir Rhyne College, Hickory, North Carolina 28601

Grain, Box 1885, Saskatoon, Saskatchewan S7K 3S2, Canada

Gramercy Review, P.O. Box 15362, Los Angeles, California 90015

Green River Review, SVSC, Box 56, University Center, Mississippi 48710

Greensboro Review, Department of English, University of North Carolina at Greensboro, Greensboro, North Carolina 27412

Harper's Magazine, 2 Park Avenue, New York, New York 10016

Hawaii Review, 2465 Campus Road, University of Hawaii, Honolulu, Hawaii 96822

Hudson Review, 65 East 55th Street, New York, New York 10022

Intellectual Digest, 110 East 59th Street, New York, New York 10022

Iowa Review, EPB 321, University of Iowa, Iowa City, Iowa 52242

Jeffersonian Review, P.O. Box 3864, Charlottesville, Virginia 22903

Jesture Magazine, Thomas More College, Box 85, Covington, Kentucky 41017

Kansas Quarterly, Department of English, Denison Hall, Kansas State University, Manhattan, Kansas 66506

Kenyon Review, Kenyon College, Gambier, Ohio 43022

Ladies' Home Journal, 641 Lexington Avenue, New York, New York 10022

Laurel Review, West Virginia Wesleyan College, Buckbannon, West Virginia 26201

Literary Review, Fairleigh Dickinson University, Madison, New Jersey 07940

Mademoiselle, 350 Madison Avenue, New York, New York 10017

Malahat Review, University of Victoria, Box 1700, Victoria, British Columbia, Canada

Massachusetts Review, Memorial Hall, University of Massachusetts, Amherst, Massachusetts 01002

McCall's, 230 Park Avenue, New York, New York 10017

MD, MD Publications, 30 East 60th Street, New York, New York 10022

Michigan Quarterly Review, 3032 Roakham Building, University of Michigan, Ann Arbor, Michigan 48109

Minnesota Review, Box 211, Bloomington, Indiana 47401

Mississippi Review, Department of English, Box 37, Southern Station, University of Southern Mississippi, Hattiesburg, Mississippi 39401

Missouri Review, Department of English 231 A & S, University of Missouri–Columbia, Columbia, Missouri 65211

Moment, 150 Fifth Avenue, New York, New York 10011

Mother Jones, 607 Market Street, San Francisco, California 94105

Ms., 370 Lexington Avenue, New York, New York 10017

Nantucket Review, P.O. Box 1444, Nantucket, Massachusetts 02554

National Jewish Monthly, 1640 Rhode Island Avenue, N.W., Washington, D.C. 20036

New, Beyond Baroque Publications, 1639 W. Washington Boulevard, Venice, California 90291

New Directions, 333 Sixth Avenue, New York, New York 10014

New England Review, Box 170, Hanover, New Hampshire 03755

New Letters, University of Missouri–Kansas City, 5346 Charlotte, Kansas City, Missouri 64110

New Orleans Review, Loyola University, New Orleans, Louisiana 70118

New Renaissance, 9 Heath Road, Arlington, Massachusetts 02174

New River Review, Radford College Station, Radford, Virginia 34142

New Voices, P.O. Box 308, Clintondale, New York 12515

New Yorker, 25 West 43rd Street, New York, New York 10036

Nimrod, University of Tulsa, Tulsa, Oklahoma 74104

North American Review, University of Northern Iowa, Cedar Rapids, Iowa 50613

Northern Minnesota Review, Bemidji State College, Bemidji, Minnesota 56601

Northwest Review, University of Oregon, Eugene, Oregon 97403

Occident, Eshleman Hall, University of California, Berkeley, California 94720

Ohio Journal, Department of English, Ohio State University, 164 West 17th Avenue, Columbus, Ohio 43210

Old Hickory Review, P.O. Box 1178, Jackson, Tennessee 38301

Ontario Review, 6000 Riverside Drive East, Windsor, Ontario N8S 1B6, Canada

Paris Review, 45–39 171 Place, Flushing, New York 11358

Partisan Review, 128 Bay State Road, Boston, Massachusetts 02215

Pathway Magazine, P.O. Box 1483, Charleston, West Virginia 25325

Penthouse, 909 Third Avenue, New York, New York 10022

Pequod, P.O. Box 491, Forest Knolls, California 94933

Phantasm, Heidelberg Graphic, P.O. Box 3606, Chico, California 95927

Phylon, Atlanta University, Atlanta, Georgia 30314

Playboy, 919 North Michigan Avenue, Chicago, Illinois 60611

Ploughshares, P.O. Box 529, Cambridge, Massachusetts 02139

Prairie Schooner, 201 Andrews Hall, University of Nebraska, Lincoln, Nebraska 68588

Present Tense, 165 East 56th Street, New York, New York 10022

Prism International, University of British Columbia, Vancouver, British Columbia, Canada

Quarry West, College V, University of California, Santa Cruz, California, 95060

Quarterly West, 312 Olpin Union, University of Utah, Salt Lake City, Utah 84112

Queen's Quarterly, Queens University, Kingston, Ontario, Canada

RE:AL, Stephen F. Austin Station University, Nacogdoches, Texas 75962

Redbook, 230 Park Avenue, New York, New York 10017

Remington Review, 505 Westfield Avenue, Elizabeth, New Jersey 07208

Response, Box 1496, Brandeis University, Waltham, Massachusetts 02154

Roanoke Review, Box 268, Roanoke College, Salem, Virginia 24513

Rockbottom, Mudborn Press, 209 West De la Guerra, Santa Barbara, California 93101

Rocky Mountain Review, Box 1848, Durango, Colorado 81301

Sahara, 297 Gordon Avenue, N.E., Atlanta, Georgia 30307

Salmagundi Magazine, Skidmore College, Saratoga Springs, New York 12866

Sam Houston Review, English Department, Sam Houston State University, Huntsville, Texas 77341

Samisdat, Box 1534, San José, California 95109

San José Studies, San José State University, San José, California 95192

Saturday Evening Post, 1100 Waterway Boulevard, Indianapolis, Indiana 46202

Saturday Night, 69 Front Street East, Toronto, Ontario M5E 1R3 Canada

Seattle Review, Padelford Hall GN-30, University of Washington, Seattle, Washington 98195

Seneca Review, Box 115, Hobard and William Smith College, Geneva, New York 14456

Seventeen, 850 Third Avenue, New York, New York 10022

Sewanee Review, University of the South, Sewanee, Tennessee 37375

Shadows, Creighton University, 2500 California Street, Omaha, Nebraska 68178

Shenandoah, Box 722, Lexington, Virginia 24450

Shout in the Street, A, Queens College of The City University of New York, 63-30 Kissena Boulevard, Flushing, New York 11367

Soundings, Salem State College, Salem, Massachusetts 01970

South Carolina Review, Department of English, Clemson University, Clemson, South Carolina 29631

South Dakota Review, University of South Dakota, Vermillion, South Dakota 57069

Southern California Review, Bauer Center, Claremont, California 91711

Southern Humanities Review, Auburn University, Auburn, Alabama 36830

Southern Review, Drawer D, University Station, Baton Rouge, Louisiana 70893

Southwest Review, Southern Methodist University, Dallas, Texas 75275

Sou'wester, Department of English, Southern Illinois University, Edwardsville, Illinois 62026

Spectrum, Box 14800, Santa Barbara, California 93107

Story Quarterly, 820 Ridge Road, Highland Park, Illinois 60035

St. Andrews Review, St. Andrews Presbyterian College, Laurinsburg, North Carolina 28352

Sumus, The Loom Press, 500 West Rosemary Street, Chapel Hill, North Carolina 27541

Sun and Moon, 433 Hartwick Road, College Park, Maryland 20740

Tamarack Review, Box 159, Station K., Toronto, Ontario M4P 2G5, Canada

Texas Quarterly, Box 7517, University Station, Austin, Texas 78712

TriQuarterly, 1735 Benson Avenue, Northwestern University, Evanston, Illinois 60201

University of Windsor Review, Department of English, University of Windsor, Windsor, Ontario N9B 3P4, Canada

U.S. Catholic, 221 West Madison Street, Chicago, Illinois 60606

Vagabond, 1610 N. Water Street, Ellensburg, Washington 98926

Virginia Quarterly Review, 1 West Range, Charlottesville, Virginia 22903

Vision, 3000 Harry Hines Boulevard, Dallas, Texas 75201

Wascana Review, Wascana Parkway, Regina, Saskachewan, Canada

Webster Review, Webster College, Webster Groves, Missouri 63119

Weekend Magazine, 390 Bay Street, Suite 504, Toronto, Ontario M5H 2Y2, Canada

Western Humanities Review, University of Utah, Salt Lake City, Utah 84112

Western Review, Western New Mexico University, Silver City, New Mexico 88061

Willmore City, P.O. Box 1601, Carlsbad, California 92008

Wind/Literary Review, RFD Route #1, Box 809K, Pikeville, Kentucky 41501

Yale Review, 250 Church Street, 1902A Yale Station, New Haven, Connecticut 06520

Yankee, Yankee, Inc., Dublin, New Hampshire 03444